P9-DMO-819

THE KAHLER FILES #5
Maxwell's Silver Hammer

To Jared
August, 2017
Eric

ERIC SAFFLIND

© 2017 Eric Safflind

All rights reserved.

ISBN-13: 9781539444251

ISBN-10: 1539444252

Library of Congress Control Number: 2016916906
CreateSpace Independent Publishing Platform
North Charleston, South Carolina
Any resemblance of any characters in this novel to persons living or dead is purely coincidental.

To BZS for her unflagging support, tireless editing, and gently made suggestions, without which The Kahler Files would have never survived, and to RCS and MAS for their thoughtful evaluation and reevaluation of the cover graphic.

CHAPTER ONE

The blue-eyed brunette perched behind the wheel of her gleaming black Shelby GT-500 Mustang convertible. She'd glanced at my twenty-five-year-old Corvette as I'd pulled up beside her. Now she nodded in approval. Her shoulder-length hair fell across her face. She flipped it back with a graceful roll of her head, and wisps of auburn glimmered in the afternoon light. The Vermont Avenue traffic light stayed red. She grinned at me as she blipped the accelerator, and her 662-horsepower supercharged engine rumbled. She looked devilishly pretty. I smiled back as I switched the ZR-1's engine to full power and slid the toe of my right shoe from brake to accelerator. I patted the wheel. My old girl wouldn't go down easy.

The light warning the perpendicular traffic turned yellow. I lifted off the clutch, just a little. My twenty-nine-year-old heart pounded. This was a perfect moment in a perfect day. The cloudless March sky held the barest hint of blue. The Mustang glistened in the early-afternoon sunlight as if elves had sculpted it from black crystal.

I caught one more look at the driver out of the corner of my eye. Her sly smile turned challenging. The light changed. Then her car blew up.

The McPherson Square section of K Street turned ugly. An oncoming cab jumped the light just as the blast came. The startled driver lost control and slammed into the Mustang hard enough to drive the three of us sideways. The Mustang pinned the 'Vette against a Metrobus that had been unloading passengers beside the park.

I craned my neck to look at the Mustang. The trunk and most everything above the rear axle had disappeared. The gas tank must have blown. Yellow flames tall as an angry giant gnawed hungrily at what was left. They worked their way forward. The girl sat slumped over the steering wheel. The airbag must have kicked the wind out of her.

Sweat trickled down my forehead and into my eyes. The world felt hot. Both Corvette doors were pinned. My hand shook as I popped the harness, and my legs felt like rubber as I worked them up onto the seat. I reached up, released the roof clasps, and pushed the panel free. I tried to will my legs to stop shaking as I climbed over the windshield and onto the hood. The 'Vette wasn't burning yet, but it had minutes to live. So did the girl.

Fire! Our garage had burned when I was seven. My collie pup had been trapped inside. I remember her frantic yelping. I'd run to the side door, grabbed the knob, twisted, and yanked it open. The hot brass seared my hand. Flames burst out at me. They snapped and crackled and leaped over my head and melted my courage. I ran. The yelping became a terrified howl that curled after me like a lariat. It tugged hard. I spun around. It jerked me back, toward the garage, to my screaming child. I reached the door. Sparks showered over me. I remember thinking each was a tiny devil, a little piece of hell. I swatted at them as I tried to climb inside. They stung my skin. I didn't care. I killed as many as I could. One last, anguished cry—cut off when the roof collapsed. Then nothing. Mom and Dad didn't let me see the body. They taped the little homemade casket closed. We'd buried her in the backyard, and I'd planted a daisy there. They'd kept my hands bandaged for a week.

I looked at my hands now and turned them over. A couple of tiny scars remained. They tingled.

Both of the Mustang's doors were blocked, the taxi on one side and 'Vette on the other. I couldn't leave her there. I climbed onto the Mustang's wide black hood and kicked furiously at the windshield. Stupid. I slipped and almost tumbled off. The glass cracked a little but didn't break. Of course it didn't break. I'm five eleven, strong for my height, and have a decent build, but I'm not Superman. I slid the knife from my belt, opened the serrated blade, and stabbed it into the convertible top. I felt a thunk, almost lost my grip on the knife, and nearly slipped off the hood. What the hell? I ran my hand over the fabric. The forward ten inches had something solid underneath. I carefully slid my hand back until I felt the fabric give. I stabbed again. This time the knife sliced through. I worked the serrated blade back and forth until I had a jagged four-foot hole. I nearly tossed the knife aside. Then I remembered the shoulder harness.

I leaned in over the top of the windshield and cut the girl free. The air inside the Mustang felt hot. When I inhaled, it burned my lungs. I jerked my head out of the car. I felt myself shaking again. *Fuck it. Not this time.* I closed the knife and returned it to my belt. Then I sucked in a breath, leaned back into the car, and reached for the girl with both hands. She stirred, tilted her chin back, and looked at me with unfocused eyes.

"Hold up your arms."

She didn't move.

"Hold up your arms!" I screamed at her. My throat burned. "Grab my neck."

She tried. I felt her hands tremble. They slipped off my sweat-drenched skin. She reached up again. This time she managed to get her hands around my neck. I felt her fingers lock. I grabbed her beneath the armpits and pulled.

The girl pulled too. For a moment I felt panic. I thought she'd drag me in, like some dying siren reaching out from a shoreline of molten rock. But she got her feet onto the car seat and finally onto the top of the backrest. Then she pushed herself up and into my arms. She smelled of sweat and gasoline.

I dragged her the rest of the way out of the hole in the top of her car and then stumbled backward. We fell onto the hood. We slid off together. We smacked the asphalt. A plume of blue-yellow flame punched through the top of the Mustang. I struggled up and pulled the girl to her feet, and we ran.

The passengers from the bus stood at the edge of McPherson Square, gawking at the flames. I pushed through the crowd and didn't stop until I felt grass beneath my feet. I turned around just in time to see flames leap from Mustang to Corvette. I thought I could smell its fiberglass skin burning. Then the 'Vette's gas tank went up. No crash of thunder—nothing more than a loud pop. My baby had survived bullets and bad judgment, but she wasn't fireproof. Now she was gone.

I glanced at the girl. Struggling to catch her breath, she lay in the grass, flat on her back. Fire had singed her hair, and black ash mottled her face. She looked made up for Halloween, or maybe she was some devil's creature, assigned to drag me to the underworld. She'd failed. I felt an insane smile capture my face as I studied her. She'd failed. I could barely hold in the laugh. Our eyes met.

She pointed a blackened finger at the flaming wreckage behind us. She shook her head. "My brother's new car. Ethan's going to kill me."

CHAPTER TWO

Launch minus Sixteen Days

We both reeked of gasoline. The girl lay on a stretcher. I sat beside her. Our ambulance wailed loudly as it leaped into the momentarily paralyzed traffic.

I glanced at the paramedic.

"George Washington Hospital Medical Center," he said. "Be there in a few minutes."

I nodded. I could have signed a paper and walked away, but there was something about this girl. She'd been ready to run a drag race on a Washington, DC, street in the middle of a Washington, DC, afternoon. I glanced at her.

She lay flat on her back: slender, close to five foot six, singed hair, smudged face, maybe some freckles under the soot. She smelled like an overworked mechanic at the end of a long day—of sweat, burned carbon, and gasoline. She turned her head toward me and opened her eyes. Blue eyes—sapphire blue—and bright as twin flames from a blowtorch.

I felt warm inside. "Hi."

"That car was my brother's brand-new toy."

"He'll get another."

"And a new sister. He might want one of those more."

"I don't think you'll be as easy to replace."

"I guess you saved him the trouble." She smiled at me. She had the kind of smile I liked.

She started to sit up. The straps held her fast. "What the f—"

"Sorry, ma'am." The paramedic rested a hand on her shoulder. "House rules. You were pretty unsteady when we loaded you in."

She collapsed back down against the stretcher. "Sure, OK. Unsteady." She took a deep breath. Her breasts pushed against the sheet. Then she coughed. A glint of fear showed in her eyes. "My chest hurts."

"Lots of fumes in burning cars," he said. "They'll get an x-ray when we get to the ER."

"Sure. Lots of fumes." She glanced back to me. "Thanks."

The sky had turned dark by the time we left the George Washington Hospital Medical Center ER. The doc had wanted to admit her overnight, but she wouldn't hear of it. He said she should keep a phone close for the next twenty-four hours and call 911 if her breathing became harder. And she shouldn't be alone.

I stood with her in the waiting area while she made a quick call from her cell. I'd heard the raised voice from the other end even though she'd held it against her ear.

She stuck the iPhone back in her purse. "I'd rather stay here than have that pain in the ass hovering over me all night."

I nodded toward the registration desk. "I'm sure they'll take you back."

"Shit." She glanced at me. "I don't suppose you've had medical training."

"I'm fair with bullet wounds."

"Sure you are."

"I live close to two hours from here and have no way home except a cab. I could stay with you. In the morning, I can get a ride. You'd be doing me the favor."

She took my hand in both of hers and squeezed it. "Thanks. Really, thank you. Most people—" She coughed hard. The spasm doubled her over. I had to grab her around the waist to keep her from falling. When she straightened up, tears streamed down her cheeks. She turned away and wiped her face quickly with the back of her hand. "I live about twenty minutes from here," she said. She coughed again. This time she covered her mouth with both hands. She pressed them tight against her face, as if using them to hold herself upright.

I stayed beside her for another minute and then turned away and started for the cabstand.

She grabbed my shoulder. "If you let me die, you'll be in real trouble with my brother. He really does care about me, you know."

I turned back and leaned toward her so that my mouth was level with her ear. "Suppose I get fresh," I whispered.

Her voice sounded hoarse, her tone matter-of-fact. "Then he'll kill you."

I straightened up and stuck my tongue out at her.

"No, really. He's done it before." Her expression turned startled for a moment. She shook her head and laughed. "Just kidding."

Our cab ride was conversation-free.

CHAPTER THREE

Launch minus Sixteen Days

Her name was Alexandra Blake. She didn't give it to me, but I stole a glance at her ER admission form. Home was Adams Morgan, a DC neighborhood best described as eclectic. Our cab pulled to a stop in front of a townhouse on Kalorama Road, a few blocks away from the pastel-fronted buildings and quirky bars, restaurants, and art merchants of Eighteenth Street. She walked to her door as I paid the cabbie, and by the time I caught up, she'd opened it and gone inside. She glanced over her shoulder and frowned, and for a moment I thought she might slam the door and leave me on the stoop. Then she went through, turned left into the living room, and collapsed onto a white leather love seat. I stepped inside, closed the door, and trotted after her.

The room had a hardwood floor, light in color, with a glossy polyurethane finish. Full-length sheer white curtains guarded the front windows. A white leather couch sat across from the love seat, and a rectangular glass-top coffee table filled most of the space between them. A white-marble fireplace with an analog clock on the mantel had been built into the far wall. "Nice house," I said.

She began to say something, but speech became a rasping cough. For a moment she breathed in little gasps. She coughed again. Slowly, carefully, she drew in another breath.

"Can I get you something to drink?" I asked.

She pointed. "Kitchen."

White appliances and black granite countertop. I found a glass and filled it with ice and water from a tap on the refrigerator door.

I held it out to her.

"Thanks," she said.

I kept a steadying hand on it. She leaned forward, wrapped her hands around mine, and tilted the glass to her mouth. She took a couple of sips and then fell back into the love seat.

"I can't manage a shower. Not now. Can you help me up the stairs? Bedroom is on the right."

"Sure."

She looped one arm around my waist, pushed off with both feet, and got vertical. Then it was one slow step at a time up the stairs.

"First door on the right," she told me.

I reached in with my free hand and felt around until I found the light switch. A four-bulb cluster hanging beneath a Casablanca ceiling fan came to life. The room had the same hardwood floor as the living room, white walls with the faintest hint of green, and a double bed with a slightly curved headboard upholstered in pastel green. The sheets were white, and the bedspread pastel green, almost a paisley. A teak night table with a white-shaded lamp and a small vase sat on each side of the bed. The vases were empty.

The stairs had worn her out. She collapsed onto the bed as soon as I had her beside it.

"No!" she yelled when I began to pull off her shoe. She rolled away from me and drew in her legs, her position nearly fetal. She glared at me and clenched her jaw.

"OK, OK." I repeated the word a couple more times, trying to calm her. I slid a pillow down to her, and she lifted her head just enough for me to slip it under.

"How's that?" I asked.

She half turned her head toward me. The muscles in her face relaxed. Her breathing became slow and regular. My drag racer fell asleep.

Behind her bed hung a four-by-two-foot canvas gallery wrap with a pastel-green background. A single bird, maybe a bluebird, stood on a thin, bare branch and gazed up and across at the only other branch in the picture. That one had a single leaf at its end, and the limb seemed to hold it out to the bird. A lattice of bamboo ran behind the branches, like the far side of a cage. That and the vases were the only decorations in the room.

I leaned over with my ear close to her chest. I didn't dare touch her. Her breathing sounded clear. At least I heard no rasping or choking.

Then I walked to the door and stood just outside Alexandra's bedroom while I took out my iPhone and made a quick call to Rawlings' Landing. Stanley Egor answered. Neither of us ever said more than "investigative services" when answering Adrian Kahler's telephone, but anyone would recognize that deep, gravelly voice. Kahler himself wouldn't pick up a phone until he knew who was on the other end.

Egor listened patiently, making no comment until I finished my tale. "Too bad about the car."

"She was my baby."

"I can pick you up at the Metro tomorrow. Call me when you have an ETA."

"Right."

I dimmed the light. I didn't want it off. I'd need to see her every time she made a sound. Then I took off my shoes and walked quietly back to Alexandra. I risked two fingers on her wrist—pulse seventy, regular. Her breathing seemed relaxed now. Still alive. Still asleep. I stole her other pillow and tossed it onto the floor beside her bed. Then I lay down—close enough to hear a gasp of distress, far enough away so she wouldn't step on me if she stood up. I drifted in and out of a half sleep, the kind I'm used to.

She could have died on me if she'd done it in silence. But my eyes went to her at every sound—a cough, a faint wheeze, a breath deeper than the rest, the soft crush of the mattress when she moved.

A little before eight o'clock, I heard her stir. I opened my eyes. Sunlight streamed in through lightly veiled windows. The same sort of ceiling-to-floor sheer white curtains used in the living room masked the bedroom windows, and I hadn't thought to look behind them to pull down a shade.

Alexandra Blake rolled onto her back and sat up. Her bedsheets were covered in the same black grime she'd worn home. She took a deep breath and then smiled. She glanced at me. "Damn, I feel better."

She swung her feet over the edge of the bed and stood up. Then she coughed, four little hacks in quick succession; leaned back; and caught the edge of the mattress with her left hand.

I leaped forward to catch her, but she sprang up, planted her right palm in the middle of my chest, and shoved me away. "Just kidding, Boy Scout."

I blinked at her and tried to clear my head.

She walked to the door.

I wriggled my feet into my shoes and followed her into the hall.

She turned to me. "I'm going to shower."

"Will you be OK alone?"

"A damn sight safer than with you leering at me."

"I'd planned to put a bag over my head. I'm sure you have one."

"Why don't you go find the kitchen and make us some breakfast?"

"Suppose I can't cook."

"Frozen waffles, Pop-Tarts, and a Keurig. You'll manage."

"You're OK? You're sure?"

"Good as new."

"Enjoy your shower."

I checked my pockets for wallet, keys, cash, and iPhone. All accounted for. I walked down the flight of stairs and waited until I heard the bathroom door close. Then I opened Alexandra Blake's front door, made sure that the lock was set, stepped out onto the stoop, and pulled the door closed behind me.

I headed for Eighteenth Street. When I reached the corner, I glanced north toward the clubs and restaurants of Adams Morgan but didn't spy any eateries that looked as if they served breakfast. So I turned south on Eighteenth and lumbered down the hill. I'd left my jacket in the 'Vette, so I had to slap my sides and hug my chest to get warm. On the good-news side, the March chill kept me alert enough to find New Hampshire Avenue, and I followed it to Dupont Circle. I remembered a Starbucks on Connecticut Avenue just north of the circle, and once I got within a block, the scent of fresh coffee drew me right to it.

One Venti-sized dark-roast coffee and a couple of scones later, I texted Egor a subway-car emoticon and then made my way to the Metro station.

The Red Line train took me to Metro Center, where I picked up the Orange Line to New Carrollton.

I pushed Alexandra Blake out of my mind. I closed my eyes. I didn't need to watch for New Carrollton. It was the last stop. I can't sleep on a train, but I dozed. Images of the new Corvette Stingray Z06 floated back and forth through my head. I wondered who I'd have to kill to get one.

CHAPTER FOUR

Thursday, March 3, 2016
Launch minus Fifteen Days

I walked out of the New Carrollton Metro Station a little after eleven o'clock. I opened my mouth and yawned. The cold air had that crisp, winter taste to it. Thick white clouds floated in a pale winter sky, and bright March sunlight shot between them like laser beams looking for something to burn. I used my right hand for a visor and squinted out from beneath it, searching for Egor. I'd called home just before boarding the train. The drive from Rawlings' Landing takes longer than the train ride from Metro Center, so looking for the mocha-brown GMC Yukon Denali was wishful thinking. I considered going back inside to find a coffee stand, but I gave up that idea when I realized I'd never seen one in a Metro station. So I resumed the slapping and hugging. I felt scruffy and dirty, but my black jeans were new, and I wore a fitted Brooks Brothers shirt. I didn't think a cop would take me for a derelict. Nonetheless, I did collect a few disapproving glances.

Images of Alexandra Blake floated around in my head like tiny letters in alphabet soup. When Stanley Egor pulled up beside me, he had to blip the Denali's horn three times to get my attention. I walked around the front of the big SUV and climbed in.

He extended a huge, muscular hand that dwarfed the four-inch-square Tupperware container he offered.

"Thanks." I pried off the cover. French toast! The thick Texas Toast kind. I picked up a piece and held it between my thumb and forefinger. It was still warm. I bit off a corner. I chewed it slowly, reverently. The world had just become a happier place.

"I thought you might need something." Egor studied me for a moment. "I'm glad you're all right." He ran his hands front to back over his thick dark-brown hair. He had it cut just long enough to comb, but I don't think he ever combed it. Then he shifted the Denali into drive and pulled away from the curb.

I stopped chewing just long enough to nod my head at him and smile.

The seven-foot-one, 325-pound engineer, one-time Navy SEAL, one-time professional wrestler sat snugly behind the wheel. His bearlike head faced the road. He didn't like to chat while driving. I think it was part of his anything-you-do-should-be-done-precisely take on life.

I felt happy just to eat and drink. I'd found a thermos in the cup holder. The black french-roast coffee warmed me from within. I cranked up the passenger-side thermostat anyway. The big SUV glided along, east on Route 50, north on I-97, and east on Route 100.

Rawlings' Landing was a privately owned peninsula that stuck out into the Chesapeake Bay a little north of the Magothy River. One and a half miles long, a mile wide at its widest point, and about sixty feet above the bay, it provided a small number of wealthy homeowners with a really nice place to live.

I must have dozed. I jolted into consciousness as the Denali hit the speed bump that sat just beyond the turn onto Rawlings' Landing's private road. Egor never slowed his SUV much for it—he would say he was testing the suspension's real-time damping. I'd always slowed the 'Vette to a crawl.

"Shit." I clutched the open thermos. "Good thing I drank it all."

"Just before you fell asleep. Hard night?"

"Nurses don't get paid enough."

"These days most people don't."

Egor slowed at the sentry booth, but the guard raised the gate and waved him on. At the apex of the peninsula is 202 Bay Drive, a Tudor house set back behind a high stone wall. Egor transmitted the coded signal as he turned the Denali left, and the hydraulic steel gates slid open as quickly and smoothly as any door on Darth Vader's command ship.

Egor drove into the garage and parked. The steel door glided down behind us. I glanced wistfully at the empty parking space to the right. Once upon a time, a Corvette had lived there. A *classic* Corvette.

I followed Egor through the laundry room and into the kitchen. I sat at the butcher-block table and mindlessly watched Egor as he filled the coffee maker and then went to work on more french toast. By then I needed more coffee. I craved it almost enough to stick a pod into a Keurig, but expedience wasn't permitted in Egor's kitchen. Neither was participation. Eat; don't touch. Violate that rule at your own risk.

"Where's the old man?" I asked.

"Living room."

"Odd choice."

"He's in a meeting."

"Really? He had nothing in the book when I left yesterday."

"Congressman Boyer called last night."

"Urgent?"

"Apparently."

"Clues?"

"I've been running a taxi service."

"I saved the life of an annoying woman."

"I thought every rescued damsel became a grateful one."

"She called me 'Boy Scout.'"

"A compliment, perhaps."

"She practically ordered me to make her breakfast."

"Aah." Then Egor returned his attention to the griddle and flipped over a piece of french toast.

I heard the living room doors open, the ones to the front hall. Kahler practically never closed them. Considering that he and his clients had been alone in the house for the better part of the morning, that seemed odd.

"I better make an appearance." I stood and walked to the front hall. I arrived as Kahler's clients were leaving.

Adrian Kahler, a sixty-four-year-old retired psychologist, ran Investigative Services Inc. His little Tudor mansion served as home and office. Egor and I lived here too. It was convenient and cheap, and nowhere else was really safe. When people asked what we did, my approved response was "industrial counterespionage." But the old man was more than that.

"Hi, Barry." Max Damron stuck out a chubby hand and gave that patented chubby smile that no campaign contributor could resist. He'd been Congressman Lowell Boyer's senior aide for as long as I could remember. I hadn't seen him for a while. An inch-long fringe of brown hair still clung to his bald pate, and neither his five-foot-six frame nor its soft girth had changed. "Sorry you missed the meeting."

"I've been damsel saving."

"So I heard."

That jolted me a little. Adrian Kahler wasn't the sort to brag about his assistants' deeds or tell anyone anything he didn't need to. I just shrugged.

"There's someone I'd like you to meet."

A lean six-footer in a perfectly tailored dark-gray suit with that Brooks Brothers look to it stepped briskly through the doorway. He wore a white-on-white shirt with buttons instead of cuff links and a striped tie in two shades of gray. He would have been good looking except that his face, while not zombie wasted, had too little flesh on it. His skin stretched tightly over bone and muscle. His sullen gray eyes sat deep in their sockets, so close together that they almost touched. Dark shadows clung to the pale skin beneath them.

"Barry, this is Drew Scofield."

He had a cologne scent. He held out his hand. "Sandler."

I took it. "Mr. Scofield."

His grip felt strong, almost painful. Those pale, bony fingers had a lot more muscle than I'd expected. "*Colonel* Scofield," he said.

I should have guessed that. He stood as rigidly as if he were saluting troops from a reviewing stand. His mouth looked too wide for his thin face and pointed chin. I got the sense that his face had been fuller once, more muscular. Then everything but his mouth had contracted. Deeply etched vertical frown lines ran from beside his nose to the angle of his jaw. The nose was aquiline but too thin to look distinguished. Except for a midline peak, his hairline had receded to his ears, which looked flat and thin. Colonel Scofield looked like a scarecrow, but one with every piece of clothing pressed to perfection and stapled tightly to the staves.

"Drew is the Joint Chiefs of Staff liaison to Goddard Space Flight Center," Max said.

That startled me. "The Joint Chiefs have a liaison to Goddard?"

Scofield smiled. His thin, pale lips didn't separate; the corners just turned up a little. "Pentagon," he said. "INSCOM. Best not to mention the Joint Chiefs."

Max nodded. "Right." He rolled his eyes at me.

I glanced over his shoulder, into the living room, and glimpsed the back of Adrian Kahler's head as he walked through the doorway between the living room and his study.

"I guess it's my job to show you folks out," I said.

Max nodded again. His chubby earlobes jiggled.

Scofield had already walked to the front door. He tried the knob, but the door stayed closed. He showed no irritation.

I wanted to know more about this guy—at least more than I did. If he was here, he was important to the old man. That made him important to me. Taking a little more time than I needed, I walked to the keypad and punched in the code. The numbers scrambled their location each time so that someone watching where you put your finger might duplicate their positions but couldn't key in the cipher.

"You live in DC?" I asked as I opened the door.

"I'd be a fool to live anywhere else." He spoke brusquely, but when I turned toward him, he surprised me with a broad grin and poked an elbow against my ribs. Before I could ask anything more, he was out the door.

Max followed Scofield out. He stopped on the small porch just before climbing down the single step to the front walk. "Today I'm a driver."

I smiled after him. "For the rest of today, I'm a sleeper."

"Nice work if you can get it."

Scofield had already climbed into the rear seat of the black Lincoln Navigator. Max and I exchanged waves, sort of a high five when your hands are too far away to touch. Then I watched Max back his SUV out of the front drive, turn around on the wide concrete pad in front of the garage, and drive out past the sliding gate. It closed behind him.

I became aware of a presence and found Egor standing behind me. You never heard him. I angled my head toward the black Lincoln Navigator. "Why didn't you get one of those?" I asked.

"They might as well stencil 'government agency' on both sides in bold white letters."

"No one would fight you for a parking space."

"Adrian wants to see you."

"Study?"

Egor nodded.

"Now?"

He laughed. Imagine the sound you might get from an amused bear tending an annoying cub—a low-pitched, mildly ferocious growl.

CHAPTER FIVE

Launch minus Fifteen Days

Adrian Kahler's study door stood open. I knocked out of habit. The nearly imperceptible scent of teak oil lingered in the air. Egor must have polished the wood earlier that morning. The old man's study was a small room with a single window set in the teak-paneled wall behind his desk. The other three walls were lined with books—English and Russian, large and small. They drank light. No matter how brightly sunshine illuminated the windowpanes, Kahler's study always felt dark. His big teak desk held a couple of landline telephones and two Macintosh computers, one hardwired to the net and the second used as an interface to the Cray supercomputer in the basement. Over the years, as the Macs had grown in size, more and more of Adrian Kahler had disappeared behind them.

For a moment all I saw was carefully groomed white hair and a bit of forehead. Then he tilted his Eames chair back from the desk, spun it toward me, and looked up. His gray-blue eyes took hold of mine. No one ever forgot Adrian Kahler's eyes. To say they latched on to you would be an understatement. Once your gaze met his, they owned you. They held you until Kahler decided to let you go. He had unruly white eyebrows, a small sharp nose, a tight mouth, and a pointed chin. His bright, pink skin fit smoothly over a hard, angular face.

"You had a close call." He had a slightly low-pitched voice, maybe a hair below a baritone, nowhere near as low as Egor's bass. It sounded as flat and emotionless as always.

I picked up a three-inch-long plastic sailboat from the top of his desk. The little model was completely black, both hull and sails. It flew mainsail, genoa, and spinnaker. Egor had crafted it with a Dremel tool. He'd learned from some guy on the Eastern Shore who carved ducks. White letters across the stern read, *Seawitch*. I fiddled with it for a moment, passing it from one hand to the other, studying the detail. It captured the wind on a port reach. Its sails billowed out, and the thin threads Egor had used for sheets were taut.

Kahler waited.

"I've been damsel saving."

"So I understand. It would be best if you report."

"Why? This isn't a case. Have you taken a sudden interest in watching fiberglass burn?"

"I have my reasons. Sit down."

The black leather easy chair facing his desk was mine. At least I thought of it that way. I'd never seen Egor use it, and it was rare for anyone else to enter Kahler's study. I sat.

"Report."

I leaned back. The cool, soft leather cushions cradled me. I closed my eyes, opened my mind, and let Kahler in. I have a photographic memory. It worked best when the old man developed the film.

I've seen him push past the defenses of people who resist. It's not a pretty sight. I didn't actually replay the day's events, at least not on a conscious level. I simply felt a gentle buzzing inside my head, almost music, not quite a lullaby. Then I drifted off. I knew he'd see and hear everything I had for as far back as he wanted to go. I was good at picking out details and filing them away, but some apparently escaped my notice. They didn't escape the old man's.

A quiet rumble tugged at my consciousness. It grew louder, as if my chair and I sat beside a desert highway, and I gradually became aware of an approaching eighteen-wheeler.

"I am sorry about your car."

I opened my eyes and nodded.

"I shall call JBA Chevrolet. I have a contact there."

"I remember. They probably have a waiting list for a Z06."

"We shall see."

"Thanks." I stood to go. If he'd picked anything useful out of my mind, he wasn't sharing—or sharing back, or whatever you'd call it. I still didn't understand why he'd bothered looking.

"One more thing."

I'd already taken two steps toward the door. I turned toward him. "Sure."

The old man studied me for a long moment, as if trying to answer a question he couldn't. Such questions were rare. "The girl."

"Yeah."

"Is she pretty?"

If the chair had been behind me, I'd have fallen into it. Instead I just stumbled backward and caught myself on the doorjamb.

I stared dumbly at Kahler. His face looked impassive. The old man's approach to women was simple—he kept them out of his house. Pretty? I'd never heard that word leave his mouth. My lips moved. They felt numb. "Yeah. I guess."

He nodded. Then his head disappeared behind the twenty-seven-inch Macintosh display.

I stumbled back to the kitchen. Egor had kept the french toast warm on the grill, or he'd given the last batch to his squirrels and made fresh. I didn't ask. Just ate. It tasted even better with butter and maple syrup. Then I climbed up the stairs to my suite on the second floor.

I peeled off my clothes, stepped into the shower, and cranked the faucet all the way to hot. I had to back it down a moment later. It took about a handful of shampoo to get the fire's grime out of my hair. Then I scrubbed off the dried sweat that clung to my skin. When I walked out of the bathroom I found a letter sitting on the desk across from my bed. I hadn't noticed it before. The stamp was Cuban. I flipped the envelope over. A return address was typed onto the back flap. It was Lisette's. We'd kept in touch.

The paper felt heavier, more expensive, than what she usually used. I took my knife from the drawer, slid it under the edge of the flap, and sliced the envelope open. A wedding invitation with embossed gold lettering fell onto my desktop. I picked it up. Lisette had handwritten under the RSVP, "Hope you'll come." Some of that degriming shampoo must have got into my eyes. I wiped them dry, tossed the invitation onto the desk, climbed into bed, and fell asleep.

CHAPTER SIX

Launch minus Fifteen Days

awoke to the annoying repeated buzz of the intercom. I jerked awake and then clumsily ran my hand along the wall. I felt for the button, found it, and pushed on it with sleepy fingers.

Egor's voice. "You have a call."

"Mmmffftt." My throat felt as dry as if I'd inhaled a burned car. I sucked up some saliva and swallowed it. I tried again. "Half-asleep. I'll call back."

"Adrian asked that you take it."

"Shit. What time is it?"

"Eight o'clock."

I glanced at the window. Black. I still wasn't sure. "At night?"

"Yes."

"It's after business hours."

"Adrian asked that you comply."

"What the f—"

The line clicked.

I sat up in bed, stood, stretched, and sat down again. I picked up the phone extension beside the intercom—no wireless remotes, no airwave-borne conversations for an unfriendly surveillance system to intercept. Everything was hardwired. Sure, telephone lines could be tapped, but that kind of tap can be detected.

"Barry?" asked a woman's voice, young and perky. I'd never heard it before.

"Right. Who's this?"

"Alex."

"Alex who?" I stretched out the cord so I could get to the window. I reached to open the shade. It was open. Night. Check. Egor had told me that. I felt groggy.

"Alexandra." The voice grew annoyingly loud. "Alexandra Blake. You pulled me out of a burning car."

I shook my head a couple of times, trying to right the universe. It didn't work.

Her voice softened, and the pauses between words lengthened, as if she were speaking to a moron. "My brother would like to meet you."

"I just woke up."

"Oh. Sorry. I guess I don't need as much sleep as you do. I should have waited until tomorrow."

"No problem. Thank-you received and appreciated. He can send me a card."

"No, silly. He wants to meet you."

"Why?"

She paused for a moment, as if she'd just thought things over and couldn't figure them out either. "He said he does. Maybe he wants to buy you a new car."

That got my attention, but I didn't fall for it. "Thanks. Already taken care of."

"For Christ's sake, Barry. I don't know. I'm the messenger. He's grateful. So am I. I was really surprised when I found you'd left."

"Had to make your own breakfast, huh?"

"Pop-Tarts. There *were* enough for two."

I looked over at my desk. Lisette's wedding announcement lay where I'd dropped it. *Enough for two? Maybe.* I pictured the hot brunette perched behind the wheel of that Shelby Mustang, that glint of challenge in her gleaming blue eyes.

"Come on, Boy Scout!"

The image crumbled. In its place lay the ash-covered waif who'd jerked away from me and drawn herself into a fetal position. I shook my head.

The receiver headed for its cradle. Then I remembered what Egor had said as I'd answered the phone. I reached for that soggy memory. *"Adrian asked that you comply."* I played it over a couple of times, trying to convince myself he'd said something else, and then accepted my fate. "OK."

"Great," she said. I guess she hadn't heard the sigh of resignation in my voice.

"When?" I asked.

"How about tomorrow?"

My jaw began to ache. Grinding your teeth does that. "Sure."

"Goddard Space Flight Center. Be at the main gate at ten o'clock. The guard will expect you."

"Got it."

"Super." She hung up.

CHAPTER SEVEN

Launch minus Fifteen Days

'd missed dinner. Egor served it at precisely seven o'clock. Adrian Kahler had diabetes, and a meticulous regimen of diet and insulin ruled the kitchen. Actually, Egor ruled the kitchen and imposed a strict schedule on the old man and on anyone near him. Kahler was a creature of pure logic in every category except food. And he had episodes. He had once nearly eaten himself to death. He had a chocolate problem.

My hours were irregular, so snacks and leftovers were always kept handy. Egor would cook for me if he had time, but Adrian Kahler was his priority.

The beechwood walls in the kitchen softened the light from the LED ceiling fixtures and imparted a welcoming glow. Egor was washing dishes when I sat down at the table. That night's leftovers were grilled salmon and broccoli. The only thing I'd ever seen Egor warm in the microwave was maple syrup. He offered to reheat everything in the oven, but I felt too hungry to wait. Anyway, I liked salmon cold. Broccoli was something I ate because I was supposed to, so its temperature didn't make much difference.

I'd finished most of the salmon and half of the broccoli when Kahler walked in through the arch from the dining room. Egor snatched away my plate while I still had a chunk of salmon in my mouth. What Adrian Kahler didn't see, he wouldn't crave.

I glanced up at the old man. He stood only five feet six inches, but his rigid posture made him appear taller. He weighed in at 155 pounds and carried himself with a bearing that made him look solid rather than stocky. That combination of bearing and posture made him appear younger than his sixty-four years. He pulled out the oak fanback chair at the head of the table and sat down.

"The meeting with Damron and Scofield proved to be productive," he said. "Payment in advance—a large sum. I insisted. Congressman Boyer agreed to the request."

"Money goes along with trouble. Something they can't risk trying to handle internally. You're the only outside contractor he trusts."

The old man nodded half a centimeter. "He is a member of the House Permanent Select Committee on Intelligence."

"Nothing new there."

"They oversee INSCOM, US Army Intelligence and Security Command."

I shrugged.

Egor placed a Wedgwood saucer holding a cup of herbal tea in front of Kahler. It came to rest silently on one of the melamine inserts Egor had crafted to avoid place mats. He handed me a sixteen-ounce glass mug filled with the same healthy swill. It had a sweet floral scent. I'd have begged the man for dark-roast coffee, but he refused to brew it after three o'clock in the afternoon.

"Keep in mind that Colonel Scofield is the Joint Chiefs of Staff liaison to the Goddard Space Flight Center."

I began to get that prickly sensation at the back of my neck. "What's Goddard doing now that the space shuttle program has been closed down?"

"They continue to design and build satellites. One design in particular is highly classified. That satellite requires a certain device, and at this point, only one of the many Goddard scientists has managed to build it. The situation is so critical that they have brought in a second scientist to run a parallel lab. He has replicated the primary lab, but he is unable to duplicate the device."

I nodded. "So scientist number one becomes a serious VIP."

"He was nearly killed yesterday."

"How nearly?"

"His car exploded."

"Injured?"

"Not at all."

"Must be a lucky guy."

"Improbably so. He was not inside the car."

A prickly sensation, as if ants had crawled under my shirt, began marching up my back. "And?"

"His sister was. His name is Ethan Blake. His sister is Alexandra."

"Shit."

"When fortune drops into your lap—"

I propped my elbows on the table and dropped my face into cupped hands. I mumbled at the old man. "It didn't drop. It fucking exploded."

CHAPTER EIGHT

Friday, March 4, 2016
Launch minus Fourteen Days

Egor's big, fat Denali did not drive like a Corvette. It rocked and rolled and used soundproofing instead of the growl of a happy V-8 to shield riders from the world beyond its tinted glass. But for music, it was a symphony hall on wheels. I'd tuned into Tchaikovsky's First Symphony on XM radio and almost found myself conducting the orchestra with my right hand. It had nothing to shift. Kahler would have been pleased. He was Russian by birth and owned a Russian's passion for Pyotr Ilyich.

I figured I'd need an hour to reach Goddard, more or less. Then I voted for less and notched my right foot down on the accelerator, wondering if the Denali could make it on one symphony.

Whatever magic Ethan Blake had worked for Goddard's satellites, Kahler wasn't letting me in on it. Need to know. Maybe he'd promised Boyer or sworn an oath on the flag, or maybe Scofield had threatened to kill me. He looked like the type of guy who went to bed wondering if the world would be there in the morning. I guess he had a right to be tense. He sure looked it.

The oddest part of this series of fortuitous events—the old man's good fortune, not mine—was that Alexandra Blake had called me. She'd said her brother wanted to meet me. Why? To thank me for saving his sister? The guy had a phone. And why ask me to Goddard? Schedule pressure? Maybe they didn't let him out much.

I'd Googled Ethan Blake right after an early breakfast. Didn't find much. Maybe the feds had wiped everything from the net. Then I'd killed twenty minutes reading the *Washington Post* on my iPad. I really liked the iPad, but when I read the wood-pulp version of the *Post*, I could passively ignore the ads. Now I had to poke a little X, and poking didn't always make them go away.

I always checked the *Post*'s crime section even though it didn't help the business much. Gangs didn't generally hire Kahler. But an occasional article caught my eye. A week or two ago, I'd read one about a couple of fresh corpses found floating in the Tidal Basin. Two young guys had been incinerated. Fourth-degree burns covered most of each body. The article speculated on a drug-trade hit, but no identifications had been made. Whoever they'd been, they'd managed to piss off someone they shouldn't have.

I'd been driving on Route 295 for a while when the NAV system spoke up. It had a woman's voice, British accent, calming and authoritative. She told me to take the Powder Mill Road exit toward Beltsville. She didn't tell me how fast to take the ramp. I probably booted the StabiliTrak computer into its idiot-protection program. Ten minutes later I reined Egor's panting beast to a stop in front of the main gate to the Goddard Space Flight Center. I needed a new Corvette. I needed one badly.

If anyone saw smoke rising from the tires, he or she had the good taste not to mention it. I lowered the driver's window as a very attractive young woman wearing an army uniform walked up to the Denali. The Beretta in her hip holster discouraged a methodical assessment.

I held out my driver's license. "Barry Sandler to see Professor Blake."

"You're expected." She handed me a Garmin GPS and a visitor's badge. Each one had my name and photograph on it. "Follow the prompts and don't deviate from its instructions," she said sternly. "Wear the badge at all times. Leave the GPS in your car when you park."

I pictured some giant laser on top of their tallest building—turret rotating slowly, tracking the Denali inch by inch, and ready to blast it out of existence at my first transgression. I clipped the badge to my sport jacket's breast pocket.

I took a moment to watch her walk away. Nice holster. Then I shifted the Denali into gear. I drove past the six-story white rocket in front of the visitors' center and then partway around a small grass-topped circle with a single leafless tree at its center, and I parked in front of a modern-looking red brick building with a row of tall, thin windows marking each of its two stories. A narrow brown lawn and concrete barriers that looked as if they'd stop anything short of a tank separated it from the parking lot.

I walked up a long, sloping concrete ramp that had a stainless-steel guardrail. It ran parallel to the building for about forty feet and then took a ninety-degree turn to the left. It extended another twelve feet and ended at a set of small black metal double doors. I stood there for a moment and glanced down at the lawn five feet below. The setup reminded me of a medieval castle. If anyone planned to storm the entrance, a battering ram wouldn't help. The numbers one and four, dull metal stampings too large to fit on the doors themselves, clung to the brick wall to their left.

As I approached, a uniformed guard opened one of the doors and waved me in. The door clanged shut behind me. Another guard sat at a small reception desk. He hit a couple of keys on his terminal and then looked up. "Dr. Blake's running late. He wants you to wait in the cafeteria." He pointed toward a long corridor. "Take your second right."

I started off.

The guard called out from behind me, "Don't wander."

They'd painted the corridor white. It had black doors along both sides. One door was marked with an electronic-access-control-system sign warning, "Must be properly closed and secured after each entry or departure. If not properly closed, an alarm is activated." A little farther along, a poster on the wall read, "Threat Awareness" and, below that, "Protecting the power of your ideas." Across from that was a Pepsi machine fronted by a full-color *Star Wars* poster showing Rey and Finn and Han Solo with the dark shadow of Kylo Ren standing menacingly behind them.

A set of swinging double doors led to the cafeteria. One of them displayed another admonition: "Badges must be displayed in this building at all times." I reflexively reached up and fingered mine.

Inside the cafeteria I felt the weight of security lift its heavy hand from my shoulder. The room felt bright and airy. About thirty glass-topped stainless-steel tables sat with plenty of space between them. Powder-blue walls lit by recessed fluorescents stood on three sides, and the far wall was fenestrated by those tall, narrow windows I'd seen from the outside. They ran floor to ceiling. Even on a winter's day, they let in enough sunlight for the room to glow. A couple of dozen people sat here and there, drinking coffee and chatting quietly. I located the food line, bought a doughnut and coffee, and looked for a place to sit.

A middle-aged woman sat alone at one of the nearby tables beside a window. She looked like as good a place to start detecting as any.

I walked over. "Mind if I sit down?"

She glanced up from her book, looked me up and down, and then shrugged. In addition to the sports jacket, I'd even worn a tie. I didn't want anyone at Goddard to think I looked like a rube.

I sat and sipped the coffee for a minute. It must have been brewed for the breakfast crowd. At midmorning it tasted flat as a sheet of cheap printer paper that had a brightness of twelve. But the doughnut was a treat. Such things weren't permitted in Egor's American Diabetes Association–spec kitchen. I bit off a small piece and rolled it around in my mouth, relishing its texture and the carefully blended flavors of sugar and saturated fat.

After a couple of minutes of doughnut pleasure, I decided I'd better get to work. I glanced across at my tablemate. She looked unreasonably slender, filling out her gray business suit in a way that made it look as though it still hung on a wire hanger. She wore her jet-black hair pulled back in a bun. It contrasted sharply with the pale skin of her broad forehead. Her long face had a gumdrop nose, a tiny mouth, and deep-set eyes.

I smiled at her. To an investigator, a disarming grin is a lot more valuable than a blackjack. "I'm here to see Ethan Blake."

She closed her book slowly, keeping her index finger between the pages to mark her place. She looked me over and then scrutinized the picture on my plastic badge. "In the cafeteria?" she asked.

"He's running late."

Her tiny mouth smirked a little. "That man." She shook her head. "He's always late."

"I don't know much about him."

"He's arrogant. Everyone says so. Thinks he's God's gift to science. He can't keep staff. At least not many. Not for long. That's a problem in a place like this—security clearance. No one just pops in the front door, says she's a lab tech, and gets hired."

"Is he good at what he does?"

"I can't discuss what he does." She took a sip of coffee and made a face. "He says he's good at it. He's got the administrator believing it."

"Have you ever worked with him?"

"No, thank goodness. I work for Dr. Seep." She straightened. Her chin rose a little. "I'm his administrative assistant."

"What does he do?"

"The same thing as Dr. Blake. That's why the board brought him here. They knew one another at MIT."

"He came from Boston?"

"No. Pasadena. Jet Propulsion Laboratory. He had a very important position there."

"Doing what?"

She shook her head.

I took another tack. "You like Dr. Seep?"

"He's a wonderful man." Her face took on a hint of color. "A real gentleman. He loves Shakespeare, you know. Not enough people respect Shakespeare nowadays. And he came back to Maryland for his mother."

"That is wonderful," I said, nodding in approval.

"She hasn't been well. She's treasurer of the DAR, you know. Strong woman. Never quits. When she became ill, her personal secretary visited her in the hospital nearly every day. The woman wasn't allowed to do a thing without Mrs. Seep's approval. I wish all people would take their obligations that seriously."

I smiled and shrugged my shoulder, doing my best to look like a simpleton. "DAR?"

"Daughters of the American Revolution, silly. You men don't know anything."

"Uh-huh." I nodded and let my face relax. If I'd held my disarming grin much longer, I'd have begun to drool. "Are you—"

A loud female voice reached out to me from the far side of the room, "Hey, Boy Scout!"

I straightened as abruptly as if someone had poured a glass of ice water into my open fly.

My coffee-drinking companion looked over my shoulder and scowled. I imagined that same expression being turned on her cat when it kicked the scented gravel out of its litter box. She shook her head. "For the life of me, I can't understand why they let *her* in here."

The legs of my chair squeaked against the floor as I stood up and pushed it back. At least I didn't knock it over. I turned toward the cafeteria's double doors.

Alexandra Blake wore dark-blue jeans and a simple white cotton blouse with full-length sleeves and buttoned cuffs. The woman certainly had curves I hadn't noticed at our last meeting. Her outfit clung to every one of them. Her dark hair swirled around slender shoulders. She had a flat belly, a narrow waist, and good hips. She ignored the turned heads and waved at me. She stood a self-assured five feet six inches and bore absolutely no resemblance to the train wreck I'd spent my night babysitting two days earlier. Even her gait had confidence in it, not showy but self-assured. When she reached us, she nodded politely to my tablemate.

The administrative assistant replied by inclining her head as little as possible. Then she opened her book. Just as well. I wouldn't have wanted her marking finger to get numb.

I smiled at Alex. I didn't need to force it. "Hi."

"Welcome to Goddard," she said.

"Do you work here too?"

"More of a mascot. Ethan got me enough security clearance so that I can park and walk between his lab and the cafeteria. I usually meet him here. He runs late."

"You don't."

"No."

"But you don't work here."

"No. Georgetown."

I pictured her as a clerk in a fashionable boutique. Those jeans probably cost ten times what mine cost.

"Want some coffee?" I asked.

"Nope. Ethan's free now. He sent me to get you."

"He could have called my cell."

"It won't work here."

We walked to the Denali, and I held the door for Alex as she climbed in. She gave me a wry smile that might have meant either "Nice to see chivalry's not dead" or "We don't do this anymore."

I drove for about a minute. The GPS directed me to a small cluster of restricted parking spaces.

I pulled in, and we climbed out.

Alex nodded toward the "Restricted" sign. "You must be more important than I thought."

"I guess your brother arranged it."

"He never did that for me." She pouted. Alexandra Blake wore no lipstick, no makeup at all. Her sapphire-blue eyes studied me for a moment. I studied back. The outer halves of her sculpted dark-brown eyebrows flared upward. A small, rounded nose sat above a small, sensual mouth with a dimpled upper lip. Her skin was lightly freckled. Even in the stark winter sunlight, it looked smooth and flawless. Her soft, dark shoulder-length hair shone like polished mahogany. Except for the sharp angle of her jaw, she might have had a pixie's face. Instead, she looked like a grown woman, some part of whom remained trapped in childhood. She was captivating. I had to force myself to look away.

The building in front of me appeared to occupy an entire block. Most of it looked like white-painted concrete, as clean and bright as if it were power washed once a week. The main section had two horizontal strips of black-tinted glass running along its face, first and second story, separated by wide bands of white, then pastel blue, and then white. The section to the left was a smaller rectangle, and its far side connected to a two-story, windowless cylindrical building with a domed roof.

The center portion of the main section rose several stories higher than the rest, giving the impression of a huge white box with a taller white box on top of it. A big circular blue-and-white NASA emblem adorned the upper-right corner. The whole thing looked expensive. Anyone getting this for Christmas wouldn't be surprised to find a satellite inside. The steps in front led to a rectangular blue archway, two stories high, trimmed in black steel and tinted glass. It dwarfed the doorway. This was Building 29.

We climbed the steps and entered a wide, circular foyer. It had a round, ten-foot-diameter courtesy desk in the center and banks of cylindrical Plexiglas restraining doors on either side. I imagined that they, and the guard station on either side of the room, had been added after 9/11. The Plexiglas cylinders had rotating doors on either side that slid open and closed. If a guard didn't like the way you looked, he or she could trap you inside as you stepped through. If you set off a bomb, the only people you'd inconvenience were the housekeepers who'd have to clean the Plexiglas.

The guard at the courtesy desk scanned our badges, nodded, and let us through. No smiles. No chatting.

I followed Alex along this and that corridor. We passed bright-white walls, sky-blue ceilings, and sunlight-mimicking recessed fluorescents. If we were tracked, the surveillance mechanisms were too well concealed for me to spot. I imagined that scientists, like other creative people, worked best in a relaxed atmosphere. That wouldn't mean a weaker security apparatus, just a more subtle one.

We reached the midpoint of a long corridor. A black steel door to the left was closed. A stainless-steel plate with black letters just above the doorframe read, "Ethan Blake, PhD." The door directly across the hall hung open. The plate above that one read, "Geoffrey Seep, PhD." The detective in me couldn't resist an open door. I looked in. A life-size bronze bust on a five-foot-high mahogany pedestal stood just inside and to the left. The plaque read, "William Shakespeare."

Alex nodded to the bust. "She would be so pleased." Then she returned her attention to the Blake door, grasped the stainless-steel lever, and pushed it down. The door swung open.

"No locks?" I asked.

Her voice took on a serious tone. "There's too much traffic between the two labs. Locks would drive everyone nuts. The security's at the perimeter."

She swung the door open, and we stepped inside.

I had to shade my eyes. Fluorescent light sparkled off stainless steel. Benches and machines, large and small, sat everywhere I looked. Men and women in white lab coats, maybe a dozen, walked, stood, and sat among them.

One of the lab coats turned a corner and bustled toward us. He looked to be in his midthirties, about my height—five feet eleven inches—and about my weight—175 pounds. He had a broad forehead and midlength dark-brown hair that he parted just to the right of center. He had a dimpled upper lip and a slightly dimpled chin. The lip didn't look nearly as good on him as on his sister. A dark stubble covered his face and made it clear no one at Goddard could insist that he shave every day. The upper half of the lab coat hung open. He wore a Pink Floyd *Dark Side of the Moon* T-shirt, the one with the prism splitting a light beam into a rainbow of colors.

When he reached us, he extended his right hand. I took it. The fingers looked long and thin, what you might expect on a surgeon. His grasp was firm.

"Ethan Blake." His voice had a take-charge tone, crisp and businesslike.

"Barry Sandler," I said. "Quite a place you have here."

He continued to grip my hand while his dark, liquid eyes studied me through round horn-rimmed glasses. His small mouth grinned at me. "It's good to be the king." Then he dropped my hand, reached past me, and took his sister's. "Thank you for what you did for Alex. Most men wouldn't have taken that kind of risk. You're either very brave or completely nuts."

I glanced to my right just in time to see Alex roll her eyes.

"Just lucky," I said. "If it hadn't been a convertible, I'd have never gotten her out in time."

"Very lucky." His deep-set eyes fixed me with an analytical gaze. I became aware of a subtle intensity about the man, like an effervescence he preferred to bottle up. Something had changed, and now bubbles had begun squeezing past the stopper. "How did you happen to be there?"

"A friend of mine cooks. He needed some imported ingredients for a recipe he wanted to try. There's a specialty grocery shop he likes. It's in the District. I was on my way home."

"Oh. Where do you live?"

"Rawlings' Landing. It's a little north of Annapolis."

"That's a long trip."

"I like to drive."

He nodded. "So do I." He pursed his lips and blew out a long, silent whistle. "Seems like we're both out of luck for a while."

"She was an old car."

"The kind you save for DC traffic?"

"Corvette ZR-1, 1991."

He whistled. "I'm so sorry. I had no idea. That's a lot harder to replace than my Mustang."

"Yeah, mostly impossible." The image of my car in its death throes filled my head. I felt sick for a moment. "Those that are left are held by collectors." Then I drove the sight of the burning 'Vette out of my head and refocused on Blake. "But you don't find a Shelby GT-500 on every dealer's lot."

"There's one to be had somewhere in this country. I'll find it. Money talks." He grinned wickedly, and for a moment his face reminded me of his sister's when she had sat in her brother's Mustang, getting ready to race an old Corvette. That picture needed no caption. It spoke without words. It said, "I'm going to win." Ethan Blake clapped me on the shoulder.

I smiled back. "I wish you luck."

He swept an arm toward one side of the huge room. "Want to see the lab?"

I shot a quizzical glance at Alex. She shrugged with disinterest.

"I don't even know what you do here," I said.

"We make crystals."

"For communication? For the satellites?"

"A form of communication." That same grin flashed across his face for a second time.

"OK. Lead on."

He turned and headed down one of the long aisles. I followed.

I heard his sister call out from behind us, "I'm heading to work. You boys have fun."

Blake turned around. "I'll get one of the guards to shuttle you to your car."

"No thanks," she said. "It's not far. I'd rather walk."

I glanced at my watch. Eleven o'clock. I caught up to Blake. "Your sister must have a great job. Nice hours."

"They don't care about hours. Just productivity."

"She must be a hell of a saleswoman."

He barked out a laugh. "We'll find out soon enough."

Then I pushed Alex out of my mind and concentrated on the job at hand.

For the next half hour, Dr. Ethan Blake showed off his lab, and he was proud of it. He led me past machine after machine, commenting on each. Most resembled large refrigerators, some dishwashers. The counters looked like granite. If the floors had been hardwood, it would have taken first place in the world's-most-expensive-kitchen contest. I fought my attention deficit disorder, but whatever secrets the place held, it became clear to me that I wouldn't come away with any.

"I make crystals," he said. "Very special crystals. Nothing quite like them has ever been grown before."

"If I see one, will you have to kill me?"

Blake stopped walking and turned to face me. He kept his face absolutely deadpan. "Scofield cleared you, so we won't need to kill you right away."

I nodded and flashed a little smile. Blake began walking again. I trotted along after him. His lab smelled like a hospital.

"NASA uses crystals in just about everything," he lectured. "Most labs rely on the Czochralski method. It uses a crystal seed on a rod to draw the forming crystal out of a melt in a heated crucible. They've been doing it that way since 1916, and they've evolved the technique to grow crystals as large as seventy-five millimeters in length by thirty millimeters in diameter. We use a newer method called 'floating zone.' Lasers create enough heat to form a molten zone at the tip of a feed rod. The molten zone is moved into contact with another rod that supports the crystal seed. Then the rods are drawn apart. The structure pattern of the new crystal formed from the feed rod will be a copy of the structure pattern of the seed crystal.

"We call the molten zone 'floating' because we can move it along the length of the sample by moving the lasers. The crystal is grown on the solidifying end of the floating zone. No crucible means a lot fewer impurities to degrade crystal function, and the floating zone can be constantly monitored with video as the crystal forms. That lets us make minute adjustments on the fly. The key to making a really large crystal is getting the growing crystal to hold together as it forms. It's as much an art as a science, a lot like crafting a violin."

"What are they used for?"

"Silicon crystals are used in semiconductors, electronics. Optical materials like ruby, sapphire, and YAG are used in lasers. What I make here is classified."

"Why?"

"My crystals are the largest and purest ever seen in this entire solar system."

The tour continued. I interrupted the monotony by running the edge of my hand over the stainless-steel countertops. They felt smooth and cold as ice. Blake pointed out this and that machine. He told me his lab still used the Czochralski method for crystals that required less purity. He pointed out a crucible. Blake led. I followed. He spoke to me over his shoulder. I couldn't tell if he cared whether or not I listened.

When we reached a far corner of the lab, he stopped, stepped in front of me, clapped his left hand onto my right shoulder, and squeezed. "By the way, Barry, what do you do for a living?"

The sensation in my shoulder was just short of pain. I refused to flinch. "Investigator."

His eyes played over me as if I were a newly discovered crystal. "You're being more straightforward than I'd expected."

I shrugged. "It is what it is."

"Why do you think I invited you here?"

I felt myself tiring of the Blake family. "Alex said you wanted to thank me. My interest in crystal is such that I'd have preferred a gift card redeemable for a pizza."

His eyes hardened. "I wanted to see if you'd get clearance."

"What?"

"How did an investigator just happen to be sitting beside my car when it exploded?" His voice sounded cold and leaden. "And by the way, this is a high-security facility. Nobody gets clearance in a day. No one. What the hell are you?"

"I've done work for the government. Clearance sticks with you."

"Not for Goddard."

I locked eyes with Ethan Blake. "You think I was following your sister?"

"No, the car. You thought I was in it."

I snapped my hand up hard against his elbow, driving his arm up and popping his fingers off my shoulder. We stood a foot apart. Neither one of us backed away. "Then why pull up beside it?" I said. "That's where I was when the thing blew. Ask your sister. Check the fucking police report."

He studied me intensely for a moment, the way card players do at a poker table. Then he took a half a step back. "Sorry. I had to be sure. A lot's going on around here right now. It just all seemed so—" He gave a short laugh. "Convenient."

"You can call Congressman Boyer's office if you like," I told him. "They've arranged security clearance in the past."

He barked a laugh. "For all I know, he's the one who wants me tailed."

"That kind of argument can go on forever. If you're paranoid enough, everyone wants you tailed."

"Just because you're paranoid doesn't mean they're not out to get you."

"Right. Henry Kissinger."

Ethan Blake shook his head. "All right, Barry. You just happened to be there."

"With groceries. They got cooked. So did my car."

Blake shook his head. "I'm sorry about that. I really am. I know what it's like to lose a car."

He met my gaze. I saw a smile take hold in the corners of his eyes and spread down his face. He laughed. A real laugh. I pretended to share it with him.

"What are you doing for a car now?" he asked.

"Denali."

"That thing is a real blimp."

I looked down at my feet and shook my head. "At least do me the courtesy of calling it an airship."

We both laughed that time. The tension between us backed down a notch.

Blake extended his hand. I took it.

"Barry, thank you. Thank you for saving my sister's life. She's annoying, but I'd be miserable without her."

"I believe you, especially the annoying part."

He led me back to the lab entrance, stepped through the doorway, and pointed down the hall. "That way out."

"Thanks."

I glanced across the hall. The door to Geoffrey Seep's lab was still open. I looked in. The bust of Shakespeare sported a black wig. It was realistic enough to look as if it had grown there. The Bard wore his new hair in schoolgirl style, with a pink ribbon tied around each shoulder-length braid.

I shot Blake a quizzical look.

"Shit," he said. "Once Geoffrey sees that, he'll be pissy for the rest of the day. As if I don't have enough trouble."

"Who's the joker?" I asked.

Blake turned and retreated into his lab. As the door swung closed, I heard him mutter half to me, half to himself, "Alex, goddamn it. Alex—Alex—Alex—Alex!"

CHAPTER NINE

Launch minus Fourteen Days

pulled into the driveway at 202 Bay Drive a little after two o'clock. Tall trees striped the driveway with dark shadows. Max Damron's gray Chevy Malibu was leaving. We lowered our windows.

"What are you doing here?" I called over to him.

"Slumming. Where'd you get the blimp?"

"What's going on?"

"Sorry, Barry. Late for a meeting. Gotta run." His car window slid closed.

I parked Egor's airship in the garage as Max drove out behind me.

I found Kahler in the den, sitting in his Eames chair and watching CNN. I walked in as a picture of a rocket launch filled the screen. A voice-over supplanted the roar of the engine, "Iran's recent modifications to the Shahab-4 have created a missile capable of reaching Israel. Sabers are being rattled. Worse yet, if development continues at this pace, Iran could have an ICBM capable of hitting Washington. That timeline is not predictable from available data."

I stood beside and a little behind the old man and rapped a knuckle against the chair's wood back. The clacking sound always annoyed him. "Nukes and a bigger rocket," I said. "Think the United States is going to permit that?"

Kahler switched off the TV with the remote built into one arm of his chair. He spun the chair abruptly. When he faced me, he said, "Events are moving quickly. If Iran strikes Tel Aviv, we will respond in kind, as required by treaty. Otherwise, whatever influence the United States has in the world will dissolve as quickly and inevitably as a cube of sugar dropped into hot coffee."

"Are the Iranians that nuts?" I asked.

The old man shook his head half a centimeter to each side. "Nothing is certain. In dealing with weapons of such destructive force, a lack of certitude creates instability. Instability is the gateway to disaster." He rose smoothly from his chair and walked to the door. In the doorway he paused and then turned toward me. He studied me for a moment. To my knowledge Adrian Kahler and the non sequitur have never met. So his next statement dropped my jaw down beside my ankles. "I need you to get closer to Ethan Blake. If necessary"—he almost winced—"use the woman."

I didn't see Kahler again until dinner. I caught a whiff of Egor's turkey chili as I jogged down the stairs. He served it over steamed broccoli. Simple, ADA healthy, and delicious. The homemade buttermilk biscuits were as good as the chili. I liked to inhale their hot-biscuit scent as I watched the butter melt into them.

As Adrian Kahler stood up from the table, he fixed me with his let-me-be-clear-this-is-an-order stare and said, "I need you to get closer to the Blake woman. Think of something. If you are unable to generate a better idea, then offer to take her sailing."

I forced a burp as he turned away.

As he walked out of the dining room, I heard him say, either to me or to himself, "Perhaps I shall accompany you."

I nearly choked.

I called Alexandra Blake an hour after the old man gave his command. I spent that hour jogging Bay Drive in jeans and a T-shirt. For the first thirty minutes, I ran hot with anger. I know the old man. He wasn't telling me the whole story—not about Alexandra Blake, not about her brother, and not about what really brought an INSCOM colonel to 202 Bay Drive. I didn't mind following orders, but I didn't like doing it blindly.

For the next thirty minutes I shivered painfully in the icy March air. When I stopped to open the gate, I looked back along the road, expecting to see little beads of frozen Barry sweat glittering in the moonlight.

She picked up on the first ring and accepted the invitation as if she'd been expecting it. That was the thing about pretty women—they were never surprised when you called. She said she'd been a member of the sailing club in college but never sailed as much as she'd wanted to. I didn't ask what kind of college trained students to work in a Georgetown boutique. Hell, I knew law-school graduates who spent the first couple of years after graduation waiting tables.

CHAPTER TEN

Ms. Alexandra Blake showed up at noon, on time to the minute. I opened the gate and watched as she parked her white Mustang convertible on the concrete pad next to the garage. Kahler had arranged for the parking spaces there to be outlined in white paint, just in case our clients couldn't figure out where to stash their cars. He didn't like our vehicles blocked.

I walked out of the garage and met her as she opened her door. The car looked brand new. I couldn't help but glance inside.

"Automatic? I figured you'd be driving a car like your brother's."

"I commute from Adams Morgan to Georgetown. That's not clutch friendly territory. Annnnd," she drew out the word as far as it would go, "it only has a V-six." She glanced up at me, that sly grin on her face again. "Disappointed?"

The sun had climbed about as high as it could in March. It glinted brightly in her dark-blue eyes. Then she bounced out of her car and hipped the door closed. She wore black jeans, white athletic shoes, and a black ski jacket with pink trim.

"Headed for the slopes?" I asked. "It's practically spring."

"But it *is* winter," she said. "That's the nature of 'practically.'"

"I didn't know you were so fussy about words."

"You have no idea."

"OK, winter. But for today, winter is bright and sunny."

"And cold."

"This time last year, I crewed the Frostbite Series. We started in early February."

"Oh, Barry, I'm so impressed!" Alexandra rolled her eyes.

I ground my teeth as I led her through the garage and into the laundry room of Adrian Kahler's little Tudor castle. It seemed silly to walk around to the front door. Kahler, with his Old World manners, would have done it. I didn't feel so gallant. This woman was a job, one I wanted out of my hair as quickly as possible.

Halfway past the washing machine, she stopped. They all do.

"Wow," she said, looking first right and then left. "Who's your Ansel Adams?"

I'd forgotten about the effect Egor's photographs had on people. I was so used to them—they were practically wallpaper. Those twenty-four-by-thirty-inch prints covered the walls. He'd tend an entire garden in the hope of growing one perfect flower. When he finally had it, the camera came out. Until last year, he'd stuck with his old Hasselblad and film, but when Nikon introduced the D800, he threw up his giant's arms and made the leap to digital. He kept his darkroom, but the enlarger moved to the closet, and balanced lighting was added to the ceiling. A Macintosh computer and a photographic printer that weighed about one hundred pounds had displaced the trays from the workbench.

"Will you look at that detail," Alex said. "And the color. It's almost as if they're growing right out of the wall. They're practically three dimensional."

"It's the lighting," I said. "He fusses with it constantly."

"How do you fuss with sunlight?"

"Reflectors, strobes with filters. He'll spend hours."

She looked from one to the other. "Wow."

"You're repeating yourself."

She shot me a dirty look.

I pulled open the door to the hall and ushered her through.

Kahler was in the den. He stood up when I led her in.

"Alexandra Blake, Adrian Kahler."

He took her hand in his. Kahler ignored most of the women I brought back to Bay Drive, and that was only when he couldn't avoid them completely.

"Ms. Blake, a pleasure. Barry tells me you will be sailing with us this afternoon."

She looked him over.

Today he wore, as usual, a white-on-white shirt, dark-blue blazer, and dark-gray pants. The contrast made his pink skin look rosier than it was. A black-and-red-striped tie completed the uniform. In the house, during business hours, which were most hours, he almost never wore anything else.

"Dr. Kahler," Alex said, "my brother tells me you're something of a mystery."

His voice held its pleasant tone. "I was not aware that I am of interest to your brother."

"Your boy here saved my life. Ethan likes to check things out. In your case, he came up with nothing. I mean less than nothing. Any desk clerk at the Marriott has a larger online persona. Same for Barry. It's as if someone scrubs you guys off the net."

"Perhaps we are simply unimportant."

"Barry told Ethan he's an investigator. He works for you. That makes you an investigator."

"I am a clinical psychologist. Retired. I occasionally do consulting work for the government. When I require data, Barry provides it."

She studied him for a long moment. The old man had immigrated to the United States from Russia when he was ten years old. For Adrian Kahler, English was a second language. He spoke it absolutely perfectly—every word, every phrase, and every inflection. His diction was textbook, without slang or cleverness. Add that to his flat, emotionless voice, and it wasn't hard to wonder if you were speaking with a highly intelligent machine.

Kahler smiled warmly. I'd never seen the old man spend so much effort trying to look harmless. "Why don't you let Barry show you our boat? We're quite proud of her."

She turned to me. "OK, Popeye. Lead on."

"Follow me, Olive Oyl." I reached to take her hand, but as our fingers brushed, she jerked hers away. I led quietly, out through the back door, across a yard still wearing its winter brown, on to the boathouse. All the while my mind kept churning. I didn't like her. I had asked her here because the old man told me to. She didn't like me, but she came. I felt my brain churning itself into whipped cream cheese.

The boathouse didn't really house boats. It was for spare cars, the kind you didn't want traced. There was also a motorcycle, a Honda CB1000R, that I used when four wheels wouldn't do the job. A large closet held spare sails, miscellaneous go-fasts, and spare parts for the sailboat's Perkins diesel. The stairs beside it ran down to the dock, eighty steps, each a wood plank, slippery when wet. I pointed. Alex grabbed the handrail and started down.

I didn't need to point to *Seawitch*. She was the only boat moored at Kahler's private pier. She lived there in the water at least 360 days a year and came out of the water only for service. The old man didn't believe in dry storage. He said the place for a boat was in the water. He had once told me that some boats, after dry storage, developed a vibration in the driveshaft. It wasn't the driveshaft that had warped. It was the hull.

Alex ran to the boat and stood at the edge of the dock, studying the big Morgan 38. She was thirty-eight feet four inches long and twelve feet across at her widest point.

"Black?" she asked. "He had them paint his sailboat black?"

"It's not paint. It's gelcoat, a kind of colored resin." I pointed to the name on the stern. "What color would you paint a witch?"

"OK. You wouldn't do pink. Red would work—ruby red."

"Kahler once told me he named her after the only woman who'd ever been a part of his life."

She turned toward me and frowned. "Nice."

I turned away quickly and pointed out at the bay. "Whitecaps," I said. "We're going to have a great afternoon."

"I'm in your hands, Popeye."

Just to prove my learning curve was shorter than she thought, I skipped the Olive Oyl retort. Instead I bowed politely and ushered her aboard. Then I pulled on the stern mooring line and held it tight while Alex climbed onto the gunwale and into the cockpit.

She called to me over her shoulder, "At least the deck's white."

"It doesn't heat up as much in the sun as black would."

I jumped aboard, walked to the forestay, and held out my Speedtech wind gauge. It read fifteen knots. I checked the self-furling apparatus on the genoa while I was there and then climbed back to the cockpit, removed the jacket from the mainsail, and opened the companionway hatch cover. Then I started the motor. The gentle vibration of the Perkins diesel coursed through the boat. I turned to the instrument cluster beneath the companionway hatch and checked the gauges. Oil pressure OK.

Alex tapped me on the shoulder. I hadn't heard her over the splashing of the water and the pinging of the shrouds. I sprang up and nearly slipped on the deck.

She laughed hard. "I thought we were going sailing," she said.

I glowered at her, but Alexandra Blake's blue eyes glowed soft and steady. The tiny, fawn-colored freckles on her forehead and across the bridge of her nose seemed to prance in the bright sunlight. She smiled impishly. My exasperation melted away.

I took a breath. "*Seawitch* displaces seventeen thousand pounds. Slamming her into the dock would be bad. She's a lot easier to control in close quarters with the motor. Once we're away from the dock, we'll raise the sails and shut down the—"

Adrian Kahler boarded his yacht. He wore a black-and-gray Gore-Tex dry suit that would keep him warm and permit no drop of Chesapeake Bay water to touch his skin. With it he wore matching boots and a yellow life jacket.

I turned to face him. "Bonjour, *mon capitaine*."

Alex had the good sense not to laugh. Maybe I hadn't been funny.

Kahler's gray-blue eyes swept from bow to stern, his gaze swift and analytic. "Do the shrouds look tight to you?"

"Not enough to matter. It's been cold."

The old man's nod was barely perceptible. Then he glanced from me to Alex. "Life jackets, please."

"The water's forty-five degrees," I said.

He scowled at me.

"OK, maybe forty. At least forty. And we're not about to capsize in a fifteen-knot wind."

"Life jackets." He didn't raise his voice, but the command was clear. The old man always acted with care and insisted that those around him did the same.

I ran below, grabbed two bright-red life vests, and climbed back onto the deck. I held one out to Alex.

"I did ask for ruby red," she said as she pulled it on.

"I'll try to do better when I'm sent out for slippers."

She smiled at me. "Of course you will. You're a fast learner."

The old man ignored us. He walked to the steering pedestal and took the wheel in one hand and the throttle in the other. "Cast off."

I stepped to the dock, freed the bowline, then freed the stern mooring line, and jumped back into the boat.

The old man shifted into forward and slowly increased the diesel's RPMs. Slowly and gracefully, *Seawitch* motored away from the dock and headed east, into the Chesapeake Bay.

The wind continued to blow from the east, so the old man simply held course, into the wind, until I had the mainsail and genoa up and luffing.

As he turned the Morgan south, Alex moved to the port bench. I guessed she had sailed before. The Morgan heeled as her sails filled. Kahler shut down the engine. Our beautiful black witch sliced through the whitecaps. The old man held her on a close reach, port tack. I kept the sails trimmed tight. I'd sailed the Morgan many more hours than Kahler had, but he paid the bills. So when he was on board, he skippered; I crewed.

Alex loved it. She leaned out over the gunwale and let the bow spray douse her. If the cold bothered her, she didn't let on. I enjoyed watching her. When you find someone who loves what you love, a bond forms between you. Perhaps that was when ours began.

After half an hour, we'd sailed well out into the Chesapeake. Alex had taken over as sail trimmer, and I had nothing to do but watch the whitecaps. I could barely make out Rawlings' Landing behind us, but I knew where we were and didn't bother turning on the navigation equipment. As long as the wind held steady, sailing back wouldn't require any more than dead reckoning. The GPS had a way of making me feel less like a Viking.

No one had said more than a dozen words since we left the dock. If this was the old man's way of getting to know Alex, then he did it by probing her mind. Maybe that was his plan. With the wind and water distracting her, she might not notice. But probe for what? Why? If Alexandra Blake knew something the old man wanted, I for one had no clue. He didn't like women, especially the young and the pretty. Yet he had used me as bait to get her to spend an afternoon with him.

I walked over to Alex and sat beside her on the port bench. The cold of the fiberglass worked quickly through my jeans. *Should have worn long underwear.*

Alex watched the sails as intently as if she were racing for the America's Cup. Every couple of minutes, she'd adjust the main sheet or the genoa, letting it out or taking it in. Her eyes sparkled. Other than the briefest of nods, she ignored me completely.

After a while I reached out to rest a hand on her shoulder and then thought better of it. My hand hovered in midair at the moment she turned to face me.

She frowned.

My arm dropped flaccidly to my side. "Where'd you learn to sail?" I asked.

"Cal Tech. I never learned much. Didn't have time."

"What were you doing there?"

Her attention had returned to the sails. She spoke idly. "School."

"School? What school?"

"Cal Tech. I just told you. Computer science, English lit."

Just then the Morgan veered to starboard and took a bounce on some heavy chop. I had to grab onto a shroud to keep from tumbling backward. If I'd fallen overboard, I'd have never heard the end of it.

Alex glanced in my direction in time to see me grab the braided stainless-steel wire with both hands. She gasped, clutched the mainsheet with her left hand, and reached out her right for me. She moved fast and had hold of my life vest just as I began righting myself.

"I'm fine," I said quickly.

"Right. You do that all the time." She rolled her eyes.

I fought for composure. "Just to be entertaining."

"It certainly does work for you."

I glanced toward the stern. Kahler stood at the helm, both hands on the three-foot stainless-steel steering wheel, watching the sails. Had he hit the chop deliberately to drive Alex and me closer together? I wouldn't put it past him. My fingers stung where they'd clutched the rough, braided wire.

"Computer science?" I asked sheepishly.

"Right. That's what I do."

"Where?"

"Georgetown. I already told you that."

"The university?"

"Well, duh."

"What do you do there?" I grimaced as I tried to quickly reformat my image of Alex from standing in front of a richly dressed mannequin in a Georgetown boutique to standing behind a lectern in a university classroom. "I mean what kind of computer science? What do you do with it?" I was babbling.

"I analyze language." She leaned toward me. "The nature of language and gender produce defined—"

I heard a single, distinct pop from deep inside the boat. Alex heard it too. Her back went straight, and she began looking around.

Kahler saw it first. His voice snapped through the cold air, "Smoke. Cabin."

I looked to the hatch. At first I saw nothing. Then a few thin wisps of gray and black curled up through the hatch and glided across the deck.

Kahler's cold, gray eyes found mine. "Engine fire."

"We're under sail. The engine's off," I said.

"*See to it.*" The command rang inside my skull as if he'd implanted a speaker there.

I raced for the companionway.

"Blake, you have the sails." That was the last thing I heard him say as I ran to the hatch.

CHAPTER ELEVEN

Launch minus Thirteen Days

I slid down the ladder, landed in the galley, and ran to the propane stove. That was where fires started. But it felt cold. The smoke thickened. It bore the caustic smell of diesel fuel. It stung my nose. My eyes burned. My vision blurred. I pulled one of the fire extinguishers from its bulkhead bracket and yanked a flashlight from another. I stuffed the flashlight into my left-front pocket and hooked the trigger of the fire extinguisher onto my right. Then I rested the palms of my hands flat against the access panel that supported the companionway steps. I jerked them back. It felt hot. The engine room sat on the other side.

I loosened the retainers. The Morgan suddenly crossed the wind, and the panel came away from the bulkhead all at once. The access panel, the attached companionway steps, and I were flung sideways as the boat snapped upright. I nearly slid into the engine room when she leaned hard over on the opposite tack.

Black smoke poured out of the engine room. Tears streamed down my cheeks. Heat scorched my face, but inside I felt cold with terror. Every

organ in my body trembled. They wanted to get away, to belong to someone else. Then I heard myself laugh. I had a second chance for death by fire.
Two in four days. Do people go mad before they die?

I grabbed onto the starboard side of the engine room hatch with my left
hand. It burned my skin, but I held on anyway. I planted my feet, held the
fire extinguisher in my right hand, reached into the engine compartment,
and squeezed the trigger. Foam poured out, covering the engine and its fuel
line. It looked like a thick white cloud settling over a mountaintop. I held
the extinguisher's trigger until only tiny bubbles trickled from its muzzle.
Then I pulled back, craned my neck toward the hatch to the deck, and
sucked in a breath. The air tasted foul, but it had oxygen in it.

I took the flashlight in my left hand and played its light around the
galley. The smoke had grown heavier. I could barely see. Then I found
the second fire extinguisher. I reached for it, but Kahler tacked the boat
again. The hull snapped upright and then leaned hard over on the opposite
tack. I stumbled and slid across the deck. I was no stranger to a pitching
boat, but my eyes straightened the world for me. In the smoke-filled cabin,
they were nearly useless. The fingers of my left hand tightened around that
flashlight like fingers of a frightened infant clutching a blanket. I crawled
on hands and knees to the second extinguisher. When I got close, my flashlight pierced the smoke just enough. I found it. I grabbed its bracket with
my right hand and pulled myself to my feet. Somehow I managed to get
myself back to the engine compartment. I dumped another load of foam.
That was all I could do.

I shone the light into the engine room. It felt like staring into a thun-
derhead. My left hand throbbed with pain. I almost yelled, "Abandon
ship," but then I sensed the smoke begin to clear. The perception might
have been visual. Perhaps breathing came easier. The burning in my eyes
might have slacked off a little. Then Kahler jibed, and the Morgan pivoted.
I fell backward. When my butt crashed to the deck, the impact jarred my
teeth. The empty fire extinguisher jerked out of my right hand, but my
left's death grip on the flashlight never wavered. If we'd died, they'd have
had to pry it out of my charred, skeletal hand.

For a moment I just sat there. I had no strength. Then the Morgan
heeled and crossed the wind again, and I slid back across the polished deck.

The smoke cleared a little more. I struggled to my feet, staggered
back to the engine room, and shone the light inside. I could barely make

out the shape of the Perkins engine through the smoke and under the foam. I saw no flames. The air smelled heavy with diesel fuel. My eyes still burned.

The diesel tank held forty-four gallons. We had to have a leak somewhere. It wouldn't plug itself. The fire had gone out. There had to be a fuel cutoff valve in the engine room, but I didn't know where. The old man had always worked on the engine alone. He would get testy at the suggestion that anyone else so much as touch it. That was the only time he ever got his hands dirty.

I could climb in, feel for the fuel line, and follow it to the cutoff valve. I'd see it when I got close. I'd be walking through a puddle of diesel fuel, but it might work. I took a small, tentative step into the engine room.

Kahler jibed the fucking boat again. I grabbed the edge of the hatch and clung to it. My mouth filled with the tastes of bile, soot, and diesel. My stomach turned into a knot pulled tight at each end. I puked and puked and then puked again.

When it was over, I limped to the galley sink, found a towel, wet it, and then soaked the diesel fumes out of my eyes. For good measure I washed off my face and then tossed the grimy, wet towel onto the little pile of vomit I'd left on the deck. Only then did I stuff the flashlight into a jeans pocket and permit my fingers to relax.

As long as the old man continued tossing his boat around, I had no chance to stay vertical in the engine bay. I didn't dare close it off. The diesel vapor had to be vented, or even the smallest spark could blow *Seawitch* to pieces. That meant I couldn't replace the companionway steps. I steadied myself, grabbed the sides of the hatch, and then pulled myself through. My burned fingers screamed. Finally I crawled out onto the deck. Kahler jibed the boat again. The boom whooshed over my head.

I yelled at the old man, "Fire's out. Leaking diesel. Hold the boat straight. Then I'll get to the cutoff valve."

He glanced at me for the briefest of moments. "A straight course will kill us."

I looked for Alex. She sat on the starboard bench. She'd clamped one hand on the mainsheet and the other on the genoa sheet. Tense as a stopwatch, she had her eyes fixed on Kahler. She looked ready to jump at his command. I crawled over and sat down beside her. Not too close. I smelled of vomit. "What's he doing?"

She kept her eyes on the sails, looking from main to genoa and back. "We're on a reach, headed in. He's jibing the boat every few minutes. Didn't tell me why."

Just then the old man cut the wheel. Alex worked the sheets and then ducked and scampered to the far side of the deck as the big mainsail snapped across. I struggled after her.

When we reached windward, she motioned for me to sit forward of her. "You take the genoa. I'll keep the main."

I kept a couple of feet between us. "Tired?" I asked.

She smiled faintly and nodded.

I could see the Rawlings' Landing pier in the distance. We'd have made it already if the crazy old man had held a straight course. I glanced at the genoa. It had filled with wind and was doing its job. My eyes still burned from diesel fumes. I squeezed them shut and then blinked and blinked again. I wiped them with the back of my hand. Then my eyes drifted down. My gaze fell to the deck, where it sat directly over the engine room. Several fine curls of black smoke rose up from it. They had a pattern. I looked more closely. They emanated from a cluster of tiny, regularly spaced holes. As I watched another group of punctures appeared in the deck. I smelled fiberglass burning.

"Adrian!" I screamed and pointed at the same time. I'd never called him Adrian before.

He glanced at the smoke. The old man showed no surprise. He snarled a curse and then spun the wheel.

"Jibing," I yelled to Alex.

We worked our sails. Alex sprang across the deck.

Then a flickering poked up through the deck, yellow and blue and yellow and blue, flames as gentle as from candles on a birthday cake. I stared at it.

Fire! I thought it. Had I said it? My voice felt stuck. I forced my mouth open and screamed. "Fire!" I pointed. A bright yellow flame leaped up from the deck. It grabbed for me like a claw. I jumped back.

Kahler barked a command, "Raft!"

A black hole took shape around the flame; it grew larger. The deck had begun to melt. I loosed the genoa. Alex followed my lead and loosed the main.

Kahler spun *Seawitch* into the wind. The sails luffed, snapping back and forth. They barked at me like dogs gone mad.

I ran aft to the lazarette and jerked it open. I hauled out the life raft. Sixty pounds. I grunted as I heaved it over the transom. It struck the water, and I yanked the tether. The raft inflated in a single puff of compressed air and then drifted aft. Its line went taut. The raft bobbled up and down, seventy feet away. I turned forward to find Alex standing beside me.

I pointed toward the raft. "Swim for it."

"The water's forty degrees."

"Stay here, and you burn!"

Her face hardened.

I tensed, ready for an argument, ready to grab her by the belt and throw her overboard.

Alex spun abruptly away, brushed past me, and executed a perfect dive off the stern. Her lithe body cut through the water. Even wearing the life vest, she made strong, perfect strokes.

I turned forward. Smoke and soot rose out of the growing breach in the deck. Black clouds poured from the companionway. Dark tendrils reached for the old man like legs of a hungry spider. I saw him cough. His body convulsed with it. His pale hands gripped the wheel. He held *Seawitch* into the wind. Flames as tall as he was leaped up from the deck in front of him. He never even looked at me. He might have spoken. I don't know. The command resonated inside my head, "Go."

I leaped overboard. I don't dive as well as Alex. I would have done better if I'd dressed for it. The shock of cold felt as if I'd jumped into a tub of melting ice. My clothing sucked up the frigid water and hauled me down. I thanked God for the life vest. I swam hard, hand over hand, kicking my feet as fast as I could make them go. My form wasn't pretty, but I swam fast enough to beat the hypothermia. My cold-numbed fingers slipped on the rough fabric of the raft as I dragged myself up and scrambled over the side.

For a moment I just lay there, gasping for breath. Then I rolled onto my back and sat up. Hypothermia could kill us in the raft just as in the water, but it would take longer. My eyes found *Seawitch*. Blue-yellow flames erupted amidships. The sails blazed like torches. What had been the deck over the cabin leaped skyward. It ran up the mast like the clapper on a carnival high striker, one hammered by a three-hundred-pound strongman. A

cloud of gray-black smoke fringed by sparks of silver and gold enveloped
Seawitch. Then the smoke cleared at the stern. A pudgy, black-and-gray,
four-limbed shape tumbled over the transom and bobbled slowly toward
us. He was floundering. Kahler was in good shape for his age, but he was
more than twice twenty-nine, and no one was nimble in the bulk of a dry
suit. I remembered he kept a knife in the utility pocket.

"Grab the tether," I yelled. "Then cut it and hang on. I'll pull you in."

I saw his arms move. The line went slack as it separated from *Seawitch.*

I turned away from the old man and pointed at the paddle. Alex understood. She grabbed it and began to propel us away from the burning boat.

Then I pulled on that line, hand over hand, eyes fixed on Adrian Kahler,
drawing him in, closer and closer to the raft. My arm and shoulder muscles
felt like dried leather, cracking and hurting and ready to snap. My knees
slipped on the wet surface of the raft. Once I slid and nearly tumbled over
the side. My burned left hand shrieked at me. I forced my fingers open
and closed repeatedly as I hauled on that line. Adrian Kahler had been my
father since my own father had died. He would survive this, or we'd drown
together.

Then the old man's gloved hands scraped against the sides of the raft.
I deployed the boarding ladder and grabbed him by the shoulders as he
struggled up and out of the bay.

Anger flowed out of him like storm clouds roiling across a dark, angry
sea. He raised his knife, and for an absurd moment I thought he might stab
one of us in an uncontrolled rage. But he reached up, sliced the raft's exte-
rior locator light from its starboard canopy support, and hurled it into the
bay. Then he collapsed onto his back.

Seawitch exploded. She made more of a loud pop than a bang. One huge
flash flared up out of that enveloping black cloud. Flaming debris leaped
skyward.

"Barry!" Alex's voice shot out at me. I understood. I grabbed the second
paddle, crawled to the side of the raft opposite her, and dug into the water
as fast and as hard as I could. We paddled for our lives. Flaming embers
clawed at us. A few brushed the sides of the raft. They hissed like outraged
dragons as they splashed into the bay.

I never saw the Morgan sink. We didn't stop our frantic paddling when
the hissing stopped. *Some say the world will end in fire. Some say in ice.* We
weren't far from either. We didn't stop until our little orange raft gently

bumped up against the dock that had been home to *Seawitch* just a few hours earlier.

I crawled to Kahler. I rested my right hand on his shoulder. He opened his eyes. The steel gray looked softer than usual. That might have been the angle of the light.

I looked up and saw Egor kneeling at the edge of the pier. "I'll take him." His huge form leaned over the raft and cast a shadow large enough to shield the old man from the sun.

The old man sat up. "No. I'm wearing a dry suit. Barry and Alex are in danger of hypothermia." Kahler crawled onto the pier. Then he extended his hand to Alex. Her fingers were blue and trembling when she took it.

Egor lifted her into his arms as if she were a kitten. She clasped her hands behind his neck as he turned and started up the steps.

The old man lashed the raft to the dock. "Seven thousand dollars well spent." Then he held out his hand. "I'll steady you on the steps."

I slipped a couple of times. Once I nearly fell backward. The old man stayed behind me, planted a hand on my back, and pushed. I don't know how he managed it without falling.

By the time we reached the house, Egor had Alex wrapped in a thick white terry-cloth robe. She sat at the kitchen table. Her hands still trembled, but she'd managed to wrap them around a steaming mug of coffee.

I glanced at her from the laundry room and then stepped to the side of the doorway and shed every piece of clothing. I dropped them next to Alex's. Egor carried in a robe, and I slipped it on. I inclined my head toward the female undergarments.

Egor's block-of-wood face nearly smiled. "I stepped out of the room and closed the door while she undressed. I had the distinct impression that she would have died there, wet and cold, if I hadn't."

The old man walked in and shed his dry suit. Then he headed for his study.

I joined Alex at the kitchen table, where coffee waited. We didn't talk.

I tried to remember details, but when I closed my eyes, I saw nothing but fire. I looked at Alex. She glanced at me over the top of her cup. She wouldn't put the coffee down. We had nothing to say.

She didn't ask me to drive her home. When Egor offered the guest room, she nodded. She actually linked her arm with mine as we trudged up the stairs to the second floor. When I pointed to the guest-room door, she simply went in and closed it behind her. I figured she'd find the shower and the closet of clothes for guests.

I bathed and crawled into bed. The old man would be fine. Egor would take care of him. He always had.

CHAPTER TWELVE

Sunday, March 6, 2016
Launch minus Twelve Days

I awoke at four o'clock Sunday morning and staggered to my kitchenette. I thought about knocking on Alex's door and then reconsidered. If she was awake, she might not want company. We weren't exactly buddies. If she awoke hungry, she'd make do. We'd stocked the guest room with a Keurig coffee maker, pods, and breakfast bars. So I fixed a bowl of cold cereal, watched less than an hour of a crappy old Dracula movie the studio hadn't even bothered to colorize, and then crawled back into bed.

My eyes popped open again at eight o'clock. Sharp winter sunlight sliced through the window glass. I'd forgotten to close the shades.

I stumbled into the kitchen. The alluring fragrance of fresh-cooked pancakes wafted over me. Alex sat at the table with Egor and chatted away. Egor glanced toward me for the briefest of moments.

"Any chance for pancakes?" I asked.

"In a minute," he answered.

Alex whispered something. Egor laughed.

"That's OK," I said. "I can fix them myself."

I made less than a step toward the refrigerator before Egor planted his massive frame in front of me. I never even heard him slide his chair back.

"Why don't you sit down," he said softly.

I slid into the vacated chair.

Alex watched Egor fussing with the griddle for a moment. Then she turned toward me. "What happened yesterday?"

"Don't know. Something went wrong in the engine bay. Insurance people will be asking the same question. Doubt they'll fish many answers out of the Chesapeake."

"OK. Just don't expect me to go sailing again."

"You can count on that."

"Any interest in playing tourist with me in Adams Morgan?"

"Why? You live there."

"That makes me a *smart* tourist."

I thought about my last trip through Alexland. I found myself staring at her. I felt the left side of my cheek twitch.

She stood up. "I'm better company when I'm not covered in soot."

Her shoulder-length, auburn-streaked brown hair framed an angel's face with luminous, barely freckled skin and sapphire-blue eyes. The blouse she'd taken from the guest-room closet was a scotch plaid of red, black, and white. Even with the top two buttons open, the soft cotton hugged every curve. She'd rolled up the sleeves to just below her elbows, and the inner lining made a two-inch cuff of bright, multicolored dots on a white back-ground. The blouse just reached her waist. The jeans were midnight blue, and the stretch fabric clung to her hips.

I began to regret my choice of clothing for the guest-room closet. I forced myself to look away. I found the microwave and counted the numbers on its keypad fifteen or twenty times. A ghost image of Alex floated alluringly in front of them.

"Barry," Alex's soft voice drifted through my self-induced fog. I heard no harshness in it.

I turned back to her. The ghost image moved with my gaze, aligned with the real Alex like a layer in Photoshop, and then dissolved. I knew what Kahler wanted. He'd made that clear. She was a job. Maybe I could take her on that way. That might keep me from being hurt. *Shields up.* "That sounds great."

She glanced down at my hand for a moment and then took it in her cool, slender fingers. "Deal." I sensed Alex thinking to herself. Her emotions felt as confused as mine.

CHAPTER THIRTEEN

Launch minus Twelve Days

We took separate cars: one Mustang, one Denali. She showed me no mercy. The blimp and I floated along behind her—way behind. Sunday traffic wasn't too bad in DC, but no way could I keep up with Alex. The drive took me an hour and a half. She'd already parked on Kalorama Road. I found her standing beside her car. She grinned at me as I lumbered past. I had to drive a block and a half farther up the street to find a spot. By the time I'd walked back to her townhouse, she'd climbed the steps. Alex Blake stood, neither blocking nor welcoming, just inside the partly open door.

I stopped on the sidewalk and waited.

Her blue eyes studied me. She smiled cautiously. "Hi, Barry."

So I climbed the stairs and walked inside. I stepped around Alex and took a few tentative footsteps into her home.

She closed the door and forced a nervous smile. All that energy, the playfulness she'd shown at Kahler's, had disappeared. At the click of the latch the shields had gone up on her own little internal *Enterprise*. I could almost feel their defensive crackle as they brushed against my own.

"Your neighbor's townhouse has a garage," I said.

"I could have bought that one. This one just seemed so..." Alex swept her eyes around her house, glancing from wall to wall, ceiling to floor. "Lovely."

"But you have a convertible."

"A car's not a pet."

"I argued with Kahler about that once. He wouldn't let me bring my 'Vette inside. Too heavy for the stairs, too big to curl up at the foot of my bed."

"I'm surprised Ethan didn't build a house around his GT-500. I read that some guy in Japan built a house around his Porsche."

"Ethan must think a lot of you to let you drive it."

"I'm the only one he's ever let drive his cars—I mean beside the mechanics. My brother would do anything for me. Has already." Alex stared off wistfully for a moment. "Want a drink or anything?"

"Sure."

"Kitchen's around that corner." She pointed. "I'm going to run upstairs for a minute."

Fifteen minutes later we crossed Eighteenth Street and walked up the hill to Adams Morgan. A cartoon picture of a duck wearing thick, black-rimmed glasses, with a head that looked like the top of a coffee mug, hung from a signpost near the corner. The little bastard looked as if he were laughing at me.

The March air felt brisk, but I was warm enough in my sweater and Coronado Leather jacket. Its built-in holster held a brand-new Colt Lady Elite .380. The tiny pistol was short and thin enough to disappear beneath the heavy leather. I'd seen no point in packing artillery on a date, but Egor had insisted. Kahler's recent dunking had caused an undercurrent of anxiety to flow beneath the surface of Egor's usually placid waters. He'd wanted me to carry the .40-caliber Glock with its thirteen-round magazine. Even inside the jacket, that one would have been a good deal more conspicuous.

I'd frowned at him. "It'll scare Alex. She'll find it the first time she brushes against me."

Egor had smiled. "Always the optimist." Then he'd made a low-pitched chuckle. If hikers ever heard a sound like that, they'd ditch their knapsacks and climb the nearest tree.

Alex walked quickly in her one-inch-heeled, calf-length leather boots. She still wore the scotch-plaid blouse and stretch jeans from our guest closet, now covered by a knee-length coat of brown fur that looked like raccoon. I'd learned to never ask if something was real fur.

We passed the Himalayan Bar and Restaurant. The wood-shingled awning on its pastel-green-painted brick looked inviting, but the sign announcing karaoke turned me away. I wanted to talk, not sing. The sign immediately to the left of the building advertised ABC Emergency Dental, and that didn't help either. We walked slowly up the hill, passing buildings two or three stories high, architecturally diverse, but all fronted in pastel-painted brick or plaster. I saw blue, purple, green, red, and cream. If Adams Morgan had a theme, its theme was pastel.

We passed shops and restaurants, all hung with colored awnings and some wearing wall paintings. Their roofs were flat or conical, and some of those cones sported short, spear-shaped spires that looked as if they might impale a passing bird.

"Columbia Station, Club Heaven and Hell," sported a sign with pointed wings and a Masonic-like eye. A sign advertising "Soul Qemistry" hung beneath it. I saw lots of pizza joints—Jumbo Slice and Pizza Mart with three Harleys parked in the cycle spaces in front. Pizza Bolis was dwarfed by the three-story-high painting on the sidewall of the adjacent building. I spotted that huge image of a woman with long red hair and large tattooed breasts from blocks away. The right breast read, "Madam's Organ Restaurant & Bar," and the left, "The Heart of Adams Morgan." The front of the restaurant sported a neon sign hung from a steer-skull-and-wagon-wheel-decorated balcony. The sign read, "Sorry, We're Open."

Across the street I spotted a small, square two-story building sitting beside the DC Arts Center Theater. It had a pink brick facade dominated by wide floor-to-ceiling windows. The upper-story windows were separated from the lower by a horizontal red band framing, "MELLOW MUSHROOM," which was written in pink uppercase letters. Protecting its red door was a brown awning inviting us to "Get mellow on the ROOF" and sporting a closed hand with its index finger pointing up.

Alex started for Madam's Organ, but I tugged gently at her arm and gestured across the street. This wasn't an evening for getting plastered. I needed to learn a lot more about Alex Blake. I had to get her talking. For some women, drink might do that. But I didn't think that was Alex. When she'd been weak and exhausted, she'd rolled herself up into a squishy but impenetrable ball. On the burning boat, she'd been quick and smart and had showed no sign of panic. The woman needed to be in control. Then she might talk. At the first sign of alcohol brain, she'd clam up tight and shove me away.

Her eyes followed my gesture. "Feeling mellow?" she asked.

"More about not feeling like skulls and wagon wheels."

"I had no idea you were so sensitive."

"Barry has many faces."

"Will I get to see them all?"

I shrugged and stepped over the curb. We were still arm in arm. Alex stayed with me.

I held open the door to the Mellow Mushroom and then followed Alex inside. A staircase led upstairs to the bar. We turned left, through the green door to the restaurant.

The ambience was not mellow. It was loud. I heard no band, but the drone of dozens of conversations created white noise with a vengeance. The exposed-beam ceiling supported hanging spotlights but no soundproofing tiles. The single large room, about eight times longer than wide, had hard-wood floors. Then the delightful aromas of oil, cheese, tomato sauce, and baking dough took hold of me, and I ignored the noise.

A small bar extended out from the wall to my left and seemed to divide the space into two sections. Unfinished red brick walls decorated with paintings of a lion tamer, a juggler, and an elephant characterized a front section composed of the bar and several tables.

The larger rear section had sidewalls of weathered brown wood with peeling white paint. Posters of sideshow performers hung from those walls, and two vertical rows of small sidelights framed each poster.

The kitchen's serving counter took up most of the rear wall, with myriad islands of stainless steel visible beyond. Mellow Mushroom T-shirts hung to either side of the kitchen. One sported a cartoonist's humanized mushroom wearing a golf cap and guiltlessly eating a slice of mushroom-topped pizza.

The place looked mostly full, but the hostess found us a table between the bar and the kitchen, neatly framed by two of the sideshow posters. Alex picked the chair in front of the "Invisible, Impossible to Behold, Bending Girl." That left me sitting in front of the "Unchainable Man."

The waiter brought us a menu, and we got Cokes to drink while I studied it.

Alex had waved it away. "Been here before. Know the menu."

I glanced at her over the top of the menu. "Know what you want?"

"You decide."

Shit. Test number one. I let my eyes cruise the pizza column, and they stopped halfway down. I was outside Egor's low-fat, low-cholesterol domain and might as well enjoy it. "Decided," I said. "The Mighty Meaty."

"I'm a vegetarian."

I drew in a mouthful of Coke hard enough to collapse the straw.

Alex shrugged. "We can order separate dishes."

I scanned the menu too fast. Funky Q Chicken, Mellowterranean, Philosopher's Pie, Maui Wowie, and Thai Dye. All meat. Must have missed a couple. Then I found it. "Holy Shiitake Pie," I announced. I read her the ingredients. "A blend of shiitake, button, and portobello mushrooms with caramelized onions on an olive-oil-and-garlic base with mozzarella and Italian MontAmoré cheese drizzled with garlic aioli." I managed it in a single exhaled breath and then looked up.

Alex smiled at me. "It's really excellent."

"Can't wait." I took another sip of Coke.

So did she.

"Your brother must be a hot property at NASA," I said.

She shook her head and narrowed her eyes pensively. "Top of his class."

"What class was that?"

"Every class. Every goddamned one. Do you have any idea what it's like to be the kid sister to number one? I worked damn hard in school. I'm smart, very smart. I got superb grades. But I wasn't Ethan. I could never be Ethan."

"How old are you?"

"Twenty-nine. Why?"

"Me too. Sorry. How old is Ethan?"

"Thirty-three."

"So you were pretty far apart in school. By the time you hit middle school, he was in high school. When you started high school, he was in college. How much would they remember about some smart kid they taught four years earlier?"

"He wasn't just another smart kid. He was amazing. Top in everything. Every class. Every science fair. Every achievement test. I think our high school got extra money from the state for having the highest average SAT score in the country. The rumor was that Ethan's score had raised the average enough to do that."

"Not everybody loves the smart kid," I said.

She grimaced. "I was the smart kid they didn't like! They all loved my brother. He knew how to make teachers feel they'd made it all possible. He once told me he never asked a question his teacher couldn't answer."

"Clever little bastard," I said.

"I was in the tenth grade. My geometry teacher had drawn a complex problem on the board, and the students were grading each other's homework. Not one of us had the right answer. Then I noticed the teacher had squared the diameter instead of the radius. Her answer was the wrong one. I said so."

"Popular girl."

"For the rest of that semester, she gave me special attention. She looked for ways to mark me down."

"What did you do?"

"I fought back. I made sure everything I did was perfect. Double- and triple-checked perfect! Every time she handed me a paper or a test, she scowled at me."

"And?"

"Every time I thought she said something that wasn't exactly right, my hand went up. They said she started keeping a bottle of Maalox in her desk drawer."

"And?"

"Got an A. Made an enemy."

"So you learned to go easy from then on."

"No fucking way!" Alex stamped her foot. A woman at a nearby table glanced at us. "The more I learned, the more I challenged my teachers. Some really liked it. Most didn't. Even in the advanced-placement classes."

"What about the other kids?"

"I thought they were on my side. I guess I didn't pay much attention to them. Too busy being right. A couple of years ago, I ran into an old high school classmate. At some point I said something about being smarter than my teachers. She laughed at me and said the whole class had wished I hadn't been."

I shrugged. "It's behind you now."

"No. It's not. It still aches."

"Regretting you made people uncomfortable. It's understandable."

"That's not it. I wanted to be valedictorian. Ethan had been. This boy and I were tied—grades, test scores, and activities. The school gave it to him. They made me salutatorian. I went to the principal and asked why they couldn't have two valedictorians. 'The school board voted.' He said nothing else. He stood up, walked out from behind his desk, walked to the door, and opened it."

"What did your parents say?"

"My father died when I was thirteen. Had a stroke."

"Oh. I'm so sorry."

"Don't be. We were never close. He was too busy making money—left us millions. NASA doesn't pay Ethan anywhere near enough to support his car habit."

"What about your mother?" I felt myself smile, as I remembered that safe place of emotional sustenance that had been my own mother.

"She died a few years ago. She really loved Dad."

Adrian Kahler always called me a poorly controlled empath. He regularly assured me that I'd improve. Now my empathic sense detected a flicker of cold emptiness deep inside Alex. My smile faded.

Alex must have seen it. She looked away.

I struggled for something to say. "I...I—"

"Pizza's here." Alex jumped up, wrapped her hands with her napkin, and held them out to a startled waiter.

He looked puzzled, but he'd been a waiter long enough to ride out nearly anything. "Careful. It's hot," he said. Then he obediently handed the pan to Alex.

I saw Alex grit her teeth, but she held on to the pan. The waiter hurriedly cleared a space for it, and Alex set it down. Then she returned to her seat and wrapped both hands around her ice-filled glass of Coke.

I studied the pizza. It had a layer of cheese covered with mushrooms, but I saw no tomato sauce. Instead, someone had squirted four concentric rings of mayonnaise on top of the mushrooms. It looked like a decoration on a birthday cake. I took the spatula and served a slice to Alex. Then I took one for myself.

Alex took up her fork and knife and dug in.

I studied the slice that sat on my plate and readied my fork and knife. Even I don't pick up a mayonnaise-topped pizza. I cut off a mayonnaise-free corner and lifted it to my mouth. Mushroom, garlic, and cheese. Not bad. I eyed the mayonnaise. Finally I dipped an exploratory finger in it and brought it halfway to my mouth.

I noticed that Alex was studying me. Her mouth made a wry smile. "It's aioli."

"What?"

"Aioli. Taste it."

I licked my finger. "Mayonnaise," I said.

"Aioli is to mayonnaise what champagne is to cheap wine."

"What about cheap champagne?"

Alex laughed so hard she nearly spit out a mushroom. I sensed that she'd needed to laugh. She sipped her Coke and then studied me for a moment. "Thanks for ordering vegetarian."

"I'm willing to learn."

"I'm glad."

Nine o'clock found us turning onto Kalorama Road. We walked arm in arm, closer than before, but she hadn't found the gun yet.

I glanced at the townhouses on either side of the street. Even at night I could tell that they were brick. Tall, old trees lined both sides of the street, and some townhouses had tiny front yards planted with bushes. Front doors sat above street level, with a flight of several stairs reaching down to the sidewalk. Most houses stood three stories high. Some looked like they had live-in attics, and a few appeared to have live-in basements. One had a full-width front porch, and one looked like it had a porch on the roof.

We walked up the steps to her front door. Alex turned her key in the lock and swung the door open wide. "After you, sir," she said. Then she giggled. She had a trilling little laugh.

She shed her coat, tossed it on a soft-looking easy chair, and sat on her white leather couch. An LCD TV hung on the wall across from the couch, high enough so that the love seat across from the couch wouldn't get in the way. I figured fifty inches. It was the guys who went for the eighty-inch screens. I parked my jacket next to the raccoon. That was the nice thing about Coronado. The gun stayed with the jacket. This wasn't the moment for brandishing a shoulder holster.

I sat down beside her, a calculated four inches away—close enough for friendship but not yet intimate. Alex smelled wonderful. Not of perfume. More like pixie dust.

She pulled off her boots, propped her feet on the glass-topped coffee table, pushed a few buttons on the remote control, and then tossed it onto the couch. The screen filled with a fireplace. A few thick logs had been carefully stacked on a wrought-iron grate, and thin fingers of dancing yellow flame curled around them. Surround-sound speakers crackled with the protests of burning wood. The noise would have convinced a blind man that the entire room was on fire. I picked up the remote and lowered the volume to the subdued snap, crackle, and pop of a breakfast cereal. Romantic? It was the best I could do.

I glanced at the white-marble fireplace built into the wall to our right. "I could make a real fire."

"Not yet." She stared into the LCD flames.

I waited a minute or so, letting my gaze go where hers went. Then I said, "So tell me about your brother. How smart is he? Really?"

"MIT. He majored in theoretical physics with a minor in mechanical engineering. They'd never seen that combination before. He said he wanted to turn ideas into something people could see. He made number one in every class he took. MIT ain't high school. They gave him a full academic scholarship. All four years. I bet they'd have paid him a salary if he'd asked."

"What about his kid sister?"

Alex stretched and arched her back. Her small, firm breasts strained against the soft fabric of the plaid blouse. Then she perched on the edge of the couch and turned to look at me. "Not as smart."

"Why? Just because you didn't go in for theoretical physics?"

"I got the same grades Ethan did in high school. I took every class he did. But there's an A, and then there's the highest score anyone had ever seen. I pushed hard. Some weeks I'd get by on four hours of sleep a night. But I could never match him." She made a self-conscious little smile. "I hated that."

"He was four years ahead—gone before you started."

"Teachers remember. I heard my name as I walked past the faculty lounge. One of the few teachers who liked me was talking. 'Of course Alex is smart,' she said. 'Very smart. But that Ethan, he was one of a kind.'"

"You're one of a kind. You're you. I'm thinking that's a very special kind. With any luck it's my kind."

Alex leaned forward and kissed me on the cheek. Then she snapped back, quick as a tetherball at the end of its cord.

We sat quietly for a while. I watched the fire. One of the logs crumbled—a great simulation. What was I—a detective, a bodyguard, a friend, someday a lover? I had no way to sort it out.

"What were your parents like?" I asked.

"Distant."

"They must have been pretty smart to produce an Alex and Ethan."

"Dad was an investment analyst. He worked for one of the big firms in Baltimore. He was pretty tight lipped about exactly what he did. He liked to drink. I guess it relieved the stress. Didn't have much time for kids, except when—" She turned away.

"What about your mom?"

"Corporate lawyer. Worked in Baltimore. She didn't like it much."

"So why didn't she quit? Sounds like your dad made more than enough."

"To Mom, life was a discipline. You don't quit. Nobody quits."

"What about with you?"

"She helped me with homework in middle school. But as I matured, we grew apart. Sometimes I'd catch her looking at me with this peculiar expression, envy or anger or something. Weird. Then she developed diabetes. Started the shots. Insulin killed her. Hypoglycemia. She died a couple of years after my father's death."

Alex stared into the fire for a while. It looked bright. It crackled. It made no heat.

She turned her head a couple of degrees toward mine. "What about your folks?"

"Dad died a few years back. Diabetes. Like your mom."

"I doubt it." Her face lost color, and she turned away.

"Sure. I suppose no two deaths are much alike."

I took a breath, long and deep. I hoped I hadn't appeared to sigh. Probably didn't matter. Alex had withdrawn. At that moment I could have tossed a bucket of water onto her digital fireplace, and she wouldn't have noticed.

I gave her a minute and then took another shot.

"Why do you live in Adams Morgan?" I asked. "You work in Georgetown. Why not live there?"

Her eyes blinked a couple of times. Then she turned toward me, all the way this time. "I like eclectic. Georgetown is wealth and college kids and wealthy college kids." Then she smiled. "And you can't get a Holy Shiitake pizza in Georgetown."

"So aioli's an Adams Morgan thing."

"It's not the item—it's the willingness to put it on a pizza. There's an enthusiasm for life here, a spirit of adventure."

"Sure is. I had to borrow some of that spirit to put a slice in my mouth."

"Did you like it?"

"Actually, yes."

"See! Life's an adventure. There's always something new here."

I glanced at my watch. "Still early," I said. "We could hit one of the nightclubs—start our adventure there. How about Madam's Organ?"

"It is the heart of Adams Morgan," Alex laughed, light and easy. "If not there, then the noisiest place we can find."

"You're on."

She reached for the remote control. I'd left it on the arm of the couch, and Alex had to lean across me to retrieve it. As she did, her breast slid across the knuckles of my right hand. I felt her nipple stiffen. Then she jerked away as if I'd cut her with a knife. She sat frozen for a moment, eyes wide. Emotion flowed out of her in waves. It wasn't anger that she felt. It was fear.

I walked to the kitchen and found a glass, some ice, and some water. I carried it back to the living room and held it out to her. She stared at me and ground her teeth. Then she regained some composure and accepted my offering.

I gave her a minute and a couple of swallows. "You OK?"

She nodded. "Of course. Why wouldn't I be?"

"Want to talk?"

"About what?"

"I guess I should be going."

"Right."

I picked up my jacket. I let myself out.

CHAPTER FOURTEEN

Monday, March 7, 2016
Launch minus Eleven Days

I looked up at the old man as he pulled out his chair and sat at the kitchen table. I'd risen early, jogged early, eaten breakfast with Egor, and paced the halls. Then I'd sat down, sipped more caffeine than needed, and waited for ten thirty. That was when Adrian Kahler would come down from his suite on the third floor. He worked until two or three o'clock in the morning, so breakfast was at ten thirty, the same time every morning. Kahler the diabetic had imposed a rhythm on his life, a template. It varied only in crises and rarely even then.

Egor placed the oat-bran pancakes, olive-oil butter, and a small ration of jam on the table in front of him. Then the sixteen-ounce glass mug of dark-roast coffee. Steam rose from the surface of the dusky liquid, and when the aroma wafted across the table, I automatically took a sip from my own cup before I realized mine had turned cold. I made a face.

Kahler ignored me. He fired off a shot from his insulin pump and buttered, sliced, and forked a piece of pancake to his mouth. He always tasted a couple of forkfuls before adding the jam. Said he liked to enjoy each flavor. When your diet was restricted, you made the most of it.

I kept myself quiet for a half-dozen forkfuls and two sips. Then I said, "Put me to work."

The old man sighed. "You have an assignment."

"It's not working."

He took a sip of coffee.

"There's something wrong with her. She's nuts. She's frigid. She's probably both."

"I do not require a romance. Become her friend."

I laughed. "Like in a buddy movie?"

"As you wish."

"They can end badly."

"I require a beginning. Definitely a middle. How your relationship ends is not my concern."

The phone rang. I picked it up. "ISI."

"Hi, Barry. It's Max. We need another meeting with Dr. Kahler."

I clicked the mute button. "Max needs—"

Kahler held up an index finger. He didn't like his meals interrupted. He chewed. He swallowed. He sipped his coffee. "One o'clock." Then he returned his attention to his rapidly diminishing breakfast. The old man didn't eat much, but he was the poster child for mindfulness.

I clicked again. "One o'clock OK?"

"We'll be there." Max hung up before I had a chance to ask for an expansion of "we."

I caught the old man's eye and gave him a questioning glance.

His gaze met mine. "You will attend this meeting. You will not speak."

At five minutes before one, Egor walked into the living room and took his customary seat. His oversized easy chair sat several feet to the right of the old man's Eames and a couple of feet in front of it. Most visitors didn't pay much attention to the silent, slumped-down form lost beneath Kahler's six-by-seven-foot copy of *Hide-and-Seek* on the wall in front of him. Pavel Tchelitchew's surrealistic painting dominated the room. His golden-haired girl rode that giant oak. Her outstretched arms and muscular legs clutched at its trunk, her face buried in its gnarled bark. That girl seized each visitor's attention, and she held it. I could usually tell when our guests finally registered those huge, fetus-like apparitions floating in the branches above her. It didn't take an empath. A tiny gasp always popped from between their lips.

The black Lincoln Navigator parked in the front driveway at 1:05 p.m. Max climbed out on the left, Scofield on the right. No congressman Boyer.

Scofield walked faster than Max. I opened the door and stood back as he marched in. He wore his tailored, crisply pressed charcoal suit like a uniform. The fabric looked expensive, and the fit did a fair job of filling out the frame to which his thin neck and gaunt face were bolted. He stopped in the foyer, and his sunken eyes looked me over. "I got orders from the Joint Chiefs this morning," he said. "You're in, Barry." He grinned and elbowed me in the ribs. "Be careful what you wish for."

"I don't wish. I do what I'm told."

"Me too." He smiled wryly. "You're not after my job, are you?"

Max stepped between us, grabbed my hand, and shook it. For him that was reflex. I couldn't help but smile back. His jacket and gray flannel trousers always looked wrinkled. They probably came from the dry cleaners that way.

I led our two clients into the living room and motioned to the couch. Scofield took the spot on the chesterfield opposite Kahler's Eames. The fabric on that couch was as soft and inviting as the old man's money could buy. Most clients grinned a little as they sank in. Scofield sat on the edge, spine as straight as if he were perched on a straight-backed chair. Max slid in after him and leaned back. Max smiled.

I took my seat to the left of Kahler's. The old man's study door opened almost immediately. He walked in, nodded curtly to our clients, and then sat down.

Max looked at Kahler, then at me, and then back at the old man. "Iran launched a missile yesterday," Max said. "It was unarmed. It overflew Israel and came down in the Mediterranean, about one hundred miles from the Israeli coast. Iran's announcement called it an engine test. That was followed by a bellicose demand for Israel to exit the West Bank and Gaza. *Theoretically*, Iran has no nukes."

"Did Israel respond?" asked Kahler.

"Jets scrambled and then returned to base."

"Armament?"

Scofield leaned forward. His thin frame looked like a bent paper clip. He grimaced. "What the hell do you think? The Israelis own nukes and have no treaty with anyone. They have them in the air. They have them under the sea."

Kahler looked at Scofield. "What does the Pentagon think?"

"It looks like a bluff, but no one in this government is one hundred percent sure what the goddamn Iranians are thinking or which Iranian is thinking what or who in Tehran might decide to go for broke, if it comes to that."

I studied Drew Scofield. His face neither smiled nor frowned. His voice neither rose nor fell. Military discipline or flat affect? I took a shot at tuning my empathic sensors to his frequency. For an instant I detected pain, unrelenting and severe, and then discipline, unwavering and intense. The signals died almost as soon as I'd picked them up.

Max broke in. "Iran did sign a treaty. No nukes. They traded them for money. The ink's barely dry on the paper. This has to be a bluff."

The old man glanced from Max to Scofield. "A bluff is a calculation. As such, each carries the danger of miscalculation. Someone in that government has a fixation on Israel. That has never been sensible from the Iranian geopolitical perspective. When things are not sensible, they are impossible to handicap."

Max shook his head. "Iran's a big country. Israel doesn't have that many nukes. Not all of them will get through. If Iran's leaders go psychotic, they might figure that they can take a few hits. Israel's small; it can't."

Scofield cleared his throat. We all looked at him. "This brings us to the impossible-to-confirm department. Rumor number one: Iran has a secret enrichment facility. They shut it down after the treaty was signed, but not before it produced enough material for six nuclear warheads. The warheads were constructed and then hidden. As I understand it, they can be attached to a delivery system in less than twenty-four hours. We don't know how much less."

I found myself staring at Scofield's thin, ragged face, fixed on his deep-set gray eyes.

"Rumor number two: a senior adviser to Iran's Supreme Leader had a dream. He awoke convinced that he must perform one great, final service for Islam. This guy is eighty-six years old. Doctors from London's UCLH Macmillan Cancer Centre have paid him several visits, probably not to play whist. After our redline fiasco in Syria, the Tehran toadies fear that old man more than they fear us. They just might figure that once we have no more Israel to protect, we'll cut another deal."

We all stared at him. The artery at my left temple had begun to throb.

Kahler spoke first. "Tel Aviv is less than twenty miles from the West Bank."

Scofield coughed. Once again I had the sense of a body wracked with pain. "Shit, I'm not in the old bastard's head. Maybe he sees those Palestinians as the lucky ones. They get to be martyrs."

He slapped the flat of his hand onto the glass tabletop. That sudden, sharp sound shattered the stillness of the room. "We need the Hammer. That's the only answer to this. If we send in cruise missiles to take out the Iranian launch sites, then we're the ones in a war. Worse, we can't be certain we've identified every site. If we do nuke them, they might get just testy enough to launch a missile at us. Maybe we shoot it down; maybe we don't." He whacked the table again, this time with the side of his fist. "We need the Hammer."

Kahler nodded a millimeter. "Agreed. Are you making progress?"

Max looked down at his knees and shook his head. "Ethan Blake's lab has produced no crystals for two weeks. The first production failure was on February twenty-second. Since then it's only been more of the same."

"Everyone has crazy moments. I've had a couple myself." Scofield ground his teeth. "But that guy's a flake. And his timing sucks."

"A brilliant flake," Max said. "It's only because of his work that the Hammer project became possible in the first place. The operational satellites have tested one hundred percent effective."

"Right," Scofield said. "But they don't control enough real estate. Not yet. The one that will cover Iran is due for launch in eleven days. The flatbed truck needs fifteen to twenty hours to drive from Goddard to Kennedy Space Center. The techies need maybe a day to mount the crystal and run the test-fire sequence. So we have nine days to stop a war."

Kahler turned to Max. "How much does Congressman Boyer know about this?"

"Almost nothing," Max said. "His committee channels the funding for surveillance satellites. He was asked to provide a liaison who could be trusted at the highest level of security. That's me. I move money into the Hammer project in a circuitous fashion. It's like money laundering. The congressman keeps his plausible deniability."

Scofield turned to Max. His thin lips smiled. "And if things get messy, it's easier to disappear an aide than a congressman."

Max nodded. "Easy as an army colonel."

"That's the job." Drew Scofield grinned at him. "I like to think of it as being killed in action but without the medal."

I shot the old man an angry glance.

Kahler regarded me for a moment. The corners of his mouth turned up a millimeter. "Patriotism has its cost."

Scofield continued, "This is all for shit if Blake doesn't come up with a crystal for the new satellite."

Kahler asked, "What about Dr. Seep?"

Scofield shook his head. "We brought him in months ago to run a parallel lab. Once we realized what we had, we knew it was too important to rest on the abilities of one scientist. So far Seep's produced nothing. He claims Blake's holding back some piece of critical information, but every member of Blake's staff swears the two labs are identical. I figure Seep overlooked something. Maybe Blake's jerking his chain. Maybe not. Once Seep gets it, we won't be so dependent on Blake. Until then, Blake remains the lynchpin."

"What's Blake's explanation?"

Scofield winced. His face contorted, and he stiffened as if a bolt of intense pain had flashed through his body. He relaxed almost as suddenly, and the barest form of a grin captured his face, as if he'd just beaten an old adversary and relished the victory. "Keeps saying it's a delicate process. They've grown a couple of crystals, but each one of them has cracked at the very last moment, just before completion."

Kahler nodded. "Does he understand the political situation?"

"He's been briefed."

"Isn't that unusual?"

"We're desperate."

"Alternatives?"

"None." Scofield pulled at his left earlobe with thumb and forefinger. "The air force gave up on crystals because they couldn't grow them large enough. Blake can. At least he could. He had the magic touch. The air force has been experimenting with gas lasers. They've been using helium. Their systems have nowhere near the power of Blake's crystal lasers, and they're way too fragile to withstand launch. No one has ever even dreamed of anything like the Hammer. It's small enough to be placed on a surveillance satellite, produces a massive, focused output from a small power source, and can fire repetitively. Most important, it's undetectable. Any missile it targets simply explodes right after liftoff."

Kahler studied Scofield. I could feel him probing the man. "What is the beam diameter?"

Scofield shrugged. "Don't know. We're compartmentalized."

The old man's gaze clung to him for a moment, so briefly that it was barely perceptible. Then Kahler turned to Max. "Do you believe that Ethan Blake is sabotaging his own laboratory?"

Max let out a long sigh. "At this point I'd believe anything."

Scofield smacked the glass tabletop again. "We need him! For now he's the irreplaceable man. It's not like we can waterboard him. He says he's doing the best he can, and all we can say is, 'Thank you.' He knows the timetable. We need leverage."

Kahler fixed Scofield with his steady, gray-blue eyes. "Like his sister?"

Scofield straightened the fingers of his right hand and chopped it against the palm of his left. "Like his balls stretched tight on a block. Like anything or anyone I might use, even if they hang me for it later."

Kahler turned to Max. "Could the Iranians have learned of this and put pressure on Dr. Blake?"

Max shook his head. "I—"

Scofield cut him off. He leaned toward Kahler again. His skin seemed to stretch even more tightly over the bones of his face, and the left corner of his mouth began to twitch. "Nobody—I repeat, nobody—knows about the Hammer, nobody who isn't supposed to. Blake is watched. We're all watched. We even run satellite control from Goddard. Manufacturing, command, and control—they're all in the same complex. We kept it out of the Pentagon. It's a small team. We're under the direct control of the Joint Chiefs of Staff." His eyes sparkled, and he chuckled as if he'd just told a joke. "Did I mention we're all watched?

"If the Iranians really knew about Blake—about any of this—they'd just kill him. So would the Russians, the Chinese. I could go on. But they don't know. And there aren't enough Iranians in Washington to host a cocktail party, let alone gather intelligence. They don't even have an embassy. They have an interest section in DC. It's technically part of the Pakistani embassy, but it has a different address. If I could do it, I'd surround Blake with bodyguards. Better yet, I'd lock him in his lab." He smacked his hand against the table again. "Shit. Even Homeland Security can't get away with that stuff."

Adrian Kahler's cold eyes swept over Scofield, then Max, and then back to Scofield. "Who named the project?"

Confusion momentarily settled on Max's plump face. "Named?"

Scofield leaned forward, across the table separating him from Kahler. "Blake named it. We humor the guy whenever we can."

Kahler stood up. "I have thinking to do. Barry will show you out. He will contact Max when I have something."

"Now wait just a damn—"

Kahler's eyes flashed battleship gray. They found Scofield's. For me the experience felt like listening to an iPod as someone cut the headphone wire. Scofield's audio stream died. Kahler stood, walked into his study, and closed the door.

Drew Scofield worked his mouth a few times, but nothing came out.

I gave him a moment to recover and then stood up and ushered him to the front door. Max followed. Scofield looked the tiniest bit unsettled, but his voice had returned. He chatted amiably as we walked. So did Max.

Scofield stood in the doorway for a moment. Max had already made it halfway to the car.

Drew Scofield was unaware anything had happened. That was how Kahler usually left the target of his displeasure. Scofield stood in the doorway for a moment. Then he turned to me and extended his hand.

As I took it, I became aware of his cologne. I'd smelled something like it in Brooks Brothers once. Sixty bucks for one of those tiny bottles. Seemed weird when men drenched themselves with it.

"I need to get home and feed my cat. He's family."

I smiled amiably. "Figured all you military guys had German shepherds."

"He's a big, ugly tomcat. Found him living in an alley behind the apartment building where I used to live. He had a limp; otherwise I'd never have caught him. Got his leg fixed. The vet said she'd treated smaller dogs. Then Shredder moved in with me. Guards the apartment. Acts like it's his. I feed him and clean his litter box, so he suffers my presence. You know cats."

I shrugged.

Scofield smiled. "They get testy when they're kept waiting." He turned and marched toward the waiting car.

I closed the door behind him.

CHAPTER FIFTEEN

Launch minus Eleven Days

Adrian Kahler's study door stood wide open. Otherwise I'd have slammed it open hard enough to bounce it off the wall. He glanced up from his computer as I stormed in.

I glared at him. "You will not speak?"

He shrugged barely enough for even me to notice. "I was concerned that you might mention *Seawitch.*"

"You let them sink your boat to test a theory?"

"I did not let them do anything. Blake's car caught fire—unusual for a new automobile sitting at a traffic light. Freak events do occur. So I presented a large, floating target to discover what might occur. In all likelihood nothing would have happened. But, in order to minimize future risk, I had to make certain. Diesel fuel is not particularly flammable. We had a fire. You put it out. We had another."

"There would have been a big hole in the deck. The laser would have had to blast through to the fuel tank."

"I suspect that the beam diameter is quite small and that the device fires repetitively at a high cyclic rate. A dozen tiny holes, each perhaps a few millimeters in diameter. In the presence of smoke and fire, they could have been overlooked."

I thought back to those patterned, tiny swirls of smoke rising from the deck, that cluster of little holes. I shouted at him. "You knew! As soon as the fire started, you knew we'd become a target. That crazy sailing—" I found myself coughing.

"Erratic maneuvers did not save us."

I took a deep breath. An icy tremble of fear trickled down my spine. "How can they target a thirty-eight-foot sailboat with no heat signature?"

"The sky was clear." The old man stared into his computer screen, as if the little Macintosh on his desk or the big Cray it connected to might hand him the answer. "The ramifications are grave."

"Could Scofield know something he's not telling us? Are the Joint Chiefs holding out?" I felt myself smile in anger. "You could slice Scofield's mind open and lay it out on the coffee table."

"I would not be able to put it back together. Were I to find nothing, the Joint Chiefs would react badly. Were I to find something, they might react worse." Kahler ran the fingers of his left hand through his meticulously combed white hair, disrupting the part on the left side. "I suspect some among them are already reconsidering the wisdom of bringing us in."

I lowered myself into the black leather of the big easy chair across from his desk. It wasn't new anymore, but when I sank into its soft cushions, a subtle leather scent draped itself around me. "Why did they?"

He smiled tightly. "Desperation. They need someone to get to Ethan Blake, learn if he is deliberately holding up manufacture of that crystal, and if so persuade him to get the processes going again. They will not risk force until the wolf is standing on their chest. He does not need money."

"And I pulled his sister out of a burning car."

"Indeed."

"Whichever member of the Joint Chiefs discovered that we have security clearance must have started believing in the tooth fairy."

"My phone rang before you left the hospital. They called Boyer first. Max and Scofield arrived at eleven the next morning. Egor had left at ten to pick you up at New Carrollton." Kahler made a face. "I had to make my own breakfast."

"Toaster challenged?"

"I dislike interruptions to my routine."

I stood up and paced the length of the tiny room, back and forth. For once I didn't mean to annoy the old man. I just thought better on my feet. "Do we really have security clearance for this?"

The old man scowled. "No one has clearance for this. That is precisely why they kept it out of the Pentagon. That place is too political, too complex, and far too hectic. A rat can't hide a crumb of cheese in a den of rats."

"So bringing us in is one hell of a risk."

"I presume Boyer vouched for us. They are in a pickle. If the clerics in Iran convince their military to launch a nuclear attack against Israel, the United States will be drawn into a nuclear war. We will be forced to make nuclear strikes against Iran, in population centers comparable to whatever they target in Israel plus every location from which they might launch a nuclear strike against us.

"Many countries live under the protection of America's nuclear umbrella. If we do not respond, if that umbrella proves to be a chimera, they will have no alternative but to develop their own nuclear capabilities. They will feel pressed to do so rapidly, and tensions will rise." The corners of the old man's mouth crept upward. "But if a laser hidden within a surveillance satellite can surreptitiously cause the Iranian ballistic missiles to explode on launch, then the entire circuit of attack and retaliation is shorted out."

I shook my head. "But the secret must be kept."

"At all cost. The moment another country learns that surveillance satellites are armed with lasers that can destroy ballistic missiles, those satellites will be attacked. We will use the Hammer to defend our satellites. That will be a giant step on the way to World War III."

I plunked my body back down into the leather chair. The cushions let out a sigh. I turned to Kahler and looked into his cold, emotionless eyes. "Think some patriot might try to rub us out when all this is over?"

The old man smiled thinly. "Perhaps the initial attempt has already been made. Perhaps someone in the Joint Chiefs' office has had second thoughts regarding our involvement." His lips were tight. His eyes looked grim. He plucked his tiny model sailboat from the top of the desk, studied it for a moment, sighed, opened the drawer beneath the right side of his desk, carefully nestled the little boat into a back corner, and slid the drawer closed.

I frowned back at him. "They'll try again."

"I doubt whoever it is will risk further exposure. He took his shot. He failed. He will go to ground, at least for the moment. However, for the time being, I plan to keep myself out of the sun."

"What about me?"

Adrian Kahler leaned back. His Eames chair tilted. He nearly smiled again. "No man who is wily enough to have climbed the ladder to the Joint Chiefs of Staff would be fool enough to kill you and leave me alive."

CHAPTER SIXTEEN

Tuesday, March 8, 2016
Launch minus Ten Days

On Tuesday I drove back to Goddard. Egor's Denali still had some of its new-car smell. Did I mention that it drove like a blimp? Wooing Ethan Blake's sister hadn't produced much of anything, so I'd been instructed to try my hand at wooing Ethan. The weird part was that I hadn't even had to reach out. He'd called me. That meant he wanted help from outside the government. He must have learned something about the old man, and he'd probably talked things over with his sister. From what I'd been able to learn about him, Blake wasn't close to anyone else. So here I sat, in the right place at the right time—available Barry.

I'd been sitting on the dock, staring at the thirty-eight feet four inches of empty water formerly occupied by *Seawitch*, when Egor walked up behind me. I hadn't heard his footsteps either on the steps or on the wood planks of the pier. The rest of us clunk.

"Mr. Blake is on the phone."

"You mean Ms. Blake."

"Not unless she's dropped her voice an octave and changed her name to Ethan."

I stood up. "It would be nice if we had wireless."

"You know Adrian. Security."

I trudged after him. Eighty steps, each nine inches high. Did I mention that I clunk?

The midafternoon traffic had been light. I'd spent the drive wondering who in Scofield's tight little team of satellite operators might have an agenda different from the Joint Chiefs'. Was it personal, ideological? If it were financial, then the Hammer secret had already been compromised, and shit was about to happen. Maybe more than the world had ever seen before. I'd begun to shiver.

At four o'clock I parked the Denali. My blue no-iron cotton shirt stuck to the leather seat even with the seat ventilation system running on full. I had to peel myself out of the car. A dour-faced guard met me at the entrance to Building 29. He looked maybe a little north of forty, maybe a few pounds north of fit, but I saw nothing soft about him. He had dark eyes and a full head of close-cropped black hair, and he moved with an air of confidence. He let his hands hang beside his baton and pistol as if the tools of his trade were old comrades. He didn't pay them much attention but was well acquainted with each. He escorted me to Ethan Blake's lab. As I reached for the stainless-steel handle, the heavy door opened about a foot and then stopped abruptly.

Ethan Blake stuck his head into the hallway. His dark hair looked damp and more slicked down than I remembered, and his receding hairline looked as if it had retreated a bit farther, leaving his broad forehead even more prominent than before. "Hi, Barry. Good to see you." He opened the heavy door a little more and then took a half step through the gap. No lab coat today. He wore an old Beatles T-shirt. "We're having a small crisis. Come back in an hour."

I stared at him. "You can't be ser—"

Blake shot a quick glance at the guard. "Entertain him. A forty-five minute tour should do it."

The door closed.

As I turned toward the guard, the door on the far side of the hall swung open. A fair-skinned six-footer, maybe six two, stepped into the hallway.

He balanced a long, thin, pale face on a skinny neck, but his perfectly tailored charcoal-gray suit made his body look solid. A white button-down shirt was embellished by a burgundy necktie. His straight white hair fell almost to his collar. He looked like a more modern, more affluent version of Ichabod Crane.

He had eyes the color of pastel-blue chalk. I once drew something like them on my folks' driveway. The two chalky disks studied me for a moment, up and down and then side to side. "I'm sorry, I haven't had the pleasure." He held out his right hand. The shiny black uppercase letters on the gold-colored name tag clipped to his breast pocket spelled out, "Geoffrey Seep, PhD."

"Barry Sandler." I took his hand. His skin felt cold, but he had a firm grip.

"Visiting Ethan?" He looked pensive for a moment. "I saw your name in an e-mail this morning. I've been asked to cooperate." He gestured me into his lab. The door swung closed behind us.

I rested my hand against the cool stainless steel of the door and leaned against it. "Thought I had a date. Told to go away and come back later."

He shook his head. I expected it to bobble, but somehow his thin neck kept it upright. "That Alex. She lives in her own little world."

"Smart, though," I said. I didn't tell him my date was with Ethan. Maybe he knew something about Alex I could use.

He shook his head. "Annoying."

I nodded. Then I said, "But lots of spirit. That can be attractive in a woman."

He pressed his thin lips into a line and narrowed his chalk-blue eyes. He spoke slowly, enunciating each word. "I prefer a woman who knows her place."

Sometimes conversation resembles a car moving through traffic. Geoffrey Seep had just slammed on the brakes, and I'd nearly whacked my head against the windshield. I fought down my distaste for the man and backtracked to plan number one. "Actually, my date's with Ethan. The powers that be are getting jumpy about crystal production."

"So am I. I simply do not understand the man. I'm beginning to think he's playing me for a fool. God knows why."

I inclined my head toward the bronze bust standing guard just inside the doorway. "How's Shakespeare?"

"Better since I burned that accursed wig."

I nodded understandingly. "Those Blakes have a twisted sense of humor."

"I think both of them like to torment me. I've no idea why. Ethan and I were classmates at MIT. I never managed better than number two to Blake's number one, but we got along. We didn't interact much. He behaved as if I didn't even exist. I probably took that too personally. To describe the situation more objectively, he acted as if no one but Ethan Blake existed. I think I moved to California to get as far away from him as possible. At JPL I was number one. I developed the tracking system those satellites use for targeting. It combines Doppler radar and infrared laser imaging. We can target the wings on a fly at—" He cut himself off abruptly. "Sorry, that's classified." He shook his head twice, slowly rotating it side to side on his pencil-thin neck. "I should have never left. But when Mother became ill—" He swallowed, bobbling his Adam's apple up and down. "She has no one else, you know. And she refused to leave the house she's lived in for forty years." He squeezed his eyes closed, covering those two chalky-blue disks for a moment. Then he raised his lids and stared at the wall behind me. "I couldn't let her die alone." His voice trailed off.

"Any suggestions as to what I can do around here to kill some time?"

Geoffrey Seep shrugged. When he did that, even his carefully padded suit couldn't hide the bony contours of his shoulders. "Tour the facility. I don't know what they hope you'll accomplish here, but you'll do it better once you have a feel for the place."

I nodded. "I best get going, then."

He held out his hand. I took it.

"Good luck with Ethan." He smiled thinly. "The man is like an alarm clock. Everyone knows he's valuable, but he's terribly annoying. No one likes him."

I worked the handle and shouldered the door open. The guard looked as if he hadn't moved.

Ichabod waved a pale hand as the door swung closed.

I followed the guard down a couple of hallways and then through a door flanked by a *Star Wars Episode I* Coke machine. It sported a top-to-bottom illuminated poster of Anakin as a child, with the shadow of Darth Vader cast onto the wall of a hut behind him. I walked out into a large open space.

"What's your name?" I asked as we climbed aboard an electric cart.

"Esposito," he said, cocking a thumb toward his ID badge.

"First name?"

"Joe."

"Hi, Joe. I'm Barry."

That was the first time I'd seen him smile.

My tour commenced. I'm not sure what I expected—maybe space station parts and a pod racer or two. Instead I got warehouses. Lots of big warehouses inside one gigantic warehouse. Open space, lots of huge open spaces, with the roof two hundred feet above. Bright-orange bridge cranes clung to the roof here and there, extending all the way across, moving on tracks that let them skate across the ceiling like huge, misshapen spiders. An eighty-foot-tall poster of the Hubble Space Telescope hung from one of them. Blue wire cages enclosed big gray machines. Toolboxes sat everywhere—big red ones with stacks of drawers, like the top-of-the-line boxes they sell at Sears. Lots of things were wrapped in silver foil. Machine shops, large and small, sat in almost every corner. Some had stainless-steel workbenches mounted with navy- and pastel-blue robotic arms. One room held a gigantic black centrifuge that must have reached four hundred feet across. It sported an American flag on one end. Whatever gravity NASA needed, NASA made.

Joe pointed to a gigantic gray metal container that looked as if it would barely fit on a flatbed truck. "Satellites ship in those. They go to Cape Kennedy for launch."

"How do they know they'll fit under the bridges?" I asked.

"The route's checked out ahead of time. Everything's measured. And a dummy truck runs in front of the container carrier. It has rods on it to check overhead clearance. Even then, things can screw up. We had a container stuck under a bridge a couple of years ago."

"Shit." I whistled. "What'd they do—blow up the bridge?"

My guide laughed. "Nah. The driver just let some air out of the tires."

I shook my head. "I hope that guy got a medal."

The guard smiled. "Better. They gave him a raise."

One section held tools for astronauts, each one stainless steel, degreased, dehydrated, sterilized, wrapped in plastic, and sporting a "Flight Hardware Equipment Parts" tag, signed, dated, and marked "NASA Goddard Space Flight Center." I saw one machine that might have been a satellite, a fifty-foot-tall, black-and-silver rectangle with a brace of solar panels folded against one side.

The clean rooms were off limits. We stopped beside one. I walked over to the glass wall and stared inside. The guard pointed. "This wall's glass. The opposite wall is made of air filters."

"The entire wall?"

"Most of it. Floor to ceiling. Final satellite assembly takes place in there. No dust permitted."

I peered through the glass. The techs inside wore head-to-toe white suits and surgical masks. Only their eyes were visible.

Then we climbed back aboard the cart. Its little engine whirred, and it rolled forward.

Joe glanced at his watch. "You'll just make your meeting."

"I already made my meeting. The good Dr. Blake postponed it."

"He does that a lot."

"Why do they stand for it?"

Joe held up an index finger and made a screwing motion beside his right ear. "Rumor is they need him. Why else?"

I grumbled half under my breath. "The indispensable fucking man."

Joe Esposito smiled broadly. "Nice work for the guy who can get it."

The cart stopped. I glanced around at lots of open space. "Something here on the tour?" I asked.

"Nope." Joe made a face. "Battery just died. Gauge read full when we started. Should have had plenty of juice."

I shrugged. "So we walk."

"Quicker if I get another cart. We passed one a little ways back. You wait here."

I glanced around. Up ahead stood a pair of huge brown metal double doors that reached halfway up the two-hundred-foot wall. One hung partially open. I pointed. "What's that?"

"Vibration test facility. Nothing much to see. I'm surprised it's open. The safety geeks want it closed tight."

"Maybe they're testing a vibration, whatever that means."

Joe shook his head. "None scheduled." He climbed down. "Safety rules say visitors stay on the cart."

I smirked at him. "If you say so."

"Listen, kid, this is a big industrial complex. Lots of stuff here can be really dangerous, especially to someone who doesn't know his way around. Think of it as the dark side of the moon. Some of it looks familiar, but it's not, not really. Some fool wanders around without his guide, and the next thing you know, he falls into a crater." Joe leveled a finger at me. "Then you're dead."

I straightened out my face and shrugged.

Joe frowned at me with all the guard-who's-seen-it-all seriousness at his command. "And they'll blame me. Stay put! Back in five."

Investigate. That was what I'd come for. I waited until Joe rounded a corner, gave it another few seconds in case he turned back to check on me, and then climbed down. One of the brown doors was closed. A white plastic sign at eye level read, "Vibration Test Facility. Used for vibroacoustic qualification; simulates the vibroacoustic environment in the launch vehicle (engine and atmosphere buffeting)." I studied the two doors—riveted steel, a good one foot thick. They reminded me of the ones those villagers had used to keep out King Kong.

The closed door's mate hung open, just a bit. I ran exploring fingertips over the surface. It felt lab-bench smooth and cold as death. The space between the two doors looked just large enough for a Barry-sized person to squeeze through. I took that as an invitation. I spy with my little eye. Neither Joe nor any other guard was in sight.

I slipped between the two giant doors and found myself inside a huge white steel box about fifty feet square and over one hundred feet tall. I felt a tingle on the back of my neck, a tiny bead of sweat. If they kept anything dangerous in here, they would have locked the door. But something not top secret but sort of secret? Maybe not. I'd hit plenty of don't-go-there spots as a kid. I let my mind drift back in time. Then I felt another trickle of sweat. Those little adventures hadn't always gone well. I shrugged. *I'm smarter now. Barry v.2.0.*

I took a few steps deeper into the huge room. Vibration test facility. Did it vibrate? Did it test something that vibrated? I looked from wall to wall, trying to figure it out. They'd painted a blue-and-gold National Aeronautics and Space Administration insignia, about six feet across, on the far wall. The door creaked. I spun toward it. Nothing. This fox would not let himself be scared out of the box. My heart ignored me and began pounding. I ignored it back.

I glanced up. A yellow gantry clung to the ceiling. For the most part, the room stood empty. It held nothing but fear. Yet my eyes returned to the narrow opening between those massive doors. If it lessened by even an inch, I'd be trapped. My heart pounded again. *Will you shut up? Please.* I remembered my meditation training and took a deep, cleansing breath. That dragged my heart rate back to normal. *Investigate, damn you.* I wiped my sweaty palms on my pants leg and got to work.

Six white spotlights shone down from the ceiling. The wall to my left was the busiest. I turned to study it. At the far end, a giant horn extended out from the wall. It looked sort of bugle shaped, about a dozen feet long. The narrow end looked about as wide as my fist, the wide end maybe five feet in diameter. It sat on a red iron cart. A twenty-foot pole to its left carried bundled wires and electrical leads. Beside that sat a normal-sized brown metal door supported by three heavy, riveted iron hinges. Next was another boom with more electrical leads. To the left of those, I found a circular depression in the wall. It looked about nine feet in diameter and six inches deep. It had a two-foot-wide blue center. A second circular depression, similar in size, sat directly above the first, just below the ceiling.

The normal-sized iron door with the three hinges was closed. I tugged on the latching mechanism, but it wouldn't budge. A tiny voice at the back of my mind whispered, *"Time to go."* I kicked it out of my mind and focused on the job. My eyes jumped from this to that, trying to latch on to anything that might give me a clue as to what had gone wrong at Goddard. I felt completely out of my element. That didn't stop me from stubbornly believing I might see something here that I'd know was out of place.

A sign beside the door read, "Notice. Emergency Cutoff Switch. Keep in Off Position When Working in Chamber." To the right of the sign were two vertical panels, each housing six round, colored buttons. Their labels read, "Power On," "Control On," "Start," "Stop," "For Brog North," "Rev Brog South," "For Trol West," "Rev Trol East," "Up," "Down," "Up Inch," "Down Inch," but I found nothing that looked like an emergency cutoff. Maybe it was on the far side of the small door. I tried it again. No go.

I perceived a squeak. I felt a pinprick of fear. My head whipped around just in time to see that giant door swing shut. The clang it made sounded long and deep and loud. It reverberated off the walls of the room like a death chant. I ran, hoping I might still escape, but the two massive doors had become a flat, nearly seamless wall of steel. The hinges, the locking mechanism, absolutely everything that could be controlled—they were all on the other side. I pounded on the door. I called out. I yelled. Then I screamed.

In reply I heard a low humming sound, barely perceptible, its pitch so low at first that I felt more than I heard. It grew louder. It inched up the decibel scale one tiny fraction at a time. I rested a tentative hand on the wall. I felt my hand vibrate. I snatched it back. The sound grew louder. I began to feel my body tremble. No. Something else. My entire body had begun to vibrate. The sensation felt strongest in my spine. It reached into the long bones and then began to stir the soft tissues of my belly and chest. I felt my intestines quiver. My legs felt like pliable wax.

My body wanted to pitch forward, but I managed to widen my stance and stay upright. I searched the room frantically. To the left of the giant doors, I spotted a small gray box with a red lever sticking out of it. I couldn't walk anymore. I dropped to all fours and crawled to it. It was nowhere near the emergency-cutoff switch warning sign, not even on the same wall. A broken padlock lay on the floor below it. The red lever had been pushed up, into the on position.

My whole body shook. Every bone felt brittle enough to shatter. *How long before my guts come apart?* I reached toward the switch. It sat low on the wall, four or five feet up. Still on my knees, I reached for the switch with my right hand. Didn't make it. Slowly I inched my knees across the floor until they pressed against the wall. I inched my fingers up the wall—first one hand, then both, clawing with one and stretching out with the fingers of the other. I tried to stretch my back, but my spine shook so hard I couldn't feel the muscles on either side of it. I grabbed at the pockmarks in the white concrete, grinding my fingernails into them. *I will not die here.*

My right hand reached the electrical pipe at the side of the box. I grabbed it and steadied myself barely enough. With the fingers of my left hand, I reached higher—one inch, another, and then I snagged the emergency lever between thumb and forefinger and jerked it down.

The shaking stopped. I still clutched the lever, afraid to let it go, as if it might laugh like a loosed demon and spring back into the killing position. I hung there, clinging to that small gray box. Vomit ran down the front of my shirt. My pants felt wet. I smelled like a sewer. But my heart beat. My lungs sucked air. A thrill pulsed through me, sudden and vital. I had survived.

The big door swung open, and Joe charged through. He tried to lift me, but my fingers refused to let go of the switch box. I saw him speak into his cell. A moment later two big men pried my fingers open and pulled my hand away from the wall. They picked me up and slung me onto a stretcher. I had a hard time hearing through the buzz in my ears, but I did register some of what they yelled at me. I'll skip the insults.

"The space shuttle produces the loudest sound ever made by a machine. This room does its best to recreate that level of sound and vibration. Every satellite leaving Goddard has to be liftoff-proof. This room is where they prove it. If you hadn't stopped the cycle, we'd be shoveling you into a trash bag."

Consciousness slipped away. I felt it go. I tried to close my hand around it, to hold on, but it felt cold and slick and smelled like shit. It trickled out between the fingers of my clenched fist. Then it went away.

I lay on my back. My eyes cracked open. Four faces stared down at me. I recognized them in an instant—Paul, John, George, and Ringo. But even in its waking fog, my brain knew two of them were dead. Was I? Good company.

A light set four stops too bright shone down around them. No, the lights hung above us. Blackness surrounded those faces. The five of us floated together—all black, worn, faded, and ill defined. Then the black began to look fuzzy. It had threads in it, like a fabric. I refocused my eyes and found Ethan Blake's face at the neck of a black T-shirt. The skin of his broad forehead was creased, and his cold, dark eyes studied me without visible emotion, as if I were a lab experiment gone wrong. My back hurt. I was stretched out on an ice-cold slab. I felt naked. It felt damp.

Ethan's mouth moved. "Barry?" He bent closer. "You OK?"

I tried to answer, but a mask of some kind was fitted over my nose and mouth. It scraped against my chin and the bridge of my nose. A cool gas flowed from it. My throat felt dry. People in white coats drifted around me like curtains in a gentle wind. I couldn't see their faces. I turned my head side to side. I tasted vomit in my mouth. An electronically synthesized voice sounded as if it had crawled out of a fifties' sci-fi movie. It called out to no one in particular, "No shock advised."

Pain stabbed into the left side of my groin. I heard myself yelp. I tried to squirm away.

"Hold him still, damn it. We need a blood gas. Good. Get this to the lab. Run it stat."

I tried to move an arm. Two strong hands grabbed it. Someone grabbed my other wrist.

"Sorry, kid. Can't let you pull out those tubes and wires. Everything stays put until we get the lab results. Sound waves can do funny things to tissue. Just bear with us."

I tried to nod. I guess they saw my chin move. The restraining hands eased up a little, held me a moment longer, and then let go. I looked for Ethan. Gone. I tried to wiggle my jaw. Felt pressure on the mask.

Another voice said, "Stays on until we get the blood gas back. Oxygen is your friend."

I glanced around, forcing my eyes left, right, up, and down, as far as I could. My world began to make sense. I lay on a stretcher of some kind. IV poles flanked both sides of my head. I felt electrocardiogram leads on my chest and then became aware of a reassuring, steady, rhythmic beep.

Ethan Blake bent over me again. Maybe a half-dozen white coats stood around the stretcher. I closed my eyes and let myself float. Just for a moment. I heard Ethan's voice again. It could have been John's. No, it couldn't. Maybe Paul's. The voice faded.

I felt the mask lift. A muscular hand raised my head, and the cool, wet edge of a plastic cup brushed my lips.

"Take a sip." Ethan's voice.

I pursed my lips and drew a few drops into my mouth. I swallowed. I took some more. The taste of vomit receded.

"If this is heaven, it needs work." My voice sounded cracked.

"No heaven this time, hotshot."

"Am I in a hospital?"

"We brought the hospital to you. Facilities like ours try to be as self-contained as possible."

I glanced around. Four white coats surrounded me. They said nothing.

"What the hell prompted you to go into the vibration room?"

"I investigate. That's what I do."

Ethan grimaced. "Didn't you see the sign? You came close to becoming a lump of jelly."

"Vibration rooms don't kill people." I coughed. "People kill people." I ran my tongue over dry, cracked lips. They felt like sandpaper. "Someone must have been following me."

"Right." Ethan shook his head. "You sure handed that someone a great opportunity."

"Any idea who?"

"Security's working on it. The director instructed them to keep the investigation in-house."

I sat up. I wobbled but didn't fall down. The stretcher had a thin black vinyl pad on it. Cold but not granite. It still felt damp.

"This thing smells like shit," I said.

"It smelled fine until we dropped you onto it."

I wore no clothes.

A woman's voice came from behind me, "All the numbers look good. Pull the pads and then the lines."

A gentle hand pushed me onto my back. I felt the cardiogram leads and then the defibrillator pads pulled away. I gritted my teeth as patches of chest hair were stripped away. I didn't feel the IV line come out. The burning below my right collarbone had begun to itch.

I sat up again.

Ethan handed me a lab coat. "Put this on."

I obeyed and buttoned up and then turned myself sideways and dangled my feet beside the stretcher.

"Thanks for the dress," I croaked. "Where are my clothes?"

Ethan handed me a white garbage bag. It had been tied with a triple knot. "You had a bit of a sphincter problem. We cleaned you up. Might want to burn these."

"I'll need my wallet and car keys."

"They're in there. Getting them is your problem."

I slid off the stretcher and stood up. I wiggled my toes. The tile floor felt cold against the soles of my feet. "How long was I out?"

"Out cold for several minutes. Damn groggy for about twenty. The good news, your heart kept beating."

I nodded to the folks standing around me. "Thanks."

Each nodded back. One of them turned to Ethan. "He's good to go, Dr. Blake." Then they turned and walked away.

I looked at Ethan. "How do I get home?"

"I'll drive you. Alex will pick me up later."

"I don't suppose you have any spare clothes here."

"You're wearing my lab coat. Don't get greedy."

"Thanks," I said.

"Feel free to burn it when you get home."

CHAPTER SEVENTEEN

Wednesday, March 9, 2016
Launch minus Nine Days

The mudroom at 202 Bay Drive reeked of chlorine bleach. So did I. That crisp, clean, toxic scent seemed to engulf me as I sat cross-legged on the cold tile floor. All those little plastic cards that identified me as a successful member of society swam lazily about in a two-gallon red plastic bucket half filled with bleach. I let my keys drop from my gloved hand and watched them sink to the bottom. The single eye of my key chain flashlight gave me a lifeless stare. Egor's Denali key fob drowned next to it. He had a spare.

A second bleach bucket held the ten one-hundred-dollar bills that had been in the back of my wallet. The old man had told me to take them to the bank after they dried out and exchange them as damaged. He'd handed me ten new ones. I'd tossed my wallet in the trash. I had a spare in my room.

Ethan Blake had driven me home in the Denali, but not before he'd had me strip off the white coat and stuck me under one of those emergency ceiling showers they use for techs who get splashed with acid. He'd even given me a second lab coat. That was two I owed him. Neither one of us had said much. After a few minutes of silence, he Bluetoothed his iPhone to the car, and Beatles' tunes stood in for conversation.

I'd already trashed the plastic bag filled with my clothes and shoes. Egor had assured me that everything could be salvaged, but I didn't have much enthusiasm for wearing salvage. It wasn't the filth per se that I found intolerable. It was that the filth had been mine, evidence that I'd lost control of my body. The soapy, hot shower last night and a second this morning hadn't washed that sentiment away. I should have felt joyful to be alive. I kept repeating that to myself. It didn't work.

The phone rang. I stripped off the gloves and picked up the handset.

The voice had a British clip to it, but it didn't sound quite British. "I would like to speak to Dr. Kahler."

"I'm his assistant. You speak to me first."

"Your name?"

"Sandler."

"Mr. Sandler, my name is Asha Talavi. I am head of the Interests Section of the Islamic Republic of Iran."

I nearly dropped the phone. I don't remember exactly what I said next, but it wasn't a gracious "How can I help you?" It was more like, "OK."

"I have information regarding a person in whom we share an interest. I wish to discuss this with Dr. Kahler."

I moved my jaw side to side to make sure I wouldn't mumble back at him. "Can Dr. Kahler get back to you?"

"It would be better if I get back to him."

"I'll see what I can do."

"I would appreciate it greatly. I'll call back in twenty minutes." He hung up.

I fished the bills out of the bleach, checked for fading, and clothespinned each one to Egor's drying rack. If I'd put them on the mesh top, he'd have probably burned it.

I found Kahler in his study. He'd finished his breakfast. Now he stood in front of his stereo cabinet and hunched over his McIntosh MT10 turntable. His fingers fiddled with its 0.5-millivolt moving-coil cartridge.

"I am occupied."

"I haven't said anything."

"You were about to."

I walked to my leather easy chair and sat. I waited. The old man didn't whistle when he worked. No grunts, no profanity, and no aha. He liked silence. I had to sit still. If I'd let the leather cushions squeak, he'd have tossed me out.

Finally Kahler straightened up.

"Shall I get Egor?" I asked.

"Unnecessary. It will track correctly now."

I told him about the call.

The old man nodded. His chin barely moved. "Curious."

"Weird."

Kahler walked to the Eames chair behind his desk and sat down. He reclined it a little and then turned to me. "I suppose we should find out what he has."

"Bring him here?"

"Under no circumstances. Meet him somewhere."

"Any place special?"

"Any location in which you will not be observed."

"Not so easy these days."

"Then make it look like a chance meeting."

"These days nobody believes in coincidence."

"Plausible deniability is better than no deniability at all."

The Tidal Basin tended to be fairly quiet in cold weather. The Iranian had suggested it. It was a pool of tranquility in a city that bustles, yet a place where anyone in Washington might happen to wander for any reason. It was as plausibly deniable as I was going to get. He'd suggested 12.30 p.m. for our meeting, and I'd agreed. I couldn't count on getting there any earlier.

Parking in Washington sucked, but I'd learned to use the Internet instead of gasoline and adrenaline. Parking Panda sold me a slot at the Mandarin Oriental Hotel. From there I hiked to the basin. Sometimes I could find a space near the paddleboats, but it wasn't something you could count on. I didn't want to be late, and I needed the exercise.

The Tidal Basin was actually a reservoir. It was built in 1949 and covered about 107 acres at the southwest edge of Washington, DC. It was an offshoot of the Potomac River, and the inlet to the basin poked through the river's north bank. The surrounding park was bounded on the north by Independence Avenue SW, and Fourteenth Street SW ran just to the east. The Jefferson Memorial sat on the southeast bank of the basin. A walking trail encircled the water, and the famous cherry blossom trees stood guard around it. I did my best not to look at them. A grassy field dotted by shrubs and trees of lesser rank extended out to the surrounding roadways.

I found the Iranian sitting on a wood-slat bench just where he'd said he'd be. He'd told me to look for a tall, balding man in his early thirties where the park widened between the water and Maine Avenue SW. He'd said he'd be wearing a black wool overcoat and eating pistachios.

The temperature at Rawlings' Landing had dipped to a few degrees below freezing when I'd left. It didn't feel any warmer here. I pulled off my gloves and unzipped my ski jacket anyway, and then I shrugged my left shoulder just enough to feel the Glock hanging beneath my armpit. I approached him from behind, making sure to step on a few small twigs to announce my arrival. Trust had yet to be established, and startling him might prove dangerous. I couldn't tell if his coat was open. As I approached, he pulled a nut out of his right coat pocket, pried it open, popped the meat into his mouth, and deposited the empty shell into his left pocket. I sat down beside him. The bench slats felt cold through the fabric of my jeans. We each faced the Tidal Basin, the way strangers do.

"Pistachio?" he asked. He turned toward me. He had a small, round face, a light-brown stubbly beard, and dark, searching eyes. His nose and mouth were small. The top of his round head was bald, and he'd trimmed the hair on the sides so close to his scalp that in dim light I might have missed it. The front of his overcoat hung open.

I flashed the friendliest, most harmless smile I could muster. "I only do pistachios on Thursdays."

"I'm a day early, then?"

"Depends on what else you have to share."

"Is this supposed to sound like code?" he asked.

I grinned back at him and then leaned close to his ear. "Trying to decode this conversation will be three hours out of someone's life they'll never get back." I straightened up.

He chuckled. His laugh had real merriment in it. "I run a small business."

"That's an odd way to put it."

"I have a small staff. Smaller still since two of them burned to death last month." He spoke as casually as if we were discussing DC traffic. "Their bodies were found here." He swept out his right arm, gesturing toward the Tidal Basin. "Perhaps they leaped into the water to extinguish the fire."

The bad taste of an old memory climbed to the back of my throat. I swallowed hard but kept my face expressionless.

"They carried ID. The Pakistanis insist on ID cards. So does your government. But the police had to use DNA to identify them." He blew out his lips. "Plastic melts. Have you ever dealt with Pakistanis?"

"Nope."

"A more dour people you will never meet." He shelled another pistachio and popped it into his mouth. He gestured toward the Tidal Basin again. "I have no idea what my men were doing here. I'm told they died in early morning. Odd. These young men had little affinity for early morning. More often than not, they were late to work."

"Around here untidy deaths usually involve drug trafficking. Could they have had a sideline?"

"Perhaps." He shook his head. "But I doubt they had the contacts, certainly not in Iran. The penalties for such activity are far more harsh at home than here. Some Iranians obtain contraband drugs from Afghanistan. Neither of my men had ever traveled there."

"Sounds like a bunch of rocks need to be overturned."

"For whatever reason, both your government and mine decided it was in their joint interest to avoid an incident. These two were—" He paused for a moment, searching for the word. "Adventurous. In the unlikely event that evidence connecting two young representatives of Iran with the drug trade did surface, Tehran would be gravely embarrassed. The deaths were reported. The details were not."

"Immolated bodies floating in the Tidal Basin. Tough to cover up here. It made the Sunday *Post*."

The Iranian shrugged. "Simple enough in Tehran. And you might have noticed"—Asha Talavi poked me in the ribs with an elbow and chuckled—"that your *Washington Post* reported neither nationality nor occupation." Then he turned away and looked out over the blue water. "Are there fish in the Tidal Basin?"

"There's fly-fishing. They eat Spam when it's offered." I turned to face him. "You plan on hiring Dr. Kahler to find the killer?"

Talavi laughed. The sound had a bright, friendly quality to it, not what I'd expected from an Iranian. "Oh, no. To be honest, they are not missed. This is not a posting that attracts the... go-getter. From the perspective of the young men from connected families, a posting here is worthless, no different from a backwater assignment."

"Is that why you're here?"

He grinned broadly, as if I'd just told a joke. "I volunteered."

"For a backwater assignment?"

His face hardened. "I have no family. The assignment is backwater. The location is not." His grin returned. He drew out his next words. "It presents opportunity."

"And exactly what opportunity do you need our help with?"

"I have a small staff. For the most part, they tend to visa requests. They are young men who wanted to see the Great Satan for themselves. They'd never be foolish enough to admit it, but they like the music here. They all speak English well enough to get by, and because they are young, their facility improves daily. They've all had military training but no fieldwork. It's really obedience training. My government values obedience. Each has the same fear that one of his coworkers will photograph him at a rock concert. So they move as a single organism. As long as the work gets done, I leave them alone.

"Anything that matters I take care of myself. I review vast quantities of data. I'm quite good at that sort of thing. I observe. When I find someone who interests me—or someone doing something that interests me—I focus there."

"That can't pay off very often."

"I have a gift for noticing the unusual. At one time I thought I might become a newspaper reporter, but in Iran—" Asha Talavi abruptly stopped talking. He looked toward the trail.

I followed his gaze to a middle-aged man with a ruddy complexion and gray-black hair. He wore an expensive-looking overcoat and black leather gloves. One hand held a leash clipped to the collar of an average-sized dog. The other gripped a stick he must have picked up from the side of the trail. I'd noticed them earlier and checked them out again when the dog yelped. No threat there.

"Sit! Damn it. Sit." The man lashed the stick against the dog's hind-quarters. Another yelp.

The Iranian stood up. I saw the corner of his small mouth twitch. He was tall, at least six two. He moved with the effortless grace of an athlete or a woodsman, sidestepping each fallen branch without appearing to notice it.

The dog beater had been glaring down at his pooch. It had long hair, brown and white, probably a collie. The man looked too well dressed for someone who'd own a mutt. He didn't register Talavi's presence until the Iranian stood beside him. Startled, he jerked his head up.

In a friendly gesture, Talavi held out his hands, palms up. Then he wrapped his right arm around the man's shoulders, bent forward, and whispered into his ear. The man's hand snapped open, and the stick clattered to the cement walkway. Talavi straightened up.

I saw no one else near them. The park was so quiet that I could hear the water of the Tidal Basin lapping against the shore. I thought I could hear the dog beater breathing. His breath came in short, heavy gasps. He stood at least sixty feet away, but I could see him tremble. He turned his head side to side, clearly looking for help. I was the only other person nearby. When his gaze fell on me, I simply shrugged. I only glimpsed his eyes for an instant, but they were wide. Then he turned and quickly jogged away. His dog liked that. It ran ahead.

Asha Talavi strolled back to our bench. I got to my feet as he approached. He stood half a head taller than me.

"You're tall for an Arab," I said.

Talavi's voice hardened for the first time since we'd met. He didn't raise it, but each word took on a sharp edge. "I am a Persian." His face had that "you ignorant bastard" look to it.

I nodded, my only gesture of apology, and sat down. It was all he was going to get.

His mouth made a fleeting smile. Then he held out another nut. I accepted that one.

"What the hell did you say to him?" I asked.

He waved it away.

"You Persians really know how to make friends. What diplomatic corps did you say you were with?"

He sat on the bench and turned toward me. "I prefer to imagine myself as a spy," he said in a stage whisper. Then his small mouth broke into a big smile. "Practically speaking, there is very little difference between a diplomat and a spy. The way one tilts is determined by opportunity."

I gave him a small nod. "And you and I are gathered here together because?"

"As I was saying, I watch people. I can't watch many, so I scan databases and look for those of potential interest. Sometimes my government can provide substantial information, either directly or through links with allies. It resembles playing a lottery, but occasionally I get lucky.

"Most recently I have developed an interest in a colonel Scofield."

I played my best poker face.

"Colonel Drew Scofield," he said.

I shrugged. "Never heard of him."

"Of course not. Nonetheless, I have a story to tell that you might find interesting. I ask for nothing in return. But if at some future date you require more, *then* we will trade."

I nodded thoughtfully. "Your deal."

"Scofield had been attached to a special forces unit, not to command but for his computer expertise. Apparently West Point does not simply train soldiers; they train engineers. Even Iranian Intelligence has never been able to discover exactly what his unit did. But it was certainly covert. When he rotated back to civilization, someone in command decided he needed a rest. So he was assigned to Kabul to train Afghan military police."

I yawned. "I just love factoids."

"Excellent. Here's another. In 2012 more than fifty Western soldiers were killed by members of the Afghan security forces. These were not enemy infiltrators. Each involved a personal motive. The first insider attack by an Afghan woman involved Scofield."

I felt myself leaning closer to the Iranian.

"Your colonel Scofield was evacuated to Landstuhl Medical Center in Germany. He spent weeks there."

I shrugged my shoulders. I felt the weight of the Glock again, but now it was just annoying. "Why tell me any of this?"

"You have an association with this man."

"OK. Let's say that I do. Why would you care?"

"We began our conversation with a discussion of dead bodies."

"Right. Someone without a shred of civic pride had the bad taste to leave two charbroiled Iranians in the Tidal Basin."

Asha Talavi regarded me for a moment. His entire face rounded up, his mouth opened until it creased at the corners, and his eyes sparkled.

"What's the joke?" I couldn't figure this guy out. Then it hit me. "You think Scofield killed your men?"

Asha Talavi stood up. I followed his lead.

"Not at all," he said. "I have no proof, but I have a suspicion." His expression became distant and unreadable. He turned toward the water. For a moment he said nothing. I waited, listening for the punch line, hearing only the faint sound of tiny waves lapping against the shore of the Tidal Basin. Asha Talavi spoke softly. I found myself leaning closer. His voice hushed to a whisper, "Could it be that my men had been working for him?"

My body jerked straight and stiff as if he'd slapped me across the face. "No fucking way!"

"Perhaps. You know where to reach me." The harsh winter sunlight glinted off his nearly bald head as he strolled casually away.

CHAPTER EIGHTEEN

Launch minus Nine Days

My iPhone vibrated against my hip as I jogged across Maine Avenue. I didn't touch it until I reached the relative safety of the far side.

"Barry? I was afraid you weren't going to pick up."

I recognized Alex's voice. "Delayed by traffic."

"What?"

"Nothing."

"Meet me for lunch."

"Where?"

"Georgetown."

"Sure. I'm in DC."

"I know. Stanley told me."

I nearly dropped the phone at that one. Apparently the old man would keep shoving us together until the crystal cracked.

"Meet me at Kafe Leopold. You know Cady's Alley? It's off M Street."

"My phone will find it. Nice day for a walk. It'll take me about an hour."

"I'm hungry. Take a cab. I'll be there in fifteen minutes." She clicked off.

Then I called the old man. He actually answered the phone. Egor must have been out.

"Things to report," I told him.

"Not over the phone. Return now."

"Alex just called. Wants me to meet her for lunch. Georgetown."

"Do it."

"What about reporting? Our friend shared."

"Is what he told you going to change anything within the next eight hours?"

"Maybe."

Adrian Kahler snorted. When he spoke, his voice had that this-is-an-order tone to it. "Make sure Ms. Blake enjoys her lunch." He hung up.

I felt as if the old man was dangling me like bait in front of a crazy woman. On the plus side, she had the face of an angel and a body that would most assuredly turn the devil's head. I left my jacket open and jogged around the east side of the Tidal Basin to the Jefferson Memorial. Then I flagged a cab and told him to head for Kafe Leopold on M Street in Georgetown. He got onto Ohio Drive SW, crossed the Potomac on the Theodore Roosevelt Memorial Bridge, drove north on Route 66 in Virginia, and then drove back across the Potomac on the Francis Scott Key Bridge. He finally connected with M Street west of our destination. That was life in the small city.

Believe it or not, had I been driving, I'd have chosen the same route. He made the trip in fifteen minutes, and I hadn't managed to tamp down all of my anger by the time we arrived. I told him to keep driving and didn't yell stop for a couple of blocks.

I walked the inlaid red brick M Street sidewalk until I settled down. Then I spent seventy dollars at the Godiva shop for a box of candy with a tote bag. On the way out, I noticed that the building that housed the Godiva shop had a couple of stories above the store. Apartments maybe? Living in one would be a chocoholic's dream.

At 3316 M Street, a pedestrian underpass interrupted the walls of painted brick. It cut through a couple of townhouses, which were left with nothing more than a second floor. It had a white arched ceiling. Its weathered brick walls were interrupted by great plates of glass that looked into the adjacent stores. I couldn't figure out what Maxalto Boffi sold, but the manager clearly understood how to make brick, glass, and stainless steel look elegant. The light at the end of this particular tunnel revealed a double-banister red brick staircase that dropped two steep flights to the brick patio below. Across from the patio was another cobblestone roadway with apartments and shops on the far side. Thirty-Third Street NW was a half block to the left.

The wall of glass and stainless steel to the left of the patio opened into 3315 Cady's Alley NW, Kafe Leopold. In warm weather the café opened outward, dotting the patio with round metal tables, each shaded by its own colored awning lettered with "Hofbräu München" and "Das Bier." Now the patio sat cold and empty, and Kafe Leopold had dressed for winter. I pushed against one of its frosty glass doors and walked inside.

The air became warm. It floated over me, carrying the scents of coffee, sugar, and baking dough. A flock of overhead spotlights made the single large room summertime bright. It looked crammed with people, two or three at a table, which was as many as the mix of round and square tiny white pedestal tables could hold. A three-tiered stainless-steel counter ran most of the length of the far side of the room. Its glass front revealed the pastries within. I expected more of a racket, but the wood-slat ceiling baffles turned the din into a kind of white noise.

Alex sat at a table in front of the pastry case. She wore a red, black, and white plaid button-down with three-quarter sleeves rolled up at the elbow to reveal a lining decorated with tiny pastel flowers. It was open at the neck, down to the third button. She held a white ceramic coffee cup in her right hand and waved it at me the moment I spotted her. She sipped as I crossed the floor of stained-wood slats. I gripped the white plastic back of the chair across from her, pulled it out, and sat down.

"You're late."

"Fashionably." I leaned across the table and presented my offering.

She tossed her head, and auburn highlights sparkled in her shoulder-length hair. "Accepted." She plucked the bag from my hand and tucked it under her chair. "I'm hungry."

I followed her gaze to the parade of pastries in the case beside us. Every tart and quiche I had ever seen or heard of was represented. "Needn't be for long. Sweet or healthy?"

She might have answered. I didn't notice. A little prickle of discomfort suddenly scratched at the back of my neck. I took another glance around the room. No one looked dangerous. No one even looked Iranian.

Alex cleared her throat. I turned to look at her. So did diners at three nearby tables. "How about if you pay attention to me. Just for this afternoon."

"Sorry. I look around. It keeps me alive."

She lifted her fork, handle between thumb and forefinger, aimed the tines at my nose, and smiled at me over the top of it. "Not if I stab this through your heart."

I ground my teeth. That kept my mouth shut.

Our waiter arrived just in time. He probably saved the afternoon. Alex smiled at him. She ordered the lemon-soufflé pancakes. I went for the bratwurst. I had no interest in keeping my breath kissing sweet. The waiter headed for the kitchen without knowing he'd already earned his tip.

Alex swirled her coffee cup and studied me over the top of it.

I looked away and then back. She looked devilishly pretty. "Clouds in your coffee?" I asked.

"Not for long."

I forced a grin. "Life should be like that."

She took another sip, held her coffee cup about an inch from her lips, and fixed me with an inquisitive stare. "What do you know about Shakespeare?"

I gaped back. Time to recalculate.

"Barry! Really."

"Not much." I thought about it for a moment. "Wrote comedies, tragedies, a book of sonnets. Maybe histories?"

"What else?"

I knit my brow, trying to look as if there was something behind it. "Born in England. Lived there. Died there."

"Good. That's more than most people know. What's interesting is that Shakespeare scholars don't know a whole lot more."

I felt myself frowning and struggled to turn it upside down. "Hard to believe. I got my bachelor's from Johns Hopkins. The English department was pretty strong on Shakespeare. The Hopkins University Press put out a journal." I tilted the plastic chair back onto its rear legs and scratched my head. "*Shakespeare Bulletin*, maybe? Something like that."

Alex knit her dark eyebrows, and her sapphire-blue eyes studied me. Her face grew thoughtful, as if she were looking at something she hadn't noticed before. "And?"

"And nothing. I wasn't an English major. I had more interest in Frank Herbert."

"A great many university English departments have a Shakespeare interest, and a fair number of academics secure their position by writing about him. For the most part, what they present as data isn't, and what they present as conclusions is conjecture."

"It's not like they're doing medical research." I shrugged. "Or designing a bridge. No one's going to die."

She brought her coffee cup down hard. The saucer survived, but some of the brown liquid splashed onto it, some onto the table. A couple of heads swiveled toward us again. In a small, packed restaurant like this one, neighbors were only a couple of feet away.

I reached across the table with my napkin, but she waved me away. "That's not the point."

"OK," I said slowly "The point is?"

"The point," Alex underscored the word with her voice, "of all academic research is to discover the truth. That, in and of itself, is important." She raised a fist and then stuck out her index finger, leaned forward, and reached across the table. Her fingertip stopped an inch from my nose. "Who was Shakespeare—the person who wrote the plays, the sonnets? Really?"

I shrugged. "I guess nobody knows. Not really."

Alexandra Blake leaned back in her chair. She crossed her legs and smiled conspiratorially. For a moment she said nothing. Then she leaned across the table and whispered to me, "I do."

Lunch arrived. Yes, there would be an extra tip. If his timing was this good with all his customers, this guy would be retired and living on his yacht in a couple more years. He even refilled Alex's coffee cup, making a point of not noticing the overflowing saucer or trying to replace it. *Note to self: a man can learn a lot from a good waiter.*

Alex studied her pancakes, cut off a tiny piece, and brought it to her mouth. She held it there a moment and then nodded and chewed. "Just enough lemon. That's the tricky part."

My mouth was full. I nodded. The bratwurst tasted great; it wasn't a tricky kind of food.

"Want a bite?" She held out her fork.

I swallowed. "No, thanks," I said. "Right now it would just taste like bratwurst."

"True that," she said.

We finished our meal without saying much. I continued to check out the room every few minutes, but now I waited until Alex had to glance down at her plate.

At one point I spotted a guy in a baseball jacket standing just inside the hallway at the far end of the restaurant: medium height, a swarthy complexion, plastered-down black hair. His dark eyes darted away from mine whenever I looked in his direction. He might have been watching us, but I couldn't be sure. At any given moment, at least 10 percent of the male eyes in the room probably lingered in Alex's direction.

The waiter's eyes widened a bit when he saw the tip, and he somehow managed to pull Alex's chair out for her the moment she stood up. The tables sat so close that he needed to inhale as he did it. Then he lifted Alex's black leather moto jacket from the back of her chair and held it as she slipped her arms into the sleeves. Her indigo jeans fit as if the cloth had been woven with a fiber made from skin magnets. I pushed open the cold glass door, and we walked out into the brisk March air. My black ski jacket would have looked bulky even without the shoulder holster underneath.

Alex headed for the stairs to M Street, and I followed. Several people stood in the courtyard, a few more on the steps. The guys wore open-necked shirts and sweaters. The women dressed like Alex. No one looked cold. A blonde and a brunette stood chatting at the top of the stairs. They glanced at us as we passed. One whispered into the other's ear. I couldn't make out the words. I imagined something like, "Oh, look, a girl and her dork."

When we reached M Street, Alex turned to face me and tugged at my sleeve. "I'd like you to see Georgetown."

I glanced up the street. "I'm looking at it."

"I meant the university."

"Why?"

She turned to face me, and the harsh winter light exposed a few freckles on her forehead and across the bridge of her nose. Then I lost them in the sparkle of her eyes. I barely noticed her scowl. "Got any better offers?"

I shrugged. "Not a one."

"Good. Come on."

She grabbed my hand and tugged me along, leading me across to N Street, along the brick sidewalks, and up the hill. Why this woman wanted to take me on another outing I couldn't imagine. But I had orders. She had sapphire eyes.

The tall spires of Georgetown University grew closer, tall and lean, stretching athletically into the crisp winter sky. The school sat on a hill, atop a great stone wall. Both Thirty-Seventh Street and N Street descended from there. The stones of the fortification, most a half foot to two feet across, were set in concrete. They were square, rectangular, or of no identifiable geometric shape, and they varied in color from gray to brown, with every conceivable shade in between. A black iron fence sat atop the wall, and the expanse from Thirty-Seventh Street to the top of that fence was about as high as a stretch limo is long.

A three-level stone staircase at the left end of the wall climbed up to the university. It was bounded by greenery on the right and the Joseph Mark Lauinger Library to the left. Adrian Kahler probably would have gone into the library and asked for an elevator. Alex jogged quickly up the stairs. I did not let her get one step ahead. At the top we entered a large grassy courtyard bounded on the right by the long wrought-iron fence I'd seen from the street and on the left by the elegant stone buildings of the university. Blue sky, powder-puff white clouds, and sinuous branches of trees were reflected in the arched windows. Ancient wrought-iron cannons flanked the steps to vaulted doorways. They offered no threat but seemed a token of the time when this construction had been new.

Alex hadn't said much since leaving Kafe Leopold. Now she swept her right arm outward authoritatively. "Healy Lawn."

Healy was showing its March brown. The sun hung winter low in the sky, and the five-story, castle-like buildings of Georgetown shadowed half the lawn. But the grass closer to the iron fence atop the Thirty-Seventh Street wall still basked in afternoon sunlight. A handful of students had spread blankets there. They sat smiling and chatting.

I struggled to match Alex's brisk pace. A couple of joggers in sweatshirts passed us, but none of the walkers did. Her boots clacked authoritatively against the red brick walkway as she hustled along. I tried to stay dead even with her but occasionally fell behind. I sensed that my getting out in front would piss her off. In addition, I had no idea where we were going. The clueless don't lead well.

We trotted by the seated statue of John Carroll, who wore a flowing robe and had kind eyes and a gentle smile. He looked as though he liked being bronzed to the past. We walked by the old stone walls of Healy Hall toward Georgetown's modern red brick intercultural center. We hustled through a stunted tunnel—Cady might have called it an alley—and then climbed the steps on the far side. Student posters plastered the red brick walls. Several clung precariously, one of them just above a recycle bin. Even the wrought-iron railing separating up steps from down had a poster stuck to it. The walkway on the far side was simple concrete. Some of the lamp-posts to the right sported hand-sanitizer dispensers. The building to the left was red brick and glass with a wide stainless-steel awning protecting the recessed glass doors. We walked on, up more stairs and over a small cobblestone bridge, and then stopped, facing a huge red brick building. It sported rows of tall arched windows flanking a pair of twin glass double doors that stood tall beneath an arched glass transom. The lettering above read, "The Thomas and Dorothy Leavey Center."

Alex swept out her arm again. "Nice place to work, isn't it?"

"As fine as Harvard Yard." I'd never been there, but the analogy coaxed a smile out of her.

We walked in. I found myself in a student lounge. I saw a large, open carpeted space with desks, tables, study chairs, easy chairs, love seats, and bronze trash cans. Beige wallpaper and subdued lighting gave it a restful air. Small square study tables and wood chairs lined the adjacent hallway. The whole place looked designed to provide comfort and reduce stress. There were computer nooks and benches outfitted with Macs. Kahler would have been pleased.

I followed Alex through a double door beneath a sign that read, "Uncommon Grounds." She ordered a sixteen-ounce cup of black coffee. A poster on one wall read, "Send us your Spotify playlist." I nearly took a couple of biscotti from one of the two huge glass canisters on the counter, but I didn't want to be the slob in the ski jacket who dropped crumbs on the carpet.

Alex led on. She pushed open one of four oak-framed glass doors, and I followed her through. The walls became white plaster brightened by a rush of sunlight that poured through an expanse of glass to the right. The floor turned to tile, and her boots clacked smartly as she walked. We passed a wall-mounted drinking fountain, with a tap for filling water bottles, and then an elevator. Vertical lettering on an oak-paneled rectangular column read, "Regents Hall." At the end of the hallway was a pair of windowed double doors. Only the one on the right had a push bar on it, and the bar sported a blinking red light.

I stepped ahead of Alex, flattened my hand against the catch on the heavy stainless-steel bar, and leaned a shoulder against the door. It didn't budge. I'd planned to say something like, "Your door is open, my lady," but the only sound that came out of my mouth was, "Ouf."

I thought I heard a wisp of a snicker, but it might have been a gasp.

"Are you OK?" she asked. Then she fingered the keys on a touch pad on the wall to the right. "Try now."

I pushed the door open and held it. She walked through. I followed.

White floor, beige walls, acoustic tile ceiling—all the same on this side of the doorway as on the other. But where there had been study nooks before, oak doors in recessed frames turned this hallway into a rabbit warren of offices. One door sported two paper signs taped up by their corners. "Observe the physicists in their natural habitat." The one directly above it ordered, "Keep this door CLOSED at all times."

Alex's office sat on the left, about halfway down. She keyed the lock, pushed open the door, marched in, and flipped on the overhead fluorescent light. I followed.

The white-painted walls looked bare except for an empty four-by-three-foot corkboard. I didn't see even one pin mark in it. One wall had filing cabinets in front of it. A long oak desk sat along the opposite one. It held a Dell workstation computer, four external hard drives, and three twenty-six-inch ViewSonic monitors, one opposite the big leather-upholstered desk chair and one flanking each side. In front of the center monitor lay an ergonomic keyboard with a numeric keypad and a big sculpted wireless mouse with lots of buttons. No notepad. No pencils. It looked like an archetype for the new-millennium office, paper-free. I ran a finger across the desktop. It felt cold and smooth.

Alex stripped off her jacket and tossed it onto a coatrack on the far side of the room. I've tried that for myself but never made it work. Then she pulled her chair out from under the desk, sat down, and waved me to a smaller one in the far corner.

My chair clattered some as I wheeled it across the white tiled floor over to hers. I unzipped my ski jacket just enough to let in some air and then sat. The Glock stayed hidden.

She fired up her computer.

"Got a pen?" I asked.

She shrugged. "Somewhere."

"What do you do here?" I asked.

She spun her chair around to face me. "Computational linguistics."

"Can you break that down a little?"

"Computerized analysis of and synthesis of language."

"Who pays for that?"

"Just about everyone. Microsoft for speech to text and back to speech. Caterpillar. Translation of repair-manual updates has been big this year. You can't sell earth-moving equipment to China if the on-site techs can't apply your latest upgrade."

"Can't they just have people do the translation?"

"Sure, if you only sell to a half-dozen language sites and you upgrade once a year. If you upgrade monthly and sell in fifty countries, that doesn't work so well."

"Is that what you do?"

"I do some of that. I have a grant that focuses on understanding how languages are put together. I do some work for the National Security Agency, but they prefer to keep as much as they can in-house. They offered me a position a couple of years ago, but I prefer being university based." Then Alex spun her chair back toward her computer. For a moment I felt like I was dealing with Kahler.

She opened Outlook, deleted a bunch of e-mails, and then turned back to me. "Besides, a university job gives me time for a hobby. And I can use Georgetown facilities as long as I don't overdo it."

"Let me guess." I smiled to myself but kept my face a blank mask. "Shakespeare."

"So you did pay attention at lunch."

"Somebody stuck a wig on Geoffrey Seep's bust of the Bard."

"It could have been anyone."

"I especially liked the braids and pink ribbons."

She grinned wickedly. Her eyes sparkled.

"Oh. Right. And there was something your brother said when he saw the Bard's new hair."

She studied me expectantly.

"It went something like this: 'Alex—Alex—Alex—Alex!'"

She closed her eyes, stretched her arms, and arched her back. The chair tilted. She exhaled a relaxed sigh.

I felt my eyes flick down to her breasts and then snapped my gaze back to her face just as Alex opened her eyes. *She's a job, you idiot.*

"Well, I'm glad you like ribbons."

"They added a certain artistic touch. You know. Something beyond simple malice."

Her eyes narrowed. "I can't stand that man."

"No argument there. Too bad, though. You have similar interests. How many people can you find to talk with about Shakespeare?"

"More than you think."

"Maybe here." I swept an arm outward.

"Lots of people outside Georgetown care about Shakespeare."

I smirked at her. "Name two."

"We meet at the Folger Shakespeare Library."

"I'll drop by next time I'm in London."

"It's right here in DC on Pennsylvania Avenue Southeast and Second Street."

I shrugged. "And I should be interested because?"

Appraising sapphire eyes studied me for a moment. Then she said, "Because I'm going to make you care."

Now it was my turn to stretch. I stopped myself halfway so the pistol wouldn't bulge. Boobs are acceptable. Guns, not so much.

"So ask me," she said. A mischievous grin captured the corners of her mouth and then spread to her eyes. "Who was William Shakespeare?"

"Okeydoke. Who was he?"

Alex leaned slightly forward in her chair. Her eyes fixed on mine. "Born in April 1564, in Stratford, England, about four days on horseback from London. We don't know the exact date, but church records document his baptism on April twenty-sixth. His father achieved success as a local businessman and a member of the town council. King's New Grammar School taught reading and writing to Stratford boys, and William most likely attended. No record exists. At eighteen he married Anne Hathaway. She was twenty-six and pregnant. They had three children. He left his family and moved to London. He lived there for twenty years, but no one knows precisely where. He visited his family only during Lent, when theaters were closed.

"Later in his life, in 1597, he purchased property in Stratford, the second-largest house in town. In 1601 he bought one hundred twenty-seven acres of farmland. In 1605 he bought leases of real estate substantial enough to provide him with a yearly income. All this time he continued to live in London. Shakespeare moved back to Stratford in 1609, and he died there seven years later, on April the twenty-third, 1616. He's buried at the Holy Trinity Church in Stratford. He left most of his estate to his eldest daughter.

"He and his partners owned the Lord Chamberlain's Company, a theater company, and he became one of the owners of the Globe Theatre. He was titled one of the king's men and a groom of the chamber by the king of England."

I nodded, trying to look appreciative. "Nice summary."

"That's not a synopsis." Alex picked up a paper clip from her desktop, held it between thumb and forefinger, and then tossed it into a small metal wastebasket on the far side of the room. I heard it ping against the bottom. "That's pretty much it. There are a few more data points, criticism by other writers, that sort of thing. At most they'd fill a couple of pages."

I shook my head. "Oh, come on. Tomes are written about this guy."

"Supposition. Ninety-nine percent of it." She read the disbelief in my face and scowled.

I held up an open hand. "His name's on all those plays."

She opened her desk drawer, picked up another paper clip, and threw it at me. I felt lucky she didn't have any rubber bands. "They didn't have bylines in the sixteenth century," she said crossly. "Plays were the property of theater companies. Playwrights were day laborers. It wasn't until after his death that two actors, Henry Condell and John Heminges, collected and published what they claimed were plays written by William Shakespeare. The First Folio came out in 1623. Only two hundred fifty First Folios still exist."

I rapped a knuckle against the arm of my chair. "When's your birthday? I'll buy you one."

She wiggled a finger at me. "Three million dollars."

"I'll get you a sonnet."

Alex stood up. "So that's the question."

I looked up at her and wrinkled my face. "The question?"

"If Shakespeare didn't write Shakespeare, who did?"

"You've got to be kidding."

She shoved my chair with the toe of her boot. The wheeled chair and I clattered across the floor. I kept it upright. Sailors have good balance.

"That's a question computational linguistics can answer. Well, with a little help from stylometry."

"And this will make you friends, right?"

"There are a whole lot of people who don't believe the William Shakespeare of Stratford wrote Shakespeare. They're called anti-Stratfordians."

"What's the term for all those academicians on the other side of the argument?"

"Wrong."

"So how do you and your little computer prove all this?"

She had a wicked look in those blue eyes. "Not quite ready to show my hand."

I smirked at her. "Aah-ha."

"Doing anything Saturday night?"

"Make me an offer."

"Folger Shakespeare Library, need to be there by six o'clock. I'd really like an escort."

CHAPTER NINETEEN

Thursday, March 10, 2016
Launch minus Eight Days

Kahler was humming when he walked into the kitchen at ten thirty the next morning. I recognized Tchaikovsky's *Winter Dreams* symphony. The old man sounded as on key as the Moscow Symphony Orchestra. Kahler didn't hum often. When he did, it made me nervous. I'd eaten earlier, but I had the feeling I should stick around.

I'd reported as usual when I'd returned from my afternoon with Alex Blake. The old man had given me only one instruction after I'd come out of my trance. "Call one of our contacts at the Metropolitan Police Department and confirm the date on which the two Iranians died." That had been easy. They'd died on Sunday, February twenty-first.

Now I sat quietly, drinking a second cup of coffee and watching the old man as he methodically picked his way through two of Egor's oat-bran waffles. I tried to catch his eye as he sipped the dark-roast coffee from his Wedgwood cup. He ignored me. Every once in a while, I thought I caught a hint of a grin. In no way did that ease my anxiety.

As Egor cleared the dishes, the old man stood up and turned toward the doorway. He spoke with his back to me. "I called JBA Chevrolet earlier. Someone there owes me a favor."

I nodded automatically. "Uh-huh." I didn't recall anyone, but as either psychologist or investigator, Adrian Kahler had helped a lot of people before I'd arrived at Rawlings' Landing. He'd stored those markers, and he drew on them when necessary.

"Your car is ready. Finding one apparently took some doing."

"Car? What car?"

"You did not think I would permit you to monopolize Stanley's. He does need it occasionally."

"Fantastic." I felt my heart begin to pound. I added hesitantly, "What kind?"

"Chevrolet. That is what they sell. Please try not to wreck this one." He stepped through the doorway and then stopped. "Perhaps Ms. Blake would be willing to drive you there."

"She works... in Georgetown."

"Her response will be an excellent indication of your success at wooing her."

"Wooing?"

"Whatever you wish to call it." Then he walked out of the kitchen, through the dining room, and into his study.

I pushed my chair back from the table and stood up.

Egor had his back to me. He stood by his sink, washing dishes. He insisted that dishwashers damaged china.

"Wooing," I said.

He turned off the water. "Perhaps you should concentrate on your new car."

"Any ideas?"

"Chevrolet."

"Thanks so much. Z06s are impossible to come by right now."

"You have an irrational fondness for horsepower. What about a Camaro? The ZL1 has five hundred eighty. Your old Corvette had three hundred eighty."

"They were friendly horses. I knew their names."

"You'd have four seats."

"I don't have that many friends."

"Perhaps you should make a start." Egor turned toward me. It could be disconcerting to see a man the size and shape of a great bear gently caressing a Wedgwood plate with his dish towel. "Call Ms. Blake."

"Sure. Why not? The old man wants wooing? What century did that come from?"

Egor turned toward me and raised one dark, bushy eyebrow. "Perhaps it sounds more contemporary in Russian."

I called her cell. She answered on the first ring. "Nope, you're not interrupting. I took the day off. Putting some finishing touches on my Saturday-night lecture."

"Shakespeare unbound?"

"Demystified."

"I doubt it."

"In the short term, you're probably right. But I'll certainly give the status quo a kick in the ass." She paused for a moment. "You're not canceling our date?"

"Wouldn't think of it. I need a favor. The old man found me a replacement car. I need a ride to the dealership."

"New 'Vette?"

"The old man's not talking."

"Ethan hasn't been able to locate a new Mustang either. He might need to factory order one. He'll probably buy something else to tide him over."

"He could buy something with four-wheel drive and keep it for bad weather."

"He lives in DC. Parking two cars at Mass Court Apartments would be extravagant, even for Ethan."

"Why DC?"

"He likes to jog the mall early in the morning."

"This is winter. It's dark early in the morning."

"He likes the dark."

"In DC it can be dangerous."

"Tell that to Ethan. Sometimes he runs all the way to the Tidal Basin. He can pretty much go to the lab whenever he wants. His techs do most of the work."

"And that's worked out so well lately."

For a moment our conversation developed one of those awkward pauses. Then she said, "Traffic's not bad this time of day. Be there in maybe an hour." She paused for a moment. "Well, less than two."

"Great. And thanks." The line might have clicked dead before I spit out the thanks.

I turned away from the phone and nearly stumbled into Egor. I had done that once. It had felt like hitting a wall.

"That went well," I said.

"It would appear Ms. Blake wants to spend time with you."

I shrugged.

Egor's heavy lids rose, and the overhead lights twinkled in his eyes. "It certainly is curious."

Alex arrived at one o'clock. She stopped in front of the gate and blipped her horn. The new video console let me zoom in on her white Mustang convertible until I could see the blue of her eyes. Then I noticed a guy sitting beside her. It was Ethan. Curiouser and curiouser.

I'd already slipped into my Kramer vest with its integrated holster. That put the Colt Lady Elite .380 inside my navy-blue denim shirt, but I could pop the snaps fast when I needed to. I didn't want to tote any unnecessary lumps of metal, and I had no intention of wearing a Michelin Man ski jacket while test-driving my new car. The .380 was a weak sister compared to the big mama .45 or even a nine millimeter, but Egor had replaced the factory-installed nubbins with real sights, and I could hit what I aimed at. The old man called it my toy pistol. Egor the photographer insisted that a gun was a lot like a camera. What mattered was having one with you.

I left the house through the garage, walking past the empty half where my old Corvette used to live. Whatever the old man had up his sleeve, it wouldn't replace a classic.

Alex had pulled her Mustang into the driveway and turned around. Ethan had moved to the backseat. I hopped in.

"Thanks," I said, turning to Alex. "This is really nice of you."

She gave me a smile. She had her hair tied up in back, and she wore an oversized red-and-black-plaid tunic sweater. "You pulled me out of one car." She rapped the steering wheel with a knuckle. "I'll help you get into another."

Ethan extended his hand over the seat back. "I didn't want to miss the birth of your new car." The front of his ski jacket hung open. Beneath it he wore a brown-and-white Beatles T-shirt with a monochrome Abbey Road graphic on it.

"More like an overseas adoption," I said. "I have no idea what she looks like."

Alex blipped the horn. "Let's go find out."

Automatically I glanced around the car. Black leather upholstery. Premium package. Nice.

The gate opened as we approached. Alex shot through. Then she spun the Mustang right and punched the accelerator.

"Speed bumps," I yelled.

She slammed the brake pedal. "Oh. Right. Forgot."

Ethan laughed so hard he nearly choked. When he stopped, he sputtered at her. "Try driving like a lady."

"That's *exactly* what I was doing."

Ethan reached over the seat back and grasped my left shoulder. "And when we get back, assuming that we have time, I'd really like to meet this Dr. Kahler of yours."

"No problem," I answered. *Curiouser and curiouser.*

Adrian Kahler's favorite Chevrolet dealer also sold GMC trucks. Egor had got his Denali there. It was a huge shoebox of a building with a front lot long enough to land a small plane. The sign at the edge of the lot sported the golden Chevy symbol on a blue background. It stood on stilts three stories tall but wasn't quite large enough to be visible from the International Space Station.

The sales floor had a faint scent of plastic, metal, and rubber. The receptionist had dark hair and long fingernails painted emerald green. They glittered in the bright fluorescent light. She smiled at me as I approached. "May I help you?"

"Barry Sandler."

She looked at me quizzically. "Yes."

"I'm here to pick up a car."

She studied her monitor, clicked a few keys, and then studied it again. Her smiling lips flatlined. Then the corners began to turn down.

"Sorry," I said. "Try Adrian Kahler."

She looked up. Her eyes widened, and her mouth popped out a little "Oh," as if she were seeing me in a beam of heavenly light shining through the clouds. "Dr. Kahler!"

"I work for him."

She stood up. "Yes, sir. Please make yourself comfortable. I'll be right back with Mr. Hudson. He's expecting you."

Hudson stood six feet tall and looked thirtysomething. He had the slightly heavy but not-yet-soft build of a high school football player who'd matured into a desk job. He had a salesman's easy smile and a firm, dry handshake that whispered, "You can trust me."

"Mr. Sandler, it's a pleasure. The boss said to take special care of you. We have your car in back. Had a devil of a time getting one. The boss said he called in a favor at Bowling Green."

I shook his hand, but as soon as he said "Bowling Green," I nearly hugged the guy. If Alex hadn't been there, I might have kissed him. Bowling Green, Kentucky, is where Corvettes are born.

"Your car's still in the shop. We were able to locate a set of Pirelli winter tires for it. Hard to find as the car. Most of our customers put their toys away for the winter. Boss says you drive yours year-round."

"Until they blow up."

Hudson maintained his smile and shrugged. "Follow me."

My heart began to race. Any courteous thought of introducing the Blakes to Hudson evaporated as soon as I heard "Bowling Green."

He led us to a brown-painted spring-hinged door with a small wire-reinforced window in it. I tried to glance through, but Hudson stepped in front of the window as he pushed the door open.

We followed him through in single file. He waved an arm to our left. That wasn't where I wanted to look, but my gaze followed his arm. He pointed to a wall of tires. The rack holding them stood twenty feet high and extended along the wall, on and on. The showroom-bright, showroom-clean service area had thirty bays lined up along the wall opposite the tires. They'd left lots of room between the two. Even a truck would have enough room to turn around. The gray epoxy-coated floor looked clean enough for them to host employee family picnics on Sundays.

Hudson led us along the wall of tires. He said with pride, "We stock just about every tire a Chevrolet or GMC vehicle might use. But winter tires for the new Corvettes—that's a special order."

He stopped us about halfway along the tire wall and pointed to the far side of the room. "Your car's just about—"

I heard four loud pops. They came so close together that they nearly made a single sound. I snapped my head around and saw a thirty-foot-wide section of the tire rack behind us lose its grip on the wall and topple forward. I swept Alex into my arms and began to run. Wishful thinking. I didn't make more than a stride or two.

The thick chemical scent of all those tires closed over me. We weren't going to make it. The black waxiness of rubber brushed my scalp. I ducked my head and lurched forward. Only a couple more feet, and I'd cheat death again. A crushing weight began to shove me down. I stumbled, pushing Alex to safety as I fell. Those couple of feet were hers now. I wondered what she'd think when she turned around and saw a pulped mess wearing my clothes. The falling rubber wall had reached my shoulders. It had shoved me down. The absurd image of a dinosaur wearing sneakers flashed through my head. I'd share that with the angels. I collapsed to my knees.

Suddenly that terrible pressure lifted. I continued to pitch forward. My outstretched hands broke the fall. The tip of my nose brushed against the gray epoxy floor as I twisted and rolled myself out of harm's way.

I pushed myself onto my knees and then stood up. My right knee ached. I turned to face the fallen tire rack. It hadn't damaged the floor. The tires stuck out beyond the steel supports and had pretty much bounced. But anything of flesh and blood caught under that mountain of falling rubber would have been crushed to guacamole.

Hudson had been the first into the big room. He'd been walking ahead of us and was already past it when the rack fell. He stood to my right, mouth gaping, eyes glassy. When he spoke, his voice was a whisper, more a note to self than conversation. "I'll be saying an extra prayer or two on Sunday."

Ethan Blake stood to my left. He faced the huge toppled dinosaur of steel and rubber. He backed up a step. Then he turned to face me. His face looked bloodless. Sweat matted his dark hair, and beads of it ran across his forehead and down his cheeks, dripping from his nose and chin. I saw a small pool of it at his feet. He trembled visibly. He looked like a bodybuilder who'd abruptly discovered that the barbell above his head carried ten times more weight than he'd ever pressed before. I walked over and rested a hand on his shoulder. Even through his clothing, his skin felt freezing cold. Emotion burst out from him. I sensed neither fright nor relief, only elation. Triumph. Ethan Blake had won. I had no idea what.

A moment passed before he acknowledged my presence. Then he pushed my hand away and took a step to his right. "I'm OK." His eyes wandered, unfocused, until they found his sister. "Alex," he said in a quavering voice, "take me home."

Alex. Shit. My mind had filled so completely with her brother that I'd forgotten about Alex. I spun around. She lay sprawled facedown on the gray floor. Then she rolled onto her back and sat up.

"You all right?" I asked.

She brushed a tangle of dark hair back from her eyes. "Think so." She wiggled her feet and then raised and lowered her shoulders a couple of times. "Everything works. Just got the wind knocked out of me." She narrowed her eyes. "Did you just throw me across the floor?"

"I tried." I gestured to the fallen tire rack.

"Oh, shit!" She studied me for a long moment. "Thanks. You OK?"

"I'll spend tonight icing bruises. We both will."

"Alex!"

We both turned toward Ethan. His voice sounded weak. His face looked pasty. I saw a damp handkerchief in his left hand. "I need to get home."

She nodded to her brother and reached for his hand. He let her take it. She slowly led him toward the door. He walked like an old man, as if every ounce of energy, all but what he needed to force one leg in front of the other, had been drained out of him. I had no understanding of what I'd just sensed in the guy. Somehow the falling tire rack hadn't crushed us, and something had sucked just about every ounce of energy out of Ethan Blake. Maybe Kahler would figure it out. My right knee began to throb.

Alex called to me over her left shoulder just before that small brown door swung closed behind her. "Call me."

I gave her a little wave.

I limped to the wall to which the tire rack had been attached. Hudson followed after me.

"When was this thing installed?" I asked.

"A couple of days ago. Brand new. The old one had rusted. This is stainless steel. The boss got a deal on it. He likes the service area to look as much like an operating room as possible. The high-end customers like that.

We're the largest 'Vette dealer in Maryland, including DC. The boss plans on keeping it that way. You need to sell a lot of Impalas to match the profit on one 'Vette, especially when a new model comes out. 'Vette customers check out the service bays."

"Yeah," I said absentmindedly. "'Vette customers." That was me. But my brain had kicked into detective mode. The toy would wait.

"A couple of days ago? Did anyone know I was picking up a car today?"

"Front office plus all the sales staff. The boss has had us calling all over the place to locate this one. These babies are damn scarce right now."

I reached the wall and swept my gaze over it, searching for the tire rack's attachment points. I found one. The bolt had pulled out of the wall, and what remained was a small crater with jagged edges and a black smear on the wall around it. I laid two fingers against the cool, smooth concrete, ran them over the black smear, and then tentatively slipped my index finger into the hole. It felt warm. The others were the same.

I turned to Hudson. "Who did the work?"

"Why do you care? Insurance will cover it. Besides, the boss has been using the same company for years. If they screwed up, they'll make good on it."

"Humor me. The workmen. Seen them before?"

"New guys. Didn't chat much. One had some kind of accent. I can get the names for you."

"I'd appreciate it."

"You a lawyer?"

"Nope. Just curious. Nearly getting crushed to death does that to me."

"No argument there. I'll have it before you leave. Want some ice for that knee? Might be a good idea before you try to drive."

"Thanks. I just killed one Corvette. Best not to kill another, at least not so soon."

Hudson gave me a funny look and then shrugged. A good salesman always rolls with it. He led me to a small office, one of the kind they use for deal closing, and pointed me to the customer chair. "Back in a couple of minutes," he said. And he was, carrying a Ziploc full of crushed ice. "We'll move your 'Vette into the showroom." Then he left me alone. I rolled up my pants leg and, for the next thirty-two minutes, practiced ten minutes on and one minute off. After that I felt better, and it hadn't gone black and blue yet. I took that as an encouraging sign.

I texted Egor on my Safeway-bought cell phone. Kahler insisted that we buy the cheap ones, bake them in the oven after a month or two, and then buy a different brand with a new contract. I told him that the tire rack appeared to have been blown off the wall with a tiny amount of C-4 and a squib planted behind each of the bolts. I know squibs. For a moment my mind drifted back to a happier time—well, happier except for the nearly dying parts.

I'd get the name of the installer from Hudson. I saw no point in trying to locate the electronic trigger or any other evidence. The old man didn't handle retribution through the courts.

I stood up and took a step, then another. I hardly hobbled at all. When I stepped into the showroom, Hudson waved to me. As I rounded a red Denali, I saw the Corvette. It crouched low, grill menacing. It glowed like black glass.

Hudson was smiling. The roof barely reached his chest. He rapped it with a knuckle. I caught myself before yelling at him, "Don't do that."

"One Z06 as requested. Double black," he announced.

My eyes locked onto a small emblem on the front fender louver. It read, "Z06."

I limped all the way around the car and then gently caressed a fender.

"It took some doing. The boss has a friend at Bowling Green. He must owe this Dr. Kahler of yours big-time."

I circled the car. My mouth hung open. The driver-side window was down. I poked my head inside.

"Six-hundred-twenty-five-horsepower supercharged V-eight," Hudson said. "Seven-speed stick. Hope you like it. Don't sell many stick shifts anymore."

"It's perfect." The words dribbled out of my mouth.

I pulled my head back. Hudson opened the driver-side door.

I didn't need more of an invitation than that. I climbed in and settled my butt onto the microfiber insert in the leather seat. I didn't get the little shock of leather cold I'd become so used to. That new-car scent blended with the fragrance of leather and surrounded me. I rested my left hand on the wheel and my right on the shifter. I depressed and released the clutch. Then I noticed the dash. Chevy had made a change. The tach now sat in the middle of the panel, in line with the center of the steering wheel, where God meant it to be. I must have been smiling. I felt my mouth stretch.

Hudson knelt down and said to me through the side window, "We disconnected OnStar. The boss insisted. That OK?"

"I don't like to be tracked."

Hudson shrugged. Then he straightened up. "The boss says we'll keep the summer tires here for you. They're on the same-style wheels. You can swap 'em out in April."

"Great."

"Can't let you drive it out of the showroom. House rules. I'll take care of that while you sign the papers."

Closing took longer than I'd have liked. A seemingly endless stack of papers had to be read. Years of practice helped me to push my attention deficit disorder aside and study every one. Today's distractions were worse than most. I had a new car to drive. And someone *had* just tried to kill me. Or they'd tried to kill Alex or Ethan, and I'd simply been part of a package deal.

When I hobbled out of the little office, Hudson stood waiting. He handed me another bag of ice. "Thanks," I said.

"Want someone to drive you home?"

I gave him a look. "Hear about any snowballs in hell today?"

"Thought I should ask."

"Sure. Thanks. If my clutch knee were bad, I'd have a problem. I don't plan on pushing the gas pedal very hard."

Hudson punched my shoulder. Cheating death bonds people, even those you barely know. "You're smarter than you look."

"She's not broken in yet."

"Keep it under four thousand revs for the first five hundred miles."

He led me to the parking lot and handed me a black-and-silver fob with the Corvette crossed-flags emblem on it. "With this in your pocket, the door will unlock as you approach the car. It's push-button start. No key. There's a manila envelope full of other stuff on the passenger seat. The spare fob is in it, so don't leave it there." He pointed his right index finger at the front of the car. "So's the front plate. None of our mechanics were willing to drill the bumper."

I nodded. "My kind of guys."

I climbed into my new car, fastened the belt, depressed the clutch, shifted into neutral, and located the start button. No mystery; it sat right where the key would have gone. Before he pushed the door closed, Hudson handed me his business card.

"I put a few more in the glove box, in case you run into any serious admirers. Oh, and the name and phone number of the company that installed the tire rack is on the back of this one. They're sending someone out this afternoon.

I pushed the start button, and a low-pitched rolling symphony of pistons, belts, and gears wafted through me. My new Z06 and I rolled out of the parking lot and headed for the highway. The gearbox was easy to get used to. The engineers had been kind. Although the old six-speed gearbox had been replaced with a seven speed, the graphic on the shift knob showed reverse still far right and back, same as always, with the new seventh gear added far right and forward. The stick shifted smoothly, and the clutch felt perfect.

I held nearly to the speed limit and checked the two tachometers frequently, the one on the dash or its fraternal twin in the heads-up display. Each was redlined just north of the four thousand mark. Hudson had scrawled a note on the envelope: "Redline moves up after break-in." I wondered if I could hit one hundred with the tach just south of the redline but decided not to try it. Even the tires weren't broken in yet.

After a while I stopped playing with my new toy and began thinking like a detective. Someone had just tried to kill me or one or both Blakes or all three of us. Alex pissed people off, but I doubted she'd pushed anyone to homicide. Geoffrey Seep didn't strike me as someone with balls enough for murder. That left Ethan as the target. Why? To stop him from making another crystal? As far as I could tell, he'd already stopped himself. And who knew that Iran was nearly launch capable anyway? No one but the Joint Chiefs, probably the National Security Agency, and the Iranians. That led me back to Asha Talavi. But why should he care about Scofield's little problems? And why tell me?

All that spun in the background as I listened to the throaty exhaust note of the supercharged Z06 engine. I never even looked for the radio controls.

CHAPTER TWENTY

Friday, March 11, 2016
Launch minus Seven Days

The bright winter sunlight carried no warmth. I jerked the covers up to my neck, buried my head in a pillow, and cursed myself for leaving the shades up. My right knee ached. Worse, it felt stiff.

I'd driven my new toy directly back to Rawlings' Landing. No side trips. I'd parked it in the garage and carried the two fobs and envelope up to my room. Then I'd iced my knee again. Someone had just come close to killing me, and a limping detective would never catch the SOB.

I reported to the old man between icings, and time spent in trance actually helped the knee. Trance always leaves me feeling relaxed.

Adrian Kahler could read minds, not all of them and not all the time. Often what he got depended on how much damage he was willing to do. As a child I had an eidetic memory, like a camera that captured whatever streamed in through its lens. My conscious mind outgrew it, but my unconscious never did. Now the old man could access what I couldn't. It felt like owning a flash drive to which someone else had the password.

He'd already spoken to the tire-rack-installation company. The installers had been new hires who'd started after two of the tire-rack company's regulars had been injured in a traffic accident. The newbies hadn't shown up for work yesterday.

Kahler had recounted this distractedly, with about as much interest as he'd shown in the new 'Vette, which was zero. The old man didn't leave his little Tudor castle much, and as far as vehicles were concerned, he had no interest in anything without a mast and sail. He seemed strangely upbeat.

As I'd turned to leave his study, I'd noticed that he'd pushed his Eames chair back from his desk and tilted it to the reclining position. He'd leaned back, eyes closed and hands folded on his belly. His extended thumbs had been describing slow, small circles against each other.

Now I rolled over, sat up, and dangled my feet at the edge of the bed. The knee ached but didn't look either blue or swollen. I ran my right index finger over it, gently at first. Then I poked at the soft tissue between the bones. No tenderness. I kicked my leg out and let it fall back a few times. It felt a little stiff. I stood up and then took a step. The ache clung to it but didn't worsen. I walked gingerly to the bathroom, found the Aleve in the medicine cabinet, and downed two of them.

I walked into the kitchen at nine o'clock. No Egor. A note sat on the kitchen table. "In the garage." Shit. I forgot about my knee and ran through the laundry room and out the door.

My shiny new toy sat in the middle of the garage. Egor had moved the Denali into the driveway. The Corvette's driver-side door hung open, and the lower half of the ex-Navy SEAL's powerful seven-foot-one-inch frame stuck out of the car, the mechanic's creeper cart nearly invisible beneath him. Joanna Dembrowski, Egor's long-time love interest, sat on the concrete floor, to the far side of the open door. She balanced a Braille Sense U2 QWERTY laptop computer on her knees, her fingers resting lightly on the keyboard. A cable from her computer ran into the 'Vette.

"That's my new car you're playing with," I shouted.

"What are you afraid of," Joanna quipped, "the blind leading the blind?"

"You're the only one who's blind," I answered, "and I'd follow you any-where. But the engineer has really big hands."

Egor's voice boomed out of the 'Vette, "The need to work in tight spaces is one of the reasons we engineers created tools."

The cart rolled back slowly, and the rest of Egor came into view. His 325 pounds sat up. "We've modified the NAV system."

I gave him a frown. "If this car blows up, I'll be really pissed."

Egor sat up on his cart. He wore his usual charcoal-gray wool trousers and blue oxford button-down shirt. I don't think the man ever owned a pair of jeans. He looked at me with sad brown eyes. They could have belonged to a puppy—a really big puppy. "Barry," he said, feigning injury, "We're California Institute of Technology graduates. Trust us."

I sighed. "OK, show me."

Egor and I had already finished breakfast when Kahler came down, but I remained at the kitchen table while Egor filled the old man's Wedgwood coffee cup and busied himself with making pancakes.

The phone rang. I recognized Ethan Blake's voice, rapped the table, and drew an uppercase *B* in the air with my finger.

Kahler pointed to the speakerphone button. I tapped it.

"I want to meet Dr. Kahler."

I glanced at the old man. "Why?"

"You're dating my sister."

"I am not. And he's not my father."

"I *need* to see him." He paused for a long moment. I thought I heard him swallow. "OK. I need his help."

Kahler's gray-blue eyes sparkled, and a tiny smile tugged at the corners of his small mouth. He nodded once.

"When?"

"Today."

Kahler held up his index finger.

"Can you be here at one o'clock?"

"See you then." He disconnected.

My eyes still held the old man's. "Curiouser and curiouser," I said.

"Indeed." His usually stony face held the faintest of smiles.

At twelve forty-five, a maroon Buick with a Hertz license-plate frame stopped in front of the gate and honked four times. I cycled through the cameras until I found one at an angle that let it peer through the wind-shield glare and then retracted the gate. Ethan Blake drove through. He drove past the pull-in spaces by the garage and parallel parked in one of the white-lined spaces at the front of the house. Then he leaped out of the car, slammed the door, and jogged up the steps to the front door. I already had it open for him.

He wore a black Beatles T-shirt. It had the faces of the Fab Four sten-ciled over a colored graphic of the British flag. A wide black leather belt supported his black jeans and the iPhone case on his right hip. No coat. He had an athletic body that looked younger than his anxious face. When he'd arrived the day before, he'd seemed as relaxed as a guy headed to a rock concert. As I thought back on it, I realized that had been a mask, a really good one. No mask today. Today would be different. He pumped my hand.

"Thanks, Barry."

I ushered him inside and then into the living room. Egor had already poured himself into his oversized easy chair, and he didn't stir when we walked in.

Kahler's study door opened, and the old man walked briskly across the hardwood floor and extended his hand. He greeted the scientist as warmly as if they'd been old army buddies who'd saved each other's lives too many times to count. Egor remained unintroduced, ignored, out of mind, and ready to snap Blake's neck at a moment's notice. The old man left little to chance. Anyone who asked for a meeting was a threat before becoming an opportunity.

I led Blake to the chocolate leather chesterfield that sat on the other side of the heavy glass coffee table from Kahler's Eames chair. He walked to the far end and faced the old man. The two of them sat simultaneously. The old man leaned back into his Eames chair. Blake perched on the front edge of a big leather cushion.

I waited a moment and then took my seat to Kahler's left. Egor's big easy chair sat to Kahler's right, but it was staggered forward so that it was closer to Blake's end of the couch than to the old man.

Kahler leaned forward in his chair and smiled his gentle therapist smile. It rolled "you can trust me" and "I can help you" into an irresist-ible invitation to share the darkest secrets from the depth of your soul. I've never figured out how a man as inherently cold as Adrian Kahler could emit warmth, but that magic smile always did it for him.

"How can I help you, Dr. Blake?"

Blake took a long breath. "I can't grow the crystal."

Kahler fixed Blake with a kind, steady gaze. "It grew before."

Blake shook his head. "No, it didn't."

The old man waited.

"It didn't grow. I grew it."

Kahler nodded slowly. "You grew it."

"That's right, damn it. It didn't just grow. That lab has the best crystal-growing technology in the world. Other NASA labs build gas lasers. Helium is a favorite. They can fill large lasing chambers with it and generate a ton of energy. But they're too big and too delicate for satellite use." Ethan Blake glanced at me. "They can't withstand the vibration generated by a launch."

I grunted my agreement. "Mmm-hmm." A trickle of sweat ran down my neck.

"Crystals, on the other hand, are sturdy. And a crystal that can lase at comparable energy levels to a gas tube can be a lot smaller. The problem was that a crystal capable of generating weapons-grade laser power would need to be dramatically larger than any lasing crystal ever produced. When they told me they wanted a crystal that large, I laughed. No one had even come close. But they were throwing money at me, and how often do you get a chance to accomplish something no one has ever done before?"

Adrian Kahler made a tiny nod, just enough to show Blake he was paying attention.

"We tried the Czochralski crucible first. Built the largest crucible ever. Didn't work. The crystals started forming and then shattered. We varied the melt, modified the seed holder, tried any idea anyone on my staff came up with, no matter how outlandish it seemed. Nothing worked. We videoed everything.

"I figured the powers that be would drop the project. Instead they doubled the funding. With the Czochralski crucible, the crystals cracked just before completion. The videos showed that when the crystals reached a certain size, often just before completion, the cracks would begin at the bottom end cone, the point farthest from the seed crystal, and then march straight up the crystal.

"So I thought we might do better with the floating-zone technique. Scrapped half the stuff in the lab. I used four CO_2 lasers as a heat source, each operating at twenty-two-hundred watts, each focused on the feed-rod assembly. Older systems use a single laser and split the beam path. I demanded better. Just the calibration and alignment for those lasers took us three months. Floating zone still needs a seed crystal but no crucible. The idea is to set the feed and seed rods apart, heat them until they begin to melt, and then move the feed rod—the upper one—downward until it contacts the seed rod. Then they're drawn apart. We had to be extremely careful, continuously adjusting the length of the molten zone to keep its diameter the same as that of the feed rod and seed rod. When the melt material on top of a seed crystal does solidify, it duplicates the seed crystal's orientation. But whenever we got close to the crystal size the satellite lasers require, the growing crystal would shatter."

I yawned. Kahler shot me a look.

Blake only smiled. "The natives became restless. I hadn't grown anything more than a longer budget flow sheet. The e-mails requesting progress reports became less and less polite. I responded tersely." He glanced at Kahler and then turned to me and grinned mischievously. "Progress: none."

Kahler nodded his psychologist's slow, patient nod. "Go on."

"One Friday I sat alone in the lab, waiting for our most recent crystal to finalize. Every step in the process had been absolutely meticulous. This part was automated. I'd sent my staff out for a long lunch. Morale had hit a new low, and I figured they'd all have a better weekend if I didn't force them to watch another crystal crack. I leaned against the wall and started to hum. I stood there, humming, thinking about John Lennon, and staring at that big machine. I began to feel a unity with my growing crystal, as if some tentacle of my mind had reached out and melted into it. Then I lost track of time.

"When the staff returned, they found me asleep, curled up on the floor. One of my postdocs went to check on the crystal. He started shouting. He sounded so hysterical I thought he'd burned himself. Then I heard his words, 'We've done it.'"

Kahler smiled and nodded. I nodded too.

"And we really had." Blake's voice held a touch of excitement, touched by the memory of better days. "It had to cool before we could test it. That was the longest wait I've ever endured. But it was the largest, purest crystal this side of Neptune. The lasing tests were perfect. The durability tests were perfect. Perfect, perfect, and perfect! They installed it in laser satellite number one, and Ronald Reagan's 1983 dream of a Star Wars defense system became a reality. The boys at the Pentagon were apparently ecstatic. I've never met them, but Drew Scofield told me that if I'd ever wanted my own island, that was the time to ask."

Kahler nodded approvingly. "And there were no further problems?"

"Not one. And from then on, I made sure to hum to every crystal we produced. Hell, I was scared not to." Ethan Blake leaned back and let himself sink into the chesterfield's yielding leather cushions. He began to hum.

"Beatles?" I asked.

For the first time ever at a client meeting, Egor opened his mouth. "'Maxwell's Silver Hammer.'"

Blake's reverie ended abruptly. "Then the magic left me!"

The fingers of his left hand trembled as they combed back his thinning dark hair. His skin turned ashen, making his broad forehead look as wide as a dinner plate.

I studied the MIT educated scientist sitting across from me. His confident, relaxed demeanor had abandoned him. His hair looked too thin, his nose too big. His eyes sank into dark pits, and his lips pressed themselves into one thin line. The veins on his hands stood out like earthworms trying to get out after a storm. Ethan Blake looked old.

"And you still hum to them?" Kahler asked.

"Always. I know this sounds crazy, but it doesn't feel the same." Blake's voice became a whisper, "It hasn't since—" Blake's mouth clamped shut.

Kahler gave him a minute. Blake just sat there, quiet as if he'd hit a mute switch.

"Exactly when did crystal production fail?"

"Monday, February twenty-second."

"You recall the exact date," Kahler said. "I suppose one would. I remember the day my father died."

Blake went rigid.

Kahler gave him a minute. Then he asked, "Dr. Blake, how can I help you?"

Ethan Blake took one deep breath. Then he said, "Dr. Kahler, I am a scientist. I speak as a scientist when I tell you that I made those crystals grow. There is no other explanation. I do not understand how, but I'm certain I did it. Until February twenty-second. Then something changed.

Something inside me. Please help me." His voice cracked. For a moment I thought he'd start to cry. "Please help me change it back."

The old man smiled his therapist smile. On a grading scale, it would rate ten out of ten. Warmth and kindness sloshed into the room as if Ethan Blake had just lowered himself into an overfilled bathtub. "Of course. It will be my pleasure."

I watched Kahler closely. Those little creases around his eyes had deepened; his eyes were smiling. That wasn't part of his therapist persona. Something new had just happened, and it had made Adrian Kahler very happy.

The old man stood up. "Barry will see you out. Please return here at one o'clock tomorrow and plan on remaining for the afternoon. I have some experience with this sort of thing. I can help you." Then he turned, walked into his study, and closed the door.

I had no idea what the hell the old man was talking about. I didn't much like being left in the dark, but I followed orders. I led Blake to the door. He pumped my hand enthusiastically. "Thanks, Barry. Thanks ever so much." Then he bounded down the front steps, hopped into his rental, executed a perfect three-point turn in the front driveway, and drove away. I waited until he'd driven clear and then closed the gate.

CHAPTER TWENTY-ONE

Saturday, March 12, 2016
Launch minus Six Days

Ethan Blake arrived at eleven o'clock. I opened the door as he climbed the front steps.

Jeans and a T-shirt as usual. This one had a picture of Janis Joplin on it. I hoped that wasn't prophetic.

"Don't you own a coat?" I asked. "It's winter."

He shrugged. "I have a couple—somewhere. I like March weather. I jog."

If he really did like the cold, it didn't show. The skin of his face looked sallow. His sunken eyes had withdrawn into the dark shadows the harsh winter sunlight cast onto his face. I waved him inside.

I punched the intercom in the front hall, connected to Kahler's study, and let the old man know his newest client or patient or experiment or whatever Blake was to him had arrived two hours early.

"Show him in." The old man's voice betrayed neither annoyance nor surprise. For all I knew, Blake had simply followed a subliminal command. His early arrival might be confirmation that Kahler had a lock on his brain.

I led Ethan Blake through the living room to the old man's study, paused outside the closed door, and then knocked.

Kahler opened the door and shook Blake's hand. "Please sit down," he said, waving Blake to *my* leather easy chair. That really pissed me off, but the old man spoke before I could think up something offensive to say. "Thank you, Barry." Then he waved me out and closed the door.

I decided to kill some time watching daytime TV. I usually did that in the den, but the living room had a sixty-inch flat-screen, and that let me sit fairly close to the study door. I muted every ad, but the conversation taking place in Kahler's soundproofed little enclave remained private.

At twelve-thirty Egor brought them a tray of sandwiches. Adrian Kahler, insulin pump notwithstanding, didn't skip meals. A couple of cloth napkins covered the tray, but I recognized the bulge of a revolver's cylinder. I hopped up and slipped in front of Egor. My left hand opened the study door for him. The shirtsleeve covering my right forearm accidently brushed one napkin aside.

The ported barrel of Egor's Raging Bull .454 Casull revolver glared up at me. That muzzle looked large enough to swallow a hard-boiled egg. The big revolver weighed over three pounds, and the cartridges were so large that the huge cylinder could hold only five. Kahler shot me a look. I closed the door without a word and then waited outside the study until Egor walked out.

When he did, I followed him to the kitchen. "What the fuck?" I said.

Egor's huge frame turned to face me. His thick brown hair fell loosely across his narrow forehead. His dark, heavily lidded eyes looked barely open. They studied me for a moment. Then he smiled the way a brown bear might smile at seeing a cub stuck in a tree. "Adrian wanted something threatening."

"You didn't load it?"

"The chamber that will rotate into firing position is empty."

"Suppose the trigger gets pulled twice."

"Adrian will not permit that to happen."

"Do you have any idea what the old man is doing in there?"

"I'm sure Adrian is in control."

"Right. Control. A wonderful thing. Solidly or barely?"

"A tightrope walker can't be concerned with how many times he slips. It's part of the show. As long as he doesn't fall, slipping doesn't matter."

"Except for a spectator whose heart stops every time the guy slips."

Egor nodded slowly. Then he fixed me with his sleepy gaze. "That's why Adrian has kept you out of the audience."

After that I gave up on the living room. I moved myself to the den and spent the rest of the afternoon watching soap operas. On two separate occasions, I felt a mild tremor rumble through the house. The TV flickered for a moment. If the old man hadn't been working, I'd have checked for news of earthquakes. At least the pistol never fired. Stopping a .454 takes three seventeen-inch-long blocks of ballistic gelatin—or a very large bear.

Alex had e-mailed me a parking pass for the university parking lot closest to her office, and by five o'clock plenty of spaces sat empty. I found one in a corner and very carefully backed my new Stingray in, hitting the brakes just shy of the concrete parking stop. I loved the backup camera. I climbed out, buttoned the jacket of my charcoal-gray suit, and straightened my tie.

Alex met me at the carded door, and this time I waited for her to open it. She wore her hair pulled back and tied up. It lay flat against the sides of her head, and the auburn streaks glistened in the overhead light. Like sapphires at daybreak, her eyes shone out between long, dark lashes. She wore a hip-length black velvet blazer over a cranberry silk V-neck tank top. Her winter-white wool pencil skirt just grazed the tops of her knees. She had Cole Haan black suede pumps on her feet. Four-inch heels! That brought her up to only an inch shorter than my five eleven. The girl had dressed to take no prisoners.

"Hi, Barry."

"Alex, you look great."

"Thanks. Maybe this outfit will keep the audience from seeing how nervous I feel."

I couldn't decide between "no reason" and "good reason," so I just nodded and smiled. "Need me to carry anything?"

"Nope."

I followed Alex into her office. She stuck a pink flash drive into her computer and opened the lecture file. I watched quietly as a stream of PowerPoint slides flew by. "Final test." She closed the program and ejected the drive. Then she repeated the process with a blue flash drive. She nodded as she ejected the second. I heard her whisper to herself, "Backup." Then she slipped both into her purse.

"Locked and loaded?" I asked.

She looked up, and her sapphire-blue eyes found mine. Alex smiled fiercely. "This battle will be mine."

"I brought the chariot."

She started for the door and then pulled up short, turned to her desk, and opened the top right-hand drawer. Then she plucked out another flash drive. That one was green. "Hold out your hand."

I obeyed, and she pressed it against my palm. "Second backup. Just in case."

I slipped it into my left-front pocket. The right was for cash and car keys. My jacket's flap pockets were fake, and I never put anything in the breast pockets, which were already covering the pistol and magazine bulges. I had the little Colt .380 in the Kramer T-shirt holster again. Even with snaps disguised as buttons on my white dress shirt, it made for a slow draw. But I didn't imagine the Shakespeare types would be driven to violence, no matter how much Alex pissed them off. If I'd simply been on a date, I'd have been firearm-free. But this woman—she was business.

The Folger Shakespeare Library was a low, rectangular building crafted from white marble. It sat at the corner of Second Street SE and East Capitol Street, a couple of blocks from the Capitol.

A large, elegant fountain surrounding a bronze statue of Puck faced Second Street. An iron-railed ground-floor balcony overlooked the mischievous woodland spirit, and from that balcony, five tall rectangular windows climbed to a dark scroll. I couldn't read the inscription in the early-evening light.

The building was separated from Second Street by a wide front lawn and connected to it by a semicircular driveway running between the grass and the building. A metal pole rose from the lawn to support a small white metal sign with red-and-black lettering and a graphic of a car being towed. It read, "Parking Area Reserved for Folger Employees Only." A huge sign framed in white marble sat across the drive from the little warning. It read, "Welcome" and "Folger Shakespeare Library."

Alex reached into her purse, unfolded a red-and-white piece of paper, and held it up. For tonight, and tonight only, we were Folger employees. She smiled slyly. "Speaker's perk."

I pulled into the driveway and parked on the left side. Curbside wasn't my first choice, but better driveway curbside than street.

Alex struggled as she climbed out of the four-and-a-half-foot-high car. That pencil skirt wasn't designed by anyone who'd ridden in a 'Vette. "Why the hell didn't you bring the Denali?" she scolded. "You knew this was a dress-up."

"Blimp."

She stretched tall on her four-inch heels, pushed her nose to within an inch of mine, and glared into my eyes.

I backed away. "The Denali. The blimp is the Denali."

She snorted at me. "Fine." She took a step back and then glanced around. "Take my arm. Pretend you're a gentleman. Act like I'm important and escort me to that lecture hall."

I hooked my right arm, and she looped her left around it. "I'll treat you just like a queen," I said.

Alex raised her chin. "Damn well better. I'm about to be."

Before I could stop it, a low sigh slipped past my lips.

The driveway and Second Street actually lay along the side of the building. The Folger fronted on East Capitol. I climbed up the few steps that led to the front of the building as slowly as a squire and as deliberately as a guy whose date wore a pencil skirt. Then we turned right and marched up a few more steps. The glass-and-stainless-steel double doors were topped by a matching glass transom taller than the doors. I pushed the right-hand door open and held it while Queen Alex made her entrance. No one noticed.

The small vestibule had walls of beige marble. A three-sided mahogany desk sat wedged into the right far corner. A young woman with shoulder-length straight black hair and black-framed glasses sat behind it. Another statue of Puck stood across from the desk, his platform inscribed with, "Lord, what fools these mortals be!" Flanked by the desk on the right and Puck on the left stood the theater entrance. Its riveted bronze double doors stood open.

I dipped my head and said, "My lady." She nodded regally. We walked through arm in arm. The floor was made of flagstone rectangles. Their size and shape varied. Rows of theater seats, upholstered in dark-red cloth, flanked the wide center aisle. Three wooden steps climbed from the front of the aisle to the ground floor of the two-story stage that dominated the front of the theater. A lectern of dark mahogany stood just to stage right of center.

An elderly woman in a charcoal business suit ran up to Alex, shook her hand warmly, and began to chat. Alex dropped my arm, and I was forgotten. The two women walked down the aisle, up the stairs, and onto the stage. A tall middle-aged man wearing a charcoal suit and bright-green tie met them there. They chatted for a moment. Then he placed a MacBook Pro on top of the lectern. Alex held up her right hand. I could see the pink flash drive between her thumb and forefinger. The man reached for it, but she jerked it away. The three of them laughed.

The theater began to fill up. I picked a front-row seat just to the left of the center aisle and sat down. I glanced around. The two-tiered balcony had dark-stained wood balustrades that reached up from either side of the orchestra floor and wrapped around the rear of the theater. Dim yellow light flowed out of wall fixtures that resembled the gas lamps of a bygone age. I glanced up and saw a white unicorn painted in the center of the high ceiling.

Five minutes later the place was packed. The guy with the green tie cleared his throat, and the room fell silent. He introduced Dr. Alexandra Blake, assistant professor of computer science at Georgetown University, to the audience. I'd never actually thought of her that way before. I regarded the slender woman in the black blazer, red tank top, and white pencil skirt. Four-inch heels. Professor Alex Blake. I thought she looked hot.

A projector screen lowered from the ceiling, center stage, just stage left to the lectern.

Green Tie handed Alex a small laser pointer and a black wireless microphone that looked like a club. She hefted it a couple of times, thanked him for his kind introduction, and thanked the audience for coming out on this cold winter evening. Until then I hadn't thought about the cold. March in Maryland. At least it hadn't been snowing.

Alex's voice dragged my attention back inside. It sounded a little deeper than her conversational speech, more self-assured. "Who really wrote the works attributed to William Shakespeare? The answer to that question has been demanded by anti-Stratfordians for years, and the list of alternatives to the glove maker's son from Stratford has grown so long that it's considered by some to have become comical."

An orange background slide with black lettering filled the screen. It held four columns of names I'd never heard of. Alex slashed a neon-green dot across it with her pointer.

"Of William Shakespeare himself, we have no oil painting, no charcoal sketch, not even a physical description written in his own lifetime. Every Shakespeare biography is five percent fact and ninety-five percent conjecture. We don't know much." She glanced around her audience, smiling at each and every one. I took a look behind me and saw more than a few grinning back.

"We believe his date of birth to be April twenty-third, 1564, in Stratford-upon-Avon. During William's childhood, his father was a successful business-man and at one point high bailiff of Stratford. Attendance at the excellent local grammar school, King's New School, was therefore available to William."

Alex shrugged. "But no proof of his attendance has been found. He married, fathered children, moved to London, lived there for a number of years, became an actor and a writer, and returned to Stratford, and at age fifty-two, he died."

She turned up her hands in a that's-all-I've-got gesture.

"But what we do have are the writings *attributed* to William Shakespeare." She smiled again. I felt the audience warming to her. "Quite a lot of them. Perhaps the words themselves can be used to identify their author."

She took a dramatic pause and then popped a slide with "Stylometry" written in pastel-pink letters on a pastel-green background. Under it in smaller font were written "Objective" on the top line and "Unconscious" on the next.

"Stylometry is a collection of techniques for identifying authorship using *objective* processes." As Alex spoke, graphics popped onto the screen and then dissolved, one after another. "It is the analysis of statistical configurations, patterns chosen *unconsciously* by authors, as measures of style. The concept is not a new one. Stylometry was used as early as the fifteenth century to identify forgery. As computational power advanced from quill and parchment to pen and index cards to keyboards and microprocessors, stylometry became capable of answering questions of greater and greater complexity. It has been used to determine authorship of some Federalist Papers. In 1982 Larsen and Rencher used stylometry to determine authorship of sections of the Book of Mormon. Limited by the computational power available at the time, they nonetheless successfully applied multivariate analysis of variance, cluster analysis, and discriminant analysis to word prints and clearly separated Book of Mormon authors from non–Book of Mormon authors.

"In 1991 Elliott and Valenza used computational analysis of the occurrence of relative clauses, hyphenated compound words, grade level, and modal tests to demonstrate that the stylistic idiosyncrasies of Edward de Vere, the seventeenth Earl of Oxford, were entirely different from those of William Shakespeare. That made de Vere an unlikely authorship alternative to the young man from Stratford.

"To date, anti-Stratfordians have collected a total of fifty-eight claimed 'true authors' of Shakespeare's dramas and verse." The orange-and-black slide with the four columns of names reappeared on the screen. Alex's luminous green pointer dot hacked at it again, one diagonal slash followed by another. "Using techniques updated from those of my predecessors to take advantage of modern computational software and hardware, I've evaluated the nine most likely alternative authors of Shakespeare's works."

A plain black-on-white slide filled the screen. Pure science, I guess. Nothing fancy.

	WS*	FG	RM	WS	MSH	HN	CM	FB	EV	ABL
M1	439/ 439	20%	42%	27%	35%	42%	58%	67%	74%	83%
M2	116/ 116	27%	59%	31%	41%	23%	61%	42%	69%	89%
M3	434/ 434	14%	52%	22%	31%	36%	56%	65%	73%	85%
M4	513/ 513	15%	39%	26%	29%	40%	49%	73%	81%	82%
M5	83/ 83	35%	44%	35%	34%	36%	65%	63%	65%	91%
M6	68/ 68	29%	51%	40%	27%	22%	60%	66%	74%	67%
M7	201/ 201	34%	36%	24%	22%	34%	73%	84%	88%	89%
M8	232/ 232	19%	42%	25%	40%	29%	71%	75%	83%	80%
M9	139/ 139	36%	61%	27%	39%	31%	67%	60%	73%	79%
M10	238/ 238	20%	56%	31%	36%	47%	65%	79%	71%	86%
Average	100%	24.9%	48.2%	28.8%	37%	34%	62.5%	67.4%	75.1%	83.1%

"Those authors are represented in each of nine columns, starting third from your left, columns three through eleven. FG is Sir Fulke Greville; RM is Roger Manners, fifth Earl of Rutland; WS is William Stanley, sixth Earl of Derby; MSH is Mary Sidney Herbert, Countess of Pembroke; HN is Sir Henry Neville; CM is Christopher Marlowe; FB is Sir Francis Bacon; EV is

Edward de Vere, seventeenth Earl of Oxford; and ABL is Amelia Bassano Lanier. Any questions so far?"

Alex studied the room. The room studied back. I discovered that I was holding my breath. I could hear the folks next to me breathing. I inhaled as quietly as I could. No one even coughed.

"OK. Column one lists the ten stylometry analytic modalities evaluated, M one through M ten. Each one is characteristic of Shakespeare's writing. Then each row in the table represents the frequency of occurrence of each of these modalities in the writings of Shakespeare and in the writings of Shakespeare's contemporaries. Some characteristics are identical to those used by previous researchers—for example, frequency of hyphenated compound words, relative clauses per thousand, and the frequency of commonly occurring noncontextual words. Others were developed specifically for this study, made possible by advances in programming theory and microprocessor speed.

"Column two grades William Shakespeare, WS star, as compared to himself. I've listed the number of times each analytic tool was found in the letters. For WS star, each cell, by definition, equals one hundred percent.

"Rather than analyze all of Shakespeare's works, I limited this study to his letters. In all of Shakespeare's thirty-seven plays, thirty-one letters are read on stage. Twenty-one are written in prose, and ten are in blank verse. I thought that if someone other than William Shakespeare had been the true author of the Shakespeare plays, perhaps he or she might have let his or her guard down when writing in the subset of letters, and a style less formal, more indicative of the true author, might come through. Comparable writings of the nine anti-Stratfordian candidates were identified and used in this analysis."

That stirred them up. A few oohs and aahs followed. Hardly a Super Bowl crowd.

Then Alex reviewed that table, cell by cell, with her audience. I glanced around. They seemed transfixed. I neither saw nor heard a single yawn. I had to stifle mine. She pointed at this or that cell, made a comment or two, and then moved to the next.

"These numbers don't lie," she told them softly. "But by themselves they prove nothing." She waved the green dot across the screen. "They do not demonstrate that someone other than the young man from Stratford wrote the works authored by William Shakespeare. But," she said. Her voice had a gentle huskiness to it, and it drew her audience in. "They do change the conversation."

The sixtyish woman beside me stared transfixed at that screen and pushed herself forward in her chair.

"If you are an anti-Stratfordian, if you believe that William Shakespeare was too untraveled or too poorly educated or too far removed from the nobility to have written the works attributed to his authorship, then the most likely alternative candidate is neither a Christopher Marlowe, who faked his own death; nor writer, lawyer, and philosopher Sir Francis Bacon; nor Edward de Vere, who died twelve years earlier than Shakespeare. If you believe that William Shakespeare, a grammar-school-educated kid from the boondocks, did not write the works attributed to him, then the person who did, the single individual best supported by objective scientific evidence, is Amelia Bassano Lanier."

Alex raised her voice to a soft feminine rumble that rolled through that room like a wave cascading over the rocks of a jagged shore. "Amelia Bassano Lanier, a woman made invisible by her times. Amelia Bassano Lanier, a *woman*, a *feminist*, and a *Jew*."

The room remained silent. A moment passed.

Then the applause began, a few isolated claps at first, then more and more, like raindrops announcing an approaching storm. When the torrent came, it engulfed the hall. It was loud. It was enthusiastic. It was cut off.

A male voice, nearly a scream, slammed into it, "Bitch! You bitch! You cannot steal him from us. You feminists think you can take whatever you want. No! Not this. Not Shakespeare! He is a man. He has always been a man. He will always be a man. You know that! You do. You just want to steal him. You steal everything. Not Shakespeare. Not now. Not ever!"

I craned my neck and spotted the source of the tirade in the back row of the theater. Tall, thin, perfectly dressed in a dark flannel suit, face red with rage, Geoffrey Seep's tense sticklike figure pushed its way to the aisle.

I began to stand up, but when I glanced at Alex, she shook her head. She would handle this. I shrugged and sat. Her people. Her show.

Seep marched forward like a wooden soldier. Each footstep clacked against the tile floor. He made about three paces. Then a short, stocky middle-aged woman in a pale turquoise dress slid gracefully out of an aisle seat, stood up, and turned to face him. He angled his shoulders a little, letting her know that she'd either move or be shoved aside. Then a second woman stepped into the aisle, stood behind the first, and glared silently at Seep. He kept coming.

A third woman stepped into the aisle, then another, then two more. By the time Dr. Geoffrey Seep reached the turquoise dress, a dozen women, young, old, and somewhere in the middle, had formed a barricade between him and the stage.

He stopped, glared directly at each and every one of them, then did an abrupt about-face, and marched away. He turned back before leaving the theater. He called out to Alex. "I knew you were planning something like this. I knew. Fool. You think you've won." I kept my eyes fixed on the man until those big riveted bronze double doors swung closed behind him.

They held a brief reception for Alex in the Great Hall. Its arched ceiling, oak-paneled walls, and terracotta floor surrounded her with elegance. The audience besieged her with questions and showered her with praise. I passed the time with the hors d'oeuvres. The blinis topped with whipped ricotta, caviar, and a slice of hard-boiled egg weren't half-bad. At one point I saw Alex nibble at an edamame wrap, but she was too busy talking to eat much. Then Alex made her good-byes, and we trotted down the steps and across the driveway. I stayed beside her. My mind grappled with potential techniques for sliding my pencil-skirt-clad date back into my four-and-a-half-foot-high car.

A Ford E-150 commercial van sat a few feet in front of the 'Vette. I turned to Alex. "If that's delivering desserts, we're going to miss out."

Then something hit me in the side of the head. My knees gave way, and I pitched forward.

CHAPTER TWENTY-TWO

Launch minus Six Days

Sharp and cold, the driveway's gravel ripped into my knees. It scraped my palms. Reflex had thrust out my hands to guard my face. My head throbbed. I struggled to one knee and forced my eyes to focus through the blur.

Two black-hooded men wrestled Alex toward the open back door of the van. She kicked at them. She screamed for help. Everyone else was still inside Folger. I reached a shaky hand toward my pistol. I stopped. My arm felt too unsteady to shoot at anyone that close to Alex. I pushed myself to my feet, bent forward, and half stumbled, half ran at the nearest assailant. Then I let myself pitch forward. The top of my head crashed into his spine just above his hips. He lost his grip on Alex, spun halfway around, and fell onto his back. I dropped on top of him, my knee on his throat. I felt something crunch.

I heard metal thump. I jerked my head toward it. The van's rear door was closed but only a few feet away. I glimpsed the second assailant as he jumped into the driver's seat. I tore off my new belt buckle, thumbed its power button to the on position, leaped at the van, and then slapped the buckle against that rear door just as the van took off. I stumbled, and my hands caught driveway for a second time.

I pushed myself up and struggled into the 'Vette. The Folger driveway exited onto Second Street SE. I stopped and stared. No sign of the van. I waited for the NAV system to boot. Egor had added a tracker. As long as that belt buckle held on, I could follow. As long as the NAV system found a signal, it would default to tracking mode.

I felt my hair growing and falling out. I had to wait for the damn thing to come online. Then, there it was, a small red dot on the display's map. The green dot was the 'Vette. I had the power-to-weight-ratio advantage. I could catch the van. But to stop it, I had to get out in front without the driver knowing. I had to figure out where he was headed, drive an alternate route, and get there first. I prayed Egor's modifications worked. I linked the navigation map to the heads-up display and engaged the probability programming. The map spread out in front of me like the tendrils of a ghost, dimly colored lines plotting the possible courses of the fleeing prey ahead. If that were me, where would I go?

The van had just turned onto Pennsylvania Avenue and was headed southeast. The southeast border of the District was the Anacostia River, and to get out, he had to cross it. That meant the Sousa Bridge. He might hide out in DC, but the District was small and heavy with surveillance. I had to gamble. I bet he'd want out.

I blasted out of the parking lot like a jet leaping from the deck of a carrier. I spun my winter-tire-shod, not-broken-in Corvette right onto Second Street NE and then slid right again onto East Capitol. Clutch in, clutch out. I ignored the break-in redline and kept the revs up. The Z06's 625 supercharged horsepower screamed. Saturday-night traffic was mercifully light. I wove around the taillights in front of me like a madman. Pedestrians were another matter—small, dimly lit, and slow. If one wandered in front of me, I'd hit him or her for sure.

I was an empath. I sensed the emotions of others. Kahler said I was poorly controlled. Time to prove the old man wrong. I segregated my psyche. Conscious for driving. With the near subconscious, I stretched out my mind, searching for even the barest hint of human emotion, scanning for pedestrians. Nine blocks. The 'Vette's heads-up display speedometer read 120 by the time I slung the car around Lincoln Park. Then I shut it off so that Egor's heads-up display map would be easier to see. I kept redlining the tach, spinning that Eaton TVS supercharger to its 20,000 rpm max.

The roads were cold but dry. I drifted the Z06 right onto Fourteenth Street SE and then roared south. Left around taillights. Right around taillights. I could sense the emotions of those they protected. Shock, fear, relief. Shock, fear, relief. Then I felt a solitary life in front of me. I stared hard into the darkness and saw nothing. Suddenly a glint of blue ski jacket flickered in the 'Vette's headlights. I jerked the wheel left, and my mind tingled with a tiny scream. In a flash it had passed behind me. No impact.

I drifted a hard right onto the Potomac Avenue circle, followed it halfway around, and then snapped another right onto Pennsylvania Avenue SE. I'd slammed the brakes so many times that the rotors had probably begun to glow. I risked a glance at Egor's map. The van still headed southeast on Pennsylvania. It was four blocks behind me.

At Fifteenth Street I spotted World Wine and Spirits. The neighborhood looked like mostly residential two-story brownstones, but businesses had grabbed the corner properties. World Wine and Spirits was a gray brick two-story brownstone with a glass double door at the Fifteenth Street corner. Across Fifteenth sat a paint-peeled, gray-green two story with fresh red paint on its Pennsylvania Avenue corner, barred windows, and a sign reading, "Pa. Ave. Market: Money Orders, Beer, Wine." Beside that was a pastel-blue-painted brick two story with matching pastel-blue awnings and a red-lettered sign over barred windows reading, "Tattoo."

The southbound roadway was four lanes here, separated from the northbound by a meridian of trees and grass at least one hundred feet wide. World Wine and Spirits was on the right side of the street. The red Dodge Challenger parked in the bus zone in front of the liquor store made up my mind. It narrowed the road to three lanes. I swung the 'Vette sideways, planted it in the middle of the road, and leaped out.

Then I saw the van, moving fast. The Challenger stood empty. I ran to it and crouched down, flat against its front bumper. I glanced at my shiny new Z06 and wished it to Corvette heaven. Alex Blake was about to become a two-Corvette girl.

I unsnapped my shirt and drew the little Colt .380 from its holster. It couldn't kill anyone on the far side of a windshield, but maybe I could blind him. I stuck my head over the hood of the Dodge. I took one shot, driver's side of the windshield, eyeball height. The glass fissured. The van swerved right. This guy wasn't going to try slamming the 'Vette out of his way. I sensed hate boiling up inside him. I'd killed his friend. He wanted me.

The van leaped forward and slammed into the back of the Dodge. I rolled into the street as the Dodge jumped at me like a hound with a bitten tail. Its trunk had folded like an accordion, but it had stopped the van. White steam poured from under the van's hood.

I glimpsed an airbag behind the marred windshield. Airbag deployment meant unlocked doors. I yanked the driver's door open. Blood streamed down from his forehead, into his eyes. He saw me anyway. He jerked his head around, reached his right hand under his jacket, swung the tip of his left-sided shoulder holster toward me, and fired through it. I felt his bullet tear the edge of my shirt above my right elbow. I shot him in the side of the head. His eyes bulged, and then he slumped forward.

The passenger seat was empty. I ran to the rear of the van. A head poked out of the liquor store's door. I yelled at it, "Call the police." If nothing else, that might keep the store owner from shooting at me. In this part of town, everyone owned a gun.

I yanked open the rear door of the van. Alex Blake lay curled up on a mattress. She looked like the image of a fetus on an ultrasound monitor. Mattresses lined the bed of the van, so whoever ran this op had wanted to keep her alive. She groaned and then straightened a leg. She'd been drugged.

I holstered my gun, dragged her to me, and bent down. Then I scooped her into my arms, slung her slender frame over my shoulder, and carried her to the 'Vette. Opening the passenger door and dumping her in was the hard part. I heard her white pencil skirt rip. For an instant that sounded like a gunshot. I thought to myself, *When she wakes up, it might as well have been.*

The sharp, chemical odor of gasoline filled the air. I found a growing puddle of fuel just beneath the rear of the van. A tiny stream of gasoline ran to it from the van's ruptured gas tank. I stripped off my suit jacket, tossed it to the asphalt, and kicked it around in the puddle. Then I caught the cuff of one sleeve with the toe of my shoe and carefully drew it out of that growing pool of gasoline.

I fished the butane lighter out of my left-front pants pocket. No, I never smoked. Yes, I carried a lighter. It went with the knife and the gun. I opened the top, spun the wheel with my thumb, reached down, and lit the jacket's cuff. My improvised fuse began to burn. The flame crept toward the gasoline beneath the van.

I slid into the Corvette and drove away fast. I don't know if the van burned or exploded. I wasn't there.

DC covered a small geographic area chock-full of surveillance cameras. I thought the same way Alex's kidnapper had. Same game plan: get out. I kept the 'Vette headed toward the Sousa Bridge. I'd hit a hundred before I realized I wasn't chasing anyone. I slowed for a moment and then down-shifted and floored it again. Now I was running.

I slowed to the speed limit when we reached the bridge. I'd put enough distance between us and the burning van. Speed would just attract atten-tion. In Anacostia I turned north on Route 295, toward Route 50. I called Kahler. The burner phone wasn't connected to the 'Vette, and Egor had dis-abled OnStar anyway. The GPS was still working. I'd just used it to catch the van. But that was a receiver. I didn't think it could be used to track me, but Egor was the techie.

Egor's voice answered, "Investigative Services."

"Alex kidnapped. Rescued. Two down. Orders?"

I heard muffled conversation. Then Egor's voice returned, saying three words, "Protect. Disappear. Critical." The line went dead.

Shit. I had to lose the car. Then I had to lose us. The magnificent auto-mobile that had just saved Alex had become an all-too-noticeable albatross. A groan rolled up from the seat beside me. Then a cough. I glanced at Alex. She began to twist side to side in her seat. I had no time to belt her in and had no way to do it now. I aimed the 'Vette toward New Carrollton and the Metro.

I headed east on Route 50. Suddenly Alex sat up. Her head jerked left, then right, and then left again. Her eyes drifted for a moment. Then they found me. "Barry?"

Alex gagged. Yellow-brown vomit spilled out of her mouth. Then it ran down her neck and onto her cranberry silk tank top. Her face looked puzzled more than surprised. She didn't look conscious enough for surprise.

I forced my attention back to the road.

"Barry?" I heard Alex retch again. I glanced over, praying her body was awake enough to keep the vomit out of her lungs. This time her white wool skirt took the hit. What the hell. It was already ripped.

Her chin dipped forward. I thought she was going to pass out, but halfway down, she jerked upright. She froze for a moment. Then her face turned slowly toward me. I recognized understanding in her eyes. Then I saw anger. Alex was back.

I wriggled forward in the bucket seat just enough to reach around with my right hand and grab the tissues in my back pocket. I reached across the center console and handed the little plastic-wrapped packet to Alex.

Her hand trembled as she pulled out a tissue and wiped her face. "What happened?"

"You were drugged. Two guys. You'll find a needle stick somewhere."

"Friends of Geoffrey Seep?"

I shook my head. "I saw a lot of Stratfordian passion tonight but not enough for a guy like that to risk life in prison."

"Then who?"

"Best guess: someone who wants a handle on your brother in case he starts growing crystals again." My fingers tightened involuntarily on the steering wheel. My palms felt wet.

Alex coughed. I glanced right. Her throat moved as she tried to swallow. "My mouth feels dry. Shit. I hurt everywhere." She wriggled her nose. "I stink."

"Yeah. Change of plans. You need clothes."

"What...plans?" Her voice sounded groggy.

"I just killed the two guys who grabbed you. Kahler says run and hide. Until the smoke clears, that's what we do."

Alex sat very still for several minutes, as if waiting for her brain and body to come back online. Finally, she said, "Smoke?"

I began to turn toward Alex, but the shoulder harness dug into my skin. It seemed to scold me. *Eyes on the road.* The Corvette had me strapped in tight. So did life. We had no easy way out. "Something big is going down," I said. "We'll disappear for a few days. By then the old man should have this figured out." My voice had the tiniest hint of a tremor in it. I remember hoping Alex didn't notice.

She pulled out another tissue and wiped her skirt. It was hopeless. Alex shook her head. "OK, fine. I need clothes."

"Yes, ma'am."

"Don't forget shoes." She pulled a third tissue from the packet and wiped her mouth again and then her neck. She glanced around. Not much of a view from inside a Corvette. "Where are we?"

"Route Fifty, east of the Capital Beltway."

"What time is it?"

I glanced at the clock. "A couple of minutes after eight. I blew the van. With any luck that might buy us an hour before whoever wants you learns that you're still alive."

She punched a finger at the NAV display, cursed, and punched it again. "Give me a minute to figure this out."

Either the drug they'd given her was a volatile one that wore off fast or Alex was as mad and focused as a queen bee that had just had her nest torched. Three minutes later she said, "Got it."

I glanced over just in time to catch her smile.

"We're west of Route Ninety-Five. There's a JCPenney in the Woodmore Shopping Center, a little east and south of us. You'll take Ninety-Five South and then Landover Road."

As if agreeing with her, a synthesized female voice called out from the speakers, "Turn right in five hundred feet onto Route Ninety-Five South."

Alex leaned back in her seat and seemed to relax for a moment, and then her face drew taut. "Can someone track us through the NAV system?"

"Shouldn't be able to. It's reading satellite broadcasts to fix our position. Egor disabled OnStar, so we don't transmit. I saw an article that claimed a car can be tracked from the signals emitted by its tire-pressure monitors, but those signals are really weak. I doubt they can be tracked from any distance or that each set of wheels has a registered signal unique to that specific car."

Alex smiled. Her lips still looked blue. "Penney's closes at nine o'clock," she said. "Your turn. My job here is done." Out of the corner of my eye, i saw her stretch and arch her back. Even with vomit on her blouse, this woman made my heart skip a beat.

JCPenney was in the southeast corner of the mall. We parked off to the side, as far from the overhead lights as I could manage. At eight thirty I helped Alex crawl out of the 'Vette. She wobbled some but didn't fall down. We cleaned her up as best we could. We ran out of tissue.

I helped her hobble to the store. Once inside Alex recovered quickly. She ducked into the nearest ladies' room and walked out a minute later, one hand filled with wet paper towels and the other with dry ones. She whispered in my ear, "Once I get these clothes off, I'll want to clean up."

She only needed one quick pass between the racks in the juniors' section. Alex pointed. I carried. In a couple of minutes, we had two pairs of black jeans, two black-and-white-checked flannel shirts, and a couple of pairs of socks and underwear. She made it to a changing room before the sales staff noticed us.

I found a cashier and paid. I double-checked that all security tags were removed, and then I returned to Alex and handed in her new clothes. A few moments later, she cracked open the door and handed me a foul-smelling bundle with the blouse and dress wrapped around the paper towels and shoes. I found a big swinging-flap trash can and tossed it all inside.

Alex left the fitting room in jeans, flannel shirt, and stocking feet. We headed for the shoe department. She picked a nice pair of black Nikes and slipped them on. "Lucky," she said. "First pair fits."

In the men's section, I went for pretty much the men's versions of everything Alex had picked, including the Nikes. A guy in a suit with a girl in jeans would look way too conspicuous. We needed to look like we belonged together.

I left the door to the fitting room open just enough so that I wouldn't lose sight of her while I put on my new clothes. I didn't need to swap underwear, so I was quick. Then we found a cart and filled it with hiking boots, black backpacks, black ski jackets, black wool sweaters, sunglasses, black wool beanies, gloves, and even acrylic ski masks. Even at checkout we kept our heads tilted down as much as possible. Many stores had security cameras that were monitored via the Internet. Those systems could be hacked. I paid in cash. We'd been quick enough to get out several minutes ahead of closing. We wouldn't be remembered for making anyone work overtime.

Woodmore Mall even had a Wegmans, the grocery store with nearly everything. They were open until midnight, but we didn't linger. In the restrooms we swapped Nikes for boots. Then we bought tissues, wipes, bottled water, a bunch of cereal bars, two ten-inch-long Maglite flashlights, and batteries. The Maglites were aircraft aluminum. If swung hard enough, they could crack a skull. I loved Wegmans.

Back at the car, I popped the hatch and dropped our shopping bags into the storage compartment. We climbed into our seats knees first and pulled the car doors closed. Then we reached over the seat backs into the storage compartment and loaded the backpacks.

When we finished, I turned to Alex and said, "We should eat something." She shook her head. "Not me."

"OK," I said. "Let's get to where we're going and lose the car." I started the engine and eased out of the parking lot. I hoped that in the dark, my shiny black Corvette would be at least a little less conspicuous.

It took about thirty minutes to reach the Courtyard Marriott in New Carrollton. Alex gave me a dirty look as I drove in. I weighed my possible responses and then decided to ignore her.

I circled around, reached the rear parking lot, and pulled into a space on the far side, away from the building and under the biggest tree I could find. No leaves in March, but the branches would break up the car's shape for anyone gazing down from above. I popped the rear hatch. We retrieved our backpacks. I fished Egor's emergency kit out of the rear storage compartment and slung it over my left shoulder. The backpack took my right. I left the car unlocked so that no ham-handed thief would set off the alarm. I didn't remove the license plate. Its absence would only attract attention. Anyone interested in the plate would have the VIN anyway.

Flashlights in hand, we walked into the narrow patch of trees behind the motel. I glanced at Alex. Her skin looked pale, even in the dim light. Our boots were mud covered by the time we crossed Garden City Drive and trudged into the New Carrollton Amtrak Station. I checked the board. We waited until fifteen minutes before the next train arrived and then bought two tickets to New York, the city for people who want to disappear. I used my business credit card. We bought a couple of sandwiches and Cokes in the club car but ate them two cars back. Alex took small, tentative bites and swallowed carefully. It took about an hour and a half to reach Wilmington, Delaware.

We stepped off the train, walked down the stairs, and followed French Street half a block to the Greyhound Station. An hour apart, we each bought a round-trip ticket to North Carolina, mine to Raleigh and Greensboro for Alex. We used cash.

I sat in one of the gray vinyl chairs on the gray vinyl floor and watched Alex do the same on the far side of the waiting area. I told her to sleep. I didn't dare. At least I hadn't been drugged.

At ten o'clock I roused Alex and then fed us each vending-machine coffee and Famous Amos chocolate-chip cookies. Potty stops were the high stress point of the morning. I could stand guard for Alex, but when my turn came, I had nothing to do except poop fast. I'd left Alex at the door with my small pistol clutched in her hand. I'd given it to her cocked and unlocked. I spent a tense few minutes on the toilet. It's tough to make things work when you're half expecting the sound of gunshots.

On the bus we took aisle seats on opposite sides of the aisle. I sat a couple of rows behind Alex. The bus jostled enough to keep me awake, but by the time we reached Union Station, the last vestiges of coffee had worn off, and my seat had begun to feel more like a rocking cradle. We arrived at Union Station, Washington, DC, a few minutes before three o'clock in the afternoon, the same place Amtrak would have taken us. I hoped this way had left less of a trail.

When you're running, where do you go to hide? For me the answer was simple. I hid in the places I knew best. Manhattan was home to over one and one-half million people crowded onto a twenty-three-square-mile island. To get out, you crossed a bridge or took a tunnel or you swam. Washington, DC, had a population of less than seven hundred thousand living in sixty-eight square miles, and although rivers bounded the southern half, to the north there was nothing to cross but a beltway. If we were chocolate chips looking for the most densely packed cookie, New York would have been the obvious choice. Maybe someone would buy that. It was where our train tickets led. But I didn't know that city very well. Trouble might look the same as shelter. DC gave me home-turf advantage. I took it. We were being hunted.

CHAPTER TWENTY-THREE

Sunday, March 13, 2016
Launch minus Five Days

The March wind felt icy cold. It stung my face, my nose. The wool beanie kept my head warm, but the cold seeped through my gloves and bit my fingers. It was my friend. It kept me awake.

Alex and I trudged along Columbus Circle and then Massachusetts Avenue. At Auntie Anne's Pretzels, we each had a cheese pretzel dog and the largest coffee they carried. Then I turned us around. We backtracked to North Capitol Street and headed north. We took our coffee with us, and it kept us awake. That and fear. I'd had no sleep. Alex had been drugged. We stumbled along. At one point I took her hand in mine to keep her close. I felt her squeeze my fingers. I liked that. But after several minutes, I let go and pushed her away. From a distance, in the bulky clothes and beanies, we might pass for a couple of guys. "Better if we don't look so affectionate," I whispered.

Alex nodded back. I thought I detected the flicker of a smile at the corners of her mouth.

I kept us walking. A cab would have left a trail. We wore those thick wool ski hats pulled low, nearly over our eyes, and we kept our heads down. All the time I was thinking, *Who is after Alex? Why?* By now Ethan didn't go anywhere without a halo of protectors, in the shadows but close at hand—military or FBI or Secret Service or some paramilitary branch I'd never heard of. That left Alex as the lever someone might use to move him, to shake him, to keep that crystal from being made. But who knew those surveillance satellites were armed? Almost no one.

Either someone who shouldn't have had found out or someone on the inside had turned. Neither seemed plausible. The Joint Chiefs were the most closely knit circle of patriots since John Hancock and company signed the Declaration of Independence. Yet someone had tried to make Ethan Blake dead. They'd failed. Second choice: grab his sister. But who? What facilities could they use? In the government? They'd leave a trail. Outside? They'd have less to work with.

I took another swallow of coffee. It had turned cold. Consciousness began to look a lot like the air at the edge of the cliff that Wile E. Coyote always runs off. For a moment I feared that I might be propped up against some building, dreaming that I was awake.

Tyler House, 1200 North Capitol Street, NW, had provided project housing, what politicians prefer to call affordable rental housing, since 1996. It sat at the corner of New York Avenue and North Capitol, eight blocks north of Union Station. It had once been new and perhaps elegant relative to its peers; now it was old and not so much. Its footprint was the size of a small city block. The outside walls looked clean. They were constructed of red brick with interspersed vertical sections of white concrete and lots of windows. The building had green metal fencing and sliding glass double doors overhung by a long, green metal awning.

Alex glanced around nervously as we approached. I followed her gaze. Everyone in sight was black. She leaned close and whispered, "We don't fit in here."

I whispered back, "Neither will anyone following us." Then I pulled out my phone and called Eddie. Adrian Kahler had helped a lot of people over the years and not always for money. Eddie was one of them. He worked in maintenance at one of the big law-firm buildings, had wrangled an apartment here so he could pay as little rent as possible, and invested the rest. He had a talent for investing. One more lunge forward for the market, and he'd be off to a very comfortable early retirement in South Carolina.

I recognized the quiet "yeah" he used as an answer.

I whispered back, "Barry Sandler."

"Trouble?"

"I'm outside."

"Shit." I waited through a long, hope-numbing pause. Then his voice returned, "Five minutes." He clicked off.

I turned to Alex. "We wait here."

I looked across North Capitol Street. It was six lanes wide here, two local lanes on either side. The center lanes dipped under New York Avenue. I saw a high-rise under construction on the far side of the street. The blue sign behind the chicken wire had white lettering that read, "WCC Construction." The orange sign on the trash can read, "Nomabid.org." NoMa is a revitalization project, a business improvement district, bringing the wealthy of Washington, DC, shoulder to shoulder with the poor. I glanced up and down the wide six lane roadway that conveniently separated those shoulders. NoMa was named for its location, north of Massachusetts Avenue.

Ten minutes later Eddie stepped through the glass double doors. At six feet two and 250 pounds, he was easy to spot: forty years old, head bald and black as an eight ball.

We walked over. He gave me a wink, nodded toward Alex, held the door for her, and then followed her through. The door whacked my shoulder as I trotted after them.

"Took your time," I said.

"Negotiations can't be rushed," he said slowly, his voice rumbling softly.

I made an effort to raise one eyebrow, but the other one followed.

Eddie frowned. "Stanley does a way better Spock."

"Buying the building?" I asked.

"Visitors show ID at the desk," he said. "But the guard's busy. A friend of mine gave him something better to do. Surveillance cameras out too." He shrugged. "Glitch in the software." His wide mouth grinned. "Happens all the time."

"Thanks."

"Keep your heads down anyway. Look at your feet. I owe your boss. This might balance the ledger."

He pulled open a dark-brown metal door and pointed a finger at the cement staircase. "Three flights up. If we run into anyone shooting up, we ignore them." He shook his head. "Don't try to save anyone from himself. Not here." He glanced at Alex. "That includes any 'herselves.'"

Alex still held her head down, but I could see her nod.

Eddie led, then Alex, and then me. We stepped over little piles of trash and past the stains on the walls. The air smelled sour.

Eddie's apartment had a steel door. He unlocked and opened it. We stepped inside. I turned toward the door as he closed and locked it behind us. I saw a tiny surveillance camera mounted on the inside of the door.

He caught my gaze. "Never put my eye to a peephole." He pointed up. He had a sixteen-inch flat-screen monitor mounted on a bracket over the door. Eddie swept his arm outward. "I can see that monitor from anywhere in the living room. There's another one in the kitchen. It has audio. I do my talking from outside the line of fire."

I nodded. "Can't be too careful."

"Some folks take offense easily, even if you don't interfere with their business."

In addition to the living room and kitchen, Eddie's apartment had two bedrooms. He pointed left. "That one's yours. Only one bathroom though." He glanced at Alex. "Hope you don't mind sharing. I keep it clean."

Alex pulled off her wool beanie and shook her head. Her brown hair swirled, and its auburn streaks glittered in the bright overhead light. "Thanks. All I want is a bathroom that's warm."

Eddie smiled at her. "They keep this building warm enough. HUD doesn't want any tenants burning the furniture."

I studied the room, checking out windows and furniture. You never knew when you might be cornered in your sanctuary. I noticed the baseboard. Here and there were small holes plugged with steel wool.

Eddie caught my gaze. "Mice," he said. "The building's crawling with them. I put a little rat poison in the steel wool. That keeps them out of here better than any carpentry. The roaches are tougher to control. If you open any of the canisters in the kitchen, reseal them right away. And don't leave any crumbs around. As long as I keep the place clean, roaches find better accommodations elsewhere. The units with little kids draw most of them."

Alex grinned at him. "If Barry spills anything, I'll see to it that he cleans up."

"Why? Do you have him in training?"

"I—" A perplexed look shadowed Alex's face. "No."

Eddie swept an arm toward his kitchen. "Food?"

I shook my head. "Sleep."

Alex swiveled her head from side to side. "Where's the shower?"

I followed Alex's lead. She took the first shower. I ate a couple of micro-waved egg-and-sausage sandwiches. While I showered, Eddie scrambled a couple of eggs for Alex. After showering Alex and I pulled on clean socks and underwear from our packs. With those exceptions we each dressed in what we'd walked in wearing. We crawled into the double bed that way. I knew one guy who was always so ready to run that he slept wearing sneakers. Alex had insisted that I take half of the double bed. I caught her checking me out before we climbed in, probably making sure I'd zipped my fly.

My head touched the pillow at six o'clock Sunday evening, probably dinnertime for most of the district. Unconsciousness hit me as soon as I closed my eyes.

CHAPTER TWENTY-FOUR

Monday, March 14, 2016
Launch minus Four Days

The machinery-like whir of automatic-weapon fire jolted me awake. I swept my hand beneath the pillow and closed my fingers over the grip of my Colt .380. I struggled to orient myself. The sound came from outside. I took a breath. A couple of seconds went by. Then another burst; this one longer. It sounded more like an AK than an Uzi; its shots were more distinct and louder. The shades were closed. No light filtered in around the edges. I felt as much as saw the movement beside me. I rolled out of bed and tackled Alex as she ran for the window. I dragged her to the floor.

"I want to see what's going on."

"I want you to live out the night."

Eddie burst through the door. His voice rumbled calmly, "Not about you." He shook his big, dark head. "Sorry. Time to go."

I holstered the Colt but left my shirt's middle buttons unfastened. "Right." I sat on the edge of the bed, bent down, pulled on my Nikes, and tied the laces. By the time I straightened up, Alex had hers tied and was pulling on her jacket. Eddie helped me with one of our backpacks. I helped Alex pull on the other.

Eddie scowled. "Drive-by. Happens around here. Not after you."

Alex gave him a frown. "Then why leave?" She zipped her jacket.

Eddie angled his big head toward her. "Pains me too, beautiful. Cops do a sweep after one of these little incidents. They'll find you."

She raised her chin. Her mouth made a soundless "Oh."

I glanced at my watch. It was just past two o'clock in the morning. I'd slept eight hours. I remembered one of Egor's many lessons: sleep is a weapon. I flexed my shoulders and then my legs. The fog had lifted from my brain. Even without our hideout, we had a chance. I zipped my jacket up to where my shirt hung open. I slipped my left hand into a glove but kept my right bare and stuck it in the jacket's pocket.

Then we were out the door and down the dimly lit stairwell that stank pretty much equally of man and beast.

"What about the guard?" I asked.

"Under his desk. The sides are lined with Kevlar panels. No one who takes that job plans to die for it. He'll wait there until he sees blue uniforms."

Eddie went through the stairwell door first. I followed. That was when I remembered the security camera. By now that glitch would have been fixed. I raised my head just enough to see the three-lens cluster on the wall over the guard desk. Shit. I reached for my pistol, hoping I could shoot it out of commission. I didn't have much faith in the little .380 slug.

A thunderclap went off beside my head, and the camera cluster disintegrated.

Eddie's gravelly voice filtered through the ringing in my ears, "Sorry, Barry. Carry a little gun like that around here—" He shot a wad of spit onto the floor beside my right foot. "You get no respect." White smoke swirled around the muzzle of the Smith & Wesson .44 Magnum revolver in his right hand.

Then he shooed Alex and me through the big glass double doors, out into the cold and black of night. We were on our own again.

A few bodies lay on the cold concrete. Some writhed in pain. A few angry-faced men looked toward the street, pistols tracking any passing car, ready for a second pass. Heads down, Alex and I angled ourselves toward the steps.

A sprawled body six feet away rolled onto its back. I turned instinctively toward motion. His features were not African but Middle Eastern. He glanced up at me. His movement was fluid, uninjured. Our eyes met. Something in his hand lit up. He drew the cell phone to his mouth.

I felt a burst of rage. I leaped at him, landed on my left foot, and swung my right with as much force as I could muster. The toe of my shoe struck his temple straight and hard. His head snapped back. His phone skittered across the pavement.

Back to Alex in a flash, I grabbed her arm and dragged her sideways toward the ramp to the sidewalk. It was a longer route than the steps but farther from the action. "Gotta go," I kept saying. "Gotta go." I didn't let go of her until we'd crossed to the far side of New York Avenue.

Big Ben Liquors was a red brick building with a four-story cone-capped turret over the entrance. It closed at nine o'clock on Sundays. I flattened against the wall, beneath its narrow awning, away from the streetlamp. I drew Alex close. I felt her shudder.

The howl of distant sirens grew louder. I waited for three squad cars to pass and then hustled us along New York Avenue, heading southwest, keeping to the shadows. I felt no wind, but the cold air bit my face, and the chill of the pavement seeped through the soles of the Nikes. I'd chosen them over the boots because they'd seemed better for running. Those little windows of the three-story brick townhouses watched us from behind narrow brown-tinged lawns.

I held Alex's hand firmly in mine. I led her left, onto First Street NW, the first street west of North Capitol, and then one short block and left onto M Street NW. We crossed back over North Capitol and across First Street NE, which is the first street east of North Capitol. The street names were one more reason why the District beat New York for hiding. If you weren't a native, maps just gave you vertigo. I kept us walking. Every few minutes I stopped and glanced around. We circled well south of Tyler House.

I felt Alex shiver. I draped my arm around her and drew her close. I wanted to offer warmth, reassurance.

She jerked away as if touched by a poisonous snake.

"You bastard." Her whisper sounded so harsh that it struck me like a slap. "You killed that man."

"Tried to."

"Are you insane?"

"Recognized us. About to make a call."

"You can't know that."

"Pretty sure."

"Pretty sure?" Her whisper screamed at me. "You can't kill a man for pretty sure!"

I grabbed her by the shoulders then. I shook her hard and then pulled her close. Our noses nearly touched.

She spat at me.

I let her go but didn't step away. "Alex," I whispered. My voice felt hoarse. "Alex! What part of running for your life don't you understand?"

She balled up her hands. I thought she'd hit me, but before I could figure out what to do, she planted both fists against my chest and shoved me away. In the dim light from the streetlamps, all I could see of her face was a nondescript blob. Something glistened beneath her left eye. She blew out a breath. When she spoke, her voice had a jagged edge to it. "'Conscience' is but a word that cowards use, devised at first to keep the strong in awe. Our strong arms be our conscience, swords our law…" her voice trailed off.

My mouth moved, but no words came out. I felt my jaw slacken.

"Richard the Third," she said, "at least according to Shakespeare."

"What happened to him?" I whispered.

"Killed. Battle of Bosworth Field. Most people think he got what he deserved."

I walked ahead. Alex followed. I kept us on M Street NE. After a while she came up beside me, close but never touching.

As we approached the NoMa Gallaudet Metro M Street entrance, Alex stopped walking. I stopped and waited. She turned to face me. "How did he find us?"

"Routine. They must have tracked us to Union Station and then expanded their search outward, quadrant by quadrant. Maybe someone just spotted us there. I don't know how many men they're using. Could be only a few, and one stumbled on us. Could be a lot."

"So he didn't know we were there."

"No way. Not until he saw me. Just lucky."

"Not for him."

"Not for us."

"He didn't contact anyone." Alex shivered. "You made sure of that."

"Doesn't matter. When he doesn't report in, they'll find him. Then they'll start the search from there."

"So you killed him for nothing?" The disgust in her voice was almost palpable.

"Bought us time. Might be enough to get us clear. Might not. No way to know."

Alex fell silent.

I ran it through my mind again. "The scary part is that they might have tracked us to Union Station. That suggests a level of sophistication a couple of hackers can't pull down from the Internet."

Alex scowled. "I know some hackers who might surprise you."

"Not likely. I work for the best. I live on top of a Cray. Kahler keeps that computer in the subbasement. You should see his utility bill. No, even the old man couldn't do this. It's government. Has to be. Everything we're doing, it's buying time. That's all. If they want us badly enough, they will find us."

"But the government's on our side. They need my brother. Killing me is no way to get him working again."

"None of this makes any sense," I said. "That's what scares me the most."

The M Street entrance to NoMa–Gallaudet–New York Avenue Metro Station was an unobtrusive glass-and-steel doorway beneath the concrete-supported Metro tracks that ran over M Street. The Florida Avenue entrance had a courtyard, statue, and arched concrete canopy. All M Street got was a rectangular black post with a red Metro *M* at its top and "NoMa–Gallaudet U–New York Ave. Station" in white lettering stenciled vertically along each side. Metro stations closed at midnight on Sundays. They wouldn't open until five o'clock. I checked my watch. Three o'clock.

Alex began walking toward the metro entrance. I wanted to go someplace warm, but even if the station doors were open, I didn't want us to be the only two people there, walking aimlessly or huddled in a corner for an hour. Metro stations had surveillance cameras.

I reached out and grabbed her hand. I half expected her to jerk it away, but she simply stopped and let me hold it. She wouldn't look at me. She didn't speak.

I glanced around. On the far side of M Street, a small ramp led upward, and a sign in the middle of it read, "Metropolitan Branch Trail." I tugged at Alex's hand and pointed.

"So?"

"We need someplace to hole up for two hours."

"What time is it?"

"Three o'clock." I pointed to the ramp. "Maybe we can wait up there."

Alex shook her head. "I'm cold." But when I began walking toward the ramp, she didn't jerk her hand away. We crossed M Street together.

The ramp ran up, curved back on itself, and then continued upward until it reached the top of the overpass. It was separated from the tracks by a tall white fence of steel tubes and wire mesh topped by three rows of barbed wire. A similar fence, a lot lower and without the barbed wire, guarded the street side of the overpass. For anyone contemplating suicide, the message was simple. *We will keep you off the tracks. Jump to the roadway if you must.*

I eyed the barbed wire.

Alex shook her head. "Even if we make it over the top without getting chewed to pieces, all we accomplish is to board a train. Whatever station we ride to, when we want to get out—" She drew out her words as if speaking to an idiot. "We'll—still—need—fare—cards."

I gave her a sullen look and then nodded. We walked back toward the ramp. On leaving the overpass, the fencing changed to a concrete barrier. "We could wait here," I said. "Sit on our packs. No one will see us from the street. If we lean against the concrete, it will protect us from the wind."

"Only a couple of nuts would do that," she said.

I shrugged. "No one will think to look for us here. It's only for two hours."

Alex turned to face me. She took in a deep breath and then blew it out. I felt the tension drain out of her. She rested a hand on each of my shoulders and smiled. Even in the dim light, I could see the upturned corners of her mouth, the softness of her eyes. Very gently she pushed me down. Then she followed. We sat on our packs and leaned against each other. I set the alarm on my watch. Alex whispered in my ear, "Only a couple of nuts."

Alex rested her head on my shoulder. Her hair felt soft against my chin. It tickled a little. I fought to stay awake. Every time I felt my mind drift, I jerked it into consciousness. Almost…

My eyes snapped open when my watch chirped. My eyes darted left and then right. Our only illumination was the sleepy light that stumbled out of the streetlamps, and not much of it reached us. My eyes had adjusted to it before, but now they struggled. I shook Alex gently. She stirred. Then she stretched against me.

"Station time," I said. I pushed myself to my feet. My joints ached. I tried to ignore the pain and concentrate on sights and sounds. All I heard were our own short gasps of breath. Icy night air stung my nose and mouth. It felt as if it had swept across a hundred miles of frozen tundra just before I sucked it in. Alex stood up, leaned against me for a moment, and then nodded for me to lead the way.

The NoMa–Gallaudet–New York Avenue Metro Station was on the Red Line. We walked through its unassuming glass-and-steel M Street entrance at five minutes after five. Heat and light embraced us. I drew warm air deep into my lungs. Entering the Taj Mahal couldn't have felt better. I pulled my jacket's zipper halfway down. We used cash to buy fare cards from a vending machine and then passed through the turnstiles. We hadn't been the first riders into the station, so it was easy to let a few people get between us on the way to the platform. We sat apart but in the same car. I sat across the aisle, a couple of rows behind—one eye on Alex.

The Dupont Circle Metro Station was the archetype for elegant simplicity. The arched walls and vaulted ceiling of honeycombed concrete overlooking floors of inlaid brick were bathed in subdued light. Colored lights between walkways and tracks announced the approach of trains and gently reminded passengers to keep back. Advertising was restricted to backlit displays and held to a minimum. The floor was clean and the walls graffiti-free. Illuminated overhead signs presented the arrival times and destinations of incoming trains. We took the escalator up, long and slow. Here the arched walls and vaulted ceiling closed in, forming a long, dimly lit tube. The pervasive regular clunk of the mechanism sounded like the heart of some great beast. We stumbled through its half-oval mouth, and the transition from darkness to light felt as abrupt as if we'd been spit from the gullet of a whale.

The winter sky looked twilight pink. I saw neither cloud nor sun. Alex leaned against me. I felt her shiver. Where to go? I looked around. The Dupont Circle Metro Station was not really at Dupont Circle, but it wasn't far. One more thing named by proximity. Sometimes all you could hope for was "close enough."

We walked south on Connecticut Avenue and found Starbucks just before we reached the circle. That green-and-white symbol looked even better than the last time I'd seen it. They'd started serving at five o'clock. The aroma of freshly brewed coffee wafted over us as I pushed open the plate-glass door. Even at this hour, a line of caffeine addicts extended back from the counter. We queued up and then each ordered a Venti, which rumor has it is about half the volume of the average human stomach. We bought slices of lemon pound cake to fill the rest. I also bought two chunks of cinnamon coffee cake and stuck them in a jacket pocket. Soldiers do travel on their stomachs. We walked upstairs and found seats with their backs to the plate-glass window.

I watched the growing crowd. We ate slowly, warming ourselves inside and out. For me, it felt like being reborn. Alex said nothing, but she kept glancing at me. Sizing me up, I suppose: monster or savior or just some male asshole. She did her best to keep me from noticing, and I took my best shot at looking as if I didn't.

Hurried office workers came and went. We sat at that table for two hours. I gave up on trying to figure out Alex. I don't know if she gave up trying to figure me out or not. She kept glancing. Then we had to leave. I didn't want anyone remembering that couple who had practically taken root. So we walked back down the stairs. I pulled open the glass door, and we walked back into winter. The cold splashed against me like a wave. The caffeine, the sugar, and the eight hours of sleep at Tyler House helped, but fatigue had become unrelenting, and my shields had begun to buckle.

Dupont Circle lay just ahead. In winter it was a park of concrete and brown grass, a circular flat area surrounded by tall buildings on the far sides of the adjacent roads. A line of shrubs guarded the perimeter, and a double-tiered, eleven-foot-high white-marble fountain stood tall at its center. Like the park, the fountain was named for Rear Admiral Samuel Francis Du Pont.

We needed shelter. Where? I had orders not to call in. Alex and I were on our own. I glanced at her slender form standing beside me. I could see her shiver. She looked frail.

We walked around the circle three times while I dug into my memory as frantically as a puppy searching for a lost bone. Kahler had mentioned a guy. I swam around inside my own head. It was a small space. I did the dog paddle, kept my nose just above water, and sniffed into every corner. I couldn't find the name. At last I came up with something so vague it seemed close to nothing at all. I took Alex's hand. I felt her tremble. We left the park and walked south on New Hampshire Avenue. All I had was something I might have overheard. It simply hadn't mattered then. It mattered now. We turned right onto O Street.

Parked cars lined both sides of the street. A small apartment building sat on each side of the New Hampshire Avenue corner. The rest of the buildings were row houses, though the term didn't begin to do them justice. "Row mansions" would be closer. The narrow, tree-lined sidewalk gave us just enough room to walk abreast. I glanced at the buildings. One had a pillar- and balcony-flanked doorway wide enough to pass an elephant. Second- and third-floor balustrade-fronted balconies shared walls with window-mounted air conditioners. On our left, halfway down the block, I spotted a pair of weathered bronze lions guarding a door to the Inn Downstairs. I turned to face them. The one to our right looked friendly enough, but the one to the left was frowning.

I remembered someone mentioning those lions. I let the internal puppy make another run through my memory. It stopped to pee. I waited.

Alex watched me closely. She began to speak and then stopped. Her face held concern.

After a few minutes, I led her up a stone staircase to our left. A small bronze plaque attached to the red brick wall at the top read, "The Mansion." A solid-looking dark-brown wooden double door stood to the right.

I looked at my watch. The LCD read 8:57 a.m. For a moment I simply stood there, watching time pass.

Alex interrupted my reverie. "Plan?" she asked. I saw her shiver.

I shrugged.

"Coffee's wearing off," she said. Her voice quavered.

At 9:01 a.m., I pushed the buzzer button to the right of the bronze-lion-head knocker. Then I turned to face the surveillance camera protruding from the wall to our right and prayed that it was wired into a local-only network.

For a few minutes, we just shuffled back and forth in the cold. Nine o'clock in DC would be late for the folks who started at six o'clock but early for the ten-o'clock contingent.

The big door swung open. A guy in his fifties stood in the doorway. He looked us over. He stood about five ten and had a slender build, a receding hairline of mixed gray and white, gray eyebrows, flat ears, and an aquiline nose. He wore a gray suit jacket over an open-collared white shirt.

"May I help you?" he asked. He projected an air of graciousness.

"Adrian Kahler sent me," I said uncomfortably.

He studied me for a long moment. His eyes looked kind. He glanced at Alex and then turned his attention back to me. "Aah," he said at last. "You must be in trouble."

CHAPTER TWENTY-FIVE

Launch minus Four Days

He ushered us into a large, bright room. It was overwhelming. Six crystal chandeliers hung from the high ceiling. Light sparkled off the glass faces of nearly fifty framed pieces of art, large and small. They clung to the walls like fireflies. A glass-door wooden cabinet protected books and engraved plates.

The barely detectable scent of freshly polished wood hung in the air. Oriental rugs covered a hardwood floor the color of espresso. A golden guitar stood on a black lacquered bench before a floor-to-ceiling mirror in an ornate gold frame. Five more guitars stood upright on a table in front of a large, white-curtained window. Several small, round wood tables draped in cutwork white tablecloths displayed books and photographs. Carved brown hardwood moldings, brighter than the floor, guarded a black ceiling embellished with inlaid triangles of gold, and golden designs surrounded each chandelier support. A round white smoke detector disrupted one of the ceiling patterns. It looked as out of place here as it would have in the palace of Versailles.

He led us through a narrow hallway anemically lighted by its own small crystal chandelier and then into a small, mirror-walled elevator. "I act as a docent for our little museum," he said. He smiled warmly at Alex and then at me. His eyes sparkled like the chandeliers. "For private tours I always start at the top." He pushed a button, and we rode up.

The door opened, and we followed our guide along another narrow, picture-hung hallway, through a room sporting barstools. The countertop held a three-foot-tall red statue of Betty Boop decked out in a bright-red jumpsuit and tall white boots. We entered a tiny mahogany-paneled elevator. The accordion gate clanked shut. The elevator rose.

We stepped out into a long rectangular room. I glanced left and right, spotting windows at either end.

Our docent looked pleased. "Penthouse," he announced.

It ran the length of the building, front to back. Recessed ceiling fixtures provided most of the light, but a little extra filtered in through the windows to our right and through the translucent venetian blinds that covered the door and window across from the elevator. The walls adjacent to the elevator, on either side, were covered in floor-to-ceiling panes of mirrored glass, each two to three feet wide and flush with the elevator door.

"Wow," Alex said. "Hell of a step up from Tyler House."

I thought I saw our docent wince, but he covered it quickly with a smile.

To the immediate left of the elevator sat a bedroom section sporting a double bed covered with a white bedspread.

I followed our docent to the right, over an oriental rug, past a partial wall stepped into shelves with vases on them, and into a living room where two white overstuffed easy chairs each sat in front of a large triangular window. A white overstuffed couch sat to the right, and several large gold-framed paintings hung from the wall behind it. A five-foot-tall painting of a standing angel, wings folded, expression beatific, dominated the rest. A ceiling fan with five large oval blades reached down from above. The partial wall across from the windows held an elegant kitchenette bar with a double stainless-steel sink. Decorated china plates hung from the wall behind the stove and sink. A microwave oven had been built in beneath the counter, and a coffee maker sat to the left of the sink. A three-foot-tall golden statue of a bear sat on a small end table between the couch and the bar. Its posture reminded me of Pooh, but its face looked too ursine. It might have been Paddington.

Our docent led us back past the elevator to the bedroom, dark except for the white bedspread covering a platform double bed. A solid-black shade shielded the large rectangular window behind the bed. He flipped a succession of wall switches, and they fired up the ceiling spotlights that clung to the tops of the walls. A ceiling fan guarded the bed. A lamp sat on a night table to the left of the bed, and a long white cloth covered a table against the wall to the right. A giant flat-screen TV hung down from the ceiling, just beyond the foot of the bed. As we walked back to the tiny elevator, I noticed a cylindrical shower stall of translucent black standing against the partial wall that bounded the bedroom. An oval white porcelain bathtub sat beside it, and an oriental rug covered the floor in front of them. A second stepped, partial wall stood behind them. I walked over and glanced around the end of the wall to find a toilet and bidet. Then I simply stood still and let my gaze track slowly around the large, rectangular space of the penthouse. That was when I realized that every—I do mean every—wall was covered with as many works of art and knickknacks as it could hold. Over the kitchenette counter, decorated china plates and glassware replaced framed art. *Every* horizontal surface that you couldn't walk on, sit on, or lie down on; *every* table; *every* shelf; *every* countertop held as many oddments as would fit—a lamp, a statue, a jug, a jar, a book, a vase, a porcelain something or other. I felt as if I stood inside a museum, one built without a storeroom.

On the wall to the right of the kitchenette counter hung a small black-and-white photograph in a foot-square metal frame. It had wide white matting, each side half the width of the photo. A border on the inner edge of the matting was stenciled with the word "Beatles," running in a repeating, continuous track all the way around the photo. Ringo sat, center stage, in an easy chair, and John, Paul, and George stood behind him. Four signatures, in black ink, were scrawled directly on the photo, three above the standing figures and one directly over Ringo's face.

Our docent must have seen my jaw dropping in its slow, notch-like progression.

"We're also a museum," he said. "But an unusual one."

I studied the photograph for a moment longer. "I have a friend who'd love this."

Out of the corner of my eye, I saw him grinning at me. "Everything here is for sale to our visitors."

I turned toward him. "Doubt I could afford any of it."

Then I got a really bad feeling. "What's the nightly rate?" I croaked.

"For Dr. Kahler and associates, one dollar." He winked at Alex and then turned back to me. "For anybody else, three thousand. This suite is secure. From inside the hotel, it can only be reached by your private elevator. Just one other way in." He walked to the venetian-blind-shielded door. It had a sturdy wood frame surrounding nearly full-height glass. The detective in me spotted the laminated label in one corner. He inserted a key into a heavy-duty brass dead-bolt lock, turned it, and pulled the door open.

I followed him outside onto a corrugated-metal platform. He swept an arm toward the rooftops of brownstones that spread out below. Winter remained cold and unwelcoming. I glanced down at a spiral staircase and then at the brown grass four stories below. "Fire escape?" I asked.

He frowned at me and gestured toward the wrought-iron table and chairs on the wider section of the platform. "We like to call this our deck."

I nodded. "Deck it is."

He faced the railing and swept out an arm, gesturing past the deck at the barren branches of the tall trees several feet away. "See those?"

I nodded.

He pointed to the left. "That one is our sixty-foot American chestnut."

I let my gaze follow his gesture to the tall trunk and gray-brown leaf-less branches.

"Most of them went extinct in the fifties. Blight. This one lived. It will bloom again in the spring."

I studied it for a moment, now noticing the myriad tiny buds that covered every branch. I nodded.

"Our museum is filled with things like this tree. Survivors."

He turned to face me, and his serious blue eyes found mine. "Do I call Dr. Kahler to let him know you're here?"

"Only if something very bad happens."

He tapped a knuckle on the metal railing. "Define 'very bad.'"

I glanced through the open door, into the penthouse. "I can't pay my bill."

He ushered me back inside, closed and locked the door, and then handed me the key and a small slip of paper with a phone number on it.

"Cell phone," he said. "You can always reach me directly." He walked into the tiny elevator. "There's food in the freezer. It's all microwavable. You should be able to hole up here for a few days." He slid the accordion gate closed. "Have a nice stay." The elevator clattered away.

Alex glanced around our new quarters and shrugged. "Well, well." Then she reached behind me and jiggled the doorknob. "I guess nobody's going to sneak up on us." She walked to the kitchenette. "Coffee?"

"Sure."

She turned on the Keurig and then knelt down on one knee and began searching the cabinets below the counter.

"Should we put in fresh water?" I asked.

"There's an empty bottle of Dasani beside it. Has today's date on the cap. They must fill it fresh every day. The empty bottle lets the guests know."

"OK."

"The pods are Starbucks. Want House Blend or French Roast?"

"House. I read somewhere it was the first blend Starbucks created."

"Go sit on the couch."

I walked to the living room and sat on the end of the couch closest to the window. I sank down into the downy white cushions. My body began to relax.

A few minutes later, Alex walked in, carrying two elegant looking gold-rimmed china cups on matching saucers. She handed one to me and then sat down on the far end of the couch. "I found some paper napkins and put a couple on each saucer," she said. "White couch. Don't spill."

I sipped at the coffee, inhaling the scent and rolling a little around my mouth to savor the taste. When I'd downed the Venti at Starbucks, I'd been too on edge to taste it. "I'll be careful," I said. "I'm used to leather. It's forgiving."

"Makes you sweat."

"Kahler makes me sweat. The fabric doesn't matter."

"You happy there? Three guys in that great big bachelor pad."

"They're family. What about you? One girl all alone in a townhouse?"

"I have no family."

"You have a brother. I swear. I've met him."

"We used to be close."

"Seems to me you still are."

"He's changed." She tapped the fingers of her free hand nervously against her cup. "The last couple of years, he's been really preoccupied."

"A lot's riding on him. That kind of pressure—it makes some people draw in."

Her shoulders rose and fell in a helpless shrug. "He won't tell me what's going on. We never had secrets. Not before. He's changed. Ever since he started growing those damn crystals."

"He's not growing them anymore."

"I know. That's made him worse. Sure, he's charming enough in public, but when we're alone, well, he doesn't really talk." The lines of Alex's face became taut; it looked drawn, almost old. "He used to talk to me. After our father died, we grew as close as twins. I practically knew what he was thinking. No more." Alex drained her cup and then reached over to the table that held the golden bear. "Move over, tubby." She gave it a push. It didn't budge. She set her cup and saucer down very carefully beside the figure's feet. "That damn thing's really heavy. Think it's gold?" she asked.

"Not even this place would let something worth that kind of money sit around unguarded."

We spent the remainder of the day sitting on the couch, eating micro-waved food, and watching the big flat-screen TV. Vanna White still looked great. We'd pulled the window shades closed, but some sunlight filtered in at the edges. Gradually it began to dim.

Alex pulled off her Nikes, drew her legs up onto the couch, and folded them in. "I'm bored."

I shot a scowl at her.

"OK, I'm exhausted. Still bored, though. Entertain me."

"How am I supposed to do that?"

"Tell me about the last time you had sex."

I'd just drained my coffee cup of caffeine shot number four, and I nearly sprayed my last mouthful all over the room. I twisted around to face her.

"Sorry. Just curious." She tilted her head back a little. The glow of the ceiling fixtures revealed light-brown freckles sprinkled over her forehead and across the bridge of her nose. Fireflies of light danced in her sapphire eyes.

"It was a while ago." I felt a tightening in my throat. "It didn't work out."

She studied me thoughtfully. "Me too. If the experience is bad enough, it can really sour you. I mean like for years."

I raised the empty cup to my lips and tried to look as if I were sipping coffee.

Alex laughed. The sound had a bright, musical quality to it. I'd readied myself for something filled with scorn.

"Still," she said, "we always wonder if it might be good the next time."

I felt as tired as I'd ever felt, cut off, and alone. I rested my eyes on her. They began to close. I forced them open, but they wouldn't quite focus. For a moment Alex looked more like a painting than a real person.

She must have seen me drifting. She raised her voice just a little, "Don't you ever wonder?" She hugged her elbows. Those sapphire-blue eyes met mine.

I spoke softly, sharing a thought that accidently turned verbal. I hadn't meant to say it to her. "We might be dead by next time." As soon as my mouth stopped moving, I regretted saying it. *Idiot.*

Surprisingly, Alex brightened. She straightened her back, propped her elbows on her knees, and rested her chin on interlocked fingers. Her eyes swept over me. Her mouth formed a mischievous grin. "Exactly!"

"What?" I felt my brain start to spin. I shook my head to clear it, wondering if I needed more coffee or if I'd had too much.

"Don't look so startled. We've already been in bed together."

"We had our clothes on."

"It was a start. Men say I'm attractive."

"That's not the point."

She pouted at me. Alex had that special kind of pout I'd seen only a couple of times before. Only women who knew they were gorgeous could do it that way.

I shook my head. "Come on, Alex. Every time I've come close to touching you, you've freaked."

"That wasn't you. It was me."

"You're still you, Alex. What makes now different?"

"Might be last-chance time. I'll make it work."

Then she stood up, closed the two steps between us, leaned forward, and kissed me on the forehead.

She took a quick step back. "Jesus, Barry. You stink. Do I smell that bad?"

"We've been sleeping on the street."

"I'm surprised that nice man even let us in the door."

"Adrian Kahler. Magic words."

"We need a shower."

"One of us has to stand guard. We can't both be wet at the same time."

"Fine," she said. "I'll shower. I hope there's a bottle of shampoo around here somewhere."

"Probably fifteen."

"You can keep your pistol ready. Guardian of the goddess."

"Sounds like a video game."

Alex stood up and stepped away from the couch. Her slender fingers unbuttoned her flannel shirt. She slid her arms out of it, one sleeve and then the other, and then flipped it away as if backhanding a Frisbee.

I pushed myself to my feet.

She reached behind her back and unhooked her bra.

My eyes jumped to her chest before I could stop myself. I forced my gaze back to her face.

Her hands remained locked behind her back, holding the straps. She studied me. No pout. No grin. I saw a tiny tremor at the edge of her jaw.

"Never too late to say no," I told her.

"No!" Alex took two steps backward and then stopped abruptly, as if her anchor had caught on a rock. "I mean yes!"

I shrugged, trying to keep my eyes off her chest, hoping to manage an expression of casual indifference. I felt my heart pounding. *Shit.*

"Oh hell." She spit out the words. "I'm not used to this." She stabbed a finger toward the door leading to the deck. "Get out! I'll shower. Then it's your turn. I'll wait for you in bed. Don't take too long. I'll lose my nerve."

"Yes, ma'am." I flattened my right hand over my eyes and turned away. "Whatever you want." Then I cracked my fingers just enough to see and walked toward the deck. "Can't close the door all the way. Have to hear what's going on inside."

"Fine," she yelled after me. Then louder, "Fine!"

I walked out onto the corrugated-metal deck and jerked the door almost closed behind me. I glanced around nervously. *I could be spotted out here. This whole deal is crazy. Anyone with half a brain would just leave Alex in that bed until she fell asleep.*

I grasped the icy wrought-iron railing with both hands and glanced nervously at the flat rooftops and red brick chimneys of adjacent brownstones and then up at the sky. It had turned nearly featureless. No clouds. Then I found myself laughing. *Spotted by what?* I studied the cold, empty yards and streets and windows and rooftops. When I looked up, I saw nothing but a faint white haze that overlaid the icy blue and kept the sky from looking clear. My mind felt like that. I couldn't quite think my way through the haze. I released the railing, interlaced my fingers, and gripped my hands together. I shivered. I felt cold again.

I squeezed my eyes closed. Alex Blake wouldn't get out of my brain. I pictured the wavy auburn hair that fell to the shoulder blades of her athletic, five-foot-six-inch frame, the broad forehead, those sapphire eyes bright with cleverness, her freckled little nose, dimpled upper lip, small sensual mouth, sassily upturned breasts, flat belly, slender legs. I'd never seen her toes.

Brilliant, probably smarter than me, certainly better educated, and irritating as hell. She'd clearly been hurt. Needed a hero. Was that me? Or was I about to take advantage of a broken little girl who had no idea what she wanted?

She acted like a puppy wearing an invisible-fence collar. Whenever she got too close to contact, it fired off. Maybe the whole hurt-before thing was bullshit. As far as I knew, the only passion she'd ever demonstrated was for an English poet who'd died four hundred years ago, and Alex thought that poet might have been a woman. Was she a lesbian? Unable to admit it to herself? I shook my head. No. Not Alexandra Blake. If she were gay, she'd have said so and been proud of it. The only other passion I'd maybe glimpsed was for her Mustang. I remembered the black wig on the bust in Geoffrey Seep's office. And she was a practical joker. That usually meant anger tucked away in some little corner of the mind, big-time anger. But she'd never mentioned anger or even hinted at it.

I stared at the door leading back into the penthouse. A shade hung over the opposite side of the glass. That and the angle of the sun had turned the window into a full-length mirror. I'm five eleven with a decent build and enough muscle to look good without sending body-builder messages. I studied my reflection. My hair didn't look as sandy blond as it did during the summer sailing season. More brown. When I'd picked her up, it had been combed as neatly as a newscaster's. Now it just looked shaggy.

"Decent enough," I whispered to the mirror. I saw nothing so special that it would cause a girl to take a look and then yank off her clothes. Certainly not Alex.

We were in danger. Sure. A lot of danger. Did the specter of death make me irresistible? I took another look at myself. Hard to believe. I raised my right arm and sniffed at the armpit. *And I stink.*

A large gray bird soared past the deck. It looked too big for a seagull, and it flew too fast to have been hunting for food. I heard no wings flap, just a whoosh of air. I stared after it.

Alex's voice sounded through the cracked-open door, "Barry! Your turn."

I swallowed hard, opened the door, and stepped back inside. I shook my head hard, trying to get her image out of my mind. It wouldn't go away. All the shaking did was make Alex's clothes disappear.

"Get moving, Boy Scout!"

I pulled the door closed. I locked it. I put the key on the small black table in front of the sunken oval bathtub.

The bathtub extended out from the base of the shower stall. It had a whirlpool jet on one side. I leaned over and started the water running. I set my small pistol and spare magazine on the red, white, and black oriental rug beside the tub—far enough away to keep it dry, close enough to reach it in a hurry. I studied the little Colt .380, wishing I'd been less fashion conscious and taken the Glock.

I stripped off my clothes, found where Alex had put hers, and dropped mine onto the pile. The two sets of filthy clothing nestled together perfectly, one on top of the other. Nothing rolled off. Maybe that was a sign. I stepped into the shower, turned on a stream of water that felt nearly too hot for my skin, and let my body sigh. I ran a hand over my face. My beard stubble felt scruffy. I glanced around the bathroom area but didn't see a razor. Maybe she liked the rugged look. I hoped she did.

I hefted the bar of soap. It smelled of lilacs. I wondered if the same scent belonged to Alex now. I felt myself smile. Maybe I'd just follow her lead, go at the go signal, and stop at stop. If worse came to worst, I'd make myself back away and finish in the bathroom. I could do that. I wasn't eighteen. Adrian Kahler had once told me there were only three things a man could really control in his life: persistence, discipline, and decency. This would be a test of two out of three.

"Barry, hurry up!"

Her voice made my penis twitch. I glanced down. Even in the hot water, it looked like a torpedo. I soaped and scrubbed. I rinsed, drained the tub, and stood in it while I toweled off. I couldn't bring myself to believe that the oriental rug one step away was for drying on. And I didn't want to risk dripping on the Colt. Dry firearms usually work. Wet ones, not so much.

Alex's voice swept out of the bedroom, "Now would be good, Boy Scout."

I draped the towel across the side of the tub and then glanced down at the Colt. Alex was already tense enough. If I walked in holding a gun—I shook my head. *I'll come back for it after she falls asleep.*

There we were. Trapped together. Cut off from everyone else. And in a few days, with or without that one little pistol, we might both be dead. As I walked past the door to the deck, I reached out my right hand and doubled-checked the lock. I was stalling. I approached the bedroom slowly and warily. The black window shades behind the bed were closed.

Alex threw off the bedsheet as I approached. She lay on her right side, right elbow propped against the mattress, forearm up, and chin braced on the knuckles of a closed fist. Her naked body looked as striking as her sapphire-blue eyes.

I walked to the side of the bed and faced her. Her chest rose and fell with sharp, rapid breaths. I let my eyes travel over her—top to bottom, bottom to top. She had full, upturned breasts, a taut belly, a narrow waist that curved into full hips, and long, muscular legs. In the overhead light, her white skin glowed like the surface of a pearl. Tiny fawn-colored freckles dusted her bare arms, shoulders, and upper chest. A muscle in her abdomen quivered. The edges of her shoulders and hips had a firmness to them, not gentle curves. Alexandra Blake did not own a soft beauty sketched in pastel or painted in watercolor.

"Hi," I said.

She shifted her body, just a little. The angle of the light changed, and for a moment, the boundary between Alex and everything around her sharpened. She looked perfect as a statue chiseled from granite.

Those blue eyes studied me. For a moment her gaze fixed on what had become an all-too-ready erection. Then she returned her attention to my face. One corner of her mouth twitched. "I've always wondered what it would be like without fear, without pain."

That stopped me cold. I stood very still at the edge of her bed, an arm's length from Alexandra Blake. I watched her. I waited for some hint of what she wanted me to do next. I spoke softly, carefully, in a tone I might use with a wild doe, as if I'd held out my hand but feared it would run if I petted its nose. "The next move is yours."

Alex reached up, took my hand, and drew me down, onto the bed beside her. She rolled onto me, and nipples hard as bullets pushed against my chest. She buried her face against my neck and made an "mmmmmm" sound. She kissed my earlobe. Then she rolled off, lay at my side, and wrapped warm, slender fingers around my erection. She ran the ball of her thumb over the head.

I felt myself stiffen even more.

Her lips brushed my ear. Her voice faltered, "Be...careful...with... me."

CHAPTER TWENTY-SIX

Launch minus Four Days

"**D**on't stop," she whispered roughly. "Don't you dare stop." This wasn't an orgasm. It was stubbornness. Alex would finish what she'd started.

Making love to Alex had almost made me feel eighteen again, back with my first serious girlfriend. Every move I made was tentative, ready to back off at her slightest flinch. I kissed her mouth and her neck, her belly, flicked my tongue into her navel, and then worked my way back up to her breasts. I caressed each nipple with my mouth. Ever so slowly I worked my way down to her slit. I slid my tongue between her labia and tasted the moisture there. Her body was ready. But when my tongue brushed against her clit, her back didn't arch; her hips didn't flex. Alex's entire body went rigid. That invisible-fence collar had shocked her again.

I moved beside her, leaned over, and kissed the center of her forehead. I waited.

Alex said to me in one short, frantic gasp, "Put it in."

I rested one palm beside each of her shoulders and held my body above the most beautiful woman I'd ever seen. I licked her nipples and then sucked each gently. I studied her face. Alex had her eyes closed.

Her mouth opened. Her voice had a husky edge to it. "Damn you, Boy Scout. Do it now. Fuck me!"

I entered her slowly, tentatively, sliding in and out a little before advancing all the way. I felt like a teenager driving a car for the first time. One foot hovered nervously over the brake pedal.

"Don't stop!"

Then my empathic sensors began to tingle. They reached out to Alex. Empathic energy surged through me more intensely than anything I'd ever felt before. It grew stronger. Its blue-yellow flame melted me into her. Skin flowed into skin, flesh flowed into flesh, and mind flowed into mind. I felt our fear, our anger, and our determination to conquer them. Ever so gently I soothed us both.

I felt her tension and her discomfort as if they were my own. The sensations from my own body began to disappear. Then I felt only what Alex felt. I saw her face and mine, blended into one. Controlling my limbs became difficult, as if I were pulling strings attached to a puppet far away, but I managed to keep my arms straight and held my body above hers. I adjusted thrust and rhythm and rate until they felt right to us. I kissed Alex on the mouth and tasted my own breath. Or was it hers? Our tongues caressed, each indistinguishable from the other.

"Don't stop!" we screamed.

Our orgasm built. Our breath came in short, rapid gasps. We moaned. Then our arms encircled us and jerked us together. We screamed. Our body bucked.

I felt a warm rush, out of me and into me all at once. Time stopped.

Then I was me again. I blinked my eyes and stared at Alex. I saw her face alone. I lay on top of her.

"Sorry," I said, panting.

"Stay right there, Boy Scout. This feels good."

I buried my head in the nape of her neck and kissed her softly. I don't know how long we lay together like that, but after a while, I felt her hands push against me. I rolled off and lay on my back, still enveloped by our lilac scent.

"Need to breathe now," she said. She rolled up onto her left side and then propped herself on an elbow, hand under her chin and gazed down at me. "That wasn't so bad."

"Sorry I didn't do better," I said. "For me, it was perfect."

She smiled slyly. "So it's Barry one, Alex zero."

"I—"

"No deal," Alex interrupted. "Rematch. I insist on a rematch."

My eyes traveled the length of her body again. My eyes were undressing a woman who was already undressed. I felt my heart pound. A drop of sweat hung from her left nipple. I raised my head and licked it off. A bead of my semen ran down her left thigh. I reached down and wiped it away with a corner of the bedsheet. When I looked at her face again, Alex was smiling.

"Sorry," I said. "Egor didn't pack condoms in the emergency kit."

Alex made a face and then stuck out her tongue. "The needle on the risk meter is already so far into the red that I can't bother worrying. You?"

I gazed up at her. "You told me I'm your first in a really long time."

"Reeeeaaaally long time," she said.

I ran my tongue over my lips. I grinned at her. "Me too."

"Good." She reached down and stroked my penis and then fingered the little opening at the head.

I felt myself twitch.

"Actually," she said, "you were pretty good."

"Not five stars?" I asked.

She shook her head. Then Alex looked away. Her eyes seemed to focus on something far, far away. She shuddered. "I wasn't thinking about stars. I was getting through it. The orgasm was an unexpected bonus. I guess my body was ready for that, but my brain hasn't caught up."

I reached up and caressed her soft auburn hair.

"Give me forty minutes," she said. "It'll be better next time." She rolled off the bed and stood up. "I saw some Pop-Tarts in one of those cabinets. Want one?"

"Sure." I stood up and stretched. My eyes wouldn't let go of her.

She turned as gracefully as a model at the end of the runway and then walked toward the kitchenette. The muscles in her legs and buttocks flexed, and the room lights played over the smooth, barely freckled skin of her shoulders. A patina of perspiration lent a soft glow.

"Thirty minutes," I called after her.

She stopped and glanced back over her shoulder. Her buttocks glistened. "Works fine for me. Just enough time to get a little more glucose into the system. As they say in chemistry, the man's always the rate-limiting step."

"I'll do what I can." I glanced down at my penis. It didn't know much chemistry. It was pointing at her.

We lay on the bed, on our backs, breathing hard and naked shoulders touching. The only sensation I had left between my legs was a comfortable ache. We'd coupled two more times, and Alex had exploded into a rolling orgasm with each. I turned my head toward her and smiled. She leaned over just enough to kiss the tip of my nose and then lay on her back again.

"You do good work," she said.

I reached for her hand and then interlaced my fingers with hers. "Team effort."

Alex's eyes found mine. I saw tears in them. "You're the second," she said.

"Wow." It was all I could think to say. Then I added, almost as an afterthought to myself, "Guy number one must have been awful."

Alex rolled onto her side so that she faced me. She planted an elbow against the mattress and settled her chin against her fist. She squeezed her eyes closed. When she opened them, tears flowed over her lids, streamed down her cheeks, and dripped onto the bedsheet. She said in barely a whisper, "Guy number one was my father."

I felt as if someone had shot a cannonball into my gut. I had no air. I tried to speak, but all that came out were tiny, gasping breaths. I rested a hand on her shoulder. I felt her tremble. We both trembled.

Alex's voice became a child's, a tiny squeak, not much above a whisper. "He came home late, drunk. Mother must have thrown him out. She must have scratched him.

"I sat in bed, reading. I heard the slap of bare feet against the hardwood floor. My head jerked up. He strode into my room and slammed the door. I saw fresh blood on the side of his face. He wore nothing but a T-shirt. He carried his shorts in his hand. He crumpled them into a ball and threw them at the wall behind my bed.

"'Tell your mother this is her fault.' That was all he said. He grabbed me by the hair with one hand. He jerked me toward him. His breath stank of alcohol. With his free hand, he pulled my nightgown up to my neck. He left it bunched up over my face. I watched him though the gauzy fabric. His face and body looked hazy, unreal, like a ghost's. I was thirteen.

"I screamed. I struggled to break free. His arms felt so strong. He wound my hair around his fist and slammed me onto my back. He forced my legs apart with his knees. Then he rammed it in. Oh, God. It hurt so bad. And he kept at it, over and over. It kept hurting.

"My door banged open. Ethan stood in the doorway. He wore jeans and a T-shirt. He'd been at baseball practice, and that little cap still sat on the top of his head. It had the school logo on it. He looked so—composed. His eyes were cool. His mouth a line.

"Father pulled out of me. He turned and lunged at Ethan. He slipped on the throw rug and fell forward. The side of his head struck the bedpost. He collapsed onto the floor. Ethan wouldn't touch him. We watched him lie there, twitching. I was bleeding. Ethan cleaned me up. He used his handkerchief and then stuffed it into his pocket.

"We sat on the edge of my bed together and waited for our father's twitching to stop. Then Ethan called the paramedics. The autopsy showed an epidural hematoma and a really high blood-alcohol level. We just told them he'd slipped on the rug. I never spoke of it again. Not until now."

I stroked her hair with my fingertips, gently, barely touching her, just enough contact so that she'd know that I was there for her. "It's over," I said. "Just a ghost from the past."

"You can't kill a ghost," she whispered. "I know. I've tried."

"You're right. You can't." I swallowed past the tightness in my throat. "But this one can't hurt you. Not really. Not unless you let it. We won't let it."

"I need to sleep now," she said.

"I'll turn out the lights." I climbed out of bed and switched off everything but a small table lamp with a mermaid-shaped base that sat on a low glass-topped table beside the door to the deck. "Just enough light for potty finding," I said. Then I slid back into bed.

Alex propped herself up on one arm and kissed me on the forehead. "Hold me, Barry. Please hold me."

I spooned against Alex, my chest against her back and my right palm holding her belly.

She let out a little "mmm" and wiggled her butt against my hips. Her naked skin felt soft, smooth, and warm against my own. Her body seemed to flow into mine. The lilac scent of spring drove away the last remnant of winter's chill. *I love this woman. I know that now. I need her as much as I need air to breathe.* That was the last thought I had before drifting into darkness.

I heard a clicking, faint and distant, a part of a dream. It hovered at the edge of consciousness. It jiggled there. I knew that sound. I knew that quick, repetitive noise. It poked its way into my sleeping mind. Who used an electric lockpick in a museum?

CHAPTER TWENTY-SEVEN

Tuesday, March 15, 2016
Launch minus Three Days

My mind scrambled awake. My eyes flew open barely in time to see the door from the deck swing inward. I swept my hand under the pillow and searched frantically for the little Colt. Shit. It still lay on the rug, right where I'd left it. Light from the open doorway spilled into the room. A man entered. Then another. Then a third. His bulk nearly filled the doorframe. He ducked his head as he entered. The sky behind them smoldered with the ruddy light of early dawn. With all the shades drawn, the room remained nearly black. The three heads turned side to side in quick, jerky movements. The intruders fanned out. They moved quickly, but they hadn't seen me yet.

I leaped off the bed, bounded across the floor, slammed an elbow into the face of the first guy I reached, and dove for the little Colt. I got one finger on the grip and then tried for two. A black boot kicked it out of my hand. I watched helplessly as my pistol bounced out the open door and over the side of the deck.

I rolled to my feet. A roundhouse punch came at me from the left. My forearms and elbows snapped instinctively to the sides of my head. I blocked the punch. I tried to grab his head and gouge his eyes with my thumbs, but he bent backward from the waist and drew his face just out of reach. I managed one groin kick before a second pair of hands grabbed me from behind.

My naked body dripped with sweat. I twisted free. I had my back to the mirrored wall as I dodged another punch. I heard a scream as a fist shattered the glass behind me. I spun away, dodging the clutter of the penthouse. I backpedaled carefully as two men bore down on me. We reached the living room. I faced two dark shapes in a dark world. One looked about my size. He approached warily. The other guy towered over him. He looked nearly as tall as Egor and every bit as solid. He moved smoothly. He didn't hurry. He was used to winning.

I stepped side to side, keeping the big guy's buddy between us. All at once he shoved the smaller man to the side and lunged at me. I grabbed a guitar from a floor stand and swung it. He grunted as he batted it away with a forearm as thick as my leg. The guitar splintered with a sickening crunch. I circled right. In the dim light, I glimpsed a flash of gold—the Paddington statue. I ran for it.

Alex cried out. I'd forgotten the third man. I glanced toward the bedroom. She sat on the edge of the bed and was shaking her head. She screamed at him, "No! No! No!"

He put a hand on each side of her waist. I heard him speak to her in a low, Middle Eastern accent, "I do not wish to injure you."

Alex thrust her head forward and bit him on the arm.

He jerked back. "Jende," he screamed. He backhanded her across the face and lifted her with both arms, nearly over his head. Then he threw her down. She screamed again.

I took a half step and a quarter turn and reached for Paddington. I grabbed the statue with both hands and jerked it from the table. It felt cold and solid, at least fifty pounds of bronze or lead or cast iron or gold. I swung it like a bat, back and forward. Then I let the bear go. It took the big guy square in the chest. He let out a cry of pain and disbelief. He collapsed onto the floor.

I leaped over the groaning body and ran toward Alex. She screamed again. The third man had wrapped her in the bedsheet. He lifted the twisting, screaming bundle to his shoulder.

I'd almost reached her when a hand grabbed my ankle. I went down. The side of my face struck the floor. Agony shot through my cheek and nose and ricocheted off the back of my skull. I felt warm fluid stream out of one nostril, over my lips and down my chin. I pushed myself to my feet in time to see a corner of white bedsheet trailing out the door and onto the deck. I leaped after it.

A silhouette stepped toward the doorway. I recognized the smaller of the two thugs who'd chased me into the living room. He didn't approach, just waited. I'd played linebacker more than once. I could get past this one. I could still save Alex. That kicking, screaming bundle would make slow going for any man negotiating those three flights of wrought-iron stairs.

I faked right and lunged left. Then I saw the big knife in his right hand. It was a pesh-kabz. Its curved blade extended at least a foot from the grip. Its long, narrow point stabbed at me. I spun sideways. One of Egor's endless weapons lessons flashed through my mind. In the seventeenth century, Persian soldiers had used the pesh-kabz's slender, reinforced point to penetrate mail armor. It would slide nicely between my ribs. Egor always started his edged-weapons lessons the same way "In a knife fight, you're going to get cut."

The silhouette backed up a step and then stood in the middle of the doorway. A hint of dawn's orange light caught half his face from the side. His mouth formed half a smile. His crooked teeth looked yellow. He sliced the air between us, once and then again. "The boss told us, 'No guns.'"

He knew I had to get through that door. I approached warily, gauging the length of his knife arm, adding the length of the blade. He held it low, belly height. He sliced the air again, once and twice. If I rushed him, he'd cut me open without half a thought. I pictured my intestines unwinding onto the floor. I stopped three feet away.

Then I heard Alex scream again. The sound seemed far away. I had to goad him.

He had the same idea. "My associates and I thank you for removing her clothes. Life is good."

My blood throbbed. "No," I whispered to myself. "No!" I heard the voice inside my head, *"Rage will get you killed."* I forced myself to an icy calm. I slowed my breathing. I watched the knife. Then I used what I had. I reached down to my dick, grabbed the foreskin, raised it up, and wiggled Johnson at him. "Hey, tough guy. Suck on this."

He glanced down. The edge of his mouth twitched. Fury suffused his face. He snapped his knife forward, making quick little cuts in the air as he moved toward me.

I backed away from the big Persian blade.

The knife wielder followed.

The little kitchenette sat to my right. There might have been a knife in one of the drawers, but I had no time to search. I grabbed a plate off the counter and spun it backhand at his head.

He jerked sideways, dodging out of its way.

Then I felt the wall behind me. Out of the corner of my eye, I saw the Beatles photo. As I slid sideways along the wall, I slipped my right hand under the photo and lifted it off its hook.

The Persian blade stabbed at me.

With both hands, I shoved the photo straight at it.

I heard glass shatter. The blade and the hand holding it stabbed through my makeshift shield. I stepped to the side, reached out with my right hand, found a corner, and spun the frame. The man's forearm stuck halfway through the jagged hole in the glass.

Blood spurted from his arm.

With a scream of rage, he stabbed at me again, still wearing the picture frame like a red bracelet.

The faint, coppery odor of blood surrounded us. I crow-hopped backward on the balls of both feet, sucking my belly back as I leaned my trunk forward. I slammed my right forearm into his elbow, sweeping his knife arm to the side. The tip of his blade scored my skin as it jerked sideways across my belly, but I had too much momentum for that to stop me. I took one quick step forward on my left foot and slammed the edge of my right foot into the back of his right knee.

His knee gave way, and he crashed to the floor. Half kneeling, he struggled to push himself up with his one good leg. I wound my body tight to the left, right arm flexed at the elbow, and then released the spring, putting all my weight behind the outside edge of my right hand. I struck just below the base of his skull. His head snapped back. The big knife tumbled from his hand. He crashed facedown onto the floor.

I felt a wet trickle of warm fluid run down my belly. Then burning. I ran a hand over my skin. It felt sticky, but nothing poked out. That would have to do. I bent down and unwound limp fingers from the grip of the big knife. I hefted it as I stepped over the dead man and ran out of the room and onto the deck. The steel grate felt cold against my bare feet. I shivered. Another scream drifted up from below.

I can hear her. I still have time.

Then a giant's hands caught me from behind. They closed around my chest. They squeezed the breath out of me and lifted me like a doll. His breath smelled sour, somehow tinged with the scent of lime. I kicked backward and struggled to twist free. Nothing. Then my body was horizontal. I reached to the side and stabbed downward with the knife. I heard a curse. Then those big hands tossed me into empty space. I flew over the railing and into darkness. I tumbled through the air, snapping tree limbs as I went. I dropped the knife and grabbed at them.

I caught one with both hands. My arms straightened. Burning pain exploded out of my shoulders. My fingers scraped against bark. It tore at my skin like sandpaper. I slipped, but I held on. My hands felt sticky. More blood. I made two tight fists around that branch, turned my head, and looked down. In the dim light I could just make out a pair of overturned plastic trash cans. They lay on their sides, two stories below me. A faint glimmer of silver sat a couple of feet to the left. It might be the Colt. If I could land on the plastic—I twisted my body. I needed to swing out, just a little, and then let go.

Alex screamed again. Her voice sounded farther away now. "No guns," he'd said. I glanced toward that little patch of silver below. Still had time. I repositioned my hands on the tree branch and then began to swing. If I could fall forward a couple of feet, I'd strike plastic instead of concrete, I'd retrieve my gun, and then I'd save Alex. I tensed my muscles and took a breath. First swing, forward and then back. Second one. Third. I heard a crack. I felt myself falling. My fingers still clamped the branch. I looked down and twisted frantically. Trash cans below. Still had time. I could get the gun and get to Alex. Falling. On target. I'd hit plastic. Still had time. Alex! Then nothing.

CHAPTER TWENTY-EIGHT

Launch minus Three Days

"**B**arry!" a voice called my name. Its anxious tone told me this wasn't the first time.

I tasted vomit. "No guns," my voice whispered. I felt it splinter. My throat felt dry. I lay on my back, on something soft. I cracked my eyes open. The light hurt. I forced both lids up anyway. A couple of four-foot fluorescent tubes stared back at me. A faint, iodine-like scent drifted in the air.

I tried to turn my head away. It barely moved. It felt too large and too soft, like a beach ball. I raised my hands to where my head should have been. My fingertips ran over bandages so thick that I couldn't feel my scalp beneath them. They surrounded my skull and extended up from ears and forehead like a small yurt constructed by a nomadic neurosurgeon. I tried to raise my eyebrows but couldn't. I stared at the ceiling again and then forced my eyes left and right. Everything looked white. *No guns.*

"Barry," the voice sounded softer now. It had a rumble to it. Egor's voice. His big, shaggy, ursine head moved into my line of blurry sight. His usually expressionless face showed subtle traces of concern. Those little smile lines at the corners of his eyes had flattened, and his lips were tight, his mouth a straight line.

"Hit the trash cans, didn't I?"

"That would explain why you're alive."

"Then how—"

"The police found you beside them. You must have bounced off. You struck your head on asphalt. The ER team picked a small piece of it out of your scalp. You're scraped and bruised, but they tell me your skull's OK. What prompted you to jump from a fourth-story balcony?"

"I got thrown."

Egor's big block-of-wood face frowned down at me.

"He was big as you."

My giant friend stood quietly for a moment. Then he said, "I hope to meet him."

"Where am I?" I asked. My voice sounded rough and groggy.

"Hospital. O Street Mansion called nine one one and then Adrian."

I heard a whir and felt the head of the bed angle up. The edge of a plastic cup touched my lower lip.

"Couldn't pay my bill."

I heard a stranger's voice. "The cops brought you in conscious, but until now you were making no sense." An unfamiliar face leaned over me: bald, glasses, light-brown eyes, clean shaven, all on a long neck that poked up from the collar of blue scrubs. "You kept repeating, 'Still have time.' That mean anything to you?"

"Doesn't matter now." I felt my body tremble.

"Your head's pretty scraped up. No lacerations. We cleaned you up. You have an IV," he said matter-of-factly. "Even if the scan's OK, we'd like to keep you a few more hours."

I shook my head. It hurt. "Things to do." I pushed myself to sitting. A sharp pain shot through my left side. I winced.

"Cracked rib. Eighth. Costochondral junction. Nothing serious. It'll heal."

"How long?"

He shrugged. "A few weeks."

"Doesn't change anything."

He looked down at me. Behind the glasses his brown eyes narrowed a little. Then he forced a smile. "I've learned not to argue," he said. "I also threw a few sutures into an abdominal laceration." The face above me turned slightly side to side. The thin lips frowned. "Straight across your belly. Superficial though. No real harm done. It'll heal faster with the sutures. The rib shouldn't become a problem, but head trauma's a different story. At least wait for the scan results."

I started to swing my legs to the edge of the bed, but Egor rested a big hand against the right side of my chest and gently pushed me back. His dark eyes flickered under his heavy lids, and he shook his head. He turned to the doctor. "Of course. We'll wait."

I'd stayed in the ER until noon. I'd been pronounced intact, sane, and stupid by the medical staff. Egor had driven me home. They'd let me keep the hospital gown. I'd complained about taking the trip to the parking garage in a wheelchair and then felt woozy as I'd climbed out of it. Egor practically lifted me into the passenger seat. My big friend had said nothing more than, "Please sit back and rest."

"Where's Alex?" I'd asked once calmly. Then I'd repeated the question with as much anger as I could throw at him. The third time I could hear panic at the edge of my voice. All three had produced no more than a shrug. I don't remember much more of the trip. I must have slept. The clatter of the garage door closing behind the Denali jolted me awake.

I barely noticed the empty spot where the 'Vette should have been. I felt too worried about Alex to care. I'd failed her. Even in my foggy, battered brain, that much flashed clear as a Vegas neon sign. That fire escape had been our way out, not their way in. We'd been safe. How had they found us? The image of a large gray bird popped into my head. Its whoosh of air. A drone? What were the chances? And who had access? Not that bunch of thugs. My brain flashed back to the big knife, the pesh-kabz. Persian. I pictured Asha Talavi. Had the men who'd kidnapped Alex been his? Did the Iranian have drones flying around DC? Did their buddies, the Pakistanis? Bullshit! None of it made any sense.

Egor had led me up the stairs to my room. With every step my cracked left rib sent a little zing of pain through my chest. He waited until I'd climbed into bed and then pulled the shades, turned out the light, and closed the door.

The intercom jolted me awake. I'd been dreaming. An angry gray bird with huge talons screeched at me. Then it grabbed Alex and tore her from my arms. It laughed as it flew away.

CHAPTER TWENTY-NINE

Launch minus Three Days

At six o'clock Tuesday evening, I sat in my chair in the living room at 202 Bay Drive. The room was brightly lit and comfortably warm, but I couldn't keep from shivering. My head throbbed, and my busted rib ached every time I took a deep breath. I'd shaved and even showered after borrowing a shower cap from the dresser in the guest room. I thought better when I was clean.

My report to Adrian Kahler had concluded ten minutes earlier. The trance he put me in for uploading usually left me refreshed and alert. Not this time. I'd jerked out of it with a start, and I'd trembled the way you did after a nightmare, after those jaws close on your neck and those teeth prick your skin. Kahler's face had looked grave.

The troops had assembled. The old man and Egor had taken their customary seats. Colonel Drew Scofield and Max sat on the chesterfield on the far side of the mahogany-and-glass coffee table, Pentagon and Congress shoulder to shoulder. Scofield sat across from the old man, and Max to

Scofield's right. Ethan Blake, back straight and eyes hard, sat in the russet-brown leather Weston chair to my left. He'd initially sat in my chair, next to the old man, and I'd had to gently but firmly suggest he move over one. He hadn't liked it.

Enough gauze bandage to reach from goal post to goal post at the Baltimore Ravens' stadium still wrapped my head.

The colonel's gray eyes looked nearly colorless. They studied me for a moment. The sweet scent of his Brooks Brothers cologne reached across the coffee table. I hated cologne. "A regular Flying Wallenda. Why aren't you dead?"

"All in the landing."

He gave me a cool, fleeting smile.

Ethan Blake fixed Scofield with a hard stare. "Dr. Kahler told me you've received word from Alex."

Scofield leaned forward on the chesterfield and angled his body toward Ethan. "Not from—about. Got a call on my home phone. It's a land line."

"Home?" Ethan asked.

"No idea how they got the number. It's unlisted, but it's not secure."

Ethan leaned forward. "And?"

"Whoever has her wants to trade. You for your sister."

Ethan slid to the edge of his chair. "Trade?"

Kahler asked quietly, "From where did the call originate?"

Scofield turned toward him. "Burner phone, District, Chinatown, high density."

Ethan squeezed his eyes shut for a moment and then opened them. "Fine. Let's trade."

Scofield shook his head slowly. His voice sounded almost gentle. "Dr. Blake, we can't do that. You are a military asset. To the people I work for, your sister—" He glanced nervously around the room, studying each of us in turn. "Your sister," his voice fell to a hush, "is nothing."

Anger crept into Blake's voice. He nearly screamed, "I'm free to do as I please!"

Scofield pressed his thin lips together for a moment, studying Blake. He had a sad look in his eyes. Then he shook his head. "Not really."

The glass top of the coffee table began to rattle. A small crack in the glass appeared at one edge. I glanced at Kahler. His eyes were slits. The rattle stopped.

Ethan unfolded his legs and got to his feet. He took a step. "I'm leaving."

Scofield fixed Ethan's eyes with his own. The skin of his face looked drawn tight, and I could sense the tension in him. He kept his voice low and steady, "To do what? To go where?"

Kahler swiveled his chair toward Ethan Blake. His voice sounded soft as silk. "Ethan, we do not know where your sister has been taken. Colonel Scofield is our only link to her captors. Alex's only hope is for us to act together."

Ethan's face looked white. He stepped backward and dropped into the chair.

Scofield studied him for a long moment. Then he said, "OK. We need one more crystal. That won't be ideal, but it will get us through this crisis. Make a crystal. After that, you can do whatever you want. Next time they contact me, I'll set up an exchange. You have my word."

Blake's eyes pleaded. "I would if I could. You know that. I can't. Whatever I had, I've lost it. Dr. Kahler is trying to help me. That's working. I have a little. I don't have enough. I need time."

Drew Scofield shook his head. His gray eyes shifted away from Ethan. He turned his head left a little, toward Kahler. "In three days Iran will be launch capable. If the crazy bastards shoot a nuke at Tel Aviv, the United States will respond in kind. The Iranians are betting we won't." Scofield raised his voice, not a lot but enough to emphasize his point, "I'm telling you we'll have to. Otherwise every mutual-defense treaty tied to the nuclear umbrella of the United States falls apart. Every one of those countries will start building nukes. How long before one gets used? Then another and another. We will have to hit Iran!"

Scofield fixed each of us in turn with an edgy stare. His eyelids twitched. He anxiously tapped his right knee with the fingers of his right hand—small, ring, middle, index; small, ring, middle, index. "It gets worse. Suppose they've nearly completed launch sites we don't know about yet. We have a list of possibles. Can't eat just one. We'll have to nuke every conceivable launch site in Iran. Some are near Russia. Some are close to Europe. That's unprecedented. The fallout, from the sky and political, is unpredictable. Once that starts, your sister will matter about as much as a raindrop striking the ocean."

Anger born of helplessness welled up inside me. *Let them all blow themselves to hell. I want Alex back.* I jammed my lips together. Saying that wouldn't help. My eyes snapped from Ethan to Max to Scofield. I studied Drew Scofield for a moment. No doubt he was willing to die for his country and let the rest of us die if that would help his Joint Chiefs. Was he holding something back? Why had the kidnappers chosen him to get their message? Why not Ethan? I unfolded my empathic feelers and waited, like a dog trying to find a scent. The only thing I registered was his fucking cologne.

Kahler opened his eyes. "I have been working with Dr. Blake. We are making progress, more than he realizes. Tomorrow he will make another try at crystal growing. If he succeeds, then perhaps we can offer a trade, or at least use such an offer to trap our kidnapper."

Scofield stood up. He had just enough space between the chesterfield and the coffee table to manage that but not enough to let him get around Max—especially Max. Kahler didn't like people leaving until he was through with them, and sometimes the little obstructions worked best. At least they were less obvious. "Nothing for me to do but go home and wait for another call. And I'll check in with the Pentagon and see if surveillance has picked up anything."

"I didn't know the Pentagon did that," I said.

"We don't. Others do. If we're nice, they share."

Max stood up. Even behind his necktie and button-down shirt, I could see his belly jiggle. "I'll do the same. Congressional connections aren't quite the same as the Pentagon's, though there is certainly some overlap."

I glanced from one of them to the other and then at Kahler. My guts felt tight and inflated and sore, like a soccer ball kicked by an angry goalie. I spit my words through clenched teeth. "One big happy government."

Max shrugged. "This time it might work for you, kid. Remember that."

CHAPTER THIRTY

Launch minus Three Days

The old man and I sat in his study, a small, dark, teak-paneled, bookcase-lined room that made me feel as though I'd followed an ill-tempered owl into his tree. I detected the faint scent of wood polish. Egor must have been in there earlier.

Ethan Blake had parked himself in the guest room. The old man had asked him to stay put until things sorted out. Since he had no way to swap himself for his sister without Scofield, no way to contact the kidnappers, he'd agreed.

Adrian Kahler sat upright in his chair, eyes fixed on one of the two Macintosh computers that sat on his teak desk. Its blank screen stared back at him. He hadn't turned it on. He removed a Godiva dark chocolate square from the larger of the two Wedgwood crystal jars that sat on the desk, unwrapped it, and deposited the wrapper in the smaller jar. The latter let him keep track. I counted. This piece made two more than his full day's allotment. He never did that. I waited for him to test his blood sugar, but he didn't. Just popped the little bundle of glucose into his mouth, chewed, and swallowed.

I couldn't help but sense the most superficial layer of his mind. I examined it for a moment but had to look away. It felt like peering at a Rolex the old man had a nervous compulsion to wind every few minutes. He shook his head a centimeter or two in each direction. For Kahler, that was practically as much of an emotional display as pounding a fist would be for anyone else. "Ethan Blake is keeping something from me," Kahler muttered, almost to himself. He never muttered. "It is profound. It is critical. Part of it is recent; part is long past."

"So pry it out of him," I said. "He's in the guest room. It's one flight up. You can probably do it without getting out of that chair. But if you want, I'll kick him a couple of times and drag him down here for you."

Kahler grimaced. He never did that either. "That would be unwise."

I didn't feel much like grinning, but I forced one just to annoy him. Sometimes, if I poked him just the right way, that got his brain moving.

But his face became expressionless. His eyes drifted past me. That was my invitation to leave him alone, but I had no intention of giving up. I'd failed Alex. They'd taken her from me, and that rested on my shoulders like a thousand pounds of lead. Every time I ran my internal video loop of the O Street Mansion fight, my heart knotted, my muscles twitched, and the space shuttle roared inside my head.

"Think harder," I said, loading my voice with as much anger and command as I could muster.

The old man sat forward in his chair and pounded his left fist against the top of his desk. "Get out."

"I'm not one of Pavlov's dogs."

Kahler stood up so violently that his chair slid backward on the hardwood floor. "Then I—" For a moment he just stood there. Then he said, "Pavlov believed that extinction is new learning, not erasure of conditioning."

I granted that my mind didn't keep up with his, but this had to be a one-of-a-kind non sequitur. On the other hand, this was a lot better than the cloud of nothing that had drifted around him a moment before. "OK. Tell me about Pavlov."

"Let us presume that Ethan Blake's singing to his crystals was a form of psychokinesis, that his mind controlled the heat or the crystal lattice or both. Then something happened that caused him to lose that ability, something he has chosen to keep from me. Researchers have experimented with the extinction of conditioned fear in rats. As I recall, a tone-conditioned stimulus previously paired with a foot shock was presented repeatedly in the absence of the foot shock. This caused the fear responses to diminish. Lesions were then placed in the rats' brains, in the medial prefrontal cortex. These lesions impaired the recall of extinction, and the fear response returned to its previous level. In addition, extinction potentiated the medial prefrontal cortex's physiological responses to the tone-conditioned stimulus. Analogously, stimulation of the medial prefrontal cortex strengthened the extinction behavior."

I nodded slowly. I think slowly. "So if something happened, if Ethan's losing his crystal-growing ability is linked to some kind of trauma, then you might be able to introduce some—" I tried to do a Spock-like eyebrow lift and failed halfway up. "Some new learning. You might be able to diminish the inhibition that occurs when he tries to use psychokinesis to grow crystals."

Kahler nodded once. Then he sat down.

"But you don't know what the original stimulus was. Don't you need that?"

"That is correct. I do not have that data. In *people* suffering from posttraumatic stress disorder, some areas of the ventromedial prefrontal cortex show morphological and functional abnormalities. This suggests that their extinction circuits are compromised. Brain imaging studies of PTSD sufferers usually show a reduced activity in the ventromedial prefrontal cortex and increased activity in the amygdala."

I raised my eyebrows at him. "What's an amygdala?"

The old man frowned at me.

"Bachelor of arts, Johns Hopkins." I gave him a sharp look. "Neuroanatomy wasn't a required part of the curriculum."

Kahler sighed. "Very well. The amygdala is a small, almond-shaped region of the brain that shows high activity in states of stress, anxiety, or fear. The ventromedial prefrontal cortex and the hippocampus are the parts of the brain that modulate brain activity. When a stimulus is misinterpreted, when something happens that causes the amygdala to fire off a fight-or-flight instruction by mistake, then the ventromedial prefrontal cortex and the hippocampus shut it down."

I shrugged, but I kept my eyes on his. "And?"

"When you hear a car backfire, you instinctively reach for your pistol. Your senses sharpen, your adrenaline level jumps, your muscles tense, and

you're ready to act. In some instances, that jolt to your body will keep
you alive. But most of the time, a backfire is just a backfire. Your senses
continue to function and tell you that the noise was not a gunshot. Then
your ventromedial prefrontal cortex and hippocampus send a signal to the
amygdala that shuts it down. Your body returns to its normal steady state.
There is good evidence that PTSD patients have a ventromedial prefrontal
cortex and hippocampus that fail to shut down their amygdala completely
once it has switched on. The result is that the fight-or-flight state per-
sists, exhausting the body and unsettling the mind. Some imaging studies
have shown that combat veterans with posttraumatic stress disorder have a
smaller left hippocampus than controls."

My own amygdala must have started firing. Gooseflesh formed between
my shoulders and worked its way down my arms. I began to sweat. "No,"
I said. "You—"

"I shall do as I please." The old man's voice sounded like a machine's,
the kind without conscience or morality or any governor at all. "I've
always approached the mind as a phenomenon, as patterns of thought.
I have never entered it as an anatomic structure. Perhaps that has been
a miscalculation.

"Let us assume that a memory of something that occurred years ago,
when he was a youth, has lain dormant until recently. It was a traumatic
event. Ms. Blake told you that her drunken father raped her and then fell,
struck his head, and died. Mr. Blake witnessed at least part of this. That
engram was stored, perhaps locked away. The subject's mind matured and
apparently evolved. During that time psychokinesis developed. He began
to sing to his crystals, and they grew. Let us postulate that something
happened fairly recently, a new trauma. At some level it unlocked the old
memory, and whatever signals that memory generated have blocked his
psychokinetic ability. Interestingly, the block is not complete. Something
held that falling tire rack until you were safe from danger. You had just
saved Ethan Blake's sister. I saw this in your mind."

The old man smiled the way a wolf smiles when it spots a lone child at
the edge of the forest.

"*Now* I have something I can work with."

"Right," I said hurriedly. "The memory of the initial event, his father's
death, was somehow liberated by this second event. You don't even need
to identify the second event. You can teach him something new that will

stop the memory of his father's death from blocking his psychokinesis. Like Pavlov said, extinction is new learning. It's not erasure of conditioning."

"And what exactly might that be?" Sarcasm shaded Adrian Kahler's voice. His battleship-gray eyes found mine. He waited.

The gooseflesh had worked its way to my waist. My underarms felt soaked. I recognized the foul odor of my sweat.

Kahler shook his head. "We have no time. I shall probe his mind. Perhaps I can isolate the index memory that is interfering. If so, I shall erase that engram."

"No! You can't. I've seen what you do. You burn things away, lots of things. There's a lot of other stuff stored in there, like maybe most of his life. You can't go fucking around with it. The last time you used your mind probe. Shit—" I shook my head. "By the time you finished getting at what you wanted, your subject had nothing much left."

"It was necessary."

"I know that. I also remember that the guy died a couple of weeks later, which probably beat spending the rest of his life as a vegetable."

The old man's face looked hard. "Desperate times."

"You really think you can find a single memory, isolate it from the rest, and then destroy it without damaging anything else?" I stood up and leveled a trembling finger at him. "You're not that good. You know it. Besides, he won't let you."

That wolfish grin flickered across the old man's face. "He wants his sister back."

I glared at Kahler. *I wanted her back.* But I knew one thing for sure. If I became part of tearing her brother's mind apart, Alex wouldn't want me. "If you just leave him alone, maybe his brain will heal itself. The body heals itself all the time."

The old man looked back with cold, dispassionate eyes. "Given time, spontaneous healing might occur, or some external stimulus might reset the system." He shook his head a centimeter. "But time is what we do not have."

I tried one last desperate gambit. "Ethan Blake, PhD, is a scientist. Explain your thinking to him. But let him decide."

Adrian Kahler turned slightly in his chair. He leaned toward me. The severity of the man, the sharp angles of his face, and his ramrod posture dominated the room. "As you wish. I shall discuss all of this with him in the morning. It will be best if he is rested when we proceed. Delay beyond that might cost his sister her life. He will understand. Scofield's people want one more crystal. If Blake can produce it, they might permit him to trade himself for his sister." The old man looked me up and down with cold, emotionless eyes. "Cooperative subjects are at less risk of damage." Then Adrian Kahler folded his arms across his abdomen and intertwined his fingers. His thumbs touched and then began describing tiny circles against each other.

CHAPTER THIRTY-ONE

Wednesday, March 16, 2016
Launch minus Two Days

On Wednesday morning Adrian Kahler got out of bed and began working two hours ahead of schedule. He had Ethan Blake with him. The study door was closed.

I'd thrown myself in front of Ethan as he stepped off the staircase and turned toward Kahler's study. I practically screamed at him. "Even if you do grow another crystal, even if Scofield keeps his word and authorizes the swap, you can't just hand yourself over to the kidnappers. You're the only leverage we've got. At least insist that they release Alex at the same time. I'll go with you."

Ethan faced me. He smiled reassuringly. "Perhaps Dr. Kahler can give me the weapon I need."

"What weapon? What the hell for?"

"To kill them."

"That's absurd." I pictured genius boy riding in with his black Mustang, shooting the bad guys, and sweeping Alex into his arms. "What's your plan? Make dead bodies, grab your sister, and then ride off into the sunset?"

Ethan turned away.

I grabbed his shoulder and spun him toward me. I clamped my other hand onto his free shoulder and dug my fingers into him. "You arrogant, goddamned idiot—you've never killed anyone."

He looked into my eyes with a complete absence of feeling. For a moment my mind synced with his. I felt a cold emptiness, a bottomless crater, as if every emotion Ethan Blake ever knew had been sucked out of him by one of those huge machines they use at Goddard when they need to simulate deep space.

"I killed my father."

My arms went limp and fell to my side.

He backed one step away and closed his hands around an imaginary baseball bat. My mind caught a glimpse of a seventeen-year-old boy wearing a baseball uniform, that little visored cap sitting half back on his head, as he watched his old man fuck his weeping thirteen-year-old sister.

Ethan Blake swung his arms back over his shoulder and then swung them forward, as if he were sending a baseball over the left field fence, right out of the ballpark.

I stepped out of his way.

CHAPTER THIRTY-TWO

Launch minus Two Days

Egor had unwound the bandage from my head, cleaned the nasty scrapes in my scalp with Betadine, and then wrapped me with fresh gauze. I ran my fingertips over it. The new bandage felt a lot thinner than the original. Now touching it hurt my scalp. My head still pounded with the least exertion, and I reeked of iodine.

I could breathe without difficulty, but whenever I coughed, my broken rib fired off a jolt of pain that shot through my left side. I took slow steps and watched where I put each foot. One more injury and I'd be out of the game. I couldn't risk that.

Asha Talavi had called at ten thirty, while I sipped coffee at the kitchen table, midway through my second cup. "We have to meet," he said. I heard tension in his voice.

"OK," I said. "When?" Just then the second line lit up. "Hold on a minute," I told him.

I switched lines. "Sandler."

"This is Scofield."

"What's up?"

"I have a lead." Unlike Talavi, Scofield spoke without emotion.

"Great. Let me in on it."

"Not over the phone. I'll show you. Pick you up at eleven o'clock." He clicked off.

I switched back to Asha Talavi, but the line was dead. I made a mental shrug. Not enough time to meet with both of them, and Scofield was far and away my best bet. The Joint Chiefs could draw on sources of information for which the concept of plausible deniability was created.

Scofield and his standard-issue black Lincoln Navigator picked me up at eleven o'clock. A light snow was falling. He blipped the horn and then stood beside the driver's door as I lumbered over, climbed into the passenger's front seat, and pulled my door closed. The sweet scent of Scofield's Brooks Brothers cologne saturated the small space. He wore a long black cashmere overcoat that looked expensive. It bulked up his thin frame. I noticed Brooks Brothers logos on the buttons.

He studied me for a moment as he started the engine. Then he said, "Turn off your cell phone. They can be tracked."

"Yes, master." I fished it out of my black ski jacket's inner breast pocket and held it up. "Already off. Besides, it's a burner."

"Sorry, Barry. I'm not supposed to let myself get jumpy." That was the most human thing I'd ever heard the man say, but his voice remained a monotone, his affect flat, and his face expressionless. He opened a box of green Tic Tacs, poured a couple onto his palm, and popped them into his mouth. He held out the box.

I shook my head. That made me wince.

Scofield noticed. "How are you feeling?"

"Great."

"Sure." He drove out of the driveway and turned right onto Bay Drive. The stainless-steel gate at number 202 slid closed behind us.

Scofield glanced over at me after he'd straightened the wheel. "You got a pretty good whack. Can you think straight?"

"Straight enough."

"Gun?"

"Yep."

"Can you shoot it?"

I grimaced. "I'll get off at least one shot before my head explodes."

"Good. Shoot the guy aiming at me."

"Whatever you say."

Conversation ended. I watched the world go past. He headed west.

"Mind telling me where we're going?"

"West."

"Details, please."

"Need to know," he said.

"Right. I need to know."

"And you will."

I could have pointed my gun at him and cocked the hammer, if it had had a hammer, which Glocks don't. Drew was military, and I wasn't. He'd have died before telling me it was Wednesday if he'd been ordered to.

We drove west and crossed Routes 97, 295, and 270. The roads held a dusting of snow, but most of the heavy stuff had been plowed to the sides. I'd thought anger and worry would keep me alert, but my eyes finally closed and didn't open again until we turned onto Route 121, Clarksburg Road. We were in Boyds, Maryland. I'd been there before. The two-laner had a thirty-mile-per-hour speed limit. For a 'Vette it presented a bumpy ride. The Lincoln barely noticed the change in pavement. Scofield slowed as we approached a sign on the right side of the road that read, "Adopt a Highway, Kingsley Wilderness Project, SWAT Team."

Just past the sign, he turned left onto a one-and-a-half-lane roadway with no name. He stopped the car. A small lake sat to our left. Its surface looked frozen. About fifty feet farther on, a yellow-painted steel traffic gate blocked the road. A sign on a pole just to the right of the gate, a big red circle with white lettering, read, "Do Not Enter." A second sign stood to the right of the first. That one was black on white. It read, "Authorized Vehicles Only by Authority of M-NCPPC." For anyone too thick to get the message, a pole to the left of the gate held an orange metal square with black letters that read, "Park Area Under Construction. Closed to the Public by Authority of M-NCPPC." One sign, it was the Park and Planning Commission. Two signs, someone was paranoid at the Park and Planning Commission. Three signs, Pentagon.

Scofield stopped the Lincoln, got out, and stuck a card in a slot.

I climbed down. A sudden gust of wind slapped my face. A thin layer of snow crystals crunched beneath my boots. I looked around. I recognized

Little Seneca Lake. I'd seen it before but from a different angle. I noticed a small sign by the water. "Thin Ice. Ice Never Safe."

The gate swung open, and Drew Scofield waved me back into the Navigator. He followed. The road on the far side of the gate had not been plowed, but Scofield's four-wheel-drive SUV didn't slip even once. Through the barren winter trees on the right, I could make out train tracks, and at one point a MARC commuter train sporting its distinctive red-and-blue horizontal stripes whisked past. I saw a dam to our left.

We drove about two-thirds of a mile. Then Scofield turned left onto a small snow-covered field and stopped the car. He turned to me. "Little Seneca Lake Dam," he said. "The lake was created by damming Little Seneca Creek. It's DC's emergency water supply." He looked extremely pleased with himself. This was the first time I'd ever seen him cheerful. His emotion was palpable.

I felt a tingling at the back of my mind. Scofield, like Star Trek's Scottie when he was trying to bewilder Norman, had too much happiness. But he didn't look as if he was about to lose his sense of *Enterprise*. I sifted through my mind but couldn't figure him out. I couldn't read the Scofield behind all that merriment.

"Come on," he said. He climbed out and walked toward the edge of the dam.

I used the moment to unzip my ski jacket and check that the Glock was in its holster. Glock kept it simple. Nothing to cock, no safety. The .45 held only six rounds, but it was thinner than most other Glocks. The extra mags were thin too—easy to conceal.

Then I struggled down to the snow and shuffled along after Drew Scofield, too proud to let the army guy see me holding my angry rib. My head would not stop throbbing. My body shivered a couple of times, but I left the jacket open.

Scofield opened a small rectangular box set into a five-foot-high metal pillar and punched several buttons. I heard the whir of electric motors and a repetitive metallic clank. Then a corrugated-metal walkway extended out, over a pipe large enough to swallow a small house. It rumbled forward and joined its companion from the far side. The little bridge looked about seventy feet long. I followed Scofield across. My boots made a faint, hollow clang with every step. He waited for me to hobble over to him. Then he tapped another rectangular box on a duplicate metal pillar, and the walk-way retracted.

The maintenance building sat on the far side. Whoever had designed the little square bunker had a sense of style. The walls were not just non-descript gray concrete. Instead the designers had built it with a variegated checkerboard of square stones set in mortar. It had a flat, concrete roof with a small gray concrete boxlike structure and a large antenna on top. Two triangular stone-in-mortar slabs flanked the doorway.

Scofield began speaking as he worked his key in the lock in the heavy-looking steel door. "We think we've found your girl. There's a SEAL team ready for extraction, but their commander wants more confirmation than we've given him. Bad press to burst in and get it wrong, especially if some-one makes a wrong move and gets shot. They want on-the-ground surveil-lance. I volunteered us. We'll communicate with the SEAL team from here. We recon, we return here, and we report. Then we sit tight and wait for orders. Any problem with that?"

The door swung inward, and Scofield held it for me as I stepped inside. Something unsettled me. Something wasn't right. I don't like dark little caves. Then the lights came on. They must have been on a sensor. Scofield hadn't touched a switch. He pushed the door closed. The latch clicked. I don't know what I expected, but this wasn't it. The walls to my left and to my right were completely covered with flat-panel computer monitors. Before each set of displays sat a wall-length workbench, a phone, and a couple of keyboards. Each also had a gray metal folding chair, the kind people carry back to the basement after card games. I guess the government had to save money somewhere.

The operant descriptor for the Little Seneca Lake Dam was "little." A part-time maintenance guy could have run it from a laptop. This place was something else.

Scofield began to remove his heavy cashmere overcoat. He had to strug-gle to get out of it. His left arm seemed stuck in the sleeve. "Hey, Barry, would you mind helping me with this?"

"Sure." I took the end of the left sleeve in both my hands and tugged it off his arm. The rest of the big coat came with it. The damn thing felt as heavy as it looked, and I had to grab it with both hands to keep it from falling to the cement floor.

Then I heard the click, that distinctive sound of the safety coming off a government-model .45 automatic. My right hand jerked instinctively toward the Glock.

"Bang." Scofield didn't need to say anything more. My hand froze. "Not too slow," he said. "Just too late. All I needed was the distraction."

"Nice to know Brooks Brothers works for you." I threw his coat onto the concrete floor and turned slowly toward him. I had to look at the bastard. He grinned maliciously. I could see why he didn't smile much. His thin skin stretched over his gaunt face to form a death's-head mask. The pistol sat comfortably in his right hand. The way he held it told me it was an old friend.

"Why?" I asked, hoping to get him talking. I inched my right hand toward the Glock.

Scofield shoved the muzzle of his pistol against my throat.

"Hands up," he commanded. "Never actually said that before." He laughed a ragged laugh. "Let's step away from my coat."

I raised my arms slowly, hoping for a chance to jump him. The muzzle of that .45 never left my skin. I felt my Adam's apple slide over the blued steel when I swallowed. I needed only an instant. Scofield didn't give it to me.

"Now, down on one knee. Now the other," he barked out the order.

The concrete floor felt icy cold. I could feel it even through the denim of my jeans.

"Hands on the floor. Now! Flat on your face."

I turned my head left as I went down. I glimpsed Scofield out of the corner of my eye. I felt my Glock flop around under my left arm. Its plastic grip clacked against the cement floor. I judged its distance to my gun hand and calculated the odds. The muzzle of Scofield's pistol never wavered. No way I could roll onto my right side and grab the Glock faster than he could squeeze his Colt's single-action trigger. We both knew it.

"Hands behind your back. Now put your wrists together."

I knew what was coming and clenched my fists as he wrapped my wrists with the zip tie. He started the job with one hand. Once he'd snugged it up, he holstered his pistol and used both hands to jerk it tight.

The edges of the plastic dug into my wrists. Instinct told me to relax my fists to reduce the pain, but I clenched harder, forcing my wrist muscles to stay thick.

"I wanted the military-spec ties, but if I'd gotten caught swiping them, this whole deal would have gone down the drain. Best to make do."

After that he bound my legs, running a zip tie over my jeans, just above the top of my boots. He jerked it tight. Then he pulled the Glock out of my holster and the Boker folding knife off my belt. He half rolled and half kicked me onto my back with his foot. Then he took my phone.

"I could shoot you now and leave your body right here. It'll be weeks before another drill. But I might need you later."

Rule number one: keep them talking. "What is this place?" I asked.

"Secondary satellite control. It's a backup in case the main station at Goddard goes down. This little bunker is home away from home to the wrath of God. From here I can fire every laser on every satellite. I'd like to boot up the monitors and show off what our little communications satellites can see. Whatever they see, they can kill."

"Is this"—I turned my head toward the workstations—"how you sank Kahler's boat?"

The corners of Scofield's mouth turned up for an instant. He began to say something. Then he cut himself off abruptly, before even one syllable slipped out between his thin lips. But his sunken, gray eyes smiled at me. "What boat?"

"Why are you doing this?" I asked. "Career military, West Point, Joint Chiefs. Whatever you're after, you're tossing all that onto a dung heap."

He grabbed the back of one of the small card-table chairs, dragged it about six feet from my face, and sat down. "I'm going to make a lot of dead Iranians," he said. "Millions."

I kept my back centered over my hands, relaxed my fists, and then began working my wrists against the zip tie. It felt about a quarter inch wide, certainly less than half an inch. Those are rated at 250 pounds. The 50-pound ones are only two-tenths of an inch wide, and they'd have dug in more. I didn't know how much time I had. I might not have any. I began to pull my wrists apart, trying to stretch the nylon, but the weight of my back pushing down on my wrists made that pretty much impossible.

"Again, why? Not to mention how."

"How is easy." Scofield smiled. His face looked drawn, hard, and thoughtful, like a rat's face—a rat with a plan. "No satellite laser over Iran, no way to blow their nuclear-tipped launch vehicle, not short of a missile strike or bombing raid. Either of those needs to be initiated well ahead of launch time, and they're very conspicuous. We'd be in a war with Iran whether we blew their missile or not. And timing can be tricky. If they fake us out, and you can bet that's their plan, they'll pull off the launch before we can stop it.

"The satellite-borne lasers, on the other hand, can fire in an instant and get speed-of-light results. The heat generated when one of their beams strikes a target is practically off the scale, and our lasers can fire as fast as a Minigun, up to six thousand shots per minute. Target the engine or the fuel, strike just after takeoff, and the explosion will be indistinguishable from a launch failure." Scofield glanced toward the ceiling, and his eyes sparkled in the overhead fluorescent light. "And they'd never suspect a thing."

He paused for a moment, as if fending off an annoying idea. Then he shrugged. "Well, some of them might, but they'd never prove it. They wouldn't even have enough suggestive data to convince their own people. Wouldn't that be cool?"

I craned my neck to look up at him. It hurt. "But there is no laser. Not on the right satellite. Time's run out."

"Not quite out, but that clock's running. As much as I love the tech, I need to kill it. See, Barry, I want those crazy Iranians to launch their nuke at Tel Aviv. So I have to keep little genius boy Blake from making another laser crystal, at least for a little while longer."

Scofield leaned to the side, scooped up his cashmere overcoat with his free hand, and draped it across his knees.

"That guy's the luckiest bastard on earth. I sent two of my Iranians to kill him during his early-morning jog. They wound up chargrilled and floating in the Tidal Basin. God knows how that happened. Lightning strike, maybe?" Scofield poked the side of my chest with the toe of his boot. "Any ideas, Barry?"

That startled the hell out of me. "Your Iranians?" I said loudly enough for my voice to reverberate off the concrete walls.

Scofield smoothed the fabric of his cashmere coat with the palm of his hand. "Bought and paid for. Well, actually, bought and promised. Iran has an interest section in the Pakistani embassy. It's like they rent space there. It's operated by this guy, Talavi, and his staff. The staffers are young, but they all received some degree of military training before being shipped over here."

He ran his tongue back and forth between his upper lip and his teeth. "So Tehran trains these kids, fills them with hate for America, and then sends them over here to act as clerks and maybe low-level spies. What happens?" He poked me with his boot again.

I shrugged, using the movement to retest the strength of the zip ties. "I'll bite. What happened?"

Scofield turned up both hands. "Barry, they acted like they'd been let out of prison! They fell in love with this place. Talk about unintended consequences. Rock music is probably the best tool we have to undermine repressive governments. All those songs about freedom, doing what you want, and sex. These kids ate it up. Not one of them wants to go home to Iran. *Ever!*

"Several months ago I followed one into a Starbucks and bought him a latte. He wanted to practice his English. We became best buds."

Scofield gave me a wink.

"We confided in each other. Move a thirty-year-old single guy from Tehran to DC, and after six months of hanging out with girls in short skirts, most of them would just as soon have their dicks cut off as return to enforced Muslim respectability. With each additional day here, he dreaded going back a little more. Said his coworkers felt the same. I threw a couple of parties for them. I listened. One day I got the first guy alone and offered the deal. 'Work for me. Let me know everything Talavi does—everything Tehran asks him to do. Do some jobs for me. When Talavi gets called home, you stay.' I promised a new identity, a real job, and personal freedom. He'd seen enough of the witness protection on TV to believe I could make that work."

"How'd you get the rest of them?"

"He *asked* if he could recruit his pals. I told him if anyone squawked to Tehran, that dude was on his own. Didn't even blink. Turns out they all wanted in. Can you believe it? So I welcomed each and every one. And they've stuck."

"So you created your own little band of monsters."

"They're not monsters. They're just kids. They fell in love with America, and now they'll do anything I ask just to stay here."

I craned my neck toward him. "You're using them."

Scofield made a dry, crackling laugh. "I'm using everyone." He mused for a moment. His left thumb and forefinger tugged at his earlobe. "All except Zafir. He's a few years older than the rest, and he's an angry guy. He acts like he enjoys violence. He applied to join MOIS a couple of years ago. That's Iran's Ministry of Intelligence and Security. He failed the exam."

Scofield barked out another laugh.

"The big test came when I sent those two after Blake. I couldn't be sure they'd kill a guy for me. Then *my guys* turned up dead. I thought that would frighten the others off, but it didn't. They wouldn't go near Blake again, but aside from that, every one of them stuck with me. It hasn't really changed, you know, not in over five hundred years."

"What hasn't changed?" I asked.

Scofield's mouth formed that tight, malicious grin. "The American dream."

"From you it's a lie."

Scofield sucked in his cheeks. The vertical lines on either sides of his mouth deepened. Then he shrugged. "The next time I went after Blake, I did it myself. Used one of the satellites. I can do that from here. I can even erase the log."

The toe of his boot dug into my side again. He knew where it would hurt.

"But his bitch sister was driving the car. Good thing you showed up, or we wouldn't have her now. She's the only leverage I have with her brother. When I sent my boys to get her, I gave two orders. First, bring her back. Second, no guns. Alive, I told them, alive and unmolested.

"Ethan Blake might never make another crystal, or he might start growing one an hour from now. So I need a hold on him. Now I have it. I owe you, Barry." Scofield drew back his left foot as if to kick me hard enough to cave in my ribcage. Then he put it down. His thin lips stretched into that malicious smile. "I figure I just paid off that debt."

"How'd you find us?"

"Drone footage. Those things are all over DC now. The government uses the small ones for surveillance. They're more like tiny jet planes than helicopters, and they fly so fast that most people don't get a good look at them—think they're birds." Scofield flapped his hands. "Some of them are even shaped to present that impression. I've had people running facial-recognition scans on drone footage since the day you and your girlfriend disappeared. Just dumb luck that we found you."

"The military flies surveillance drones over DC?"

"Of course not. That would set off all kinds of paranoia. But other agencies do. I told you before, if we're nice, they share."

I looked him up and down. "So why does a guy with all your charm want Iran to launch a nuclear missile at Tel Aviv? Doesn't that make dead Israelis?"

"They're collateral damage." His tongue flicked between his lips for an instant. He scratched the tip of his nose with the back of his hand. I sensed his mind momentarily running backward, over the puzzle pieces he'd assembled so carefully. "It's Iran I want. Seventy-seven million Muslims, eight million in Tehran alone.

"Latest intel says the ayatollahs figure they can nuke Tel Aviv and get away with it. They don't believe Washington has the balls to nuke 'em back. But you know—and I know—we will. World's leader or world's pussy. No president has *ever* stepped into the history books as choice number two. Iran's headed back to the Stone Age, and most of those stones will glow in the dark. And once we start, well, we might just keep going. Everyone knows the only way to win in Afghanistan is to burn all those places where the Taliban hide. When your enemy goes to ground, make his ground radioactive. I know plenty of officers at the Pentagon who wouldn't weep if those orders came down."

I struggled to raise my head up off the floor. My voice felt hoarse. "Why do you want this?"

He stood up and dropped his coat on the chair. He looked so thin. Then Scofield's skinny fingers unbuttoned his shirt. He pulled the flaps from under his trousers and lifted the shirt to expose his belly. Pale skin clung to his lower ribs as tightly as Saran Wrap stretched over the threads of a jar; it looked nearly as transparent. A colostomy bag clung to the right side of his abdomen. He poked it with his right index finger, and the dark-brown fluid inside sloshed around.

"This isn't the worst part," he said. "The worst part's inside. *Four bullets.* They had to take out so much small intestine." He shook his head. For a moment he just ground his teeth. "Afterward I lost nearly half my body weight. I've never been able to put it back on—not much of it anyway."

"What happened?"

Scofield began to speak in a monotone, his voice emotionless, with neither peaks nor valleys. "After West Point I worked with the US Army Rangers. I was the computer geek at school. I wanted more experience as a soldier. Combat opportunities were spotty, so I grabbed that one. Ranger school made combat ops at West Point feel like playing nice with small children. I loved jump school. After that, I became the rangers' go-to tech guy. You'd be surprised how much covert ops rely on tech. That was my job. 'Jump ready' meant chute, laptop, and pistol, in that order. The other guys carried the M-16s. I led the way in and led the way out. My guys kept me alive. I had one close call. The sly bastard slipped through our perimeter and got off a shot. He knew who to aim for. My laptop shattered. The round tore a hole in my shirt and left a score mark on the side of my chest. He never got off a second shot—hit the ground with six slugs in him. My guys were that good."

I found myself staring at Scofield's colostomy bag. "Then that's not what did the damage?"

He shook his head several times, slowly and almost dreamily. "A couple of years ago, some Pentagon genius decided that a computer whiz with a dozen HALO jumps to his credit would be more valuable as a trainer than in the field. They assigned me to fucking Afghanistan."

For an instant Scofield's hands squeezed the ends of his shirt so tightly that the pale skin of his fingers turned nearly white. Then he let go, unclasped his belt, tucked in his shirt, rebuckled, and returned to his chair. That cashmere coat found its way to his lap again.

"Kabul, by the way, is a shithole. Though I grant it's the most tolerable shithole in a country of shitholes. It became my new home. Command assigned me to training Special Forces. They work in teams of about a dozen. It was my job to figure out who got the laptop and then do the training. Those soldiers learn fast, so I had lots of spare time."

He began running his hand over his coat, petting it again and again.

"In 2012, command noticed that, and some genius decided to fill my empty hours. They assigned me to help train Afghan Uniformed Police. Not that what I'd been doing had any relevance to policing, but that was true for most everyone they selected for the job. Instructors got a crash course in police work and training. Then we trained.

"I called my trainees cadets and addressed them that way: Cadet Abdali, Cadet Kalakani. Thought that a title would give them some esprit de corps. A few were women. Believe it or not, over eighteen hundred female Afghan Uniformed Police officers were trained between 2002 and 2012. That's unusual for a Muslim country. A lot of Muslim men didn't take to the idea, but for the most part, the male students tolerated women in their midst. Becoming a cop and getting a cop's salary was too good a deal to pass up.

"I made it my business to run a gender-blind class. I told them that on day number one. This would be meritocracy, plain and simple. For anyone who didn't like that, the door was open. A couple of guys actually stood up and walked out. Most simply glared at the women. For their part, the women kept their eyes down and heads bent. Things went well for a while. None of the women ever raised her hand when I put a question to the group, but when I called on one, she'd answer. Head bent, eyes cast down, voice barely above a whisper—but she'd answer. They used their body language as an apology to their male classmates. 'Sorry, he's making me do this. It's not my fault.'

"I pressed on. Then I gave them a hypothetical tactical problem and told them to write a paper detailing how they'd handle it. Most of the solutions were absurd. One stood out, really brilliant. It showed the kind of thinking I wanted from them. I spent one entire class period reviewing that paper with them. 'Listen. Learn how to think.' That's what I told them. The paper had been written by a woman. That didn't click in my gender-neutral brain until I announced her name to the class and asked her to stand up. No one moved."

Scofield stopped petting his coat. For a moment he just dug his fingers into the fabric.

"At the start of the next class, my new favorite cadet stood up, walked to the front of the class, and stood at attention before me. She saluted. Then she stuck a pistol in my gut and pulled the trigger four times. I had just enough consciousness left to watch her calmly raise the muzzle to her right temple. The last thing I remember is the dark-red plume that blew out of the left side of her head.

"After I came out of anesthesia, one of the nurses at the hospital told me that my little performance had insulted several of my brilliant cadet's classmates. Word got around. So a couple of their brothers or cousins or whoever gang-raped my cadet's fifteen-year-old sister. The kid made it half-way home and then threw herself off a bridge. In Afghanistan's Muslim culture, it's the woman, not the rapist, who's considered dishonored. Rape victims don't have much of a future there. The whole thing was my fault. That's why her sister shot me."

"Jesus," I said. "That's awful. The whole thing's awful."

Scofield's sunken gray eyes drifted over the wall on the far side of the room. "Afghan security forces, men with a beef of one sort or another, have killed Western soldiers before." He inhaled slowly and then blew out a breath between thin, pursed lips. "I was the only one ever attacked by an Afghan woman."

He squeezed his eyelids shut for a moment and then opened them. His eyes seemed to have withdrawn farther into their sockets, into those dark little caves they called home. "As far as the rape was concerned, the Afghanistan military did nothing." Scofield leaned down to me, his nose an inch from mine, so close that I could smell his mint-tinged breath. "Even the nurses at the hospital knew who the rapists were. Nobody bothers keeping that kind of secret there. No penalty, no need."

He straightened up. His monotone continued, a uniform drone lacking audible emotion. But now and then the left corner of his mouth twitched ever so slightly. "I've thought about going back to Afghanistan and tracking down those Muslim monsters, but the truth is I'm in no shape for it. I used to be six feet and two hundred pounds of solid muscle. Now I'm garbage." The corners of his mouth inched upward. "And I don't shit. Not anymore. I don't fuck either. The urologists, and I've gone to a bunch, tell me I've got no physical impediment. It just doesn't work anymore. Besides, not many women flock to a beanpole with a bag on his belly. Time was when the girls found me irresistible. Now I have a cat."

I craned my neck off the floor and found his eyes with mine. "If it's Afghanis you hate, why go after Iran?"

Scofield stared at me for a long moment.

I thought I'd brought him back. "You haven't killed anybody," I told him. "Not yet."

He waved it away. "It's not the people," he whispered. "It's Islam. It's the belief system and the vicious way Muslims go about implementing it. Iran presents an opportunity, and that's all. And it's a target-rich environment."

I took one shot at reaching whatever humanity was left in the man. "You can't generalize the actions of a few Afghanis to all Muslims everywhere."

Scofield's eyes drifted. "I was at a med station once after the Taliban shelled a village. Lots of civilian casualties. The fathers would carry in their wounded kids and scream at any doctor who treated a little girl before all the boys' wounds had been cleaned and dressed. The extent of the injuries didn't matter. A male child with a cut finger got a Band-Aid before a little girl with her guts hanging out got plasma. The whole fucking country thinks like that. It's all Muslim fucking bullshit. Afghanis, Iranians, Arabs—they're all the same. The world will be better off without them."

"They're just people," I told him.

Scofield rolled his eyes. For an instant they sparkled in the light of the overhead fluorescents. "Just people," he said. "And very soon there's going to be a lot fewer of them."

Scofield stood up and pulled on his coat. He walked toward the door. "I'm going to go and collect Dr. Blake now. I don't know why he hasn't made that crystal yet. I never figured that his project might implode on its own. But I can't risk any sudden recovery. This whole deal rests on keeping him out of that lab for a little while longer. Then it won't matter.

"That satellite will launch on schedule and without its top-secret laser on board. The Joint Chiefs won't delay the launch. To do so would prompt an investigation. Then the entire Hammer program might be discovered. We already have laser-armed satellites that can target China and Russia. No one's going to put those at risk for a bunch of Jews and Muslims."

I heard my pistol scrape against the concrete floor as Scofield picked it up.

"Kahler has a rep. He's dangerous. A good combat op has preparations for the unexpected. Might need you to bargain."

He stopped and turned toward me.

"You got lucky at Goddard. That guard found you. They pulled you out of the vibration room. Not this time." His drawn, usually expressionless face broke into a grin. His lips stretched tight against his teeth again, and his cheekbones showed beneath his thin, taut skin. He wore the same smile the devil wears when he's collecting a soul. "No one will find you here." As he pulled the heavy door closed behind him, a roguish lilt replaced his habitual monotone. "Bye, Barry. Kill you later."

I had only one thought as he pulled the heavy door closed behind him. *If this is what he planned for me, what is he doing to Alex?*

CHAPTER THIRTY-THREE

Launch minus Two Days

The cement floor felt as cold as hard-packed snow against my legs, and it pushed relentlessly against the back of my head. At least the lights stayed on. I raised and lowered my legs a couple of times so the motion sensor would know someone was still in the room. Pitch black would not make things better. I saw no windows.

Scofield had bound my hands behind my back. I tried relaxing the muscles and wiggling my hands out of the zip tie. No dice.

Escape method number two required hands in front. So I rolled onto my right side, bent my knees hard, and inched my feet up along my back until my fingertips felt the heel of a boot. Working my bound wrists over the combat boots was the toughest part. I do plenty of stretching exercises, but this was well beyond the level of no pain, no gain. My head kept drumming. As my wrists worked their way around my boots, the broken rib begged them to stop. I cursed at it. *Shut the fuck up. When you're dead, you're dead for a long time.*

Then I had my hands in front of me. I took a look at the black plastic that encircled my wrists: just like any zip tie but thicker. The key to escape was the little tongue inside the catch. It was called a locking bar. That was the weak point in the system, and although the locking bar on a 250-pound zip tie was stronger than the one on a 50-pounder, it wasn't all that much stronger. Give 'em a sharp, sudden shock, and they'd snap.

With my hands in front of me, it was easy to roll until my ass sat on the concrete and my legs stretched out in front of me. Then I bent my knees, sat forward, grabbed the end of the zip tie around my wrists with my teeth, and pulled it as tight as it would go. Locking bars on loose straps don't snap. Then I raised my bound hands and brought them down hard against one knee.

My broken rib shrieked. I felt like a skewered salmon, as if a black bear had swung its paw through the water and plunged a claw into the side of my chest. For a long moment, I couldn't breathe. Then I raised my hands to my face and stared at the little tongue inside the zip tie. It looked as good as new. If that tongue had had a mouth, it would have laughed at me. I felt tears on my cheeks. I wiped them away with the back of one thumb.

I stared down at the paracord laces in my boots. He'd bound my wrists and legs, but my fingers were free. I bent forward, untied my left shoelace, and then worked it free. The paracord was a little thick for the eyelets, so I had to work it off the boot hole by hole. Bending forward put pressure on the broken rib. It got even. Finally I had my prize: forty-five inches of paracord.

I tried to work one end of paracord between my bound hands and around the lower half of the zip tie that I'd so cleverly yanked tight a few minutes earlier. I held my hands straight up, pulled my wrists apart as far as I could, and used my fingers to push the paracord between my bound wrists. The more I tried to pull my wrists apart, the less room I had for my fingers to move. Once I had the paracord partway through, I used the tip of my tongue, and millimeter by millimeter, I licked it through while I pushed with my fingertips. Slow, tedious, painful work. At least I hadn't walked through a cow pasture. After about ten minutes, I had enough poking out from between my wrists to grab with my teeth. I pulled it through.

The taste of copper filled my mouth. I spat between my knees and then spat again. A foamy mix of blood and saliva spattered onto the floor. The concrete looked as if it had begun to bleed. I couldn't feel my tongue. I played it around each cheek, then against the backs of my teeth and the root of my mouth; it felt like a big chunk of leather.

Thankful for being a sailor, I used my fingers to fashion a bowline knot at each end of the paracord. Then I turned each bowline into a lasso and worked the toe of each boot through the loop. Finally I had my rough paracord saw blade looped around the bottom segment of the plastic tie that bound my wrists and had each end secured to a boot.

Heels against the cement floor, I moved my legs forward and back in an alternating rhythm. The zip tie that bound them left just enough slack for me to do that. At the same time, I pulled my hands up hard, forcing their zip tie around my wrists tight against the paracord. Micrometer by micrometer my paracord shoelace began to cut through the plastic zip tie.

Slow, painstaking, anxious work. I froze every time I heard a sound— maybe a key in a lock or a door creaking open. Back and forth, back and forth, and back and forth. Some part of my body yelped with every movement, but I got a rhythm going. Pain wasn't so bad when it was predictable.

I focused my mind. Kill Scofield. I watched him die a dozen different ways, by my hand always. I rocked my feet back and forth. My rib whimpered. Focus. *Scofield! I'd jerk his head back and whisper in his ear, joking with him as he died.* My body whined like a flogged animal. I tugged harder at the paracord. Saw left, saw right. *Scofield!* Pain was nothing—would be nothing. Saw left. Saw right. I kept at it for twenty minutes.

The paracord snapped.

I stared at the torn ends. A bolt of fear shot though me. I had another shoelace. I didn't have another tongue. I tried to roll it around in my mouth. It felt as big as Alley Oop's club. I spat past the lump of dead meat in my mouth, and another foamy, red glob spattered against the floor. I felt tears in my eyes. My body began to shiver.

I forced myself to take one deep, cleansing breath and then another. I raised my hands to my face and studied the zip tie. The paracord had sawed through more than halfway. I accidently twisted a little at the waist, and my rib poked me hard. I yelled at it. *Oh, fuck you!*

Adrenaline born of rage pulsed through me. I planted my feet, snapped my wrists over my head, jerked them apart as hard as I could, and slammed them onto my left knee. I heard myself scream. I heard a snap. My hands sprang apart.

The broken black plastic lay at my feet. My wrists burned like hell. I studied them. Big, mottled purple welts looked like tattoos gone bad. The skin looked abraded but not cut. I wiggled my hands and flexed my fingers a few times. Everything hurt. Everything worked.

My hands were free. I unlaced the paracord from my right boot, wrapped one end around each hand, and used it to saw through the zip tie that bound my legs. That went faster.

I laced my left boot as best I could with the two pieces of paracord, tying one midway and one at the top. The paracord from the right boot hadn't broken, so that one was easy. I stood up and took a couple of steps. I felt unsteady at first, but I could walk. I could kick.

The desks had drawers. They were properly secured, but Scofield hadn't taken my belt, and the lockpicks inside its hidden pocket made quick work of their little tumblers.

I rifled through each drawer. No weapons. I pulled the caps off a couple of cheap ballpoint pens and stuck one in each front pocket. Almost anything could become a weapon. I saw two phones but couldn't risk using them. At best, my call would be monitored. At worst, the little bunker might blow up. Scofield was crazy. I didn't know how crazy.

I found only one interesting item—or five, if you're a splitter. Five sheets of typing paper with line drawings on them. Lots of little stick-figure cartoons had been scribbled just inside the edges, and some on top of the lines, so at first glance, the whole deal looked like some engineer's doodle. But most of the lines looked straight, ruler drawn. To me they suggested a road map. Scofield might have been nuts, but he was smart. The more I studied the papers, the more I convinced myself that he'd hidden them in plain sight.

I stared at them for several minutes, but nothing clicked. Then I realized that one line on one sheet was crosshatched. I remembered the MARC train I'd seen on our way in.

The desks were too small. I lay the papers on the floor and arranged them so that the straight lines running toward the edge of one sheet matched up with the straight lines running toward the edge of another. I covered the cartoons where I could. Then I focused on the crosshatched line and backed away. All at once a pattern clicked into place, and I recognized the route Scofield had driven to get here. I dog-eared the top right corner of that page so that it would be easy to pick it out from the others.

Why would a computer guy spend hours tracing maps on paper? Covert often meant keeping it simple. What wasn't in a computer couldn't be hacked, stumbled on, or picked up in a routine security sweep. His subordinates wouldn't pay much attention to a few doodled papers lying in a drawer. In the new millennium, paper didn't count for much. If it wasn't digital, it wasn't important.

Scofield had studied the area around this substation. He must have needed a hiding place nearby for something he couldn't risk bringing here. Or someone. He'd brought me here, but that had to have been a last-minute improvisation. He couldn't keep the real prize where he faced even a remote chance of one of his subordinates stumbling in. As soon as he went undercover and out of touch, that had become a risk.

I examined the map. He must have traced every street. Clean white paper, clean black lines. Then I noticed the smudge. He'd erased something. It had been done so neatly that I barely noticed. Had he made a mark and then erased it so a prying eye wouldn't notice? Or had he corrected a mistake? I pictured that West Point computer whiz kid for a moment, his rigid stance, and his precise way of speaking. His only mistake had been letting his pencil move with his brain. And he'd fixed it. He just hadn't fixed it quite enough.

Erasers at the ends of pencils can leave marks. That was why artists used kneaded rubber. I imagined the perfectionist in Scofield bothering over it, working at the smudge, worrying that he was making it worse. "If I keep this up, I might tear the paper." Would any of his subordinates do more than just glance at this stack of papers anyway?

That bastard had Alex, and he'd stashed her. Not at the substation but close enough so that he could move between the two places quickly if he had to.

I studied the map again, edge to edge and corner to corner. I found three more erasures, each ever so faint. I had no mileage scale, but I could estimate distance relative to the route we'd driven. The erasures were all within a few miles of the dam. I needed a real map so that I could make better sense of the overlay. I searched the room again. I didn't find one.

My eyes swept the room one last time. Then I stacked the five pieces of paper, rolled them into a thin tube, found a couple of rubber bands to secure it, and slipped as much as would fit into my left-front jeans pocket. The end of the tube stuck up out of the pocket, but I zipped my ski jacket closed over it.

I turned the heavy steel dead bolt and unlocked the door. At least it unlocked from the inside without a key. Then I walked out into the late-afternoon cold. I had one huge piece of luck. The bridge control on the maintenance building's side of the dam had a simple red button. No code required. The military had no reason to lock people in. I extended the cor-rugated-metal bridge and clanked across. Without the key code, I couldn't make it retract, but I just didn't give a shit.

Then I began walking across the small field and along the road. A sul-len gray sky began to spit out sharp, nasty crystals of something between snow and ice. A cold wind blew sideways, and the crystals pricked at my face. I could see my breath. Each shallow gasp came with a nip of pain, as if from an angry rat trapped deep inside my chest.

A little farther on, I began glancing left for train tracks, but a MARC train roared past and saved me the trouble. Once I reached the intersection, I'd thumb a ride. Then all I had to do was find a map. The fire in my wrists still smoldered. I walked to the side of the road, scooped up a handful of snow, shook some into my empty hand, and rubbed my wrists with the soothing powdered ice.

I trudged on, pushing away the pain. I'd save Alex. I would kill Scofield. I fixed my inner eye on that gaunt, angry face and let my hate for the man smolder. I shivered only once more, a single spasm of icy pain that melted away. *Save Alex. Kill Scofield. Save Alex. Kill Scofield. Save Alex. Kill Scofield.* The two thoughts echoed in my head with each slow, painful, trudging step. They blended into a single mantra. After a while I didn't know which mattered more to me. That really scared me.

I lumbered along the frozen, snow-dusted road. The ski jacket kept my torso warm, but the wind cut right through the denim of my jeans and nipped at my skin with icy teeth. That busted rib poked at me with every step—sometimes a gentle tweak, more often an ice pick's jab. The erratic nature of the pain made my gait hesitant and unsteady. Fear of slipping on a hidden patch of ice slowed me more. I'd walked for nearly an hour before I spotted the metal gate Scofield had swung open back when we'd been hunting buddies. The sun looked pale as it hunkered low in the blue-black sky. Wispy gray clouds fluttered between us like flocks of geese. I wiped away a growing string of snot with the back of my hand. My nose felt like some frozen carrot I'd borrowed from a snowman.

I walked around the yellow gate and stared up the hill in front of me. The sign at the right of the roadway read, "West, Maryland 117." A couple of buildings sat near the top of the hill, to the left of the roadway. They looked old and weather beaten. One of them sported a large rectangular sign that hung from a long horizontal pole sticking out from the roof. I squinted at it with tired eyes. Its white letters stood out from the orange background. It read, "Toro." I smiled, took another shallow breath, and climbed up the hill.

CHAPTER THIRTY-FOUR

Launch minus Two Days

Boyds Country Store was a small two-story building with a squared-off, worn-but-still-white brick facade in front. The white-painted brick on the side looked brighter. The "Boyds Country Store" sign was fastened just above the roof of a full, four-column front porch, and a small single window peeked out above the sign. "Coca-Cola," printed in retro white script on a red background, flanked each side of the faded Boyds Country Store block letters.

I plodded between a few Toro snowblowers in the parking lot. The floorboards groaned as I stepped onto the porch. I shivered as I passed the ice machine to my left. I tried to stand erect as I pushed the door open. I didn't want to look like a bum. At least I had money. Scofield hadn't bothered taking anything but the pistol, my knife, and my phone. He'd even left me the spare magazines. He hadn't figured on my getting loose. Even after I had, the most I could do with the bullets was to throw them at him. I hadn't thought to bite on one during my walk. Just as well. I probably would've stumbled and swallowed it.

The Toro sign meant that this place sold, and I hoped repaired, snow-blowers and lawn tractors. That meant tools. Tools could become weapons.

I walked inside. The air felt warm. It had a faint musty smell. Yellow light shone down from the ceiling fixtures. I glanced around. The place appeared clean but timeworn.

An old man stood behind the counter. He looked about the same vintage as his place of business. He'd probably been my height once, but his stooped posture left him shorter now. He had close-cropped white hair and a ruddy complexion covered by a day or two of white stubble, the kind some old people wear out of indifference. His eyes were half-closed.

I bought a large coffee, a couple of packs of Twinkies, and a Dinty Moore Big Bowls beef stew. I didn't even try to speak. Just poured the coffee, picked up the rest, walked to the counter, and held out a twenty.

He didn't talk either—just pointed a thin, worn finger at the microwave.

I pocketed a couple of plastic spoons that sat in a utensil rack beside the microwave and then nuked the stew. The instructions stated that the metal edges of the container would be hot after microwaving, so I wrapped it in a few paper napkins before lifting it out. I didn't need another injury. I spotted a faded brown door with a white unisex-restroom graphic and headed for it.

I glanced at the old man. His eyes followed me as I carried my food into the restroom and closed the door. At least the toilet had a lid. I spent ten minutes sitting, thinking, replenishing my blood glucose, and then relieving what needed to be relieved. A little of the pain drained out of my body.

I tried making my mouth speak, testing to figure out if I still had a voice. I kept it to a whisper so that the clerk wouldn't think he had a nutcase in his bathroom and call the cops. I didn't know what Scofield might have been able to load into the police feed. If I were arrested now, by the time I got out of jail, this game would be over. My tongue still felt too big for my mouth, but it moved. Demosthenes had managed to speak clearly with a mouthful of pebbles. My task was easier.

The old man studied me as I left the bathroom. "Hurt your head?" he asked.

I'd forgotten about the bandage. I gave that friendly, harmless smile I keep stashed for just such occasions. "Just a flesh wound," I said.

If he'd ever been a Monty Python fan, he didn't let on. He shrugged.

I shrugged back. I looked like a bum, but I'd proven I was a paying customer, the only one in the store. I walked to the counter.

"Repair engines here?" I asked quietly. I spoke slowly, forced my tongue to move slowly, and tried not to mumble.

He rubbed his white stubble with the fingertips of his right hand. "You want Poolesville Small Engine," he said. "That's the red brick building next door. They're closed."

I'd walked past it. The building was set back a lot farther from the road than the store was. I'd given it a glancing inspection. I'd seen a few snow-blowers and one snowmobile out in front. "Sign says, 'Boyds Professional Center.'"

"Ain't been any professionals in there for years," he said. "Sign hasn't been changed yet, that's all."

"Thanks. Sell any tools there?" I asked.

"Doubt it," he said. "They use 'em; don't sell 'em. We sell some." He pointed one long, skinny finger. "Over there with the car stuff."

I walked over to a rack at the far end of the little building. It held a treasure trove. I found a slotted-head screwdriver with an eight-inch blade, a D-cell flashlight, batteries, a good-sized hammer, two cans of Sterno, and a butane cigarette lighter.

I gathered up my improvised weapons and carried them to the counter. "Any knives?" I asked. I had a streak going.

"Kitchen section," he said, pointing to the far end of the store. He shook his head. "Local folks in a hurry don't want to drive to Home Depot and stand in line for ten minutes. You know. Something comes loose, and you don't have a screwdriver that fits, and you just want to be right quick done with it. They come here. A couple of years ago, my tool rep conned me into adding a kitchen rack. Claimed kitchen stuff would sell the same. Never happened. Should've figured. When you cook, you get what you need before you start. If your spatula breaks, you're not about to drop every-thing and run out for a new one. Someone's hungry. You make do."

"Thanks," I said. "Be right back."

I found the rack. A big black-and-white sign labeled "Kitchen Section" stuck up from the top of it. Mostly it held measuring spoons, measuring cups, spatulas, and such. The trophy item hung from the bottom row of hooks. I took the shrink-wrapped package from the rack and practically hugged it to my chest. It held a chef's knife with an eight-inch blade and a black plastic grip. I thought about buying scissors, a spatula, and a set of measuring spoons to make the knife look innocent, but who was I kidding? I didn't look as if I were about to throw a dinner party.

I returned to the counter. He took the knife and went about ringing up my little treasures.

"Want a bag?" he asked.

I shook my head. I loaded the batteries into the flashlight and then placed each item into one or another pocket of my ski jacket. I made a point of leaving the knife inside its packaging.

The prices were high, but I had money and was short on friends. I handed him two fifties and told him to keep the change.

"Thanks, buddy," he said.

Kahler had once told me, "Friends are where you find them." Then he'd added, "Money hastens the process."

"Got any maps?" I asked.

"Magazine rack." He pointed.

He had quite a few. I found two that showed the streets of Boyds in fairly good detail.

"Mind if I spread this out on the floor over there?" I asked.

"Ain't no one here but us." He waved out an arm. "Use the counter."

For a moment I feared he might become too interested. But time was running out, and a local could tell me a lot more about the area than black lines on white paper would.

I spread out the first road map on the glass countertop, slid the tube of white papers out of my pocket, and unrolled what I hoped really were map tracings. I held the first one above the road map and turned it first one way and then another. The scale looked wrong, and I couldn't make anything match. I tried the second map. Better, but not one of the tracings lined up with the roads on the map. After ten minutes of my repeated failure with each of the five tracings, the old man walked away. I figured that his attention span had diminished with age, but he returned a few minutes later with a rusted metal-shade desk lamp. Without saying a word, he removed the candy bars from the shelf beneath the countertop, flipped over the shade so that light from the lamp would project up, and stuck the little lamp into the case where the candy had been.

"Used to work a darkroom," he said. His eyes sparkled. "Before all this digital crap caught on." He plugged in the lamp and switched it on. "Now try it," he said.

He'd improvised a light box. We went to work. The third tracing fit. He saw it first.

"Routes One Twenty-One and One Seventeen," he said. "Match the intersection." He took each of my hands in his and twisted the paper. "Set it down like that." The lines on the tracing came very close to matching the roads on the map. The overlay wasn't perfect, but it looked close enough.

The old man stepped back and smiled.

"Thanks," I said.

I bent over the tracing. This one had the single smudge on it, so faint that I had to ask the old man to turn off the lamp before I could find it. When I did, I scored the paper with a fingernail. My new buddy handed me a short pencil with its end chewed off. I drew an X. When I straightened up, I nearly backed into him.

"Hand me that pencil," he said.

He took it, gently shoved me away from our light box, leaned over it, and drew a second X. "That's us here," he said.

I blew a soft whistle past my swollen tongue. The two marks sat less than a half mile apart.

"Know what's there?" I asked, pointing to the X I'd drawn.

"Temple, maybe. It's close by anyway."

"A synagogue?"

He shook his head. "Nope. Some kind of foreign temple. Zoro something or other."

"Zoroastrian?" I asked.

"Maybe. Sure as hell ain't no church, not by the look of it. Brand new, though. I drive by it every day. I think they're still working on the inside. No congregation yet. Never any cars 'cept for workmen. Plumbing. Electric."

Something tickled at the back of my brain.

"Got a computer?" I asked.

"Nope."

I must have grimaced.

He rested a fatherly hand on my shoulder. "Cheer up, son. Got a cell phone." He reached into his back right pocket and then held out an iPhone 6 Plus.

"Thanks." I took the phone and pushed the button. "Find Zoroastrian."
Siri ignored me.

The old man took his phone from my hand. "Something's wrong with
your voice," he said sympathetically.

"Yeah. Burned my tongue."

He said into his phone, "Siri. Find"—he paused for a moment, narrow-
ing his eyes—"Zoro…astrian."

The screen lit up. "Zoroastrianism is an ancient, monotheistic religion
of Greater Iran. It is one of the world's oldest monotheistic religions. It was
founded by the prophet Zoroaster thirty-five hundred years ago. Beginning
in the seventh century, it was gradually marginalized by Islam. Today there
are approximately two and a half million Zoroastrians, most living in Iran
and India. There is a significant population of Zoroastrians living in the
United States of America. A fire temple in Zoroastrianism is the place of
worship for Zoroastrians."

I took the phone, tapped Google, and typed "Zoroastrian Temple,
Boyds, Maryland." The address lit up the screen: "15316 Barnesville Road."

"What's the address here?" I asked. "The street number?"

"One five one one zero."

I looked back at the map. My heart raced. This had to be it. *Close to
Scofield's substation, empty, and Iranian. He'll probably burn it down when he's
through, just for spite.*

I glanced back at the street map. An envelope icon sat between the old
man's two Xs. I put a finger on it. "This?"

"Boyds Post Office. Nothing else from here to there 'cept houses. Not
many. Big yards."

"OK, if I make a call?" I asked.

"Sure."

I began to key in Kahler's number and then stopped. Between the mili-
tary and all those agencies that "help out," Scofield had unlimited tech.
He'd found us on a drone scan at O Street. Compared to that, bugging
Adrian Kahler's phone was beyond simple.

I handed the iPhone back to the clerk.

His hazel eyes studied me. They held an intelligence I hadn't noticed
before. If I lived long enough, maybe I'd become smart enough to stop
prejudging people.

"Got to be going," I said. "Thanks for your help." I held out a fifty-dollar bill.

He held up a hand. "You might need that."

I shook my head. "Not likely."

"Fair enough." He reached out and plucked the bill from my hand. "Thanks."

I nodded and then turned away and zipped my jacket closed. I heard him call out as the door swung closed behind me.

"Good luck, young fella."

I walked off the porch and stepped to the side of the building. While I'd eaten and studied maps, more snow had fallen. Sheets of it stuck to the white siding, transforming Boyds Country Store into a great square igloo. My fingers ached as I pried the clear plastic bubble pack off my new knife and dropped the packaging into a four-foot-tall yellow recycle bin that stood against the wall. Then I slid the blade, point up, inside my left sleeve, between shirt and jacket. The grip had a slightly rubbery texture covered with tiny nodules. It rested nicely in my palm. I dropped my arm to my side, keeping the fingers curled. I reached across with my right hand and caressed the knobby plastic. *Draw straight out and then slash. Make it work. By the way, idiot, don't bend your arm.*

CHAPTER THIRTY-FIVE

Launch minus Two Days

I crossed the parking lot and walked to the street. I missed the light and warmth of the store. A part of me wished I'd stayed there. The night had turned fully dark, the air frigidly cold. Streetlights had become bright blue-white halos behind a curtain of falling snow.

The Zoroastrian temple wasn't far, maybe a third of a mile. I glanced left and right. A car drove by. Its headlights flicked out into the darkness and licked my face. Then another. I saw no other pedestrians. If Scofield or one of his men drove by, they'd win the Kewpie doll with one shot.

I looked to my left. Flat, white terrain ran to a tree line about fifty yards away. Those trees looked fifty to one hundred feet tall. Then I remembered the MARC train. Its tracks had to lie on the far side of those trees. I turned toward the tree line and began to trudge across the snow-covered field. The light from the streetlamps barely reached me. The snow fell faster now. A roll of thunder broke from the sky, then another. I glanced around. I stood taller than anything else in that open field. I quickened my pace to a jog. My broken rib screamed at me, but now I had a goal. I carried a weapon. I moved within a rolling balloon inflated by the heat of anger. It insulated me from pain, from cold, from fear, and from the falling snow.

I reached the tree line and pushed between the branches. Dislodged clumps of slush pelted me from above. About two inches of the stuff stuck to my head. I brushed it off with the edge of my right hand. Near total darkness surrounded me, and when I reached the MARC tracks, I almost tripped over them. I steadied myself and took a step back. I gasped through an open mouth that sucked in the falling snow with every breath. I tried to spit it out, but I still couldn't feel my tongue. I stood still and drew in a breath—long, cold, and slow. Then another.

I fished out the flashlight with my right hand, flipped it on, aimed the beam at the tracks, and marched toward the temple. I made decent time. No need for stealth as long as that line of tall trees separated the tracks from the field. The light had a focused beam that didn't drift far from the tracks, but just to play safe, I angled it slightly to my left, away from the road, from where the temple would be. Every couple of minutes I stopped, killed the light, walked to the tree line, and peered through. I had no idea what a Zoroastrian temple would look like but figured it would look different enough from anything else in the neighborhood.

A footfall, light as a ghost's, whispered across the snow behind me.

CHAPTER THIRTY-SIX

Launch minus Two Days

I dropped the flashlight, grabbed my knife, and whirled toward the sound. An arm the size of a python snaked around my chest from behind. I struggled against it. My injured rib felt like it would explode. Another arm encircled my neck. The first wrapped tighter. It crushed the air out of me. I managed about as much resistance as a kid might get from a bathtub toy.

"Shhhhh," was the only sound the creature made.

The carving knife slid out of my hand.

The voice, low pitched but soft as a snake's whisper, said, "Barry?"

I coughed out his name, "Egor?"

The two huge arms relaxed.

"Sorry. You drew that knife." His whisper had the hint of a laugh in it.

I turned around to face him. I coughed a couple of times, trying to clear my throat.

With the snow covering his white sniper suit, Egor looked as much like a polar bear as a man. The most striking difference was his white tactical backpack.

"I have a tale to tell," I said.

Egor nodded. "Yes. And we have work to do." He slid the backpack from his shoulders, rested it on the snow, and opened the compartment containing his VSS rifle. He glanced inside, grunted in satisfaction, and then began to assemble the suppressor-integrated barrel, receiver, butt-stock, twenty round magazine, and nightscope.

The Vintovka Snayperskaya Spetsialnaya, or Special Sniper Rifle, was manufactured by the Tula Arsenal for use by Russian Spetsnaz units in clandestine operations. It weighed just under six pounds and when dis-assembled was small enough to fit inside a briefcase. A nine-millimeter round with a tungsten tip, about twice as heavy as a nine-millimeter pistol bullet, left the muzzle at just under the speed of sound and could penetrate a 0.2-inch high-density steel plate at one hundred yards or a standard army helmet at over five hundred yards. That relegated body armor to the world of wishful thinking. Neither the wearer of that helmet nor his comrades would hear a sound or see a flash. As for accuracy, the Russians nicknamed their little jewel "Vintorez." English translation: "Thread cutter."

Adrian Kahler still had contacts in the land of his birth, and he'd had a couple of VSS rifles, with ammo, sans serial number, shipped into the United States by way of Denmark. They'd arrived labeled as audiophile-grade stereo gear. The separately wrapped components of each rifle sat inside a crate graced by a picture of a Dali Euphonia MS5 loudspeaker and filled with enough lead to bring the package up to the 162 pounds an MS5 weighs. To me that seemed risky. The old man had never purchased an audiophile component that wasn't McIntosh.

"Colonel Scofield called," he whispered. "He told Adrian he'd located Alex and that the SEAL team was in place. He said he'd made a deal to swap Dr. Blake for Alex."

I spat out a blob of glop, a warm mix of saliva and blood. I watched for it to splat against the snow, but in the dark I saw nothing. "The old man will never OK that."

I thought I saw Egor's dim outline shake its massive head. "Adrian agreed to it. That's what Dr. Blake wanted. He can't grow the crystals. Adrian believes he was able to implant a subroutine of sorts in Dr. Blake's ventromedial prefrontal cortex, but he could not activate it. Dr. Blake must do that for himself. Adrian actually rested a hand on his shoulder when he told him to go. I remember what he said.

"'Your mind is like a pistol, cocked and locked. You squeeze the trigger, but nothing happens. The safety is engaged. You search and search, but you cannot find it. I could not find it for you. It is small and easily overlooked. A button, perhaps. A tiny lever. *Find it*. Push it to the red dot.' When Adrian said, 'Find it,' my brain rang as if a small bell had been struck by a surgeon's hammer."

"The old bastard is using Alex," I said. "He wants Ethan to watch her die. He figures that's what it will take to push Ethan's little safety to the red dot." My voice trembled.

"Barry!" Egor grabbed me by the shoulders and shook so hard I nearly bit my swollen tongue. "She was already in play."

I felt darkness upon darkness close in around me. I nodded anyway. Maybe Egor felt my movement. He still held my shoulders.

"Dr. Blake and I drove here together in the Denali. I got out at the post office and told Dr. Blake to give me at least an hour—drive out Clopper Road and then back. He'll be late, but in this weather, that shouldn't arouse any suspicion. He can always say he got lost in the storm. And setting them on edge will be to our advantage. This seemed the ideal spot for me. Colonel Scofield said, 'The SEAL team will take up a position on the far side of Barnesville Road, across from the temple. Dr. Blake will walk up to the temple, and the SEALs will storm it the moment the door opens.'"

My mouth had filled with spit again. I felt light headed. I dropped my head between my knees. When I spat this time, I saw my glob of saliva plunge downward and melt its way into the snow. For a moment it won its little fight with the elements. Then the snow engulfed it, and it disappeared. I straightened up, tried to clear my head, and looked up into Egor's dark eyes. "I'm your SEAL team."

"What?"

I filled him in. He shook his massive head. A few clods of snow slid off his white hood. He stared down at the ground for a moment. The polar-bear likeness held. "Same plan," he said. Egor rested a big paw on my shoulder. "As you said, you're the SEAL team. I'll back you up. We have no time for anything else." He straightened up, led me through the trees, and then handed me his binoculars.

The white phosphor image intensifiers, same as in his riflescope, turned the Zoroastrian temple into a great white specter enshrouded by the fallen snow. It sat about one hundred yards away. A steeply pitched roof rose up from the back wall. The building looked to be more than 150 feet across. Left to right I saw four huge framed windows, a pair of french doors, and then four more windows. Not far from the tree line stood poles for street-lights that must have outlined a parking lot. Under its blanket of snow it looked the same as the field. The lights might have had bulbs, but the power was off. The temple's sidewall to my left had four doors in it and might have been forty feet long. It ended in an outcropping of the front section of the building that stuck out about fifteen feet beyond that wall. A good-sized shed, maybe twenty feet wide, sat about five feet to the left of the outcropping. The side facing us had one small window.

The snowfall slacked off. Egor nudged me. "Get to that shed. Then fol-low Dr. Blake into the temple." He leveled a finger at those tall windows at the rear of the temple. "If you meet resistance, lead them there."

I nodded, understanding.

"When the time is right, I'll follow you in." He handed me a nine-millimeter Glock 26. "That's my backup."

I knew he carried a Desert Eagle .50-caliber pistol in a shoulder holster under each arm.

Then he returned my knife. "Not bad," he said. "Use this first." Then he unslung his Val rifle, switched on its scope's image intensifier, and raised the rifle to his shoulder. The bolt clacked home.

The last thing I heard as I tensed for my dash to the shed was, "Conserve ammo. No double taps."

I had one knife and ten bullets. No kidding.

CHAPTER THIRTY-SEVEN

Thursday, March 17, 2016
Launch minus One Day

I ignored the pain and ran. The fresh, clean scent of falling snow surrounded me. Faster. I kept to the left side of the parking lot. I headed for the shed. As I ran, the snowfall slackened. By the time I reached the shed, it had nearly stopped.

I'd become easy to spot. I dropped to my knees and flattened myself against the wall of the shed. It gave off a musty smell. The air felt colder now. I shivered. Every few minutes that broken rib gnawed at my side like a sated wolf that just couldn't ignore available flesh.

The temple sat to my right. A pair of french doors faced the shed's single entrance. Their venetian blinds were closed. To the left of the shed, the parking lot narrowed to driveway width. Beyond that a few feet of snow-covered yard was bounded on its far side by a chicken-wire fence that held back a forest of close-packed bamboo. Glistening in the wet, freezing air, those stalks had become a second fence, one that looked like a row of inverted icicles reaching fifty feet into the sky. If anyone spotted me, I had no place to run.

Hugging the wall of the shed, I crawled to its door on hands and knees. I glanced up. The black letters on the door were just visible. "Fire Pump House." I reached up, closed my bare hand over the ice-cold knob, and turned it slowly and quietly. The door swung open. I scuttled inside and carefully pushed it closed. An anemic glow from a streetlight filtered in through the window facing the road. The musty smell grew stronger.

I bumped a knee against something hard. I lowered my hand to it. Freezing cold to the touch. I'd found the brass end of a fire hose. I worked my hand along its length until I felt the hose itself. I stood up. At the back of the shed, I found huge coils of the stuff. Fire hose. I remembered the blurb Siri had found for us. "*Fire* temple." For an instant I became a child again, awake in my bed and alone in the dark. An orange light shimmered at the edges of my mattress. A dragon licked its tongue along the bed frame. Then another. They'd come from underneath, from where monsters live.

The shed door creaked open. My heart nearly stopped. I flattened myself against the wall and readied my knife, holding it low, to slash or to jab. A tall shadow slipped inside and closed the door. The shadow stepped in front of the dimly lit window. He snapped on a small flashlight. I knew the face.

"Asha," I whispered, "kill the light!"

The light went out. "Barry?"

"Right. What the hell are you doing here?"

He whispered back, "My staff never showed up for work today. I picked up one outside his apartment and followed him here."

"They work for Scofield now."

"All of them?"

"Best I can tell. They think they're about to become rich Americans with nice homes and new identities."

"All of them?"

"Iran must be a great place to live."

Asha Talavi let out a sigh. "The rule of the mullahs can feel oppressive. We all occasionally fear that someone is asking, 'Is he Muslim enough?'" Asha turned away from me for a moment. I heard him swallow. "For the minorities it can be much worse."

"Ethan Blake, a scientist at Goddard, is about to show up," I said. "Scofield's boys are holding his sister inside. If Scofield gets Blake, very bad things will happen to your country. I'm going to try to stop him."

Asha's obsidian eyes glinted in the dim light from the window. The rest of him remained a tall, slender shadow. "How can I help?"

"You believe me?"

"Oddly enough, yes. I believe an American. But that is not the issue. Two of my staff died mysteriously. The others have been co-opted by a foreign agent. I either throw in with you and get lucky, or I return to my office and wait to be recalled in disgrace."

"Give me five minutes. Then follow me in. You have a gun?"

He shook his head.

I fingered the carving knife. *If I just kill him now, there's one less wild card.* I reached out my empathic sensors and tried to read the tall shadow standing before me. I got nothing.

"The guy at the Tidal Basin, the one with the dog—what did you say to him?"

"Dogs are sacred in Zoroastrianism. He was treating his badly. I asked him to stop."

For a moment my mouth wouldn't move. I gave my head a quick shake to break the spell. "This your temple?"

"I have no temple. I am a devout Muslim."

I sensed something there, discomfort and a restlessness. "There's more to that story."

Asha spoke in a hurried whisper. "My parents were Zoroastrian. I was born in Yazd Province. It is an arid land, the driest part of Iran, less than four inches of rain per year. Most of the green patches are watered by springs. When the queen and the last Sassanian royal family fled from the invading Arab armies, they fled to Yazd. Zoroastrians and others who did not wish to live under Muslim rule followed. I imagine they believed no one else would want it. But Iran engulfed it.

"Although Zoroastrianism is permitted, my people live under Muslim rule. In my teens I converted to Islam. That made college possible for me, then the military, and then the diplomatic corps. Washington was not a choice posting. Perhaps, to my superiors, I am indeed not Muslim enough. I thought this might give me an opportunity to prove myself. Technically my agency is part of the Pakistani embassy. We call it the Interest Section of the Islamic Republic of Iran. We file visas. I thought I might collect intelligence, but my staff has neither the requisite brains nor talent. And your government watches us. And the Pakistanis watch us. My only accomplishment has been designing a website. Even that must list us as part of the Pakistani embassy. But I am patient. I have waited—for opportunity."

I shook my head. "This ain't it. Best-case scenario, no one ever learns about what goes down here. Worst case, you and I wind up dead."

"At least I'll die in a Zoroastrian temple." He might have smiled. "Back to the beginning. Destiny perhaps. God's will?"

"God's will, huh? Is that what Zoroastrians believe in?"

The tall, shadowy figure turned to face me. I heard melancholy in his voice, "Zoroastrians believe in God and the fight of good against evil, in order, and in the battle of order against chaos, in—"

A car ground to a stop on the snow-covered driveway. I took a quick look out the window. The snowfall had stopped. Ethan Blake climbed out of the Denali and strode toward the temple's main entrance.

I walked around Asha Talavi and stepped toward the door. I glanced at my watch. "It's ten after twelve. Wait five minutes and then follow my footprints. Blake's going in through the main entrance. If I get lucky, there'll be a pistol waiting for you just inside. If I don't, you'll know it. At that point, if you live long enough, you can take mine." I turned and took Asha by the shoulders. I squeezed hard enough to hurt him. "Whatever happens, keep the girl alive." Then I opened the door and crept out into icy darkness.

CHAPTER THIRTY-EIGHT

Launch minus One Day

The sky had cleared. Freshly fallen snow glowed in the moonlight. My breath formed a bright-white plume that stretched out in front of my face. It pointed at me like an arrow. I ran in a crouch to keep below the windowsills of a round, turret-like structure and then passed two double french doors with full-length glass covered by closed venetian blinds. I slipped past a big double window. Ethan had his hand on the door handle by the time I reached the two-story arched portico that led to the main door. A huge cylindrical lamp hung from the portico's ceiling. No one had turned it on.

Ethan pushed down on the door handle and slammed the toe of his boot against the brass kickplate. A startled, swarthy face with a short, scruffy beard jerked his head toward Ethan as the door swung open. Ethan raised his hands. I heard him say, "Alex."

The Iranian stood about five seven, and the rolled-up sleeves of his black shirt revealed muscular forearms covered in thick black hair. I leaped up, ran for the door, and didn't stop until I'd body-slammed Ethan into him. They both went down. I stepped left, dropped to one knee, and jabbed my kitchen knife into the side of the Iranian's neck. In and out fast. Blood burst from the wound in a gusher. Then I dropped the knife, grabbed either side of the guard's head with my hands, and twisted it sideways. A fountain of blood sprayed across my jacket. I couldn't risk another guard seeing any of it on Ethan.

Ethan pushed himself to his feet. He glanced down at the twitching body and then looked at me. "Is he dead?"

The body on the floor lay on its back. I stood up and kicked it hard, driving the toe of my boot into its ribs. The left arm twitched a little. Blood still spilled from the wound. "His brain is."

"Now what?" he asked.

We stood in a large, brightly lit atrium with a vaulted ceiling, white-painted walls, and a white tile floor. I looked for a closet or someplace else to hide the body. Nothing. And it kept bleeding. I'd planned on being Ethan's invisible backup. Thanks to ADD impulsiveness, that was over.

Now, best case, I was the wild card. My entire body began to tremble. I couldn't let Ethan hear fear in my voice. I kept my mouth shut and pointed down at the Iranian's pistol.

Ethan shook his head. "If you get shot, I still have me to trade for Alex. If I get shot, you've got nothing."

I held out my hands and turned my palms up.

Ethan made a sad little smile. "That's all I've got."

I rested both my hands on Ethan's shoulders. "Scofield's behind this. These men are his. The crazy bastard wants a nuclear war with Iran." I pointed toward the white wrought-iron banister along the pine staircase to the left. I took a long, slow breath before I said, "If you find Alex and can manage it, get her out. If they find you first, say the guard told you to go upstairs. For all we know, those were his orders. If they weren't, well, a little confusion won't hurt. You're the prize. No one's going to shoot you."

Ethan made a sharp laugh.

"They won't!" I shook my head. "No, they won't. Not one of them will dare to touch you."

Ethan walked to the staircase. Then he stopped. He turned toward me. "Sure. Not until Scofield gets here."

"That buys us time." I tried to sound confident, but I'd already made one mistake. The dead man in the foyer. A lake of blood. I'd have gladly traded a pistol for a mop. Egor would have killed him smarter.

Ethan turned away, climbed up the stairs, and disappeared around the curve of the staircase.

I took another look at the Iranian's pistol. A long, double-stack-sized grip stuck out of his holster. It held more rounds than my Glock 26. *You just can't have too many bullets.* I knelt down on my right knee, leaned over him, and reached for it. A sudden, brutal pain shot through my right thigh.

CHAPTER THIRTY-NINE

Launch minus One Day

I hadn't killed the guard. He'd picked up my knife and backhanded it into my thigh. No time to think. I pivoted right, grunted with an uptick in pain, and let my left knee drop. I heard the crunch as it struck his windpipe. His body twitched once. I didn't move until I'd felt every bit of life seep out of him.

I took hold of my knife and slid it out of my thigh slowly and carefully, remembering what Egor had taught me about knives doing more damage on the way out. I held the blade straight. The guard had only had enough strength to shove it in less than an inch, but when it's yours, all real estate is priceless. The tip of the blade cleared the hole in my jeans. An expanding red stain followed it. I tore apart the fabric so that I could examine my wound. Blood ran out of the gash, but it flowed slowly. It didn't spurt. The skin around the wound had already turned purple. I yanked the guard's shirt out of his pants, found his T-shirt, and cut off several long strips. Then I tied them together, wrapped the makeshift bandage around my wounded leg, pulled it tight, and knotted the ends. All I could hope for was to slow the bleeding. It didn't appear that an artery had been cut, so that should be enough. I took his pistol, checked that it had a round in the chamber, and stuck it under my belt behind my right hip. I checked for spare magazines, but he didn't carry any.

I nearly screamed when I stood up. I had to reach down slowly, but I retrieved my knife. The lettering on its plastic packaging popped into my head as I slid it back into my left sleeve. *Classic chef's knife, eight-inch blade, Kray-Ex handle.* It had two blood types on it already, and the night was young. I used the remaining strips of the dead man's T-shirt to clean the soles of my shoes.

Stairs to the left, big black metal door straight ahead, smaller door to the right. For a crazy moment, I imagined myself as an avatar in a video game. Then I took a step. Pain shot up my thigh. I walked slowly forward, opened the big door as slowly and quietly as I could, and slipped through. I glanced back just before I closed it behind me. No bloody footprints marked my path. One plus in the Barry column.

The door latch clicked shut. In my head it sounded as loud as a crowbar striking a concrete floor. Stupid. Stupid.

I found myself in a huge, open room, maybe 150 feet side to side and 40 feet front to back. A red exit sign sat over each doorway, the one I'd come through and one at either end. They were closed. Each sign cast jagged shadows on the walls. Faint, silvery moonlight flowed around the edges of eight large venetian-blind-covered windows set into the far wall, four of them on either side of a pair of french doors. I'd seen this from outside. Those windows faced the field I'd crossed and the tree line beyond. Egor might still be out there, or he could be standing two feet behind me. No one could hear him move. I took a quick glance over my shoulder. Nope. Still alone. He'd never told me his play—one less thing someone could beat out of me.

I plastered my back to the wall and moved slowly to my right, away from the door I'd just closed. Two more doors, one at each end of the room. Was Alex behind number one or number two—or neither one? I moved away from the exit sign. I should have felt safety in darkness, like the feeling that the ocean gives a SEAL, but all I sensed was danger. Cold sweat and warm blood trickled down my right leg, competing for attention like restless children in a kindergarten class. The Chicken Little voice at the base of my brain began squeaking at me, "Go back. Go back." I froze and listened. I heard no sound but my own ragged breathing. I held my breath. Still nothing.

Then I thought I heard a scream. Faint and muffled, but the voice might have been a woman's. It came from my left. I reversed course. My back slid across the wall and then across the door I'd shut a moment before. The huge room offered me as much cover as an open plain. My heart pounded. Stupid, stupid, stupid, stupid. The stillness of that great open space seemed to close in around me. I felt it creep over my skin. The hairs on my arms stiffened. I shivered. I worked my way along the wall. I tried to melt into it, sideways step by sideways step. Now mine were the only sounds. That great room stood all around me, quiet as death. My wounded thigh throbbed each time I lifted a foot and put it down. The broken rib nipped at the inside of my chest. I had no speed. I reached the corner, turned left, and worked my way to the door in the sidewall. The light from its exit sign looked bright as a searchlight. *Alex, I'm coming.* Then I had my back against the door. I started across—my spine flat against the cold, black metal. As I reached for the knob, I heard a click. The door swung away from me.

CHAPTER FORTY

Launch minus One Day

I stepped sideways fast. A man strode through the doorway. He was my height, my build. His long hair covered his ears. He wore jeans, a dark shirt, and boots. He had his back toward me. I had to turn away from him to grab the knob. Tension tightened every muscle as I pulled the door closed. I couldn't keep the latch from clicking. It sounded loud as a coffin lid slammed shut in a tomb.

He'd been turning to his right, probably looking for a light switch. Now he whirled toward me. We stood close, nearly touching. I could smell sour spice on his breath. The knife was still under my left sleeve, but I didn't have space enough to draw it. I had no time. I punched him in the nose with my right fist—one quick jab, then another, and then two more. I hit him in the mouth. Once, twice, and again. I saw the pistol stuck inside his belt. I leaned forward and grabbed it by the slide. He reached for my wrist. Fingernails scraped my skin as I flipped his pistol into the air. It crashed against the tile floor and slid away into darkness.

He started to call out. I chopped at his throat with the edge of my right hand. He managed no more than a gurgle. I swung at him again, but he took a step back. I couldn't reach.

I drew my knife and readied myself to lunge. Then I froze. The Iranian held an Applegate-Fairbairn combat knife in his right hand. I'd have thrown myself right into it.

We locked eyes for a moment. His looked black as coal. We circled one another. My blade was longer. His was six inches, but it was combat strength and double edged. Streams of blood ran out his nose, from his mouth, and down his chin. But he smiled at me. He nodded. He made a little gesture with the upturned fingers of his left hand, beckoning me closer.

Before I could stop myself, I backed away. My hands felt slick with sweat. Only those little rubber bumps on its handle kept the chef's knife from slipping from my fingers. He feinted a slice at my face and then stabbed down at my belly. I crow-hopped backward on the balls of both feet. My thigh screamed at me again. I sucked in my gut as the tip of his blade sliced through my shirt. As he shifted his knife, I leaned farther forward and stabbed back. We played our little game of death, dancing with each other. Stab and slash. Stab and slash. I had to finish this. As soon as he got his voice back, even one loud syllable, I'd be toast. I kept repositioning myself between him and the door. He tried to work around me.

Somehow training engrams switched on. Tiny bubbles of memory popped open inside my head. After Egor had left the SEALs, he'd studied combat technique in West Virginia with John Kary. He'd taught me knife fighting based on the American Combative system, and he'd made me watch Kary's DVDs until my eyes had burned. We'd trained with rubber knives, but Egor had coated the edges of the blades with lipstick, so every strike showed. Lipstick was a good motivator. No man wanted to finish a workout covered in it. Those countless drills had done their job.

Panic ebbed. A calm resignation took its place. *Attack, attack, attack.* I moved in, letting muscle memory do its work. I flexed my left arm across my chest, my hand in front of my throat. The only thing I had for a shield was myself. My knife arm began to describe a circular track. The motion came from my shoulder, blade edge moving down when in front of me and up when behind. It felt like a wheel at my side. Its arc protected my chest.

He kept trying to work around me to reach the door. But I pivoted on my front foot and kept myself in his way. I slashed sideways at every opening, never allowing my blade to go farther than the width of the Iranian's shoulders. He nicked my left forearm once, but he paid for it with a slash across his chest. Then I feinted down, slashed right, and drew a bright line across his forehead. Just a trickle of blood, but it ran into his eyes. He tried to blink it away. His smile faded. He slashed frantically at my throat, but I managed to get my left forearm under his wrist. I arched my back, pulled my head back, and drove his blade hand up. I turned my blade sideways, reversed its circular movement, and drove it up from below. I felt the blade flex as it slid between the ribs on his left side.

He gave a little gasp. He staggered. I shoved my blade deeper. He fell backward, and I followed him all the way down. I lay on top of him. I pushed my knife harder and harder, not letting up until I felt his breathing stop.

I stood up. I was breathing hard, gasping for every little wisp of air. The space around me wouldn't surrender its oxygen. I fought for it. I stared down at the dead man at my feet. I remembered Scofield's words. "They're not monsters. They're kids. They fell in love with America." I'd just killed two of them. My bones ached. My muscles trembled. Tears ran down my face.

I limped slowly toward the door. I left my knife in the dead Iranian: once critical, now irrelevant. I didn't have another knife fight in me. I checked my two pistols. I left the larger one under my belt and pulled out the smaller—Egor's Glock 26. I knew that one would work. They called it the Baby Glock. I hefted the little pistol in my right hand. I rested my index finger just above the trigger guard. It felt at home there. Anyone I ran into now, if I couldn't shoot him, he would kill me.

My eyes had adapted to the dim glow from the exit signs. Moonlight still trickled in around the edges of the venetian blinds set in the french doors and in the four big windows. I glanced around the huge auditorium.

My thigh throbbed. Pretending to ignore the pain, I limped across the floor toward the far side, toward the french doors that led to the backyard and the windows on either side.

I reached the door. I found the rod that opened the slats, turned it, and pulled on the cord that raised the blinds. One side, and then the other. Then I limped to the next window and repeated the process. Finally, I'd opened every blind.

I glanced around the room. Either my eyes had adapted to the darkness or they were helped out by the moonlight wafting in through the uncovered windows. I could make out shapes I hadn't recognized before. The wall to my right was lined with folding chairs, stack after stack of them. When opened, they'd fill the huge room.

As quietly as I could, I carried one chair at a time several feet away from the wall and then restacked them. I built a tiny fort—just like a little kid would make, except my life depended on this one. The muscles in my arms burned, my rib ached fiercely, and my thigh throbbed. I had to fight for enough strength to finish. Finally I had protection on three sides, each barrier four feet high. A double-depth stack faced the doorway in the far wall. I didn't need to worry about the doorway behind me. Someone had ignored the fire code in favor of easy storage. They'd blocked it with layer atop layer of stacked chairs. I took eight more chairs and dragged two in front of each big rear window. I was ready to execute a plan laced with insanity.

CHAPTER FORTY-ONE

Launch minus One Day

oud, angry voices carried through the door the dead Iranian had used. I crept closer. I rested my ear against the cold black metal.

"Let her go." I recognized Ethan's voice. I heard panic in it.

"After the launch."

"You don't need my sister now."

"She's a handle. I can move you with it."

"That's ridiculous."

The second voice dropped to a hush—Scofield's. "I can move my men with it."

"You filthy son of a bitch!"

The sound of a fist striking flesh and bone rushed through the door. A second blow followed, louder than the first, more solid. A body slammed against the door. I heard Scofield's ragged laugh. Then his harsh whisper, "None of us has a future now. These Iranian kids haven't figured that out. I might need a distraction. A woman like your sister." Scofield laughed again. "That's the stuff dreams are really made of."

My chest tightened.

I ran. If my thigh hurt, if it moved, if I dragged my leg, I don't remember. I grabbed a folded metal chair and hurled it through the lower-left pane in the closest window. The sound of breaking glass shattered the stillness of the huge room. I jerked up the second chair and threw it at the pane on the lower right. Then I worked my way back to my improvised fortress, throwing chair after chair through each windowpane as I stumbled by. I prayed Egor was still where I'd left him.

The door I'd had my ear against moments before slammed open. Men poured through, shooting at me as they ran. I dove behind my makeshift barricade. I returned fire, but they had me pinned. I'd be outflanked in seconds, or one or another nine-millimeter projectile would just pass between the cracks in my improvised fortress. *I'm sorry, Alex.*

One of the Iranians collapsed. Then a second. Egor had seen the windows break. With the shades open, he could see every attacker, each a tiny bright outline in the white phosphor image intensifier of his sniper scope. With the glass out, each tungsten-tipped bullet fired from his VSS rifle found its mark.

My ears rang with gunfire. I could hear nothing else. I saw Scofield. His mouth bellowed at his men, but I couldn't hear his words. I saw sparks as a round ricocheted off the metal of one of my folded chairs. I popped up to return fire. In the dim light, the Iranians looked like fallen logs in a field. I couldn't tell the dead from the living. I saw a flash. I fired back.

I sensed a presence behind me. I jerked around, but it turned with me, quick as my shadow. Arms as big around as giant pythons encircled my chest and pinned my own arms to my side. My pistol could point only down. I fired anyway, hoping to hit his foot, not caring if I hit my own. He lifted me off the floor. I kicked backward. Those arms squeezed. I gasped for breath. I jerked my head sideways and tried to bite. The skin of my face scratched against his stubble. I recognized his smell, still sour and tinged with lime. My lungs struggled. I felt them quit. The blackness came.

CHAPTER FORTY-TWO

Launch Imminent

Heat surrounded me. It came from everywhere, as if my arms and legs had been staked to the sand on an empty beach cooked by noonday sun. The bandage on my head felt wet. My scalp throbbed. I tried to touch it. My hands were two willful children lying naked on the hot sand. I told them to rise. They ignored me.

My lids felt heavy. They wouldn't lift either. Something hard pushed against my back, or maybe I pushed against it. I could feel its surface through the fabric of my shirt, not sand but warm and curved and smooth as glass. Fat beads of sweat, like snails exhausted by the heat, slid listlessly over my ribs and down my belly. I tried to draw a breath. Something rough dug into my chest. It hurt. I wriggled an arm and then a leg. Those were the only freedoms I had. I forced my eyes open. Peaks and valleys of orange light flickered in the shadows.

I craned my neck to one side and then the other. I had to touch my chin to my chest to look down. Yellow nylon rope encircled me from chest to ankles and held me flat against the curve of an enormous cylinder. It felt hard, metallic—but metal should be cold. This felt hot. Tendrils of warmth swam under my shirt, slid over my skin, and dove into my flesh. I smelled a fire burning.

Fully awake now, I bent my head backward as far as I could and looked up. The flickering yellow-orange light of an open fire wrestled with shadows against a domed ceiling. Here and there I could make out a wisp of white smoke. Fire! I strained in panic against the ropes. My busted rib screamed. I twisted an arm. I squirmed a leg. Nothing moved enough to matter. I craned my neck to one side and then the other. No guard. They had fled the fire. No escape. I was about to burn.

"Scofield!" I screamed his name. "You sick bastard. If you're going to kill me, use a bullet. Do it now."

"Barry! Shut up!"

I tugged at my bonds. I struggled to find the source of that voice. I whispered her name, "Alex?"

"To your left."

I jerked my head toward her voice and strained against the smooth metal until my ear began to cook. I couldn't see her. "Where are you?"

"Beside you, tied to the urn. Ethan's on your other side."

"Urn?" I asked.

"Contemporary interpretation of a Zoroastrian fire urn—simpler in design, maybe a thousand times larger than the original, sort of Americanized. It's a plain brass cylinder, about six feet tall and three and a half feet in diameter. It sits on a marble platform, same diameter, about two inches high. No fancy base. No ornate handles. But the sacred fire burns inside, just like it did in Zoroastrian temples a couple of thousand years ago. I saw flames flickering at the top when they dragged me in here."

I took as much of a breath as the yellow nylon rope allowed. "What's Scofield's play?"

"Says he'll let us go after the launch."

"Not going to happen."

I heard a man groan.

"That's Ethan," Alex said. "They dragged him in before you got here. He was out cold. His face looked bloody, bruised." Her voice trembled. "Scofield said Ethan killed one of his men."

"He didn't do it. I did."

Alex's voice fell to barely a whisper, "Oh."

"We have to get out of here," I told her.

A harsh, military voice reached out of the darkness. It had taken on the ring of command. "I can't permit that."

CHAPTER FORTY-THREE

Launch Imminent

I smelled Scofield's syrupy Brooks Brothers cologne before he stepped into view. I heard a click. Cool fluorescent light flooded the room. It reduced the impact of the flames in the urn to barely visible flickers against the ceiling and blue-white marble walls. Scofield stood in an archway in front of me, and another blue-white marble wall stood several yards behind him. I glanced down at the marble floor and then up at the arched ceiling. I found no means of escape. I fought the ropes again anyway.

He studied me for a long moment. Then he looked to the side. I watched his sunken, gray eyes drift over Alex. Scofield's narrow, taut face grinned at her. "You never thanked me for the clothing. When my boys told me you'd dressed in a sheet, I figured I'd better find something. Only a man's jeans and shirt. Beats a bare ass, though. Discipline's half-decent, but I couldn't risk a gang bang. Not yet, anyway."

"You've got Ethan," I told him. "You don't need Alex anymore."

"Sure we do. One of my boys has taken a liking to her." Scofield laughed. It was a low, guttural sound, like a wild boar's snorting.

My heart pounded hard enough to explode. I squirmed left and right like an eel caught in a snare.

He walked over to me and stopped less than a foot away. His entire face grinned, as if he could feel me squirm. "Who don't we need? Take a guess, Sandler."

Scofield reached his right hand behind his back. It came out holding a pistol. It looked like the one Egor had given me.

"Embarrassing to get shot with your own gun," he said. Scofield's smile couldn't have grown wider, but now he had a lilt in his voice. "My guys want to kill you themselves. You sure know how to make friends. I told them the only fair way is for me to do it."

I stared back at him. "They could draw straws."

"Shit. Why didn't I think of that?"

Scofield walked around the fire urn, out of sight. I heard a slap. "Awake now?" he asked. "About time."

I heard Ethan's voice. He sounded hoarse. "You son of a bitch."

Scofield laughed again. Then he walked back into view and stopped several feet away. He leveled the gun at my head. The muzzle looked big and black as a manhole. He rested his index finger against the trigger. He flexed it slowly. I stared at his finger so hard that I could see the skin blanch.

I felt my breath catch.

Scofield smiled at me. His lowered his voice to a hush. I had to strain to hear it. "Barry, Barry, Barry, Barry."

I found myself trying to lean closer to him, focused on that whisper, hoping I'd hear something I could use to get us out of this.

"Bye, Barry."

CHAPTER FORTY-FOUR

Launch Imminent

In that marble-enclosed space, the sound of the gunshot was deafening. Blood spurted from Scofield's right shoulder. The Glock fell from his hand, crashed onto the floor, and skidded across slick marble. It stopped six inches from me. It might as well have been a football field away. I strained against the rope. I winced. I strained again.

Asha Talavi stood in the archway, a pistol in his hand. He walked to Scofield and kicked him in the knee. I heard the crunch. Scofield dropped to the floor.

Asha stabbed the muzzle of the pistol against Scofield's temple and glanced at me. "I was never much of a pistol shot, but I can make up for that."

"Not yet. A friend of mine will want to talk to him."

"He has created a problem. Things will go badly for me in Tehran."

I gave Asha a hard stare and tried to hold his gaze the way Kahler might have. I had to make him believe me. "Unless you get us untied quickly, there won't be any Tehran."

Asha studied me for a moment. Then he clubbed the barrel against Scofield's head and stuck the pistol under his belt. He glanced around the room as he walked toward me.

"Cut the rope," I said.

"With what? I have no knife."

"Then shoot it."

"The bullet will bounce. It might strike one of us."

The heat from the urn felt hot against my back. Beads of sweat ran down my sides. "I'll take that chance."

Another gunshot echoed off the marble walls. Asha staggered. Then he crumpled to the floor.

"This is *not* over." Scofield coughed out the words.

He'd climbed to one knee. His right arm hung limp at his side. The long, thin fingers of his left hand wound around a small two-barrel derringer. A thin wisp of white smoke issued from its upper muzzle.

Scofield's mad eyes glistened. He grimaced with pain. "Second time's the charm."

He leveled his derringer at my head.

The big Iranian who'd thrown me off the O Street Mansion's forth-story deck half ran and half staggered through the archway. The holster on his belt was empty, his right eye had swollen closed, and blood streamed from his nose. His eyes fixed on the gun in Scofield's hand. "Shoot him. Shoot him," he screamed. His bellowing voice nearly shook the room.

Egor, bruised and bleeding, charged in after him. The big Iranian stood between him and Scofield. Egor never saw the derringer.

"Egor," I yelled. "Gun!"

Blood soaked Scofield's right side, and repetitive spurts of it burst through the hole in his shirt just below his armpit. But he swung the derringer in his left hand toward Egor. He wobbled, but I could see him fight for control. The oscillations diminished. I focused my mind on Scofield until I could feel his hatred. Time froze.

For once my empathic ability worked when I needed it. But I needed more. I willed him not to squeeze the trigger. I tried to reach into Scofield's mind as Adrian Kahler would. I tried to make my thoughts belong to Scofield. I pushed the limits of my brain until I felt it might explode.

Our minds touched. *Scofield, you bastard—I have you now. Lower your arm.*

His eyes lost focus. His left arm fell to his side.

Open your hand.

"Shit!" I yelled. Something hot as an open flame burned into the skin on the back of my left hand. I lost the link.

Scofield's face hardened. I felt the intense discipline of the man fight against me as he raised his left arm.

The big Iranian dove out of the line of fire and slammed against the floor with enough force to shake the urn.

A blue-yellow flame burst from the lower muzzle of Scofield's derringer. The blast from the gunshot echoed from marble wall to marble wall.

Egor's left leg jerked. He went down. I heard his head smack the marble floor.

CHAPTER FORTY-FIVE

Launch Imminent

S omething had caused several sections of the rope that bound me to catch fire. The acrid smell of burning nylon surrounded me. A tiny, molten blob had dripped onto my hand. I shook it off. A few coils of rope gave way. I began to wiggle free. I had a chance.

Scofield tossed his empty derringer onto the floor. He took a half step toward me and nearly collapsed. He steadied himself and then pointed toward the pistol at my feet. "Zafir, get that for me."

The big Iranian stood up, brushed himself off, and walked over to the pistol. He looked even larger than the last time we'd met. He stood nearly as tall as Egor. His body looked every bit as wide, but atop it sat a large angular face with flat ears, dark angry eyes, and a hooked nose that pointed down like a beak. Zafir swiveled his head side to side. He stooped and swept the pistol into his big hand before I could reach it. When he straightened up, he backhanded me across the face with his free hand. For a moment the entire room disappeared. The world returned in time for me to watch him hand the prize to Scofield.

Scofield took the pistol in his left hand. He smiled at it the way a kid would smile when handed that first present from beneath the Christmas tree. "See, Barry, there is absolutely nothing that can stop me from killing you."

He leveled the pistol. This time his entire body trembled with effort. His arm swung wildly. He kept compensating—left, right, up, down. I watched that swaying muzzle as if death had one good eye that searched only for me.

He turned to Zafir. "Steady my arm, will you. I'm a little light headed."

The big Iranian smiled. "Hey, boss, let me tourniquet your right arm. I'll shoot him for you."

Scofield screamed at him, "No, goddamn it. He's mine!"

A concerned look captured Zafir's face. He shook his head. That big, brutal ape actually cared about someone.

Scofield screamed again, "He's mine, I said." Then his thin lips grinned. He lowered his voice to almost a whisper, "This one's mine. You can have the girl."

The big Iranian shrugged. "As you say." Then he knelt beside Scofield, extended his right arm, and cupped Scofield's left elbow with the palm of his hand. "Mine to keep?"

Scofield laughed. He answered in a stage whisper, "For as long as she lasts."

I heard Alex gasp. A few coils had loosened, but the nylon rope still bound us to that huge brass cauldron. Now it jerked tight, and one coil bit into my chest as Alex struggled frantically to get free.

Zafir's dark eyes gleamed. His thick lips parted. He smiled. He had yellow teeth.

Ethan's voice, shrill with fury, called out from the far side of the fire urn, "Scofield, you bastard. I'll kill you first." His voice grew louder, more intense, "I *will* kill you."

Scofield laughed at him. So did Zafir.

My empathic sensors felt a jolt, like a chain snapping, as if something dark and mysterious had broken free.

The tone of Ethan's voice changed. It became calm, emotionless, matter-of-fact. It was the voice of a professor lecturing a class, explaining a math equation. "I'll kill you both." He might as well have been telling them that the circumference of a circle equals pi times the diameter.

I felt Alex jerk. A coil of rope dug into me again. Then it came loose. Another slackened. That one fell away. I lowered my chin as far as I could, looked down at the yellow rope, and then slid one arm out from under it. The room had become thick with the acrid smell of burning nylon. My hips and legs remained bound to the urn. I tugged frantically at the rope.

The pistol in Scofield's good hand pointed a few inches to the left of my chest. Zafir coaxed Scofield's elbow to compensate. Ever so slowly the muzzle swung toward my heart. I had no time.

Then Ethan Blake began to sing.

Scofield stared past me. His face held an expression of disbelief. Zafir's mouth gaped. His big hand fell away from Scofield's elbow. Scofield's arm dropped to his side. Then they both began to laugh.

I strained to look to the right, but I couldn't see Ethan beyond the great curve of the tire urn.

His voice echoed around the room.

"Back in school again Maxwell plays the fool again.
Teacher gets annoyed.
Wishing to avoid an unpleasant
Sce-e-e-ene

"He tells Max to stay when the class has gone away,
So he waits behind
Writing fifty times 'I must not be
So-o-o-o.'

"But when he turns his back on the boy,
He creeps up from behind.

"Bang! Bang! Maxwell's silver hammer
Came down upon his head.
Clang! Clang! Maxwell's silver hammer
Made sure that he was dead."

I heard a sudden crack, like the splintering of a log in a bonfire. The ceiling brightened. I looked up as a torrent of yellow flame burst out of the fire urn. It sailed over my head and dropped onto Scofield like a net. It engulfed him. He made half a scream. Then his features melted like those of a wax statue caught by a blowtorch. The air filled with the smell of burned hair and then the odors of piss, shit, and grilling meat. I glanced up. Tall flames reached out of the cauldron like the hands of eager students competing for a teacher's praise, each stretching higher than the one beside it. The ceiling began to burn.

Zafir turned, bolted through the archway, and disappeared.

I freed myself from the nylon rope and swung toward Alex. She snapped the last of her bonds and jerked away from the fire urn. A great blue-yellow plume of fire exploded out of it.

I glanced at Alex and then at Egor's inert body. He lay facedown on the marble floor. I'd need her to help me drag him out, if the two of us could manage that. We might all burn. To keep Alex here was to risk watching her die. Sending her away might be Egor's death sentence, and my own if I stayed to help him. Sweat poured off my forehead. It ran into my eyes. My heart pounded, jerking itself repeatedly from side to side within my chest. My eyes darted from Alex to Egor to Alex to Egor. The skin on the backs of my hands felt scorched, but sweat like droplets of ice ran across my palms. I couldn't breathe. My eyes stung. I blinked and then blinked again. Risk! This kind of risk was what Egor and I were paid for. *Not Alex. Not her job.*

My eyes found her. Streaks of sweat ran through the mottled black-and-gray ash that clung to her skin. I might never see her again. She was beautiful. I pointed toward the archway. I struggled to hide the tremor in my voice, "Get out."

"But Ethan—"

"I'll take care of him." I glanced at the flames towering over me. I screamed at her, "The ceiling's going to cave. Get the fuck out of here!"

Alex spun away from me. She raced through the archway.

Ethan had freed himself from his bonds. He stood rigid, head tossed back, smiling up at the mounting firestorm above us. I slapped him hard.

His eyes stared ahead blankly for a moment. Then he focused on me.

"Time to go," I said. "I need your help."

He followed my gaze. Egor and Asha lay facedown, each in his own pool of blood. That faraway look left Ethan's face, and understanding shone in his eyes. "Right."

Blood stained Egor's trousers, but there wasn't much. None of it had pooled beside him. When I pressed two fingers against his carotid artery, he stirred. He opened his eyes and then rolled slowly onto his back and sat up. He had a flat purple bruise on his left temple. He surveyed the room. His gaze settled on the pile of crackling meat several feet away.

I nodded toward it. "Scofield."

He gave me a puzzled look.

"I'll explain later. We need to get you out of here."

"Help me up. I can walk." Suddenly Egor's eyes looked left. He jerked his head around.

I followed his gaze.

Asha Talavi had pushed himself up onto his hands and knees. He raised his head and looked around the room the way a wounded animal might. His eyes found mine. He called out to me, "Still alive!" His shirt was soaked with blood, and small, red droplets collected just above his belt and then let go and fell into the burgundy pool on the blue-white marble beneath him. His face looked ashen. The soft lines and creases at the corners of his eyes were gone. Every muscle tensed; every angle hardened. The growing fire reflected in his eyes. I'd seen a gut-shot cougar once. Asha Talavi looked like that. He refused to die.

"Can you walk?" I asked.

"I can try." Asha straightened his trunk, put one foot onto the floor, and pushed himself upright. He gasped in pain. He wobbled for an instant but didn't fall.

I looked from Asha to Egor and back. I glanced at Ethan. "I told Alex to get out."

He nodded. His skin flickered yellow in the light of the towering flames. His eyes glowed like a demon's. "I'd have killed you if you'd kept her here." Then he walked to Asha. "Friend of Barry?"

Asha nodded.

"Good enough for me," Ethan told him. "Drape one arm around my neck. Good. Now lean on me." Ethan put an arm around Asha's waist, and they started toward the archway. Ethan called back over his shoulder. He had laughter in his voice. "Last one out's a—"

"Dead," I said. "Get the fuck out of here."

Then Egor and I stood alone in the midst of a mounting inferno.

"I can walk," he said.

"You'd better. Dragging you would be like towing a bear."

Egor pushed himself up and grabbed my shoulder with one massive paw. I locked my knees as he hauled himself to standing. Then my 325-pound closest friend used me as a cane. Even stooped with pain, Egor's seven-foot-one-inch frame towered over me.

We lumbered through the archway, out of the fire chamber, and then down a long corridor. That's when panic shook me. Did this corridor lead to an exit? I'd never been here before. I didn't know. The fire grew behind us. Fire! So much of it. I wasn't standing outdoors on the hood of a car. I was lost inside a huge building, and fire had begun to eat it. That crackling sound grew louder. It smacked its lips. Flames licked out of the archway behind us. Fear pounded in my ears. I nearly dropped Egor and ran.

We turned a corner. Ethan and Asha had stopped in front of us. Alex faced them. She stood a few feet away. So did Zafir. His big left forearm practically encircled her. His right hand held a pistol.

CHAPTER FORTY-SIX

Launch Imminent

At Zafir's feet lay another of the Iranians. That one didn't move. His head looked crooked.

Zafir locked eyes with Egor. "This was a friend of mine," Zafir said.

Egor nodded weakly. Under his breath, he whispered, "He was in my way."

Asha Talavi, head of the Embassy of Pakistan Interests Section of the Islamic Republic of Iran, took a step away from Ethan. He stood straight as a general reviewing his troops. He faced Zafir. The side of his right trouser leg looked stained with blood, and drops of it fell from the cuff and spattered against the marble floor. He spoke slowly, in English, his words firm, clear, and evenly spaced.

"Zafir! You work for *me*. You will stand down. You will surrender your weapon." Asha held out his hand, palm up, and waited.

For a moment I heard no sound but the crackling of the fire behind us. The two Iranians just stared at one another. Then Zafir snapped at Asha in Persian. His tone was far from obsequious. His arm tightened around Alex.

I saw her wince in pain. Then Alex screamed at him, "You piece of shit. Fuck you." She twisted her body violently. Zafir's grip loosened, and Alex drove her knee into his groin.

Zafir's gun arm wobbled.

Asha charged him.

Zafir fired.

I saw Asha's body jerk when the bullet struck, but I sensed that he wouldn't stop. Zafir shot him again. Asha pitched forward. But he'd closed the distance between them. As Asha fell, he drove his shoulder into Zafir's right side.

Alex twisted free, threw herself onto the floor, and rolled to Zafir's left.

A white-hot ball of fire streaked past my head like a meteor, so close it singed my hair. It looked smaller than the one that took out Scofield, maybe softball sized. It struck Zafir in the gut, knocking him away from Asha and sticking to the big Iranian like a great glob of napalm. He tried instinctively to grab it and pull it off. He screamed as his fingers turned to charred sticks. It burrowed into him, gnawing like a burning rat. It advanced slowly, through skin, then muscle, and then intestines.

We all watched him die, spellbound by the slow horror of it.

Zafir screamed and screamed and screamed. Then he whimpered. Then he wheezed. Then blood exploded out of him, hissing past the flames.

Asha raised his head. He was still alive. Ethan ran to his side and knelt over him. Asha raised a trembling hand. Ethan took it in both of his.

Asha's eyes looked glazed. They roamed around the burning building. Then they locked on Ethan's. He squeezed Ethan's fingers white. "Please," he said. "Please rebuild it. I beg you. Rebuild this temple for me." He coughed once. Then his jaw slackened. Asha Talavi's mouth hung open, wide and unmoving. A golf-ball-sized bubble of blood sat between his lips.

Black smoke billowed around us. The smell of soot clung to the air. I could taste it. Alex screamed, "We're all going to burn!"

Ethan's voice sounded relaxed, almost soothing. "It's fine, Alex. We'll be fine." He walked to his kid sister and held out his hand. Alex grasped it, and Ethan pulled her to her feet. "Everything will be fine."

Alex looked over his head, then left, right, and back at her brother. "The fire! It's everywhere."

Ethan pointed down the hallway. "Just find us an exit."

"But the fire!"

Ethan rested a hand on each of her shoulders, smiled gently, and looked into her eyes. "I won't let it hurt you."

Alex nodded. She turned and ran down the hallway.

Ethan dropped back for a moment. He faced the fire chamber. I heard several popping sounds, and with each one, the heat behind me seemed to intensify. Then he wedged himself under Egor's other arm, and the three of us hobbled after Alex.

"Thanks," I said to Ethan. "This guy's no daisy."

Egor grunted at me.

Ethan laughed. "I owe you, Barry. I'll always owe you."

Ethan and I struggled under our heavy burden, but we managed. The flames never touched us. The sound was barely audible under the crackling of fire, the snapping of beams, and the crashing of marble, but I know I heard Ethan humming softly to himself, a Beatles song, the one he'd sung before killing Scofield: "Maxwell's Silver Hammer." That melody still plays inside my head whenever I watch a fire burn.

I used Egor's cell to call Kahler as soon as we cleared the burning temple. A military helicopter came for Ethan and whisked him back to Goddard. A swarm of firefighters and medics arrived. The medics didn't have much to do. Egor and I were their only customers. An ambulance carried us to the emergency room at Holy Cross Germantown Hospital. They cleansed, sutured, bandaged, and x-rayed us both. This time Egor and I both got turbans. Alex kept me company.

CHAPTER FORTY-SEVEN

Dr. Ethan Blake grew his new crystal faster than the floating-zone process had ever produced a crystal even one-tenth its size. The flatbed truck that normally would have transported the laser-armed satellite from Goddard to Cape Kennedy traveled only as far as Joint Base Andrews. Then the satellite was loaded onto a modified C-5C transport and flown to Kennedy Space Center. The launch rocket lifted off on schedule and deposited a locked-and-loaded "surveillance" satellite into an orbit from which it could watch Iran.

Three days later, Benjamin Netanyahu, prime minister of Israel, threw a diplomatic monkey wrench into the carefully laid plans of the Joint Chiefs. He flew to Tehran and met privately with Ayatollah Ali Khamenei.

They spent four hours together. Max Damron swore to Kahler that no one at the US State Department or in the Central Intelligence Agency had seen that coming. Since then, diplomats had been shuffling back and forth between Tel Aviv and Tehran. Lips were officially sealed, but it appeared that the Joint Chiefs might not get to play with their new toy after all.

The diplomatic shit hit the fan when no one answered Tehran's calls to the Interests Section of its Islamic Republic. The US State Department mobilized every agency it could tap to scour first DC and then the entire United States, including Alaska and Hawaii. Not one of the missing Iranians was found. Tehran might have interpreted the disappearances as an attack, maybe even an act of war, except that their mission to the United Nations hadn't been touched. That was where the important people worked. Apparently no one on either side could imagine what anyone would gain by dispatching, or granting asylum to, the staff of Iran's Interests Section. Even the web-enabled conspiracy theorists came up empty.

The US Interests Section in Tehran was part of the Swiss embassy. It was staffed by Swiss nationals, so Tehran didn't have a tit-for-tat option. That didn't keep sabers from being rattled, especially by the antirapprochement forces in the Iranian parliament, Iran's Guardian Council, and in the US Congress. But the missing Iranians stood low on the Islamic State totem pole. They only really mattered to their families. The US State Department continued to pursue rapprochement. They denied responsibility but arranged for reparations to be paid. The Joint Chiefs continued readying itself to sweep Iran from the face of the earth. In the end, the entire affair wound down to an embarrassment for both countries. Ronald Reagan's Star Wars satellites would continue to populate the sky, watching and ready.

EPILOGUE

Alex drove the 'Vette. I sat beside her, periodically glancing at the rearview mirror, still feeling thankful that no one had stolen my new car from the Marriott's parking lot. Ethan, in his new black Mustang, kept close behind. They weren't really racing. At anything close to fast, the speed humps on Bay Drive would have demolished both cars.

We'd visited the Zoroastrian temple earlier in the day. I sensed from Ethan a genuine sorrow as his gaze swept the destruction around us. He'd spoken with the temple's dastur a couple of days after the fire. Ethan had explained that he did anonymous philanthropic work, had learned of the tragedy at the temple, and would like to help. Then he'd offered to pay whatever rebuilding costs the temple's insurance wouldn't cover.

Today was their first face-to-face meeting. The Zoroastrian priest graciously accepted Ethan's proposal. He'd shaken his new benefactor's hand enthusiastically, but I thought he'd held it a bit longer than necessary. I could see him studying Ethan's face.

The temple's destruction had been blamed on some malfunction in the fire chamber. No bodies or weapons had been found. They must have melted or been incinerated to ash. The fire marshal's report stated that it had been the hottest fire he'd ever seen. The temple had been completely destroyed. I suppose the Joint Chiefs might have had the bodies and weapons removed, but I suspect Ethan's fire had saved them the trouble. I never asked.

I punched the remote as we closed in on 202 Bay Drive. The steel gate snapped open, and the garage door rose. Alex sped through and planted my car on the epoxy-coated garage floor two inches from the concrete wall. Ethan did a 360 and stopped with his rear bumper a couple of feet outside the door. Yes, they were both still crazy.

Adrian Kahler had instructed me to bring our guests to the pier, so I led Alex and Ethan to the boathouse and then to the eighty wood-plank steps leading down. The old man had recently replaced the old planks with teak, and they shone in the bright spring sunlight.

Egor waved to us from the pier below. Moored to two new posts, fore and aft, a mean-looking sailboat pointed out into the bay. It looked sleek and fast. Measured against the dock, it appeared shorter than the Morgan had been. Black hull. Black spars. White cabin. The deck looked like teak. They'd furled the jib, but the black mainsail had been hoisted out of its V-boom, and it luffed loudly in the cool, fresh breeze. The sail had a bright-red underscored uppercase letter *J* stenciled just below its head and a "97" below the underscore.

Alex must have spotted the new boat before I did. She flew down the stairs, her fingers barely touching the rail. Ethan and I hurried after her.

Adrian Kahler, white hair flashing in the sunlight, stood at the helm, one hand on the huge black wheel. The boat had an open transom, but when I reached the dock, I spotted lettering on the hull. Electric-red print, bright enough to start a fire, spelled out *Seawitch II*.

THE END

ACKNOWLEDGMENTS

1. GODDARD SPACE FLIGHT CENTER—I am extremely grateful for the wonderful tour I was permitted to attend and for the courtesy and patience Goddard scientists extended to this nonphysicist.
2. JOHN KARY AT AMERICAN COMBATIVES INC.—I used John Kary's instruction videos as a basis for much of Barry's fighting technique.
3. ITS TACTICAL IMMINENT THREAT SOLUTIONS—I used the ITS Tactical YouTube video as the basis for Barry's zip-tie escape. (http://www.itstactical.com/intellicom/tradecraft/how-to-escape-from-zip-ties/)
4. "MAXWELL'S SILVER HAMMER"
Words and Music by John Lennon and Paul McCartney.
© 1969 Sony/ATV Music Publishing LLC
Copyright renewed.
All rights administered by Sony/ATV Music Publishing LLC,
424 Church Street, Suite 1200, Nashville, TN 37219.
International copyright secured. All rights reserved.
Reprinted by permission of Hal Leonard Corporation.

46613816R00176

Made in the USA
Middletown, DE
04 August 2017